Colorado Promise

The Front Range Series, Book One

By Charlene Whitman

UBIQUITOUS PRESS

Boulder Creek, CA

Colorado Promise

ISBN-13: 978-0615909264
ISBN-10: 0615909264
LCCN: 2013953150

Cover designed by Delle Jacobs
Interior designed by Ellie Searl, Publishista®

UBIQUITOUS PRESS

Boulder Creek, CA

Praise for COLORADO PROMISE

"With her debut novel COLORADO PROMISE, the first of the Front Range series, Charlene Whitman is sure to become a favorite among fans of historical romantic fiction. Well-drawn characters, a solid plot and just the right mix of action and romance makes this story set in Greeley, Colorado a page-turner. An adequate writer of historical fiction will include minor bits and pieces about the setting of their story. A good writer will do a bit of research to make sure there are historical facts included in the pages of their novel. A superb writer will create characters that could have actually lived during the time in which the story takes place and allows them to act as people in that time period would have really acted. Charlene Whitman is a superb writer. She had this reader wanting to learn more about Greeley, Colorado . . . Whatever story is told in future books in the series, they will be worth reading."

~ Examiner.com

"A fresh new voice in Historical Romance, Charlene Whitman captured me from the beginning with characters I won't soon forget, a sizzling-sweet romance, a love triangle, spiteful villains, heart-throbbing heroes, and a plot full of intrigue that kept me guessing. Ms. Whitman's magnificent research transported me to the Colorado plains and left me longing to join the characters amid the wildflower-dotted fields, rushing rivers, and panoramic Rocky Mountains. Fans of Historical Western Romance will not soon forget COLORADO PROMISE."

~ Best-selling romance author Marylu Tyndall

"Ms. Whitman's writing on the page pleases the senses and the mind. Words roll on the tongue and fill the reader with wonders of the countryside and olden times of living wild on the frontier. You can feel and smell the scents of wild grass, the warm ranch fires in the evenings, and cattle mooing in the background. A most enjoyable book that merits five stars! I didn't know I could fall in love with Western Romance, but I did. This beautifully written story is a breath of fresh air."

~ Romance author Lillian Gafni

"If you are expecting this Western to be a wild shoot-em-up with bar brawls every other chapter you will want to look elsewhere. This is a realistic story, rich with the nuances of first loves and old loves and the love of the country. The pace is quick where it needs to be and slows for her readers to catch their breaths before the plot begins to unfold fast before their eyes. It is never dull during the action scenes or gentle scenes. I believe much research went into this book. It reads realistically without a lot of unbelievable drama. I will be first in line to grab a copy of the next book and read it. Don't miss this book. You won't regret reading it."

~ Author Marianne Spitzer

Away Out in the West

There's a little western city,
Of which I presume you've heard
Many strange and wondrous stories,
And perhaps some quite absurd;
'Tis the one which M. C. Meeker
Founded on the barren plain,
Where they farm by irrigation,
As it seldom ever rains.

'Tis away out in the west,
Yes, away out in the west;
Oh! This model town is Greeley,
Where my home is in the west.

~ Mrs. Annie M. Green, 1876

Chapter 1

New York City, June 1875

"EMMA, DEAR, I BELIEVE THIS heat is about to make me faint." Camilla Bradshaw fluttered the silk fan close to her flushed cheeks as the carriage jostled along the bumpy streets of the Upper West Side. Emma reached over and dabbed her mother's perspiring brow with a lace handkerchief, frowning over her propensity for melodrama.

She glanced out the window. "We're nearly home, Mother. I'll have Josephine bring you some sweet tea in the parlor as soon as we arrive." Hoping to stem the tide of complaints sure to follow her mother's remark, Emma said, "Weren't the florals beautiful? I especially enjoyed the still-life oils from Venice—"

"Yes, oh yes, Emma, dear. A stunning exhibition." She turned and looked at her daughter. "But your paintings are just as delightful. Perhaps one day we'll see your works of art hanging in the prestigious Metropolitan Museum."

Emma refrained from shaking her head at her mother's imagination. "I do botanical illustrations. Not something anyone would hang on the walls of a museum. But I hope someday my drawings will be good enough to be used in reference books."

Her mother made a little noise of disapproval, but Emma turned from her and looked through the window at the bustle of the city, letting the sound of the horses' hooves on pavement and the rhythmic turn of the carriage wheels lull her in the balmy afternoon, the heat matting her coifed hair against her head.

As she watched the passing of gleaming black Hansom cabs drawn by sluggish, heat-weary horses, she thought about the lovely book her father had given her for Christmas, a book she cherished above all others and one that had inspired her to take up pen and ink and watercolor to capture the fine details of plants. Which led to her growing passion to study botany. The artist, a Belgian woman named Berthe Hoola van Nooten, did more than just paint flowers and trees; she somehow captured their perfection in a way that made each living species fascinating and magnificent. Emma wished she could portray creation with such precision, but knew she still had a long way to go. She longed for a studio in which she could paint for hours, uninterrupted.

Her heart thrilled at knowing her opportunity to reach her dream was at hand. Soon, in a scant two months, she would be off to Vassar College—seventy miles away. Away from the stifling heat of the city and the suffocating scrutiny of her parents.

She chided herself for such thoughts, but she yearned for room to grow, for more space than their small but elegant brownstone home afforded, where she had little privacy and even less say in how she spent her time. She loved her parents truly, and although some of her friends had already found their escape through marriage,

Emma had yet to find a suitable beau. Like them, she yearned for love and often fantasized what her future husband would be like, but none of the young men her parents had arranged for her to meet were at all what she hoped for in a husband. Stuffy, arrogant, well mannered—and oh so dull.

Upon her sixteenth birthday, her father had seemed determined to marry her off as quickly as possible, but after the last disastrous dinner, at which her father nearly pressed the poor man into a corner with his unrelenting questions, Emma begged her father to give her a little time off from the arranged meetings with potential suitors.

She scoffed. She knew why her father was anxious to marry her off, and it had nothing to do with *her* happiness.

Their carriage drew to a stop. Emma glanced out the window and said, "Mother, we're home." The coachman pushed the lever and opened the door, then helped her mother down to the sidewalk. She then extended her own gloved hand, careful to gather up her skirts as she stepped out. Emma took her mother's arm and walked with her to the door, which opened briskly to allow them entrance.

"Madame," Thomas, the butler, said, offering his arm to escort Emma's mother inside. Emma nodded her thanks to the older gentleman who had been serving her family for as long as she could recall. Thomas led her mother into the drawing room, and Emma blew out a breath. She enjoyed these outings with her mother, and knew once she went away to college she would no doubt miss them, but her mother had been especially annoying today. On and on about her cousin's lovely wedding they had just attended last week upstate. And what a beautiful wedding she would plan for Emma once she became engaged. It seemed all her mother talked about these days was her inevitable wedding. But they knew her plans to go to college. It was as if no one listened to her or cared what she wanted.

As she willed herself to calm down, her personal maid, Helen, came hurrying the length of the hall and took Emma's lace gloves from her as Emma peeled them from her sticky hands. The house was a mite cooler than the outdoors, but perspiration still dotted her brow, and her blouse and petticoats stuck to her skin. Her corset had seemed to swell from the heat, and she longed to unlace the stays and breathe freely again. She pushed back a stray strand of long ebony hair that had come unpinned, looking forward to washing up and changing into something cooler for dinner.

"Helen, would you see to it that Mother gets some sweetened tea?" She saw no sign of Katherine, but assumed the maid was upstairs and hadn't heard them arrive.

As she handed her purse to Helen, she caught a glimpse of her brother standing just inside the door to her father's study. The sight gave her pause, and she drew in a deep breath. "What is Walter doing here?" she asked in a quiet tone.

Helen, who was not much older than Emma and easy to glean secrets from, pursed her lips in agitation. "Your father has been waiting for your return. He asked to send you directly into the study."

Emma's throat clenched. *What now?* What could possibly be so important that he called for Walter to come over in the middle of a workday? And why was her father home? He should be at one of his textile mills, where he often stayed late into the evening. Something must be terribly wrong.

Her first thought turned to Lynette, Walter's petite and frail wife. Had something terrible happened? She dared wonder—another miscarriage? She hoped not. The poor woman already had had three in three years, much to the grief of Emma's brother. But her failure to successfully bear a child seemed more tragic and upsetting to Emma's father, who had no qualms about reminding poor Walter how important it was that the Bradshaw line continued.

Her heart went out to Lynette, who wanted a child terribly, and who seemed to be getting more and more withdrawn year after year. And it was apparent the waiting was trying on Walter. His patience had been worn to a thin veneer, and Emma worried at some point it would crack.

Emma could hardly imagine the disappointment and heartache of losing a child, albeit early in pregnancy. But three? Would Lynette ever successfully bear a child? If not, Emma hated to think how her father would react. And what that would mean for her, his only other child progeny of continuing the Bradshaw name. Although, once she married, she would no longer be a Bradshaw. But if her brother failed to provide any grandchildren, Emma knew she would be pressured more than ever to marry and have a family.

She scowled at the thought. She was little more than a brood mare to her father—like the many horses he owned. Someone to whom he could pass along his wealth and investments and race horses and properties, labeled with the reputation and prestige of the name Bradshaw. She would not be allowed to marry whomever she wanted. Nor would she be allowed to marry for love. She gulped back tears as she walked slowly to the study, dreading every step. She had no doubt if Lynette failed to provide her father an heir to his estate that she herself would be forced into a marriage solely to his liking, and not hers.

All the more reason to hurry off to college, where the long arm of his authority could not fully reach. Maybe while at college she would meet a man she could love with all her heart. A man she would choose—not one picked her father.

As she entered the study, she saw not only her mother already seated on the settee, a sweating glass of sweet tea in her hand, but also Lynette, who appeared fine—albeit a bit pale—much to Emma's relief. Lynette, dressed in a light-blue crinoline skirt and white button blouse, gave her a smile from the small sofa she sat upon, but a reserved smile, and Emma wondered about that. She nodded hello to her brother, who had a big grin on his face as he towered over his wife from behind the sofa, his chin jutting and his arms crossed.

What could that possibly mean? Maybe Lynette was pregnant again? But if she was, they would not be sitting here in the middle of a Thursday, and her brother's face would be more worried than joyful. No, there had to be another reason for this mysterious gathering.

"Please sit, Emaline," her father said, smoothing out his silk vest and gesturing to the velvet wingback chair next to the settee. His tone was firm but held a spark of excitement. Emma dreaded what was coming. Her father had the look of someone who had just made an important decision. And usually those decisions did not take anyone else's opinion into consideration.

Oh no . . . He couldn't have . . .

"As you know," he began, his eyes lighting on each person in the room, "I've been in correspondence for a while now with my longtime friend Nathan Meeker—who used to work at the *Tribune*—ever since he started the colony in Greeley, Colorado . . ."

Emma's head suddenly spun. The room grew claustrophobic and hot, and she grasped the sides of the chair to steady herself, afraid she might faint.

Her father gestured enthusiastically. ". . . For five years now they've been building a wonderful town, based on morality, high values, family, and church. Ever since the last presidential election, you know how upset I've been with the disturbing state of affairs. With Greeley's loss in the election, and then his death, I'd lost all faith in the current administration. And these last few years of depression have shown that the economy is getting worse. All that overspeculation in the railroads, the closing of the stock exchange for ten days, the whining and lying and corruption everywhere, particularly in Grant's cabinet—"

"Darling," Emma's mother said, patting her husband's hand a little frantically, "we all know how you feel about President Grant. And the economy."

How many evenings at the dinner table had they all been subjected to her father's rants about the loose and shameful morals of those running—and ruining—the country? More than Emma could count. But why was her father going on about this now, in the middle of a hot June day? She wished she had her fan so she could cool off her face, but she dared not move for fear of swooning.

Walter spoke up. "What Father means is we are going to leave all this . . . chaos behind. A new life awaits us."

"What?" Emma blurted out before she could catch herself. She stole a quick glance at her mother, and then Lynette. They did not seem surprised at all by Walter's words. Which meant . . .

"I don't understand, Father. What are you talking about?"

Charles Edwin Bradshaw gave his daughter a smile filled with confident assurance. "In two weeks we are moving to Greeley. You remember our good friends, the Turnbulls, who moved some years ago to Albany? Well, they've recently moved out there, and Ernest has been after me for two years now to join them."

"Colorado . . ." Emma barely whispered. Colorado Territory was all the way across the country, halfway around the world. Images of cutthroat Indians and mangy cowboys shooting rifles at poor homesteaders ran through her mind. Snakes, buffalo stampedes, dust storms, dirt. "But, Father, how . . . why . . . ? It's the middle of nowhere." Why in the world would her family want to move there? She would never go to a place as wild as that. Just the thought of living in a house without indoor plumbing, and having to venture the elements to wander out to an outhouse . . . She sucked in a deep breath. Thank God she had been accepted into Vassar and her classes were already secured.

"Turnbull's company has finally brought the railroad up to their colony. The town is a short train ride from Denver—a booming city with everything you could possibly need. He's already had two houses built for us in town, and they are nearly finished—"

Emma gasped in horror. "You've been planning this for months, then. And never told us?" She could hardly keep the ire and shock out of her voice. From the corner of her eye she saw Lynette drop her gaze, no doubt embarrassed for Emma over this outburst. Emma seethed in silence. How long had Lynette and Walter known? Emma rarely dared to speak up to her father, but she had to. They were abandoning her, or so it felt.

Her father stroked her mother's head. Only then did she realize her mother, too, had not only known this secret but approved. She asked her mother pointedly, "How can you give all this up? Live in the Wild West like some outlaws?"

Walter chuckled. Emma scowled at him. "What's so funny?"

He waved his hand in the air in an arrogant manner that so reminded her of her father. He was slowly but surely becoming just like him, the way he would disdain those who had the misfortune of a lower station in life, as if it were somehow their fault. Sometimes she felt sorry for Lynette having him as a husband. It couldn't be easy. But Lynette had come from a family that had lost much of its wealth in bad investments. Her status had been greatly improved by marrying into the Bradshaw family. She didn't doubt her brother loved Lynette, but Emma did not miss how he often treated her in a cool and condescending manner, much like Father treated Mother.

Walter got up and stood in front of Emma, shaking his head as if she were a silly child. "Greeley is a forward-thinking community. Founded by men of great education and skill. In the last few years they've built flour mills, tanning factories, and opera houses. The original group of six hundred all come from wealthy families from New York and other East Coast cities. Hardly a bunch of country bumpkins. They heeded Greeley's cry to go west and restore this country to right morals and ideals."

He sounds just like Father too. Emma sighed, knowing it was foolish to try to dissuade her family. Clearly they had made up their mind to leave. But why hadn't they discussed this with her before now?

"Emma, dear," her mother added, "a wonderful land of promise awaits us. A place where we can live in the fresh air surrounded by beautiful mountains. A town with culture, values, integrity. No more humid, crowded city to endure." She looked over at Lynette. "And the doctor says the climate change will be good for Lynette's health."

Emma nodded. *So she would be in better health to bear a child.* She could see now why her brother had jumped on the bandwagon like some political supporter. But didn't they even consider all the dangers? Did they really think they could transport this comfortable, wealthy lifestyle to the frontier?

"Well, I suppose if you've made up your mind to go, I can hardly stop you," Emma said, conceding. It would be much more inconvenient for them all to visit each other, but in a way, the idea began to appeal to her. Perhaps with them so far from New York, she could truly live the life she dreamed of without hindrance. She would dutifully write them, and assure them in the way they'd expect, but she would be free.

A lengthy silence fell. She looked up from her musings, only to find puzzled, stern expressions. "What is it?" she asked, a terrible feeling creeping into her stomach. Once more the heat constricted her breathing, and her corset felt about to burst. She fidgeted on her chair.

Her mother smiled sweetly and laid her hand on Emma's wrist — not all that lightly. Emma sensed tension and chastisement in her touch.

"We know it's not what you had planned, dear, but we feel it's for the best . . ."

Emma's hands clenched, and she shut tight her mouth. *No . . .*

"What your mother is saying," her father interjected, "is we are *all* going. As a family, together."

Her father's words sounded as if coming from underwater, but they made their way into her heart, piercing her like tiny darts as she drew in short, shallow breaths. No one noticed her distress.

"But . . . I'm going to Vassar. I'm already enrolled — "

Her father smiled, but it held no warmth. Emma knew by his look he would not brook any argument from her. The realization of what he had done descended upon her like a storm cloud, and tears fell like rain upon her cheeks.

"I've taken care of all that. The school knows you will not be attending this fall."

An uncomfortable silence flooded the small room, stifling Emma more than the heat. "Please, Father . . ." she managed to eke out.

"There will be no further discussion." Then her father clapped loudly, a boom of thunder to add to her storm, startling Emma, who had her eyes pinned on the gold brocade drapes drawn to keep out the noise and heat of the city. "We have two weeks to pack. I am having trunks and crates delivered tomorrow, so we can begin going through our things and instruct the servants what to pack. Our furniture will be shipped, as will your horse, Emma. Once we get settled in, you should feel right at home. So no need to fret."

With that last brusque announcement, her father strode to the study door. "I must get back to the office. I'll be home late." Emma lifted her face and met her father's stern gaze. He forced a smile, but his eyes warned her against any more objections. She knew nothing she could say would change his mind. Without a word or gesture of support, the rest of her family quietly vacated the room, leaving her alone in her misery.

Her dreams were now dashed, she realized as she wiped her face with the sleeve of her blouse. Maybe Colorado was a land of promise to Father and the rest of her family, but it felt like a death sentence to her.

Chapter 2

EMMA LOOKED UP FROM WHERE she was sitting on a cushion and glanced out the window. From her second-story bedroom, she could see the servants and movers emptying out her house, one trunk, one piece of furniture, at a time. As four men hefted the heavy pieces onto flat platforms attached to draft horses, her mother looked on from the front stoop, calling out to them, although Emma couldn't hear what she was saying. No doubt warning them to take great care with her precious china and collectibles. Her father was finishing up at his office, leaving Emma and her mother with the last bit of packing.

A few neighbors strolled by eyeing the goings-on with curiosity. What had Father told them? Who would soon buy their lovely house? Who would soon be sleeping in her room? Emma had lived in this charming high-ceilinged brownstone her whole life, and although she had planned to leave for college, she'd assumed she'd always have a home to come back to. Now, she felt unmoored, like a ship floundering the waves, directionless.

She wrenched her gaze from the window and returned to her packing. Helen had offered to help her finish, but she wanted to be alone. To sit in her room one last time and try to prepare herself for what lay ahead. If it were possible.

What would she do without Helen each day? Mother had assured Emma a placement agency in Denver would provide them with suitable help, but Helen had become more of a friend than a lady's maid over the last few years. It had brought tears to her eyes saying good-bye to the young woman who had provided not just a listening ear but kind compassion at the times Emma needed it. And she'd hardly been able to spend a few last hours with her closest female friends with whom she rode on Saturdays in Central Park.

A lump lodged in her throat as she pictured the life she knew beginning to slip from her hands. She let out a trembling sigh, holding back the tears pushing to the corners of her eyes. At least she'd have Shahayla, her Arabian mare, to ride to counteract the loneliness she was bound to feel.

Emma looked around her bedroom. The pretty blue-striped wallpaper appeared barren without the pictures and drawings hanging upon them. With the furniture already loaded onto the wagons, her room was now an empty, impersonal space that gave little indication anyone had occupied it in the last seventeen years. It hurt her heart to think of walking out the door, never to return.

As much as her father's decision had blighted her dreams, she would find a way to turn this disaster into something worthwhile. She was determined to continue her studies of botany, and to hone her illustrative technique. She knew she had talent as an artist, but that wasn't what mattered to her. She had a longing to understand plants—how they grew and reproduced. And no doubt there were going to be plants in Colorado that she could study and draw.

She got up from the floor and went to her little glass atrium off her room and set the space to memory. She would miss this haven of solitude the most. After she had read a book on the Royal Botanical Gardens in Kew, England, two years ago, at her pleading her father had had this glass-paneled space added to her room, extended out over the back roof a few feet. Just like the Palm House at Kew, the addition was framed in wrought iron, with hand-blown glass panes to allow light to stream in. The small transom windows could be opened to regulate the temperature and bring in a cool breeze. Here she grew her orchids and violets and other flowers, but her most cherished plant was the crape myrtle she'd ordered from England, which originally came from Asia. She had planned to plant it in front of the brownstone before heading for college, as a way of leaving something of herself behind. But now . . .

She knew myrtles could withstand some winter weather, but would it survive in the harsh Colorado elements? She had cut back on watering and fertilizing last fall, to increase its hardiness and help it survive the cold. It was only three feet tall, and it seemed silly to bring it along on the train, but she couldn't bear the thought of leaving it behind, not knowing if anyone would tend to it properly. Her mother chided her for her request but thankfully had given in.

Emma let her fingers brush the shiny smooth leaves of the tree as she looked at all the various potted plants and flowers lining the shelf against the back glass wall. She had told Helen to keep them or give them away. Or perhaps she could even sell them and make a few pennies. If only Helen could come to Colorado along with her; she would so cherish her companionship in a place where she knew no one. But her maid had family in New York. In fact, none of the servants, although offered continued employment and reassurance they would be well taken care of in their new residence in Greeley, were coming—except for Josephine, her mother's longtime maid.

Emma didn't blame them. Who would want to give up the comforts and familiarity of New York for the wild frontier?

Emma smirked. As much as her family believed they would be picking up their life of class and ease and transferring it all to Colorado Territory without any trouble, Emma doubted it would be such a smooth transition. She had heard and read plenty of stories of those who had moved out west as if taken by a fever — searching for a new life, hoping to strike it rich in the gold fields. So many hopes and dreams dashed when faced with the rigors and challenges of the frontier. And what about the Indians? She'd read of massacres and continual skirmishes with native tribes in Colorado. When she mentioned this to her father, he assured her the "hostiles" had all been removed to Oklahoma. They were no longer a threat. But Emma wondered if that was truly the case. And the thought of forcing people off their land to make way for others that wanted the land for themselves . . . well, that just didn't sit well with her.

Emma shook her head and gathered up the few last drawings lying about. She tucked them into her leather portfolio and collected the stack of journals and books she still needed to pack. She would not leave behind Bantha's *Handbook of the British Flora* or Schleiden's *Principles of Scientific Botany.* They would be a source of encouragement and comfort to her in her new home. A reminder of her dreams. Maybe, in a few years, she would find a way to attend college. Without her father to pay her tuition, though, she didn't see how that would be possible. But she would not give up hope.

As she placed her portfolio and books into the small trunk at her feet, her mother came into her room.

"Oh my. It looks so empty." She came over to Emma and stroked her cheek. Emma said nothing as her throat tightened. Her mother took in the bare walls. "I remember when I decorated this room to be your nursery. Do you remember the wallpaper with the little flowers and rabbits?"

Emma nodded, smiling at the memory. They had replaced that paper many years ago. She recalled counting the rabbits that jumped over the hedges as she lay in bed, fighting sleep.

Her mother gave her a sad smile. "Where have all the years gone? You've grown up. Now you're a woman, old enough to marry and start your own family—"

Emma had no patience this morning for one of her mother's long dreamy visions of Emma's inevitable marriage and subsequent childbearing. She closed the trunk's lid and said, "Mother, how long did you know about these plans to move to Colorado Territory?"

Her mother seemed taken aback. "Why, your father only informed me of his decision the night before he told you. He'd spoken of moving many times, of course. But really—I had no idea he'd made up his mind—"

"But didn't he care to ask you what you wanted? You seem so happy here in New York, with your social circles and friends and all the events and charities you support."

"Emma," her mother said in a tone that made Emma feel as if she were a naïve child, "you need to understand a woman's role in marriage, in society. Your father is the head of the family; it is a divine charge for him to be so. A woman must concede to her husband's wishes."

"But aren't husbands also to love their wives, and make concession for their needs and wants?" Emma knew her father loved her mother, but he rarely asked for her opinion on anything, and his hard-handedness often seemed more oppressive than loving. And her mother never dared cross him or disagree with his decisions, although Emma could tell by her mother's frequent "illnesses" that she suffered from such restraint. Mother's way of coping with unpleasantness was to develop a migraine or shortness of breath, often excusing herself to her room—probably to take a dose of laudanum.

COLORADO PROMISE

Her mother paced the room, a look of discomfort flushing her cheeks. "This is not the time for such a lengthy discussion. The carriage is out front to take us to the train depot. Your brother and Lynette will be meeting us there at eleven." She twisted the pair of gloves she held in her hand and stopped to look at Emma.

"In time, when you're married, you'll understand. How it's a woman's place to support her husband. That the greatest fulfillment a woman can have is found in being submissive and obedient to his leading. Women are meant to be wives and mothers, not to take a man's place in the working world. Expressing such strong opinions . . . isn't proper."

Emma could think of nothing to say in reply. She'd read of the suffrage movements gaining momentum. Of women taking on positions of authority only men once held. Even at Vassar there were women who were members of scientific societies. How could her mother forget Victoria Woodhull's run for presidency in 1872? Times were surely changing for women, and her mother just didn't want to see it. Nor did her father, Emma thought bitterly.

When Emma failed to say anything in reply, her mother curtly nodded and left the room with an admonishment to hurry up and finish packing.

Emma listened to her mother's shoes clicking on the oak stairs as she headed downstairs. The sound echoed solemnly through the empty house, mirroring the emptiness she now felt in her heart. She turned and picked up the small pot that held the crape myrtle. The poor plant was nearly bursting from its container, yearning to grow into a tall and magnificent tree full of beautiful crimson blooms. She knew exactly how the tree felt.

She hugged the pot close and made a promise—more to herself than to the sapling. *I will find a place for you in Colorado, where you can stretch out your roots and flourish under a wide-open sky.*

She walked to the threshold of her room, and after a final glance back, set her face to her uncertain future and made her way to the carriage waiting to take her to her new life.

Lucas Rawlings felt someone staring at his back. He stopped walking the thoroughbred mare, turned and looked over at the paddock gate, and pushed back his wide-brimmed beaver felt hat. Two bright-eyed faces stared back at him. Lucas smiled and resumed walking the horse in a slow circle.

"Whatcha doing, Doc Rawlings?" one of the twins asked. Lucas studied the ten-year-old's face. He knew most folks couldn't tell the boys apart, but he could. Thomas always had a more mischievous look on his face, and Lucas figured he was the instigator of most of their misbehavior. But he knew these boys had good hearts. Lucas chuckled. They just had an abundance of energy. Good thing their parents let them run a little wild, although Lucas could tell many of Ed Edwards's neighbors did not approve. Those who lived here in Greeley tended to be very set on proper manners, and particularly in having well-behaved children.

"This horse has colic," he told the boy. "And you don't really have to call me 'Doc.' I'm a veterinary physician, Thomas." He knew those "big" words would make the boys frown in puzzlement.

Thomas shook his head adamantly. "My name's *Tex*. Not Thomas."

Lucas snickered but tried to keep a straight face. "Oh, right. My mistake . . . Tex. And how are you doing today, *Bandit*?" Lucas wondered if Henry had come up with that name for himself or if his more aggressive brother had thought of that one. The two boys, although identical in looks, were anything but when it came to their personalities. Henry was soft-spoken and shy, and Lucas could tell he deferred to Thomas in all matters. But he too had an eagerness to learn, and Lucas made a point to teach these boys as much as he could about what they loved the most—horses.

"What's colic?" Henry asked.

Lucas looked over the mare, pleased with how she was now faring, after he'd administered the medicine and been walking her for the better part of an hour. "It's an intestinal problem. Oftentimes it's just a stomachache, but it can be deadly, so you want to take care not to let your horse get sick like this."

"That's the Wilkersons' horse, ain't it?" Thomas asked. "How'd it get sick?"

Lucas looked back at the boys. "You recall how I told you about horses having sensitive stomachs?" The boys nodded. "Now, a horse that gets hot and thirsty will want to take a long drink, but if it drinks a lot of cold water, it can get colicky. Or even if it spends too much time in cold water, like wading across a deep stream. " He noticed the boys listening with their usual rapt attention, and a familiar pang of sadness rose up in his heart. *Push that thought away, Lucas Rawlings. It will do nothing but give you heartache.*

He cleared his throat, swallowing past the lump lodged there, and put on a serious face. "Now, some folks here, coming from the East, aren't aware how cold our Colorado rivers are. The water coming down Cache la Poudre is snowmelt—"

"And that's really cold," Thomas added with a twinkle in his eye showing he was pleased with his remark.

Lucas nodded, then brought the gleaming black horse over to the boys. They eagerly reached their hands over the top railing of the gate and stroked her head and muzzle. "So," he continued, "after a long ride across the prairie on a hot day such as today, a rider might let the horse take a long drink before bringing her back to the stables. But too much of that cold water too fast—"

"Will make the horse real sick," Thomas finished in his high-pitched voice.

"Right," Lucas answered. He ran his hands along the mare's flank and belly, then patted her on the rump. "I think she'll be fine now." He unbuckled the halter and let the horse loose, then came toward the gate. The boys jumped down and swung it open for him, and he came out into the long corridor inside the livery stable. Lucas ruffled Henry's hair, and the boy laughed and pulled back with a sour expression. He figured the boys thought they were getting too old for such affection.

He looked out the open stable doors to the beautiful warm summer day. Sarah's ranch dog, Hoesta, was waiting patiently for him, sitting on his haunches with his tongue lolling out the side of his mouth. The half-wolf loved to run, and just about every time Lucas headed to town, the dog loped along at the horse's hooves. "You boys out of school already?"

"Yep," Thomas said. "For the *whole* summer." Henry gave an enthusiastic nod in agreement.

All the more opportunity to get into more trouble, Lucas mused with a smile. He closed the latches on his medical bag and straightened up. "So, how are those ponies doing? You taking good care of them?" He gave both boys a stern look.

"Yes sir," they chimed in unison.

"Good." He took a last look at the mare, marveling at her beautiful conformation and gentle nature. She'd been shipped out here in the spring from Massachusetts—Hugh Wilkerson had bought her on the recommendation of one of his neighbors who owned a horse farm. He'd made a good purchase. She surely was a magnificent creature. Much like the horses he had been around in his childhood in Kentucky. Although he loved all horses, he had a special fondness for thoroughbreds, since he'd grown up with them, and most of his veterinary training was on the race horse farms near Lexington. *That life feels like a hundred years ago.*

"Well, boys, I need to be off. Things to tend to at the ranch." He tipped his hat and started walking toward the graveled path that led to the street.

Thomas tugged on Lucas's sleeve. "But when are you going to take us out to see the buffalo? You promised."

Lucas shook his head. "Now, Thomas—"

"Tex!"

"Now, Tex, I can't control when or where the buffalo roam. But if I catch a whiff of them anywhere around Greeley, I will come get you. So long as your folks say it's okay."

"They will! They will!" Thomas answered. "Hey, did you know that buffalo can jump six feet in the air? And they can run forty miles an hour!"

"Nope, didn't know that," Lucas said, amused at Thomas's beaming face. "All right. Now run along."

Lucas sighed and shook his head as the two boys ran out the stables and down the road. Ever since their father had taken them to Denver to see Bill Cody's Wild West Show, they wouldn't let up about wanting to see the buffalo. Well, it wouldn't be too hard. The plains were overrun with the beasts. And they were the cause of a lot of the Indian wars, Lucas reminded himself, thinking how not that long ago the Indians and white settlers had seemed to live peaceably together—until the disputes arose over the buffalo hunting grounds. Sarah had told him plenty of stories back when he'd come down from the mountains three years ago and began working for her. Her father had been a buffalo skin trader for two decades.

Three years. He'd pushed it out of his mind this morning when he woke, but the anniversary date of his arrival on the Front Range made him realize how quickly the time had passed. And how slowly the pain ebbed away. But he refused to indulge in the sadness that threatened to engulf him. He had to move forward, leave the past behind and find purpose and meaning in his life. Even though at times he wanted nothing more than to give up.

My son would have been three years old . . .

He steeled his resolve and pushed the image of Alice and the baby out of his mind. But every time he did so, a knife stabbed his heart. What hurt more than anything was how her face was fading more and more each day. All he had was the one daguerreotype they'd taken that weekend they'd gone down from Leadville to Denver. It had been Alice's idea to pose for a picture, as she wanted to frame it and put it on the mantle. Now it sat buried under a pile of clothes in his small cabin, where he lived alone and lonely.

Sarah had recently been hinting he should think about "getting out." Meaning, to start looking for a wife. But how could anyone ever replace Alice? No one could. He had loved her so much, and it had been his fault she'd died . . .

Stop thinking like that. You know it gets you nowhere. He'd hoped by now he'd have stopped blaming himself. He knew he'd done everything he could to save her and the baby. It was just a bad set of circumstances. The blizzard, her going into labor early, the doctor sick, not able to clear the snow and get any help. He'd tried everything. God knows he'd tried.

Lucas hurried his pace over to the hitching rail outside the stables. His mustang opened its eyes, awaking from a lazy nap in the sun at his approach. He patted the gelding's neck, then tightened the cinch and looped the headstall over the horse's head. After removing the halter, he tied it to the side of the saddle. He tossed the reins over the railing and fastened his medical satchel behind the saddle's cantel. Then he led the horse down the hard-packed dirt street toward the Wilkersons' house on Eleventh Street, to let them know how their mare was doing. Hoesta trotted with his head hung behind them, looking every bit wolfish.

Earlier, when he arrived at the stables after Miz Wilkerson had found him at the mercantile, he'd explained to the couple about the colic and the need to take care not to let their horses drink so much after a long, hot ride. They'd only been in Colorado Territory a year, and this was their first summer on the Front Range. He liked Hugh and Cora very much, and unlike some of the other wealthy residents of Greeley, they treated him with warmth and acceptance, uncaring of any class difference between them. So many of the folks that had founded this town had airs. But the ones he'd become closest to were Ed and Ginny Edwards—the parents of the wild twins. *Tex and Bandit.* Lucas chuckled.

As he walked along looking at the finely dressed ladies strolling the well-swept wooden sidewalks, he reflected on some of the names folks used when referring to Greeley, like "City of Saints" and "City of Churches." Some of the local ranchers and farmers joked about the high-mindedness of the Greeley residents, but Lucas felt all in all they were a decent bunch that loved their families and lived by good moral principles.

Now, he knew some who lived around Evans and Fort Collins didn't want any reminding of how low or lacking their own morals were and so rightly kept their distance from the town. But there were plenty of places for ruffians and low-minded individuals to spend their time and money without having to enter inside Greeley's fenced community. Sometimes Lucas thought they'd erected that wood fence in hopes of keeping more than just free-ranging cattle from wandering into their fields of wheat or trampling their rows of vegetables. But trouble and bad intentions regarded no boundaries. Lucas knew that all too well from his years entrenched in the Civil War—more memories he hoped the crisp Colorado air would eventually whisk away across the open range.

He stopped along the side of the road and looked out over the impressive acres of thriving crops, intersected with weed-free irrigation ditches, filled with water brought from the river by way of a wisely designed system of flumes and pipes. Although Lucas had no interest in moving to town, preferring his solitude along the South Platte at the northeast edge of Sarah's ranch, he couldn't help but admire what these industrious and talented folks had built here. It amazed him to see how the town had grown over the last few years, with more and more settlers from the East moving in. Why, they had three opera houses! And at least a dozen churches. Ed Edwards was kept very busy designing and building new homes, and had showed him just last week two new houses he was finishing up for a family moving out from New York. *More rich folks bringing their fancy clothes and horses and furnishings.* Paying top dollar and more to ship lumber out from as far as Chicago, due to the shortage of trees on the Front Range.

All these folks, coming to Colorado Territory, with hopes and dreams—the frontier offering the promise of a new start. He wondered why they'd up and leave such a comfortable, easy life behind. Adventure? A sense of belonging they just couldn't get in a big city?

Lucas frowned as sadness welled back up in his heart. This time he let it, too tired to fight the surge sweeping him under. He pushed back the tears threatening to erupt and pulled his hat down to hide his eyes. He'd gone out to Colorado seven years ago with plenty of dreams, but they'd all melted away, like snow under the hot Colorado summer sun.

After Alice's death, when he stumbled down from the mountains to the Front Range, he hadn't seen anything but a vast empty prairie, as flat as the top of a stove, bursting with colorful wildflowers that seemed inconsiderate of his pain. The sight offered little solace and even less hope. But he'd had nowhere else to go, and he couldn't foster the thought of staying in Leadville, where he'd buried his wife and infant son. No, he had to leave it all behind, though the memories trotted after him like a pesky unwanted dog he couldn't shake off.

Yet, somehow over the last few years, the edge had softened on the pain. Most days. Some days he truly enjoyed his life. He had learned to find fulfillment in his vocation and the simple joy of pleasant acquaintances with those who shared the land. And the wide open space of the Front Range afforded him room to breathe, to heal. The majesty of the mountains as a backdrop, the hard sky so blue it hurt your eyes, and the sweeping panorama of the miles of unspoiled river valley often served as a balm to his wounds.

He only hoped one day the pain and guilt would flow away, the way the golden aspen leaves in the fall danced on the ripples of the river, carried off to faraway places, leaving the bare limbs to sprout new greenery in the spring. He had been similarly stripped bare, his heart numb and raw both, left wondering if he could ever love again. His heart ached for the kind of love he'd shared with Alice, but would he ever again find anyone he could love that much? He hoped so. He knew he couldn't spend the rest of his life alone like this; he was only twenty-eight.

Maybe Sarah was right. Maybe it was time to open up his heart. At least entertain the possibility. It wasn't like he didn't notice the attractive young women that made subtle advances toward him. He appreciated their interest, and he'd be lying if he said their comely smiles and womanly attributes failed to stir his slumbering passion. But none yet had even come close to having that spark of life and vibrant personality that had attracted him to his former wife. And he couldn't settle for just anyone, no matter how lonely he felt.

No, if he was going to open his heart and be willing to risk pain *and* love, it would have to be for someone truly meant for him. And somehow he knew he'd know her the moment he laid eyes on her.

Chapter 3

___

"OH, THERE THEY ARE. DARLING! Walter, over here!"

Emma turned around on the train platform and saw her father standing alongside her brother and Lynette at the doorway of the next train car. They were all dressed in their light woolen travel clothes, their many suitcases and travel bags piled at their sides. The sight of them amid the noise and bustle of passengers eager to speed off to far-flung destinations enhanced Emma's despair. Her sadness over losing the only home she'd ever known and the trepidation for what lay ahead seemed a silent cry in all this heyday of adventure around her. She felt anything but adventurous.

Two porters came down the short steps from the train car and began transferring her family's things on board. Emma hurried after her mother, both of them threading through the thick crowd of awaiting passengers to greet the rest of the family.

Her father stood tall in his elegant beige three-piece suit, glancing down at his gold pocket watch and smiling. Excitement shone in his features, and she had to admit it was good to see him so happy after many months of his grumbling and gloomy forecasts over the economy. He had left able men in charge of his many textile factories, but she wondered how restless he would get out in Colorado without men to order around and the affairs of industry and business occupying his days. Once they were out in Colorado, he and Walter would still oversee all of Father's investments through telegraph and mail correspondence. She hoped that would keep her father too busy to focus on finding a husband for her. Just the thought made her spirits sink even lower.

She politely greeted her father and brother, but they hardly acknowledged her presence. That left her free to go speak to Lynette, leaving behind her mother, who was fretting in her usual way—now worrying over which seats they'd been assigned and whether the sleeper cars would be roomy enough.

"Hello, Lynette," Emma said, noting her sister-in-law looked terribly pale. Was she ill? Emma felt a stab of guilt. Maybe moving west to drier air and cooler summer temperatures would be beneficial for Lynette's health. Although Emma was certain that was not the primary reason for the whole family to move to Colorado Territory—not by any means—it encouraged her to see their concern over Lynette's well-being.

"Emma." Lynette smiled and reached out with her white-gloved hands, clasping Emma's lace ones. Emma admired the lovely travel hat Lynette sported—a pale gray felt trimmed with ribbon that bordered her pretty heart-shaped face. She wore a smart lightweight gray travel suit with a ruffle-trimmed white blouse. Lynette always made simple fashion look elegant, although the pale gray color only emphasized the wan tone of her skin.

"I'm hoping we can spend some time together on the train," Emma said, "and perhaps we can sneak off and have tea in the dining car. I feel like we've had so little opportunity to visit with each other." Emma had taken many short trips on trains, but this would be the first time she would actually sleep on one—and for many days. She worried how unpleasant they might all feel—and smell—after so much time without a proper bath. Well, a few days was surely manageable.

"I agree," Lynette said, giving Emma a reassuring sisterly smile. Emma had always wanted a sister, someone to confide in and share secrets with. She knew Lynette could never truly be a sister like that—not with Walter standing between them. But she hoped maybe this trip—and this move—would provide a way for the two of them to finally become close and get to know each other better. Lynette seemed to be the only one in her immediate family that didn't judge her or make plans for her future. Maybe that would be one benefit to this forced move.

They'd had little opportunity to become more than acquaintances, what with her brother living miles away, just outside the city across the East River—where the heat was often blown away by the currents off the water, and Lynette often being too frail to come visiting. Emma now realized she could have made a greater effort to visit her sister-in-law, but truth be told—her brother never made her feel welcome in his home. Ever since he married, he'd devoted all his time and energy to helping their father grow their business empire. And she had to admit—he doted on Lynette, but he often seemed to treat her as if she were a delicate caged bird, keeping her close and never letting her really spread her wings. Emma wondered what dreams Lynette harbored in her heart—aside from wanting a family.

Emma again felt a pang of sympathy for her sister-in-law. She told her in a quiet voice, "I do hope this move will be a good one for you. And now I'll be living close by, so I can be more of a friend than an acquaintance."

Lynette responded with a genuine smile. "I'm looking forward to that." She leaned close to Emma's face. "And I have to admit I'm a bit excited to see some of the West. I've read so much about it; it hardly seems like a real place."

Emma chuckled. All she could imagine were the eccentric descriptions of vengeful Indians and ruffian cowboys she'd read of in magazines and those dime novels her childhood neighbor, Randall Turnbull, used to read to her when they hid in the corner of his father's study hoping to avoid being shooed out of the house to play. Beadle's Dime Novels—that's what they were called, Emma now remembered. How enthralled little Randall became in the stories of the daring men who risked death in their call to adventure. Although, he was never one to take risks at all. He preferred reading about them from the safety of a comfortable chair.

"I'm sure Colorado will be full of surprises," she conceded to Lynette, watching the crowds of people boarding the trains around her.

Lynette's face grew serious, and then Emma caught a curious mischievous spark in her sister-in-law's eye. In a whisper she said to Emma, "Speaking of surprises . . ."

Emma spun around to see who Lynette was tipping her head toward and noticed a dashing-looking young man walk with purpose directly toward them. How odd. Then she caught his eyes, and realized with embarrassment the man was looking straight at her and smiling.

He looked somewhat familiar, but she could not place his face. His burnished red hair peeked out from his tan bowler hat, and thick side-whiskers ran down the edge of his round face. He presented a very fine figure, Emma had to admit, although a bit broad and hefty, and the cut and fabric of his suit bespoke wealth.

His face emanated a kind demeanor, and his smile revealed white, straight teeth.

Emma felt her face heat up as she watched the man make a beeline right toward them. She turned her head toward Lynette. "A friend of yours?" she asked her.

"No," Lynette answered with a sly grin. "Apparently an old acquaintance of yours. Walter introduced us moments before you arrived, and your father sent him to watch for you at the curb. He must have missed you in the crowds."

"But . . . who is he?" She dared take another quick look at this man, whose warm brown eyes were bright with excitement. A slightly crooked grin rose up on his face, making dimples appear on his cheeks. Dimples she remembered well. "Oh . . . it can't be . . ."

As the words left her mouth, the man came up to her, lifted her hand to his lips, and planted a kiss on her gloved fingers. She nearly pulled back in horror at his forwardness, then when she saw the twinkle in his eyes, burst out in a laugh.

"Oh my goodness. It's you. Randall . . . you're so . . . tall. What happened to the pudgy little boy I used to chase in the park?"

She covered her lips with her hand, wishing she could stuff the words back in her mouth. How could she talk so familiarly in public, and in front of her sister-in-law? It was so improper and unladylike. But she could hardly think of Randall Turnbull as a gentleman—or even a man. To her, he was the funny little boy with whom she'd spent long summer days while growing up, who'd live just three doors down and been her best friend—and cohort—in all their mischievous enterprises.

"Well," Randall said, interrupting the flood of delightful memories that rushed through her mind at seeing him. "You are hardly the little scrawny tomboy that liked to climb trees." He blew out a breath, took both her hands in his, and stepped back to look at her. "In fact, Emaline Bradshaw, you are quite stunning."

Emma's cheeks burned hot at his words. But for the first time in her life, she didn't mind such manly scrutiny. She knew his gaze held only affection, no hint of lechery or condescension. Oh, what a wonderful surprise to see him again.

Lynette cleared her throat politely and nodded to where Walter was in animate discussion with Emma's father. "If you'll excuse me . . ." she said, and left Emma to speak privately with her longtime, nearly forgotten friend.

"What are you doing here? I'd heard you were at Yale." Emma felt suddenly flushed from all the excitement and smothering heat of the depot, and drew back, putting distance between them so she could breathe easier. Randall dropped her hands and stepped back as well, as if suddenly aware people were watching.

Emma glanced quickly over at her parents, and immediately her stomach twisted in a knot. One look at her father's keen gaze upon them told her Randall's appearance here was no coincidence. Leave it to her father to arrange such a meeting.

But for once she was glad. She turned back to Randall and took him in. Never in her life had she ever imagined he would have grown up to be so tall and handsome. His pudgy features had mostly gone, leaving in their place a man with stature and poise, although he wasn't what she'd consider a muscular type. He gave her a smile that was wholly genuine, and she had to resist touching his dimples, remembering how she used to tease him and poke his dimples just to annoy him.

Oh my, he's very attractive . . . and I'm guessing very available, if Father arranged for him to see us off. But why bring us together now, when I'm about to leave on a train out west? Is he going out to see his father? The thought suddenly struck her, and she had to ask.

"Will you be joining us on the train?" Perhaps he was taking the summer off between classes. "Are you still attending Yale?"

He nodded yes to both questions, then frowned. "Well, I've taken a leave . . . for the moment."

Emma could tell he was upset about something, but didn't want to press him for answers. Not here, and now her father was waving them over, signaling they needed to board.

"And your sisters—how are they?" she asked as they headed toward her family. Randall had been the baby, with four much-older sisters.

Randall smirked. "All married—living along the Eastern seaboard, from Boston to Charleston. I'm an uncle five times over, although I rarely see them all. Holidays, of course." He shrugged. "I'm the last one to marry off, and Father has been needling me to no end in that regard, but I want to finish my last two years of school first."

How alike they were. *Still.* But he at least had gotten to go to college, she thought with bitterness. Then another thought crossed her mind unexpectedly. *Would he really wait to marry until he finished school—if he found the right woman?* She felt a little flutter in her chest and wondered at the surprising feelings of attraction she felt for him. Or was it just because he was so comfortable to be around?

She stole a glance at his profile and once more saw the little boy he had been, and it cheered her immensely. He'd always stood up for her and gallantly took the blame when they got into trouble. And she remembered the hours they spent riding their horses together on family outings to the countryside, daring each other to jump the hurdles, while pretending to be riding bucking broncos in the Wild West.

And here she was now—about to head out into that Wild West.

To her surprise—and she had to admit, pleasure—Randall entwined his arm around hers so that she rested her palm on the back of his hand. As he led her over to her family, she said, "I was just remembering those dime novels we used to read. About the West."

Randall threw back his head and gave a hearty chuckle. "Oh, yes, those." He stopped suddenly, narrowed his eyes, and stared hard at her. "*Maleaska, the Indian Wife of the White Hunter.*" He crouched and pretended to stalk her, forcing girlish giggles to erupt from her mouth. "Ah, those were priceless. Worth much more than a dime, I'd say—for the hours of entertainment they offered us."

Emma shook her head as their laughter quieted. Those carefree, halcyon days of childhood—where had they gone? It seemed like years since Emma had had such an unrestrained laugh of utter joy. These recent years of living with her parents' constant stress and worries—over everything, it seemed—had stripped her of so much spontaneity and fun. This was the first time in a long while she'd felt so lighthearted and unburdened.

She looked into Randall's face—so familiar and yet so full of surprise. His eyes then snagged on hers, and her heart raced at the penetrating gaze. No longer were these the innocent, boyish eyes of a ten-year-old. No indeed. These were the eyes—Emma realized, a bit startled—of a man capable of love. She was so used to being invisible, of feeling so unloved for so long, this attention felt like a long drink of cool water soothing a parched throat.

She suddenly found herself at a loss for words, aware of the feel of the back of his hand under hers. She was glad when her father ushered them all onto the train. It afforded her the chance to wrench her gaze away from Randall and mull over these unexpected, unsettling feelings growing in her heart.

Chapter 4

LUCAS COULD TELL SOMEONE HAD entered the barn, but he couldn't turn around at the moment, as he had one hand calming the mare by rubbing her abdomen and the other hand reaching carefully along the cervical wall to determine the position of the foal's legs and head. The fetal membranes bulged out the vulva, signaling the impending birth, but for the last ten minutes, Lucas had been waiting for the sac to rupture. It was time to help the mare along, as she was showing undue agitation.

A splash of light spread across the stall, crisscrossing the lamplight shining from the lantern Lucas had hung on the wood siding. Sarah's quiet presence filled the intimate space, although she said nothing. He felt her watching; she must have sensed this delivery was taking longer than usual. He'd never known anyone with such an intuitive sense about everything, but he chalked it up to her Cheyenne blood, and the fact that her grandmother had been a medicine woman in her tribe. *A tribe that was mostly wiped out, and the rest "relocated" to where they could cause no trouble to the settlers moving west along the railroad lines.*

He hadn't lived here when all the wars and skirmishes broke out, but he'd heard plenty of stories, and although most of the Cheyenne and Arapahoe were gone from the Front Range, fervent hatred toward Indians was far from eradicated. The sting and shame of the Sand Creek Massacre lay fresh on many folks' minds, although it had taken place a dozen years ago, draping the land like a foul odor. He wondered why Sarah and her two sons stayed here and tolerated it. He was sure her many refusals to sell her late husband's choice acreage and established horse ranch were prompted more by stubbornness and defiance than anything else.

He didn't blame her for standing her ground, though. In fact, he greatly admired her and Eli and LeRoy. Their ranch had been supplying quality horses to ranchers, miners, and settlers across the state for many years, and neither intimidation nor threats lessened Sarah's resolve to continue doing just so.

A sudden eruption of warm fluid gushed all over Lucas's arm and soaked into his shirt. Relieved, he pushed aside the mare's tail and made room for the hooves to emerge. One hoof, then the other, then the nose . . . He blew out a pent-up breath upon seeing the expected normal presentation of the foal.

Sarah came alongside him, the sleeves of her blouse rolled up — which was enough of a sign — and he glanced at her face that gleamed in the firelight. But instead of smiling at the birth of this last foal of the season, her expression was streaked with worry. She said something under her breath: *"Haatano."* Which he knew meant something like scared, possible trouble. Her look made his body flinch, and he rubbed his chin. Something was wrong. What was it?

He strained to watch as the foal slipped out of the birth canal with ease, wet and . . . covered with bloody red membrane tissue. *Great. Premature rupture of chorioallantois.*

He muttered under his breath and clenched his teeth. Without wanting it to, his mind raced to that tragic night. The difficult delivery. Alice's screaming and moaning. His bloodied hands as he tried to stem the hemorrhaging. His tiny infant son emerging lifeless into his trembling hands.

He shook his head hard and narrowed his eyes at the task before him. *Breathe. The placenta has burst, cutting off the foal's oxygen. Get the foal breathing. That's it . . .*

Sarah knelt down beside Lucas, pushed her skirt aside, and with steady hands helped rip the membranes from around the foal's face. She then handed Lucas a rough cotton towel to wipe the fluids and mucous from the newborn's eyes and mouth.

After an unbearable moment of stillness, the foal finally jerked its head, then pedaled with its hooves, seeking purchase in the straw bedding around it. Lucas scooted back to make room, and felt a hand on his shoulder. It only added to the heavy guilt weighing down his heart.

"She's small," Sarah said, her tone even. Lucas wasn't surprised she knew the gender of the foal. He didn't even bother to check when the rest of the body slid out of the mare and plopped onto the straw. "But she has determination. You can see it in her eyes."

Lucas looked up at Sarah, who went over and patted the mare's neck with a satisfied grin, then muttered encouraging words in the language of the Cheyenne to the new mother. "She did good. Her first. Maybe her last." She gave Lucas a questioning look.

"I'll know more once the placenta delivers." He didn't see enough blood dripping out to worry him.

Sarah straightened and smiled. "Coffee?" She had witnessed — and no doubt assisted in — hundreds of births on her ranch over the years. She well knew the many complications that could arise with a mare in labor, as did he. He often wondered if she'd helped deliver more foals than he had. No doubt she had. Most mares birthed effortlessly, but like humans, from time to time things just went wrong.

Way wrong.

Another pang of sadness struck him, but he forced it down, focusing on the filly, who had now fumbled to her feet and was searching for milk. He noted the umbilical breaking and checked to make sure it wasn't bleeding, and he was pleased to see it wasn't. The mare nickered affectionately and stood, then nuzzled her newborn. A smile rose on Lucas's face. He turned back to Sarah.

"Coffee sounds good," he told her. She knew he'd be here awhile, to make sure the mare was out of danger and didn't begin to hemorrhage. It could take hours for the placenta to be expelled. The nursing would help.

When she left the barn, Lucas dabbed antiseptic on the end of the umbilical stub and looked the filly over. She had nice paint markings, like her mother, who was a paint–quarter horse mix. He was pretty sure Wildfire was the sire. He always threw handsome paint colors and strong-spirited offspring, and he was Sarah's favorite stud. His own horse, Ransom, had some of Wildfire's bloodline. *Vooveheva* was his Cherokee name, but Sarah didn't mind him calling the horse by the simpler English word. A bit easier on the tongue, he told her.

Sarah had given him the gelding when he began working for her, insisting this was the horse for him. The name was not lost on him, for she had ransomed Lucas, in a way. Even without telling her what had happened to bring him stumbling down out of the mountains that spring, he had a feeling she knew. How—he didn't know and didn't ask. He had been grateful for her offer of employment and room and board. He must have looked pitiable indeed, having gone without bathing or eating for days. Days he hardly recalled.

While the mare nursed her newborn, Lucas stood next to her hip and took her temperature. He let his thoughts drift into silence, willing his heart to settle in the warm stall glowing with light and new life. The strong stench of the amniotic fluids mixed with hay and straw and horse smells gave familiar comfort even though it stung his nostrils. His earliest memories were ones of being in a stall not much different from this one, gazing upon the new foals in wonder as they got to their feet and soon ran playfully in the Kentucky bluegrass stretching for miles over rolling hills. He'd spent long days, and some long nights, alongside Giles Forsythe, one of the most highly esteemed veterinarians in the state—a transplant from Britain—famous among race horse circles. Forsythe had taught him so much, not just mentoring him but serving as a substitute father when his own father had died in the flu epidemic of '58. Those years had ingrained in him a deep love for horses and respect for life—giving him the dream that led him to attend veterinary school years later in Philadelphia, once the war ended and he'd left the fields of bloodshed and death behind him. *Or so I'd thought.*

He'd had an idyllic childhood, one full of promise and prosperity. All which disappeared like a puff of smoke overnight with the onset of the Civil War and its horrors. Sometimes the haunting images woke him with a start in the late-night hours. But not as much lately. Sarah had made him a tincture to help dispel the nightmares when he'd first come to the Front Range. He was grateful for her knowledge of plants—which far surpassed his own. It was one thing to read and study plants in medical school. Quite another to live in harmony with the land, where you were intimate with all that grew around you, and you depended on that knowledge for survival.

As he gathered up his supplies and towels, Sarah came back in holding two steaming mugs, Hoesta at her heels. The dog came over and sniffed him, then plopped down in the straw with a grunt. Lucas wasn't sure why Sarah was staying up late with him, but her expression no longer showed worry. Maybe she was in the mood for conversation. They'd often talked late into the night over a cup of coffee, or an occasional shot of brandy when the deep cold of winter threatened to sink into their bones. Sometimes when snow half-buried the buildings, he and Sarah and her sons would play cards, although Eli hated it when LeRoy cheated, and ended up calling him all sorts of names, which only made Sarah laugh. Eli had little patience for cheating—and for most anything that rubbed him the wrong way. And that worried Lucas. Because lately there were some serious things rubbing Eli raw. And Lucas wasn't sure Sarah had been told. But someone had to tell her.

"You talk to Eli lately?" Lucas began, keeping his tone even.

"I noticed something's been bothering him. Thought it was that girl over in LaPorte giving him grief again." She chuckled. "He'd do well to marry her already. She'll keep at him until he buckles."

Lucas forced a grin, hating to bring up what he knew had to be told. He never kept anything from Sarah when it concerned her, the ranch, or her family. Sure, she knew about the animosity some of the ranchers and farmers in the area had toward her sons, although they were honest and hardworking young men. The problem was they were one-quarter Indian. And, to some, that was the same as 100-percent enemy. It didn't seem to matter to some that Sarah's husband, John, had been a respected horse breeder whose family had lived in the area for decades. John's father had been a pastor in what was now Fort Collins, fifteen miles to the east, and his grandfather a well-known, if not legendary, beaver trapper who had been the principal supplier of pelts to the many outposts and traders.

The hat Sarah wore had been made from beaver John's grandfather trapped and skinned.

What did matter to those dissenters, though, was that John Banks had married a Cheyenne squaw. And he wasn't the first by any stretch. Many white settlers had married Indian women. Kit Carson had married two—first an Arapaho, then a Cheyenne. Sarah had actually met Carson, who had been appointed superintendent of Indian Affairs for Colorado Territory, just before he died in '68. She spoke of him as an outstanding man—honorable, upright, and kind.

But plenty of folks hadn't liked Carson's friendliness toward the Indian peoples either.

Lucas sipped his coffee as he and Sarah leaned against the barn siding and observed the mare and foal in the ensuing stillness of the quiet night. A light breeze wafted in through the open windows, stirring up dust particles that danced on the refreshingly cool air. The scent of hay and damp grass—sprinkled on by the passing thunderstorm that afternoon—lent a soothing aroma that mingled with the strong coffee in Lucas's hands. At moments like this, peace pushed its way into his heart, bypassing the many protests and arguments against it. Tonight, he was too tuckered out from spending dawn to dusk sinking all those fence posts with Eli and Leroy—not to mention the late-night birth—to resist. But a thin layer of guilt lay underneath that tenuous peace. He would be a fool to if he thought he could vanquish it.

About an hour after delivering her foal, without much effort, the mare passed her placenta, and Lucas gathered it up and put it in the barrel for disposal. A barn owl hooted softly from the rafters, and Lucas looked out the nearby window at the star-splattered sky. He wished he didn't have to disrupt the pleasant peacefulness that had settled around them like a warm blanket, but there was something he needed to tell Sarah, and he supposed he couldn't put it off any longer.

Lucas cleared his throat and brushed bits of straw off his brown denims. "Eli's been exchanging words with Rusty Dunnigan." He'd tried to word it delicately, but there was no softening the meaning.

Her reaction was knee-jerk. She slapped the siding with the palm of her hand. "That boy—sometimes I wonder if he doesn't have a lick of sense in that big head of his." Sarah seethed and shook her head. "I told him . . ." She pursed her lips and made a disapproving sound. With a nod, she encouraged Lucas to continue. He could tell she wanted to listen about as much as he wanted to speak.

"We were picking up that load of barbed wire at the depot the other day. Dunnigan, Caleb Dixon, and Gus Woodson came over and watched. LeRoy said nothing, but you know Eli."

Sarah slapped her thigh this time. "That trap of his will get him killed one of these days."

Lucas recalled the venom in those men's eyes. This new fencing manufactured in Kansas was controversial, and good reason the cattle ranchers didn't like it, as it was harder for cattle to detect and caused a good deal more injuries than wood fencing. But with the railroads required to construct fences along right-of-ways, and farmers—and ranchers like Sarah—given the legal burden of fencing out free-range cattle that were permitted to graze unrestrained, what choice did many have? Wood was scarce and expensive, and building and maintaining split-rail fences was time-consuming. Not to mention they rotted and often broke under heavy snow loads—and heavy cattle determined to push through to greener pastures. Sarah had grown tired of her back eighty of alfalfa being invaded by the encroaching herds of cattle—Sixty thousand head of which belonged to one Rusty Dunnigan, who made little effort to conceal his hatred of the red man.

"Dunnigan's just waiting for Eli to take the bait," Sarah said. "When he was young, I could lock that cantankerous boy in the cellar, make him cool down. Now? My words slide right off his back. Like a *shi'shi* with its slick feathers." She entreated Lucas with her eyes. "Would you talk to him? I know you can't beat any sense into him, but maybe remind him what's at stake."

Lucas clenched and unclenched his jaw. "Eli believes none of that lot will let up until you sell the ranch."

Sarah grunted. "Those ranchers know I'll never sell. I've told them a thousand times if I've told them once."

"Their grazing land is shrinking. All these new towns springing up, expanding. The railroad cutting through prime land and obstructing access to the rivers. You told me yourself—you saw it coming years ago."

Sarah pushed back her long straight hair streaked with gray over one shoulder. "You'll talk to Eli?"

Lucas didn't need to give her an answer; she knew he would do his best to keep her younger son from detonating a small-scale Indian war of his own. If he could contain the growing conflagration seeking to erupt into a prairie fire that would only go out when everything in sight was incinerated and turned to ash.

"Well," he said, knowing no more words needed to be spoken over this matter, "best we leave this pair to get some sleep." Sarah said nothing more, only peeled off a flake of hay from the bale on the long bench outside the stall and tossed it over by the mare. Lucas walked over and took his lantern down from the hook on the siding. Giving the mare a gentle pat on the neck as she tucked into the hay, he thought how grateful he was that mother and baby were going to be just fine.

He'd just hoped and prayed Sarah and her sons would be likewise.

Chapter 5

AFTER FOUR DAYS ON THE swaying, jostling train, Emma felt weary beyond belief. Although the bed in her private berth was somewhat comfortable, her mind had been in a preoccupied turmoil, which robbed her of much-needed sleep. She imagined she looked horrendous; it was so difficult to perform her daily toilet at the tiny sink in a curtained-off space she could barely fit in, and she longed to soak in a hot bath and wash her hair. Despite the overall cleanliness of the train carriages, the grime from the steam and stirred-up dust filtered in through every crack and open window and coated the surfaces with a patina of dirt. Finally, to Emma's relief they had entered Colorado Territory, and before noon would arrive in Denver. From there, Randall had assured her, it would be a short jaunt to Greeley, their destination.

The closer they got to their new home, however, the more agitated Emma felt. It seemed like each mile that took her further west erased just a little part of her past back east. She wished she could share her father's excitement over the unknown that lay ahead, but Emma liked to limit her adventurous jaunts between the pages of a book.

The scenery out the windows had gradually changed. Once they crossed the great Mississippi River, the landscape shifted from the hubbub of cities and towns, to woods and patches of farmland, to miles upon miles of rolling plains. But just this morning she felt she'd awakened in a wholly new world, with the sun streaking the sky in pink and gold light that shone across the open prairie land and the tall grasses billowing like a verdant sea. The crystal shimmering quality of light was like nothing she'd ever seen before.

Kansas Territory was flat and more flat. Hours and hours the wide open country sped past her window as she tried to draw in her sketchpad, having gotten up much earlier than usual, anticipating the day of arrival. However, she found she couldn't concentrate on her sketches, and finally abandoned the effort and let her gaze wander along with her imagination. Could she ever come to feel at home here? She doubted it. She was a city girl, through and through, and although she hated to admit it, she liked her comforts.

She'd read about the pioneers spreading west—thousands of them. Seeking adventure, gold, a new life. Escaping troubles—only to find more, no doubt. Emma found it difficult to comprehend why so many would exchange the comfort and security of an established life fraught with little danger for one surely replete with danger. Did her parents really think they could keep the Wild West from their front steps? Why, an article she'd found in a nature journal of the West told there were more than fifty species of snakes indigenous to the Great Plains. Including four types of prolific pitvipers and rattlesnakes whose bite would cause death in mere moments. Just the thought of encountering any such creature made her shake all over. It was one thing to examine a snake through a thick pane of glass at the Central Park Zoo; it was another thing entirely to step on one while taking a morning constitutional.

Yet, staring out the window at the breathtaking mountains dusted with snow in the distance stirred something in her soul—a sense of awe and wonderment that she had never felt before. She never imagined so much country so unspoiled and untrampled by civilization.

Randall had told her at length about the golden spike driven into the ground in Utah Territory that had linked the eastern and western railway lines, now providing a complete transcontinental railroad. Now travelers could journey from one coast to the other without getting off a train. What a remarkable achievement. Randall noted how his father had helped finance and organize this enterprise, the celebration of which he attended along with an estimated three thousand witnesses made up mostly of government and railroad officials, as well as track workers and supporters. The senior Mr. Turnbull had been key in coordinating three private railroad companies to build this nineteen-hundred-mile-long line, which took nearly seven years.

Thinking of Randall brought a smile to her face. Reminding herself he would be coming shortly to fetch her for breakfast set her heart beating a little faster. They'd had many pleasant conversations these last few days—over tea or a meal in the dining car—which seemed to please her parents. She now had no doubt her father had a hand in arranging for Randall to accompany them out west. But Emma was glad. Surprisingly, her mother had left her quite on her own upon boarding the train—no doubt trusting Randall would keep her company. And he had—although it was apparent he tried to respect her privacy and not make demands on her time. Although, what else was she to do, hour after hour, as the train chugged and rumbled along? She'd read some, and drew in her sketchbook, but the hours had dragged on, making her look forward with impatience to her social visits with her former childhood friend.

Just as he had when a boy, Randall loved to talk. For hours he regaled her with stories about college, and about the only other trip he had taken west—two years back to visit his father in Denver. He'd taken the trip by himself, as his mother disliked traveling so far. From what Emma could gather, Mr. Turnbull's business ventures required he be gone a good part of the year, leaving Randall's mother alone in her huge mansion in Albany. Although, she was far from alone, Randall explained—surrounded by at least a dozen servants. And she kept herself busy attending endless societal events and fundraisers for charities, when she wasn't visiting for months at each of her daughters' homes. She'd taken up grandparenting as a new vocation and seemed to love every minute of it. Emma hardly remembered Randall's mother. Most of the time she played at his home, his nanny had watched over them and fed them.

Randall's comfortable manner set Emma at ease, and she often listened quietly, enjoying his enthusiastic recounting as they drank tea and ate cucumber sandwiches. For the most part he allayed her concerns about the journey, and navigated through the train carriages with the familiarity expected of a railroad baron's son.

It frankly astonished Emma to see how mature and gentlemanly he had become. She could still see the boyish spark in his eyes when he spoke, but when she looked at his stature and manly comportment, she realized he was no longer the little boy she'd known.

A knock at her door sent butterflies fluttering in her stomach. The self-conscious feelings that arose around Randall surprised her. Just thinking about his warm smile and the gentle touch of his arm against hers as they walked in close proximity through the train carriages made her pulse race fast. Could she really be attracted to him? It was such a strange new feeling to have for this man who had once been her playmate. Now she chose her words with care, aware she wanted to make a good impression upon him.

She stood and smoothed out her skirt, then checked the buttons on her blouse to make sure she looked presentable. "One moment," she called out, sneaking a peek at the mirror over the sink to check that her hair was still nicely in place. Josephine had been coming in each morning to help her dress and pin up her hair. What a godsend she was! Emma could barely manage to find her clothes in this cramped space, and was completely helpless when it came to tightening her own corset.

As she opened the door, Randall's face lit up with an unabashed smile. He looked her up and down, which caused her to tingle all over and feel exposed somehow. Maybe it was because he didn't put on airs or worry what kind of impression he would make on her. And his gaze held no lechery or judgment. He seemed completely and unreservedly pleased to see her. And that felt so refreshingly wonderful. Such a change from the way most men looked at her.

And how handsome he looked. The color of his broadcloth suit brought out the simmering warmth of those molasses eyes. He took her arm, and the touch sent tingles all over her body. Randall led her gently through the train cars, seemingly unaware of the effect his proximity and touch were having upon her. As she followed behind him, her eyes on his broad shoulders, she wondered at how she felt so drawn to him in a way she never imagined she would. She pictured his large, comforting arms encircling her waist, his hands running through her hair, stroking her neck . . .

She uttered a barely perceptible gasp and shook the images out of her head, her heart fluttering such that she found it hard to draw in deep breaths. Her imagination both surprised and excited her. She'd never allowed herself such feelings when in the company of the many suitors who had come to call, even though she found a few quite attractive. But she wanted more than a handsome face and impressive stature. She wanted her heartstrings to be plucked.

Was that what she was now experiencing with Randall? Was she possibly falling in love? How silly. Randall would always be a childhood friend in her mind. A husband? Yet Randall was smart, gentle, respectful, hardworking, wealthy. Could she truly want anything more in a husband?

But did Randall even feel at all attracted to her, or was he just being cordial and obedient to his charge to keep her company? Did he still see her as little Emaline, a friend to while away the hours with, engaging in pleasant conversation? Maybe he had no desire for marriage and children.

Emma sucked in a breath, her corset feeling suddenly too tight although the morning weather was mild and cool. She was grateful when the waiter seated them, and she sipped a glass of water. She worked to relax her breathing as Randall ordered coffee, toast, and soft-boiled eggs for them both. A quick glance around the dining car showed neither her parents nor her brother was here. She imagined her mother fretting over packing their things and primping to make sure she looked impeccable upon deboarding the train.

Worry simmered again in Emma's heart, thinking about Lynette. She had hoped to spend time with her on this journey, but her sister-in-law had been sick the whole time, never leaving her berth, and politely declined Emma's offer to visit, sending word through Walter. The few times Emma saw her brother, he put on a brave face, expressing confidence Lynette would feel much better once they arrived at their new town, that the shaking of the train nauseated her. But Emma saw through Walter's tense comportment, and his exhausted eyes were fraught with concern. A horrible dread came over her as she wondered if Lynette would be able to make the adjustment to a new life in a strange place.

"We only have about an hour until we arrive in Denver," Randall said, drawing her attention back to his face. "So light fare will sit better than a heavy breakfast, I think."

"I agree," Emma said, her eyes widening in delight as the waiter came over and poured coffee into her porcelain cup. She sipped gratefully—both for the stimulating warmth of the drink and for something to focus on that would wrench her eyes away from Randall.

A silence hung between them, and Emma chanced to look at Randall. A mood seemed to have come over him, draping him in serious thought as he stared out the window and sipped his coffee. Emma wanted to say something, curious and concerned, but the waiter then appeared with their breakfast. Randall stirred from his concentration on the landscape rushing by and thanked the man, who gave a respectful nod and asked if there was anything else they needed.

Randall questioned Emma with his eyes, and she was moved by his consideration. Her father never asked if there was something she wanted. He just told her what she should have. Again, she felt herself drawing closer to this man whom she was learning to know anew.

"Nothing more, thank you," she said to the waiter with a smile. Upon leaving, Randall let out a sigh, and a frown formed on his face.

A tendril of panic sprouted in her heart. Was he bored with her? Tired of her company? She dropped her gaze and looked at him under her lashes, but he seemed to sense her concern.

"I apologize. I'm a bit distracted."

She dared speak her heart; better to know now if he had some reservations about being with her. "Is . . . something bothering you? Have I said something . . . ?"

Randall straightened and his eyes widened. "Oh, good gracious, no. Sorry. Please don't take my sudden gloomy mood personally."

He seemed to fumble with his words, and suddenly Emma understood what was troubling him.

"It's your father, isn't it? You haven't seen him in years, and you . . . don't seem happy about going to work for him."

Randall's expression confirmed her suspicions.

Emma had only met the senior Mr. Turnbull on a few occasions, and she recalled him as an imposing, overbearing man whose presence overpowered a room. Of course she'd been small and young at the time, but his domineering personality and loud gruff voice greatly intimidated her, and often she and Randall would make themselves scarce when Ernest Turnbull was in the house. She hadn't realized it at the time, but now she understood Randall had been afraid of his father. Had the man been heavy-handed with his only son? Had he beat him? Treated him mercilessly when Randall failed to live up to his father's expectations? Was Randall now afraid he would somehow fail in his father's eyes?

Emma surely knew just how that felt—to be glared at and found wanting. She never seemed to meet her own father's approval, and she longed for him to say he loved her, and to hold her close. But her father was not a naturally affectionate man, and she suffered from the absence of his affection. Randall shared the same lack of love and support in his relationship with his father as well. And in this way she and he were well met.

She dared lay a hand on his arm. He pulled back a bit and glanced down at her hand, then met her eyes. A flash of understanding and gratitude shone in his gaze, and Emma's heart beat wildly in her chest.

"If it turns out you don't like working for your father, you could just go back to New York, couldn't you?"

Randall let out a sound of bitter defeat. His face drooped and he clenched his jaw. "No. That is not an option for me. He sent me off to learn business management and accounting so I would be a worthy partner in his business. And I've applied myself dutifully and more than met his expectations."

Emma sensed a "but" dangling after his words, yet he said nothing further. He spread jam on his toast and cracked a spoon against the eggshell to break it open. Emma felt Randall's fragility at that moment, as if his thin shell threatened to crack. If he was so unhappy about working for his father, why wouldn't he stand up for himself and say so? She doubted Randall would care if his father cut off his financial support. Or would he?

When Randall had dreamed of heading west as a child, surely these were not the circumstances he'd envisioned for himself.

Randall nodded toward the window as he finished off his toast. Herds of brown cattle with short horns grazed across miles of open range. Emma had never seen a cow before this trip, but they'd passed hundreds in the last few hours.

"We'll be coming into Denver any moment. And then we have just two hours' layover until our train to Greeley departs. It will be a short jaunt north, and we'll arrive before the dinner hour." He mustered a smile, but Emma could tell his melancholy hung heavily over his heart. It was as if the closer they got to their destination, the more trepidation Randall felt. She caught a glimpse of Randall's hands wringing the napkin in his lap.

To be polite, she averted her gaze. Off in the distance, the Rocky Mountains rose majestically into the heavens like the bony backbone of some great beast. She had never seen such towering peaks that practically punctured the sky. Snowy caps glistened in the crystal-clear sunlight, although dark storm clouds churned and roiled to the north, as if drawn to the mountaintops. The verdant, velvety foothills were blanketed in color. Wildflowers, no doubt. But what kinds?

The thought of setting out into the fields and drawing the flora began to excite her. So much different than sketching in Central

Park, where familiar flowers were planted in perfect rows. Here in Colorado Territory she was bound to discover countless species of plants she'd never before seen. Maybe she would even draw plants no one else ever had. She could even compile a portfolio of the plants of the prairie land—a comprehensive collection not unlike the botanical cataloging the Belgian artist van Nooten had done.

A surge of excitement filled her as she pictured herself steeped in fragrant wildflowers, a bright sun overhead and the wide open sky spreading around her. She wouldn't have to travel to some botanical gardens or order exotic plants in order to have something unique to draw.

Suddenly she couldn't wait for this interminable train ride to end. She looked back at Randall, who seemed lost in troubled thought, and wondered just what dreams, if any, he cherished.

Perhaps she was prying, but she felt a sudden need to ask.

"Randall, do you remember how we used to sit out in the gazebo and fantasize our futures? I told you when I grew up I wanted to be a singer on the stage. And you said you wanted to learn magic tricks and run away with Barnum's Traveling World's Fair—"

Her words had the desired effect of lightening Randall's dour mood. He let out a laugh. "The greatest show on earth. Oh how I longed to run away. But I imagine every boy dreams of doing that at one point in his life."

Some more than others, Emma mused, knowing now, with mature hindsight, why Randall had embraced such a dream.

"What I really wanted was to learn how to be invisible. To utter a magic word and disappear. That would have been quite a feat," he said wistfully.

Emma sensed, ironically, that this was exactly what Randall still wished for at this moment in his life.

"What would you rather pursue—should you have the opportunity?"

He smoothed his wavy hair. "Maybe you'll think this odd, but I'd love to go into publishing."

"Publishing? What in particular?"

"Books. Big, colorful, beautiful books. Books about exotic places with artwork and daguerreotypes that could transport readers to faraway places. I once visited a publishing house. The smell of ink, seeing the drums spinning and spitting out sheets of printed pages . . . it was glorious to watch."

Books. Why would that surprise her? He'd always loved books and had stacks of them in his room. Often they'd gone to the public library escorted by his nanny, where he searched the stacks for new adventure stories to check out. Now Emma realized much of reading had been to escape the emptiness and lack of love in his home. Much the way she retreated to her paints and pens.

"Well," she said, hoping to sound encouraging, "maybe one day you will have your chance to be a publisher."

Randall scoffed as if the idea were ludicrous, causing Emma to shut tight her mouth. Since he'd made this choice, though, to work for his father, she hoped in time he'd find joy in his role as accountant. Maybe once he settled into his work . . . and perhaps if he married and had a family, he'd grow to enjoy the routine and challenge. Maybe, Emma thought with a flush rising to her cheeks, if he found the right woman to love him, who understood him . . .

Emma changed the direction her thoughts were heading and instead listened to the *clickety-clack* of the train wheels rolling along the tracks and the muted conversations of the other diners around them. Outside the window, the outskirts of the city appeared. Clusters of buildings that looked like huge barns, factories, and storage facilities made of weathered wood and brick sped by, followed by huge pens of crowded cattle lowing and making a racket. The odor of the animals mingled with the increasing dust, and the waiters hurried to close all the windows in the dining car as patrons wrinkled their noses in annoyance.

In the distance, thunder rolled, and looking at the wide streak of gray hovering over the foothills to the northwest, she could tell rain was pelting the hills.

Randall finished his coffee and said, "I imagine this is all quite overwhelming for you. But in a few days, once all your furniture has been moved into your new home and you get settled, I'm sure you'll adjust wonderfully. I'm told Greeley is a fine town. And no doubt you'll make friends. You were always good at that."

A loud crack of thunder followed by a bright flash of light out the carriage window signaled the storm was coming their way. Emma caught Randall's eyes and saw another storm—one brewing in his soul. A feeling of doom and trepidation lay over him, like a heavy black cloud about to deluge the earth. She hoped though, like this storm, this mood would soon pass and he'd feel the refreshing breeze of hope and promise wash over him.

Wash over both of us, she added somberly.

Chapter 6

LUCAS GOT UP FROM THE table and took his plate to the sink to wash, glancing at the sparkling morning that emerged outside after a hard rain. He was glad the skies had cleared for now; he planned to make good progress on setting in the rest of the new posts for the fence. And then he had some patients to check over in Greeley.

He turned his head as Eli and LeRoy came stomping in, the dog easing in beside them and heading straight for his bowl of food. Lucas chuckled. Sarah liked to describe her sons as a whole herd of buffalo on four legs. He said good morning to them, noting they even resembled a bit like buffalo this morning — shaggy, unwashed, and smelly.

Sarah didn't miss a beat as she spooned eggs and bacon onto their plates and slid the food across the table as they sat down.

"What pigsty have you two been wallowing in this morning? You could show the decency of washing up before coming in."

"Too hungry." LeRoy pushed his shoulder-length straight dark hair out of his eyes and set his hat on the empty chair beside him. He grabbed a piece of brown bread toast off the plate in the center of the table and talked as he chewed. "That rainstorm that rumbled over us this morning dumped at least three inches. We wanted to fix that gate early before we headed to Evans to pick up those two new water troughs—"

"And, Ma, we did wash our hands," Eli protested, holding up his palms for her to inspect.

Sarah tsked and sat down across from her sons. Lucas dried his plate and set it on the cupboard shelf, then poured some more coffee into his cup from the pot percolating on the wood stove. The kitchen radiated warmth, chasing out the early morning chill.

LeRoy continued, a mischievous smile rising on his face. "And Eli had a little tussle with the latch." He threw his brother a smirk. "The latch won."

"So I slipped," Eli said good-naturedly while stuffing eggs into his mouth. "So did you."

LeRoy waggled his head and laughed as he reached across the table for the cream pitcher. Sarah slapped his hand.

"Where're your manners? Haven't you learned anything I taught you?"

LeRoy ignored her, and Sarah scolded him with her eyes. He pointed a finger at Eli. "Yeah, I only fell in the mud because you grabbed on to my sleeve to catch yourself. You owe me, Brother."

Lucas allowed a slight smile, careful not to let Sarah know he enjoyed these antics in the morning. He was glad to see Eli in a good mood too. Maybe he wouldn't have to have that little talk with him about stirring up contention with the cattle ranchers. If he and Sarah kept him busy enough, maybe he'd stay out of trouble. LeRoy wasn't much help in that department. Although the older brother never instigated conflict, he wasn't one to back away when it met him head-on.

The banter died down quickly as both young men stuffed food into their mouths and chased it down with coffee. Lucas used the dishcloth to take the hot skillet off the cast-iron stovetop and set it in the sink to wash. He threw Hoesta a piece of bacon, which the dog gobbled down in a flash without chewing.

"You can leave that," Sarah called over to him.

"You made breakfast." How many times had they said that to each other? Lucas knew Sarah considered the kitchen her domain, but she also ran a horse ranch of about fifty head, and helped her sons keep up all the property. She was strong and hale for being nearly fifty, but Lucas knew she pushed herself to exhaustion often, so he liked to lighten her load where he could. She'd drawn the line, though, when she caught him one time washing the floor on his hands and knees. She'd slapped him upside his head and whisked him out of the room.

After scrubbing the stubborn crust of eggs off the inside of the skillet, he leaned against the sink and sipped his coffee.

"When you think you'll be back?" Sarah asked LeRoy.

He looked at his brother and shrugged. "If'n you don't need us to pick anything else up, by mid-afternoon, I s'pect."

She nodded. Like another four-legged herd of buffalo, Eli and LeRoy pushed their chairs from the table, took their dishes to the sink, and grabbed their hats. Although the brothers looked enough alike, Lucas guessed Eli took after his father. His hair was a light brown, streaked with gold from hours in the sun, and it curled where it hung above his amber eyes. Girls could hardly resist his boyish grin and unusually straight teeth. You could hardly tell he had Cheyenne blood; whereas LeRoy looked mostly Indian, with his gleaming bronze skin and nearly black irises. Both were handsome young men, just a couple of years younger than he was, and although they hadn't seen the hardships or been through the suffering Lucas had, they had a tough, weathered nature to them. Lucas figured some of that was posturing, but the rest was the result of taming a hard land amid hard and often intolerant folks.

It often struck him odd how the West had gone through the war years practically untouched and unaware of the horrors of the battles raging east. While hundreds of thousands of men fought and died and lay bloated and rotting across a dozen states, those living life in the Western frontier had their own daily concerns over surviving. Yankees killed Confederates while white settlers killed Indians. And vice versa. Lucas had seen more death in a few short years than any man should ever have to witness in a lifetime.

He chewed his lip thoughtfully. No wonder there was such a big influx of folks from the East coming out west, buying up large parcels of land, and trying to start a new life—create a utopian society in which they could live peacefully and push away the ugliness of the war years.

"You are going to clean up and change your clothes." Sarah made the declaration sound like an order instead of a question.

Eli feigned shock. "What? You think we'd head out looking and smelling like this? Wouldn't want to offend the ladies."

Sarah chuckled. "Heaven forbid."

Lucas knew both her sons were wont to gravitate over to any pretty young woman who even glanced their way. And Eli especially knew how to butter them up and get them all flustered. Lucas had seen it on many occasions and was, frankly, impressed with his talent. But Sarah wanted him married soon. Both her boys. She felt that would make them settle down and defuse some of their wildness. Lucas wondered if that would do the trick.

"Well, bye," LeRoy said. Eli tipped his hat at his mother and nodded to Lucas. Then they tromped out the door. Sarah sat sipping her coffee as the stampeding faded in the distance.

Lucas was about to grab his hat and coat hanging on the hook by the door, but Sarah stopped him with her hand as he passed her chair.

He looked at her, and she gestured for him to sit. He took the chair across from her and questioned her with his eyes.

"I had a dream last night. *Ovaxe.*"

Lucas knew that meant something more than just an ordinary dream. He imagined it more like a vision, or premonition. She sometimes had them, and they often portended unpleasant things. He gulped and waited to hear her out, knowing she might take a while in the telling.

Much to his relief, a smile tweaked the sides of her mouth. She stood and took something off the shelf on the wall behind her, and Lucas recognized it as her small wooden box in which she kept various dried plants and herbs. But these weren't spices for food; they were ceremonial.

He watched in silence as she pinched out some gray crumbly matter and set it on a smooth, flat stone the size of her palm. She then used tongs to bring over a tiny ember from the stove, then dropped it onto the plate. The plant fibers smoldered and gave off a sage-dust smell that he found calming. She'd never burned anything in front of him like this, but he knew she did so at night sometimes in her room. He'd pass by her windows, outside the ranch house, and smell strong aromas of burning plants. He never asked her about it though, thinking to respect her privacy and traditions, figuring if she wanted to tell him about them, she would.

Clearly she meant to now.

As a tendril of smoke twisted up toward the ceiling, she looked at it instead of at him. "Two blue pools. Blue like the water under ice. Round and identical." She waved her hand slightly in the air, spreading the smoke across the table. "But not cold. Although the ice covers the water, it is thin and will easily crack. It needs to crack for the blue water to flow freely. Under the ice is heat—great heat that will not only melt the ice covering the water but the ice chilling your heart." When she spoke these last words, her head jerked up, and she caught Lucas's gaze.

He startled as smoke canted into his face. Something flared in her eyes, like a spark.

"Your pain is like ice," she told him in a strange faraway-sounding voice. "It encases your heart, and even the hottest summer sun cannot penetrate. But this heat—of the blue pools—can melt the ice."

Lucas waited for her to explain. She shook off whatever spell she was under and let out a long sigh. "In my dream," she said, "you stood next to the pools and stared in. You saw your reflection gazing back. But you also saw through the ice to the life-giving water. You longed for that water, and so you stepped onto the ice. And as heat from beneath rose up, it melted not just the surface you stood upon but also the ice holding your spirit trapped."

A shiver ran down Lucas's spine. He wasn't at all sure what she was talking about, but he felt the ice around his heart. That, he was familiar with. It had appeared that winter three years ago, after he held his wife in his arms one last time and kissed his infant son's forehead for the first and only time. He thought he'd left winter behind when he came down to the Front Range in the spring, but apparently he had taken it with him.

At that image of Alice, his heart clenched, as if unable to bear the cold fist tightening around it. Sarah nodded and stirred up the smoke more, and Lucas drew it into his nostrils, feeling in seep into his limbs all the way to his feet. He felt something crack, the way ice did under the spring sun. A tiny crack that dulled the pain.

He shook his head, as if flinging away these strange sensations. "What does it mean? Your dream—the two pools?"

"I don't know about the pools, but I'm certain the understanding will come to you when it's time." She exhaled long and reached for her coffee, then sipped it thoughtfully, her ordinary action breaking the pall of mystery hanging over him. "But what I do know is it's time."

"Time?"

"To find a wife. To remarry." She held up her hand as if expecting him to protest, but this time he didn't flinch at her words. She searched his eyes, pinning him in his chair. "I think the dream means she is here, somewhere, and it is time for you to find her."

Lucas blurted out a chuckle. He didn't mean to offend Sarah, but her words evoked a funny image of him out tracking an elusive wife across the open prairie. "Did your dream tell me where to go find this wife?"

Sarah gave a quiet snort and shook her head. "You know it doesn't work that way. But . . . maybe she'll find you. Who knows? She is out there."

"Two blue pools."

"Yes."

"Whatever that means."

Sarah nodded.

Lucas couldn't think of anyplace within a hundred miles where he'd seen two round, identical blue pools side by side. "Okay."

Her eyebrows raised. "I have a dream for you, and all you can say is 'okay'?"

Lucas stood, feeling a bit stiff and suddenly tired. "Thanks?" he tried.

Sarah grinned. "You're welcome." She stood then. "Well, time to get to work. I've got horses needing to learn some manners."

Lucas laughed. She might not be able to get Eli and LeRoy in line, but she surely knew how to get a horse to listen to her.

"I'll see you around suppertime," he told her, stuffing his hat on his head and grabbing his coat. She nodded and smiled at him, then he walked out the door to the front yard that opened to miles of shimmering river and rolling prairie land. The dog stuck close to his heels, his eyes eager for some adventure. Lucas patted him mindlessly, glad for his company.

As he made for the storage barn to load up more fence posts onto the buckboard, he shook his head. *Blue pools. Ice.* Then he frowned. *Marry? Again.* He'd never wanted to consider it, but at the thought, a surge of loneliness struck him hard, filling him with yearning and need.

He brushed it away with determination and quickened his stride. There was a load of work to be done, and the morning was quickly slipping away.

"It's a short ride from the train to your hotel," Mr. Turnbull announced in a loud voice so they all could hear him over the boisterous noises of the train depot around them. "You'll be pleased to see what a fine town we've built here, due to the dedication and industriousness of its hardworking citizens. Why, in just the last year we've seen the opening of a furniture emporium—which imports quality furniture from Chicago—and a proper tonsorial parlor, with a man who is the best tailor this side of the Mississippi. There is also a haberdashery, and for the ladies, Ashton's Fine Fashions. We've brought culture and class to the West."

Emma stood, tired and overwhelmed by the flurry of activity around her. When they got off the train, she'd met up with the rest of her family on the platform, Randall stiffening as he watched his father approach. Emma recognized Mr. Turnbull—he was a hard man to forget—with his large stature, round face sporting huge red moustaches, and wide shoulders that reminded Emma of some of the bulls she'd seen out the train window. He truly fit his name, Emma thought, hiding a sudden grin behind her hand.

She'd hardly had time to say two words to either her parents or Walter and Lynette before Randall's father whisked them to the waiting carriages. She overheard her father talking with Mr. Turnbull, who reassured him that their possessions—including her Arabian horse that had taken the journey with them in one of the box cars—were in good hands and would be loaded up and taken to their new residence directly. Emma had learned a barn was being constructed in the back of their property and would be completed within the week. She hadn't considered she might have Shahayla so close, instead of boarded at a stables she had to travel to, as she had in New York. This way she could go riding on a moment's notice. The thought made her happy.

The town, from what she could tell, was not all that big. The train depot seemed situated right in the center, and the main street was lined with shops and other one-story wood buildings painted mostly white or beige. A wooden boardwalk fronted the shops on both sides of the wide street, and Emma made out a mercantile at the corner. A large two-story weathered building stood out a few blocks down the street. An effort had been made to give the main street of town some character. Benches were placed along the boardwalk, and elms and maples grew out of pretty brick planters on the corners. Their size attested to the newness of the town, but Emma could picture how full and pretty they'd look after a few years.

The afternoon sun shone warm on her shoulders, but she drew in fresh, crisp air that smelled sweet. Hay? She detected floral scents as well, and noticed the people of the town had planted flowers in small beds in front of many of the shops. Not a lot of people walked the streets, but Emma figured most would be busy at work—whatever it was they did.

As much as she'd have liked to explore the town, she was tired. She longed for a hot bath, to scrub the grime accumulated on her skin.

As if reading her thoughts, Mr. Turnbull bellowed to his charges, "No doubt you are all weary from your long journey." He pointed to the two-story building she had just noticed. "That's your hotel, and I've secured you the best suites. Used to be a barracks in Cheyenne, but it's now the Hotel D'Comfort. Randall and I will see that you get properly settled, and then we'll return to join you this evening in the dining room for dinner."

Emma glanced over at Lynette, who was clearly pale and tired but perhaps none the worse for wear. But it was evident she longed for a hot bath and long nap on a soft bed as well.

"Lovely, lovely," Emma's mother said to Mr. Turnbull. "We are so thankful to you for arranging all this. For our houses, our hotel—"

"Think nothing of it, my dear," he said, patting her hand, his chin jutting out in arrogance. Emma could tell her mother was anxious to get off the train platform and into her carriage. Josephine, her mother's maid, came up to Emma's mother, having just gotten off the train, and stood alongside her, carrying her mother's handbags and a hat box.

The two carriages, each attached to one large draft horse rigged with breaching, looked very much like the ones in New York. Perhaps they'd been shipped out from there.

Mr. Turnbull led Emma's mother and father to the first carriage, followed by Josephine. The coachman—who was dressed in only brown trousers and a button-down blue chambray shirt topped with a dull-brown leather vest—opened the side door and helped them board.

"Randall," Mr. Turnbull barked, "please ride with Mr. and Mrs. Bradshaw, then help them to their rooms."

Emma noted Randall's sunken face. Maybe he had hoped to ride with her to the hotel. Mr. Turnbull then whisked her into the carriage with Walter and Lynette. Before another word was spoken, they were off.

The carriage bounced and shook as the horses trotted down the dirt street, their hooves kicking up dust. Lynette coughed and buried her head in Walter's shoulder. Emma wanted so much to speak to them both and ask how they were doing, what they thought of the train ride, and their first impressions of the town, but seeing Lynette's distress made her keep quiet. They would have time later to talk and catch up—over dinner. So she politely looked out the window at the passing storefronts and people, who were dressed much differently than New Yorkers.

Women wore simpler dresses—with petticoats and no doubt corsets underneath—but without any bustles. And some women wore what looked like plain cotton dresses, in checked or calico patterns—without any petticoats at all. All wore bonnets or sun hats, although hardly the latest fashions. And the men wore wide-brimmed hats and bowlers. None wore suits that she could tell, but she guessed these were mostly laborers or cowboys that worked in the fields and ranches. No doubt the men of upper classes wore suits, and were busy at work in the many offices they seemed to be passing.

When they arrived at the hotel, exhaustion hit Emma full force. She could barely walk in through the front door of the hotel without shaking. She imagined her legs were wobbly from days on the train. Hopefully she'd get both her land legs and her energy back.

As much as she'd have liked to talk more with Randall, he went off with her parents to their room. Mr. Turnbull strode into the lobby, not at all politely instructing the hotel staff what to do in order to see to her family's needs. Two men who looked Chinese shuffled quickly at his command to unload the luggage from the carriages and take the bags to their rooms. The hotel was spacious, with high ornately trimmed ceilings and deep-red plush carpeting. Emma was glad to be out of the stuffy train and breathing fresh air once again.

Soon she was being led to her own room—around the corner on the first floor. The young housemaid in a pert black uniform dress with white ruffles at the hem handed Emma the key after opening the door to her room.

"Here you go, miss. Is there anything else you might be needin'?"

"A bath?" Emma now worried if she would get one.

"I've already set it up for you, miss." The young woman pointed to the small room past her four-poster brass bed. "Would you be wantin' some assistance?"

Emma breathed out a sigh of relief. "Oh yes, I would. Thank you so much. If you could help me undress and brush out my hair so I can wash it, I'd be utterly grateful."

"Yes, miss."

While the attendant went to prepare for Emma's bath and hair washing, a knock came at the door. Emma opened to a porter, who brought in her suitcases. When he left, she locked the door and went over to the large ceramic claw-foot tub that sat steaming with hot water. A lavender fragrance filled the room, delighting her senses. Already she was unwinding from the stress of travel.

She undressed, thrilled to be out of her corset, and slipped into the glorious hot water that quickly soothed her aching limbs. The housemaid with her brilliant red hair pulled tightly into a bun on her head, whose name was Katy, hummed quietly as she brushed out Emma's hair.

Excitement and worry mixed in her heart, but knowing Randall would be nearby to talk to, she felt more confident that she'd be able to weather the changes that lay ahead.

Emma closed her eyes and let the week's tumultuous travels melt away, and as she drifted off in relaxation, her mind dwelled on the dinner she would attend later with her family and, hopefully, Randall.

Chapter 7

A S THE MORNING SUN STREAMED in through her windows, Emma stood in the middle of her new room and turned in a circle. It was a bit smaller than her former room and smelled of fresh paint, and of course did not have the delightful glass greenhouse she'd enjoyed in New York, but it would be nice once the painting and wallpapering were finished. With her familiar furnishings around her—and her books and sketches and even her pathetic-looking crape myrtle tree that looked like it had hardly survived the journey west—she felt at home. Although, the town was still a mystery to her, and she worried if and when she would meet other young women her age and make friends. Surely there had to be some around.

These last three days, her mother had nearly driven her—and her father—crazy with her fussing and fretting over the house. The decisions—on how to decorate each room, what drapes to buy and in what colors, where to put each piece of furniture — seemed monumental tasks to her. Her mother often collapsed dramatically in a nearby chair or flung herself onto a sofa, wiping her forehead in consternation. Emma noted that she had lost weight, and streaks of gray tinted her hair. With Emma's father conveniently at work each day — from sunup to sundown — that left Emma at the mercy of her mother and her worries.

Mr. Turnbull had managed to find some temporary help, to assist her mother with all that needed doing, but when her mother learned there were no maids or butlers or cooks presently available for hire, she nearly swooned. Poor Josephine did what she could to help out, but she was only one woman — and knew nothing about cooking. She had been trained as a lady' maid, and that she did quite well, thankfully. Emma was grateful to her for coming out west with them.

In response to her mother's visible panic that first day they'd moved in, Mr. Turnbull graciously lent his servants to them for a few hours each day — "until proper help could be found," he said, consoling her as the men carted in their loads of furniture. Ernest Turnbull lived about a mile away, on the other side of the town, and Randall was, of course, living with him. Emma had yet to be invited over to the house, but she hoped she would soon.

Her spirits dropped thinking about Randall and how she hadn't seen him since that first day. She could only assume his father was keeping him very busy getting familiarized with his business ledgers and books. Mr. Turnbull was a prominent, busy, ambitious man, from what Randall had told her, and he had high expectations of Randall to perform well for him. She wished she could go to the office where he was working and inquire of his well-being, but she knew that would be forward of her. She would suggest to her father to perhaps invite him and his father to dinner soon — if they could be certain they'd have a cook to prepare a nice meal.

She had hardly seen her father. Since their arrival he'd been busy setting up his own office in town. And when she did have a few minutes with him—usually at the breakfast table, where he ate a hurried meal and rushed out—he said little other than to give her tasks to do. Most involved helping her mother and making sure she was adjusting. And his temper was often curt and short, making Emma again feel miserable and unloved.

Emma suspected her father had not anticipated the near-hysterical reaction of his wife to this move. *At least he can leave the house and get some breathing room*, she mused, feeling trapped inside these last few days. She'd only been outside a bit to visit her horse, which was stabled temporarily on the next block in a neighbor's barn.

She'd briefly met the Turners and found them cordial. They'd been here since the colony began—she learned its prior name was Union Colony, since the founders had supported the Union army in the war—and William Turner was a grocer who had a large warehouse in the more industrial area of town. He was one of three men who grew food crops and shipped their products out by train to other towns. His wife was an avid gardener, quite obsessed with her roses and perennials. She had a stunning garden that wrapped entirely around their modest one-story brick home. With a cheery smile she had said to Emma, "Life is quite a bit different out here and takes getting used to. But we have a saying here in Greeley: 'Bloom where you're planted.'"

Those words stuck in Emma's head, and she thought of her transplanted crape myrtle. Somehow she would have to find a way to not just survive the drastic change in her life but find joy. To bloom. And to do so she would have to develop a hardened skin while being flexible and open-minded to adjust to new ways of doing things. She didn't want to end up like her mother—hysterical and fretting over each new challenge. The West could never become the East—no matter how hard anyone might try to make it so.

Emma's thoughts were interrupted by her mother calling for her.

"Emma, Emma, where are you?"

"Here in my room, Mother." Where else would she be?

Her mother walked briskly into her room, and her eyes darted around. Emma could almost feel the tension radiating off her mother's skin.

"Why are you just standing around, when there is so much to do?"

Emma's jaw dropped. She pursed her lips together to prevent saying something she'd regret. "What is it you'd like me to do right now? Everything has been put away. The furniture and dishes are all exactly where we had them in New York. I even made my own bed." Which she'd never had to do before coming here.

Her mother's head shook spastically, and she clutched at her skirts. "There is so much dirt here." She flapped her hands in the air as if about to take flight. "I-I just can't bear all this dirt. Josephine has been cleaning nonstop, bless her heart, but there seems to be no end to it."

Emma blew out a breath. "Mother, you are out on the frontier. On the Front Range. There is dirt everywhere. No paved or cobblestone streets. Father said if you keep the windows and doors all closed, it will minimize—"

"But the house gets too stuffy and hot. Perhaps when we find someone to plant a garden around the house, it will cut down on the dust. But, the horses and carriages going by all the time stir everything up . . ."

Her mother dropped down onto Emma's bed.

"So . . . what do you want me to do?" Emma asked nervously. She hoped her mother didn't have plans to turn her own daughter into a scullery maid.

Her mother stared across the room. "What if we have company? How can I make a proper first impression to the important people in this town if they step into a dirty house? Oh, when will your father find us proper help?"

Emma waited for her mother's fretting to slow down, but it only appeared that she was gaining momentum.

"Emma, you are going to have to help with this until we find the proper servants."

What? Emma's fists tightened. "Mother, surely we can allow a little dirt. We have to make adjustments."

Her mother slapped her hands on the bed, startling Emma. "No, we will *not* make adjustments. I will not tolerate lowering our standards. We have class. And money. There is no reason for compromise. I won't see my reputation ruined before we are even properly moved in."

To Emma's surprise, her mother sobbed, and tears began spilling down her cheeks.

Oh, for goodness' sake. Emma tried to put her arm around her mother to offer some kind of comfort—although it felt quite awkward to do so—but her mother pushed her away. Her expression shifted from one of distress to one of anger. She waved a hand wildly in the air.

"Walter has had to hire some . . . Mexican woman to clean his house. Lynette cannot do a thing to help, of course, and why should she be expected to—"

"But you expect me to. To be a charwoman for you. Mother, what has gotten into you? And what is wrong about hiring a Mexican woman? Or a Chinese or Indian—"

Her mother turned abruptly and looked at Emma with an utterly shocked expression.

"What is wrong? What is *wrong*? Emma, didn't I raise you right? To understand your place in society—"

Emma seethed, unable to rein in her emotions. "Yet you want me to get on my hands and knees and clean the house—all so *you* can make a good impression."

Emma didn't wait to hear her mother's reply. She'd heard enough. With her mother's ranting chasing after her through the hallway, Emma stormed out of the house, needing to get as much distance from her mother as possible.

She threw open the door to an erratic warm wind that whipped at her hair, pulling strands loose from their pins. But at this moment Emma did not care how she looked. She just wanted to escape. Dark clouds roiled to the north, mirroring the rage she felt churning in her chest. What in the world was going on with her mother? Was all her careful control over her life coming apart here in this new land? She knew her mother was easily agitated when anything was out of place or not going as expected, so Emma supposed it was no wonder she was having a hard time adjusting. But no one bothered to ask Emma how *she* was adjusting.

Tears stung her eyes. She ran to the neighbor's barn, battling the gritty dust flying into her face. Why had her father demanded she come out here to Colorado? Why couldn't he have sent her off to college as planned? Oh, everything was so different from the city life she was used to. She had no friends here, no direction, no one who truly loved or cared for her.

She wiped her face with the sleeve of her blouse as she entered the barn. Shahayla nickered at her as she hurried to get her mare's saddle and bridle. Anger simmered in her heart as she threw the saddle over her horse and latched and tightened the cinch. She knew she was being foolish, going out riding in these clothes instead of changing into her riding habit. She had on one of her favorite dresses, with layers of petticoats, and her expensive lace-up walking shoes. She hadn't even bothered to take a shawl or a hat. But she didn't care. She just wanted to run with the wind, run as far as she could.

Shahayla seemed to sense her thoughts and began pawing the ground in anticipation. The Arab loved to run. Well, she would give her her head and let her do so. Maybe after they both had a good exhausting ride, Emma could return home and face the disaster her life had become.

After fitting her mare with the bridle and throwing the reins over her neck, Emma led her horse out of her stall and over to the mounting block, her riding crop in hand. The stirrup attached to the sidesaddle was already adjusted from her previous ride, so she mounted and threw her right leg around the pommel, observing her skirts riding up her legs. She winced at the thought of someone seeing her like this, but hopefully, in this weather, no one would be out on the streets.

Raindrops splattered her as she picked up the reins and urged her mare to head down the narrow lane to the street. A few people were out in front of their houses, scurrying about in the wind. A couple of carriages were heading up and down the street nearer to the center of town. Emma didn't know her way around yet, but she was aware that some of these streets led east out of town. And the sooner she left Greeley behind, the better.

Her throat choked up, making it hard to swallow. As she urged her mare into a gallop, the bite of grit and wind stung her eyes more and made tears stream down her face. A great ache lodged in her gut, prompting her to push the horse harder. She tapped her mare's rump over and over with the crop, and they picked up speed. No doubt her neighbors were watching this spectacle go by—her riding through town in such improper riding attire, her hair coming loose and flying all around her face. She imagined her father hearing of her impulsive behavior. Would he become angry? Her mother wasn't the only one concerned about their family making the proper impression in this "city of saints."

Emma scoffed as she tucked her head down and pulled Shahayla into a turn that would lead her across the railroad tracks and out of town. They had moved to a colony proud of its temperance and high moral standards. Where everyone behaved just so. A town small enough that no doubt everyone knew everyone else and all their secrets. In New York, Emma could be herself, and go mostly unnoticed among thousands in such a large city. As much as she'd disliked feeling invisible, now she longed to be such. Had she moved from one stifling environment into another—perhaps an even worse one?

Emma tightened her jaw and clenched the reins tight. Her mare, apparently thrilled to be running free, galloped along the dirt road and over the tracks, and Emma let her mind grow still. She settled into the rhythm of her horse's gait, hardly feeling the bumps and unevenness of the ground beneath her. She felt entirely at home in her saddle, and after a few minutes some of the rage seeped away.

She closed her eyes and let the warm rain pelt her face, imagining what a dirty, wet mess she would be when she returned home. But suddenly the rain turned cold, and then she felt the drops hit hard against her cheeks and head. She opened her eyes and saw a wide ribbon of river to her right as the houses and shops of the town slipped further behind her. Tear-sized drops of white smacked her arms and her horse, and Emma realized it was hailing.

Hail—in summer? She glanced up at the mean, imposing clouds the color of slate that were now choking the sky. How quickly this storm had gathered. She'd never seen anything like it.

She slowed her mare to a trot, and spotted a narrow trail that led to the river. The water barely flowed in the wide channel bordered by tall wild grass. Its water looked gloomy and foreboding, reflecting the angry sky overhead. But Emma was drawn to the river and the flocks of small gray birds gathered along its banks, so she pressed her panting horse onward, aware Shahayla could feel the pinpricks of hail hitting her.

Then unexpectedly, the sky let loose. A squall erupted directly overhead, and hailstones rained down upon her the size of eggs. With each smack of a stone, pain shot through her. Her mare reared up and whinnied in fright.

Emma screamed, trying to control her horse, who kept rearing and prancing in terror. She held the reins tight and tried to utter words to calm her horse, but she was so frightened herself, she could only hang on tight, aware Shahayla's feet were now becoming mired in mud, which caused the horse to struggle and panic even harder.

Emma held on for dear life, but she knew she was in trouble.

Lucas stopped and raised his head and listened through the howling wind and pounding rain hitting his head and horse. He had just finished sinking the last fence post when this squall blew in, thankful to have beaten the storm and gotten his chores done. But as he made to mount his gelding, he thought he heard a scream.

There. Another one. Coming from the river just over the rise from where he stood. And it sounded like a woman's voice. And a horse in distress. Lucas well knew that sound after witnessing thousands of horses injured and killed on the bloody battlefields of war.

Without another moment's hesitation, he threw his leg up over the saddle and yelled at Ransom to run, leaning forward and kicking the horse's flanks hard with his boots as he headed off down the road in the direction of the cries. When he ran out of road, he galloped hard through the grass, gritting his teeth and praying his horse didn't get tripped up in a prairie dog tunnel or rabbit hole. He could tell by the way his horse was running that the ground was soft and uneven. He held his breath, craning to peer through the sheets of rain smacking his face to navigate along the driest path he could make out through the mats of sagebrush. But with such thick, high grass, bogs could be underfoot and he wouldn't see them.

Please, he prayed, *let me get through this potholed lowland without breaking Ransom's legs—or mine.*

Fortunately he reached a bit higher, drier ground, and he could feel Ransom get better purchase with his hooves. There, along the bank of the South Platte, was the source of the commotion. He spurred Ransom on faster when he saw a woman struggling to control her horse.

He grunted in annoyance. He could tell this had to be one of those women from Greeley. Riding sidesaddle and in entirely inappropriate dress. And she rode an Arab. That said it all. Anything would spook a horse like that. When a barrage of huge hailstones whacked Lucas in the face, he guessed that was what had set the Arab off.

And why in the world was this woman out riding in weather like this? Some people had no sense.

Lucas blew out a breath as he hunkered down and kept his horse at a steady canter, carefully checking the ground to make sure he didn't trip. He'd be no help to this woman if he tumbled facefirst in the mud.

The woman screamed again, and Lucas watched in horror as the horse reared up again—but this time he could tell the Arab's back legs had gotten mired. And the woman's skirts blew up and flew over the horse's face, making it panic and rear back so far it began to fall.

Lucas watched, feeling utterly helpless, as he saw the horse go down on its back—taking its rider with it. The woman screamed one more time as she was catapulted—thankfully—to the side of the horse as it fell in the mud.

He finally made it to her, yanking Ransom to a halt and leaping off his saddle to run to her aid. Her eyes were closed, but he could tell she was alive and breathing hard, and that sent a wave of relief rushing through his limbs. But before he could tend to her, he had to first make sure her mare didn't trample her to death, so he ran to the Arab's side as it flailed in an effort to get up, and grabbed the reins.

Speaking in soothing tones, he calmed the horse enough to get her to look at him and stop snorting frantically. Lucas noticed the hail stopped—thank God—and he threw his hat off to better assess the situation.

Once he got the mare to her feet, he could tell she hurt like the dickens. A long gash ran along her front leg leading down to her forelock, and blood dribbled out, but didn't gush. Good, that wasn't too bad. With a quick assessment he determined the horse would be okay, but all he really cared about was getting her far enough away so that Lucas could safely tend to this woman.

He looked around, trying to figure out where he could tie off the mare, but of course there were no trees or branches or posts of any kind along the muddy riverbank thick with brush and weeds. So he led both horses a dozen feet away, then tied the mare's reins to Ransom's saddle strings. He told Ransom to stay put, but he could tell his horse had no interest in going anywhere. Not when he had an abundance of grass around him to eat. The Arab, in her distress, quickly followed Ransom's lead and found comfort in tucking into the vegetation as well. All right, one problem solved.

Now, with trepidation, Lucas turned his attention to the woman lying on the ground. She was curled on her side, her skirts a muddy mess and her hair wrapped around her head and face. Carefully he rolled her onto her back on the soft grass, and as the wind died down to a gentle breeze and the clouds began to part and let in streaks of sunlight, he gently pushed the hair from her face and neatened her clothing, covering her legs, which exposed muddied cotton bloomers.

He sucked in a breath upon seeing her face. Despite the smears of mud and dirt, he could tell she was stunning. Clearly some young woman from high society—the quality of her clothes and shoes made that evident. Her hair was long and as black as coal. And her face was like an angel's—creamy white with full lips and high cheekbones. He couldn't help but notice she resembled Alice—how she'd looked when he met her years ago. She'd been about this age too. He figured the girl lying next to him couldn't be more than about eighteen.

He shook his head, wondering again why she'd been out here alone, along the river. It was dangerous enough for a woman to ride on the open range by herself, but clearly she either didn't know that or care. Or know how muddy and slippery the Platte's banks got in the summer. He figured she'd recently moved here. He hadn't seen her before, but then again, he didn't know everyone in town. But the fact that she'd ridden a high-spirited Arab out onto the Front Range told him she had no idea what she was doing. He snorted. Probably thought she was back in some pretty park back east, where the bridle paths were perfectly smooth and the weather predictable.

Without being disrespectful, he carefully checked her over, trying to forget she was a beautiful young woman and just concentrating on assessing her injuries the way he would any hurt creature. His breath trembled in his throat. *But what a creature . . .*

He resisted the desire to stroke her cheek, instead cradling her head and trying to get her to come to. From what he could tell, nothing was broken, but it greatly concerned him that she hadn't yet opened her eyes.

"Miss. Miss," he said softly. "Can you hear me? Open your eyes?"

Lucas waited but he got no response. He clenched his jaw and calmed his pounding heart. This was bad. He couldn't leave her here to go get help, and the closest doctor was back in Greeley. Which meant somehow carting an unconscious woman three miles in his arms on horseback. Sarah and her ranch were less than a quarter mile from here. And he knew Sarah could do as good a job of helping this poor girl as any doctor.

He made his decision. He looked over at the girl's horse. The Arab favored her right leg but she was clearly limping. He needed to get back home quickly, and the mare would slow him down. He didn't feel right about leaving the horse behind to wander off—and that leg probably needed stitches.

Lucas blew out a frustrated breath, feeling the urgency squeezing him like a vise. Back over that rise was a stand of cottonwoods. He would pony her horse that far, then tie her off until he could come back to her. Hopefully she'd fare until he returned or sent one of Sarah's sons to fetch her. He'd have to tie her loosely, knowing she might spook at just about anything. Which meant removing her bridle and fixing Ransom's breakaway halter on her. Thankfully, he always carried it with him. If she broke free and ran, maybe she'd head back to her home. Most horses would. Well, that was the best he could do under the circumstances.

With that decided, he fetched his hat from the ground, then bent over and positioned his arms to scoop the girl up. What he hadn't expected was the rush of emotion that surged through him upon lifting her into his arms. Instantly he was back in Leadville, and a strangled cry snuck out of his mouth. The last time he had held Alice, she had lain lifeless in his arms like this.

Lucas stood there, unmoving, under the cool rays of sun now streaming down on him, as his boots sank a bit into the mud, frozen by the memories assailing him. This girl's arms hung down by her sides, her head lolled against his chest. All he could see was Alice, dead in his arms. Her sweet face pale, her eyes closed—never again to open. Suddenly he couldn't breathe.

He almost dropped the girl but steadied himself. He hadn't held or even touched a woman since then, and it was as if his arms burned with the contact of her skin.

But it was warm skin, he reminded himself. This girl was alive. She wasn't Alice. And she needed medical attention. Now.

Lucas swatted away the images of his wife along with the buildup of tears threatening to rain down his face. He sniffed hard and ordered his legs to move. But as he walked over to the horses, he couldn't help but draw in the sweet smell of this girl in his arms. Her hair smelled like lavender and the rich loamy aroma of earth. He closed his eyes for a precious second to indulge in the soothing scent, even though his heart ached so bad he thought it would crack open and bleed. He allowed himself a long look at her features. She had a strong but gentle face. He imagined she had a determined spirit and a joyful laugh.

Gently he brushed her lustrous hair back over her shoulders and noticed his arms were shaking. Oh, how he missed Alice, missed her in his arms, the touch of her soft hands, the way her laugh made her eyes sparkle.

He batted away his thoughts and turned his attention to the matter at hand. He wished he had someone to hand her up to him on the horse. He couldn't just flop her across the saddle. He worried she'd had a bad concussion, so needed to keep her upright and not let the blood rush to her head. The only way he figured to get her to the ranch was to put her in front of him on the saddle and wrap his arms around her as he took her to Sarah's.

His efforts to get her up on the horse would have been laughable if it wasn't such a serious predicament he was in. But somehow he managed to balance her in front of the saddle and mount up behind her without letting her slip off and back onto the ground. He picked up the reins and had Ransom walk a few steps, checking back along his right side to see her mare was walking well enough to make the short jaunt to the willows.

It felt like it took hours, but Lucas guessed it only took ten minutes to get to the copse of trees and tie off her horse. He was satisfied she was secure enough there, although if she spooked she could break away and not get hurt. He hated leaving the animal there, but it was a matter of priorities.

Freed from that burden, he once more clambered up onto his horse after balancing her in front, then put Ransom into a soft canter—which the gelding did with his masterful smoothness. Lucas was grateful for Ransom's buttery smooth gaits. Like riding on a sofa, hardly feeling any jostling at all. He hoped all this moving around wasn't making this girl's condition worse. *You're doing all you can*, he reminded himself. Although, he worried he'd taken too long.

As he rode down the road toward the house, Sarah came rushing out of the hay barn with Hoesta barking at her heels. One look at him got her feet running, so by the time he brought Ransom to a halt in front of the main stable, she was there at his side, helping slide the girl slowly off the horse's neck.

Sarah made her usual tsking sound and studied Lucas's face. He knew her worried look reflected his own.

"Her horse threw her over by the river," he said, and he jumped down and took the girl back into his arms. "Nothing broken as far as I can tell, but you can see she's unconscious."

Sarah kept up with Lucas's fast pace as he took the girl inside the barn to the room where he treated the horses. He figured this was the best place to bring her, as all his medical supplies were in here.

"Where's her horse?" Sarah asked, as LeRoy suddenly appeared inside the barn, his eyes quickly sizing up the situation.

Lucas looked at LeRoy. "I tied her off on some cottonwoods. Directly east of where I was setting those fence posts."

LeRoy nodded and adjusted his hat. "I'll get her."

"Take Ransom. He'll lead you there. He's already saddled up." He added, "The mare's leg's got a gash in it. She's limping, so bring her slow. She's a white Arab."

LeRoy snorted and shook his head. Lucas almost wanted to laugh. He knew what LeRoy thought of the fancy horses some of the settlers brought out with them. Especially Arabs.

"Do you recognize her?" LeRoy asked, nodding to the girl Lucas had carefully laid down on the cot against the wall. Lucas had spent many hours sleeping on this cot waiting for mares to foal or for the recovery of a tenuously injured horse.

"Nope. I figured due to her riding out in a storm by the river she hasn't been out West all that long. That, or she was just looking for trouble."

"I'll say," LeRoy answered wryly. He gave a quick nod and left, and Lucas was grateful LeRoy was off to fetch that horse. Maybe if he got to that gash in time and put some stitches in it, the horse would heal without a hitch.

He looked down at the angelic face of the girl lying on his cot, aware of Sarah's eyes on him.

He hoped this girl would come through too. He hated to think about her family worrying about her and wondering where she was. But they'd be way more upset if she never opened her eyes again.

He didn't have any magic cure for waking someone up who'd been concussed. She could be in a coma for all he knew. He looked to Sarah, who studied the girl's face thoughtfully.

"Maybe you could clean her up and get her comfortable while I ride off and fetch a proper doctor," Lucas suggested.

Sarah grunted, and to Lucas's surprise, a grin rode up her face. "You're more proper a doctor than most I know. And besides," she said tipping her head in the girl's direction with a strange knowing look on her face, "she's awake."

Lucas spun back around to look at the girl. Her eyes were indeed open and staring at his.

Piercing blue eyes the color of water under ice.

Like two identical round blue pools.

Chapter 8

EMMA STRAINED TO OPEN HER eyes as the throbbing pain in her head pounded and blood pulsed in her ears. Where was she? She could tell she was lying down and struggled to sit up, but the slightest move sent her head into a spin.

"Whoa, miss," a husky male voice said. "Don't try to get up."

Her vision cleared, and the fuzzy outline of a room came into view. And the face of a man in a cowboy hat who stood above her, leaning a bit too close. She smelled mud and sweat and winced.

Two emerald green eyes searched hers—stunning eyes laced with concern. She knew she should be frightened with a strange man standing so close, and her lying down in some strange place . . . but for some reason his kindly gaze comforted her. She could tell he was genuinely worried for her.

What had happened? She sifted through her memories and recalled riding along the river. Then the hail came deluging down and her horse reared—

She bolted upright, but the stab of pain that cut through her skull forced her to lie back again. "My horse—"

The man—who Emma couldn't help but notice was strikingly handsome despite the smears of mud all over his face—gave her a reassuring smile. Her gaze settled on his strong jaw and nice straight teeth as he said, "LeRoy's fetching her now, miss. She's got a gash on her leg, but I'll see to it when she gets here. But for now, let's see how you're doing."

Emma suddenly became aware of the state of her appearance. She glanced down at her dress and shoes, which were caked with mud. Her skirt was torn along the hem, and upon lifting her hands, she saw she was a filthy mess. The sight prompted another bout of dizziness. *Heavens, what an impression I must be making.*

A wave of embarrassment washed over her—more for her stupidity than for her appearance. But how did she get here—wherever *here* was?

She noticed movement in the corner of the room and looked to see an older woman—an Indian?—enter. She was dressed in a simple skirt of calico print and a plain white button blouse made of cotton, similar to the clothing she'd seen women around the town wear. Her long dark hair was pulled back in a thick braid over one shoulder, and as she came over to her, Emma was warmed by her smile.

She realized she was shaking, more from shock than cold, she guessed. The man seemed to notice as well.

"Here," he said, reaching over to a bench and grabbing a brown wool blanket. "You need to keep warm; can't have you going into shock." He wrapped the blanket around her shoulders with the tenderness of a mother coddling a child.

She couldn't seem to stop staring at his eyes, and she wondered at the odd expression on his face. He studied her intently—not in any lecherous way, but more out of curiosity, as if she were a mystery to him. The Indian woman then came over and offered her a wet towel.

"For your face," she said kindly. Emma thanked her and took it and started rubbing her forehead and cheeks. The towel smelled wonderful—it had been soaked in some refreshing fragrance—and it felt heavenly to wipe off all the caked mud. The woman gave the man a nod and said, "I'll go make some tea." She smiled, and Emma wondered at the sparkle in her eyes. Was this man her husband? He seemed much younger than she, but perhaps he was.

"You took a nasty fall," the man told her, "out along the Platte. I heard you scream, and by the time I got to you, your mare had thrown you."

"So . . . you brought me back here. Wh-where am I?" She managed to sit upright, her back leaning against what appeared to be a wooden barn wall. The strong smell of hay and horse confirmed she wasn't inside a house.

"You're at Miz Sarah Banks's ranch." He tipped his head toward the door, indicating the woman she'd spoken to. "And pardon my manners, miss. My name is Lucas Rawlings." He tipped his hat at her and gave her a smile that for some reason caused her stomach to flutter. He stood tall, with strong broad shoulders and nice posture.

"I'm . . . I'm Emma Bradshaw. I'm deeply grateful for your kindness in rescuing me and am pleased to meet your acquaintance, Mr. Rawlings," she said, then added with a wry smile, "although I'm quite embarrassed by these circumstances."

She caught a flare of irritation in the man's eyes and wondered if he thought her a fool. Surely she was. And what were her parents going to say when they saw her like this? Panic flooded her as she thought of them. A glance outside the window showed a sunny day. Clearly the storm had passed, but how long had she been unconscious? She needed to get back home.

"How long have I been here?"

"Not long," he said. "About a half hour."

Another stab of pain erupted behind her eyes as she made to stand. But the cowboy quickly grabbed her by the shoulders and urged her back to sitting. "You shouldn't try to get up just yet. You're probably concussed. I'd like to observe you a bit before we take you back to town. You live in Greeley?"

Emma nodded, although that simple gesture felt like rocks were rattling around inside her head. She just then noticed the bottles of medicine and boxes of bandages on the shelves. Was this man a doctor? He was dressed in faded brown denim trousers and wore a threadbare chambray blue shirt covered with mud, with the sleeves rolled up to his elbows. He didn't look like any doctor she'd known. But then again, she had no idea what doctors in the Wild West wore.

"Just rest awhile. Sarah's bringing you tea. That'll make you feel better."

"I'm grateful, thank you." Emma leaned back again and wrapped the blanket tighter around her shoulders. Although the day was plenty warm, she was shaking all over. Her throat tightened as tears welled up in the corners of her eyes. She hoped her horse was going to be all right. She chided herself for her impetuous, foolhardy behavior. As if reading her mind, the man glanced over at her as he fussed with something at the far table under the window.

"You could have been killed—you know that? What were you thinking riding out alone along the river? Aside from the rattlers and gopher holes your horse could have tripped over, the riverbank turns into a quagmire at the slightest flash of rain." His attention was caught by something out the window. "And Colorado Territory is no place for a high-strung Arab like yours. Best to get yourself a quarter horse or a mustang if you want to ride. And a proper saddle."

"Excuse me?" Emma felt her face grow hot despite her chills. Well, he sure felt at liberty to put her in her place. Ride a quarter horse? And what did he mean by a proper saddle? Did he expect for her to ride astride, like Calamity Jane? What a preposterous idea. Clearly this man had no understanding of how a proper lady was expected to behave. Just because women moved out west, it didn't mean they should abandon their civility or compromise their behavior.

But he was right on one account, she conceded, mulling in silence over the fact that she could have died from her stupidity and recklessness. The Front Range held untold dangers, and here she was gallivanting around, not paying attention.

Just then Sarah returned with a mug of sweet-smelling tea. "Here, this will help ease any aches and clear up your headache."

Emma thanked her, wondering how Sarah knew about her pounding head. Maybe it was evident by her wincing in pain. She wrapped her hands around the warm mug and sipped, the licorice-flavored drink soothing her throat as she swallowed.

She looked over at her rescuer, who was washing his face in a white ceramic basin. His back turned to her, his golden-brown hair curled around his ears and fell to his shoulders. She could see the outline of his firm back muscles through the thin shirt he wore. She knew she shouldn't stare, but she was drawn to the confident, gentle way he moved. As he dried his face with a towel, he paused and his chin lifted. Emma heard a dog barking.

"Your mare's back." He set the towel down and shot Sarah an inquisitive look as he made for the door.

"I'll stay with her," she said, taking a seat on a bench next to the bed Emma sat on.

Emma frowned. "I should go out and —"

Sarah laid a hand on Emma's wrist. "Lucas'll tend to her just fine. He's been fixing horses most of his life. She'll be as good as new when he's done."

So, he's more than just a hired hand. Emma heard Lucas talking outside, probably to Sarah's son, LeRoy. She turned to Sarah. "He's a veterinarian?"

Sarah nodded. "Came out here three years ago. He lives in a cabin on my property and takes care of my horses."

So she's not married to him either. "He said you have a ranch."

"My husband started this horse ranch thirty years ago with two dozen head. We grow hay and breed horses. When he died ten years back, my sons and I kept it going. LeRoy's my older son. My younger is Eli."

Emma wanted to ask more about her life and her background but Mr. Rawlings strode in, his boots thumping on the dirt floor, and went over to the shelves lining the back wall.

"How is she?" Emma asked, afraid to know. "Will I be able to ride her home?"

The vet chuckled but it lacked humor. He gathered up supplies—bottles, bandages, thread—and turned to her. "Your mare should stay in a quiet, clean place for a few days. That gash is pretty deep, and I don't want those stitches pulling out. I'll return her to you when she's had a chance to heal up."

"A few days?" Emma gulped. "Will . . . I be able to ride her after that?"

Mr. Rawlings gave her a smile that shot warmth right to her chest. Her heartbeat sped up at his penetrating gaze. "I believe so." He studied her, and Emma felt suddenly self-conscious. "You feel well enough to go home?"

"I think so." The tea was helping. Her headache was clearing, and the pain had lessened to a dull throb against her skull. She knew her mother had medicine at home, for her frequent headaches. She could always take some of that if her headache persisted.

"Sarah, would you mind seeing Miss Bradshaw back to her home? I'll get this horse stitched up and put her in the foaling stall in the back."

Sarah nodded. "Let me go rig up the buggy." With the supplies in his arms, Lucas went back outside. Sarah turned to Emma. "You want to try standing?"

Emma carefully got to her feet, grateful the room hardly spun at all. "I'm so sorry for troubling you."

Sarah looked her over and smiled. "Would you like to change out of your clothes? I'm sure I could find a clean dress for you to wear—"

"Oh, no. That won't be necessary. But thank you for offering." She hoped she could slink down low enough in the buggy so no one would see her come through town in this condition. Would she be able to sneak into her house and up to her room before her mother spotted her? She hoped so.

Again another wave of embarrassment washed over her. She drank her tea while Sarah went to prepare the buggy, watching this intriguing man through the open window. From where she sat she could see Shahayla tied up at a post. Her mare seemed calm, clearly trusting this man tending to her, and that surprised her.

Mr. Rawlings knelt by her horse's leg as he dabbed something on her skin and gave her an injection. Probably some kind of anesthetic. He worked steadily with precision, all the while patting her horse and keeping her subdued. Emma was impressed. Most vets had a hard time getting her mare to relax and submit to any treatment at all. She'd once kicked a vet just for trying to get her to swallow her worming medicine. At one point, although she couldn't hear what he was saying, Emma noticed him draw close to the horse's face and speak to her. The tenderness in his eyes attested to a man with a compassionate heart. She felt a smile inch up her face.

What had brought Lucas Rawlings out to Colorado? Where had he come from? Did he live in that cabin with a wife and children? She imagined he must have a family. A man that good-looking, kind, and responsible couldn't stay single for long.

She realized with a shock that she was attracted to him. How silly. The man was a cowboy, rough around the edges and living a life she could never tolerate. Not to mention he must be years older than she. And he was from a class much below hers; probably didn't know which fork to use at a dinner party. What she needed—and wanted—was a man like Randall. A man accustomed to money and raised in high society like she'd been. Someone who could really understand her and her needs.

Thinking of Randall made her wistful. When would she see him? Did he even want to see her? She couldn't imagine why he wouldn't, but maybe she had read into the way he had looked at her on the train. Maybe he'd just been polite, keeping her company, following his father's instructions.

Emma's heart sank as loneliness seeped into her heart. She longed for a man to love. Someone she could share her life and dreams with. Raise a family with. She had to hope Randall felt the same way. She couldn't bear to think of living in her parents' house for years. And if she didn't find someone proper to marry soon, she'd be considered an old maid and no one would want her. Then her father would probably force her off on some old, doddering widower with a gigantic belly hanging over his belt. The thought sent a shock of panic through her.

She would just have to go pay Randall a visit at his office. She winced as she looked down at her dress. Of course, once she properly cleaned up. She could steal Josephine away for an hour to help her do her hair and dress, then walk downtown and pay Mr.

Turnbull and his son a neighborly visit. Maybe invite them over for lunch after church on Sunday—if she could arrange for a cook to prepare a nice meal. And, she thought with exasperation, get her mother to calm down about the dust in the house.

Emma let out a bitter sigh. How in the world would she be able to lead a normal life—the kind of life she'd had back in New York— in such a place as different as Colorado?

Just then a buggy pulled up behind the vet and her horse. She took slow steps out of the room, down the dim corridor, and outside, grateful for the warm sun shining overhead. Her horse nickered upon seeing her, and Emma walked over, a little shaky but so glad to see she was alive and mostly unharmed. As she stroked the mare's neck, Mr. Rawlings stepped back, allowing Emma to inspect the neat line of stitches running down the horse's left shoulder all the way past her knee.

Emma didn't have the heart to sell her, but maybe this cowboy was right. The open prairie was too dangerous for a horse like her. Maybe Emma would just ride her around town and eventually get another horse for rides outside town. If she ever wanted to attempt such a thing again. For now, she'd be content to limit her forays on horseback to the packed-dirt streets of Greeley.

"You ready?" Sarah called down from the bench seat on the buggy. A sturdy draft horse snorted and pulled at his breeching that attached to the buggy. A shaggy dog with black and white patches sat on the bench next to Sarah.

"Here," Mr. Rawlings said, taking her arm and leading her over to Sarah. "Let me help you." Emma put her hand in his and allowed him to help her up to the bench. But her footing slipped as her head spun in a little dance again. Immediately, warm arms encircled her waist, and she blushed.

Lifting her effortlessly, he gently set her down on the bench beside Sarah, and she nervously smoothed out her muddy skirts. *I must look so awful,* she thought, wishing she could do something about her hair splaying down over her shoulders. She figured this man must think her pathetic.

But his eyes said otherwise. They seemed to be filled with kindness and . . . something else. But what? A shiver rippled down her back as he laid his hand lightly on hers in her lap.

"I'll take good care of your mare, Miss Bradshaw," he said, then gave her hands a slight squeeze. "Now, take good care of yourself."

She nodded, unable to say anything as she got lost in his emerald-green gaze. As Sarah clucked at the horse and the buggy jerked forward, Emma saw that he kept watching her. She then figured out what it was she'd noticed about his eyes. She'd seen that look before, but never with such innocence. It was a look filled with longing.

Lucas stood watching until the buggy turned left down the lane and disappeared around the corner. Then he untied the mare and led her to the back stall, where he gave her some hay and filled the large water bucket at the water pump outside. He checked her leg one last time and, satisfied, headed to his cabin to throw off his filthy clothes and wash up. He'd planned on riding over to Greeley to check on a few of his patients, but he felt suddenly weary and decided to take the rest of the afternoon off.

As he pulled off his shirt and pants, he noticed a few scratches. Nothing serious. He thought about heating water for a bath in the old tub alongside his cabin, but contented himself with a bowl of lukewarm water and strong soap.

He washed up, all the while thinking about his encounter with one Emma Bradshaw. Just picturing her sent tingles across his skin. When he'd lifted her up into the buggy, it was as if his hands burned at the touch. He'd felt her warm skin under his fingers, and an urge to pull her into his arms had startled him so much he nearly dropped her again. Her sweet, expressive face enticed him. He read so much emotion underneath her features, and clearly she had a zest for life. And a love of horses. He'd wanted to ask her so many questions—about her life and how she'd come to Greeley and who with—but he knew it wasn't his place. And surely not after the girl had just suffered a concussion.

Girl? Hardly. Although she was years younger than he, she was 100-percent woman. And not just beautiful on the outside. Sure, he couldn't help but notice her slim waist and attractive curves. But plenty of women had those. What captivated him, though, was what he saw in her eyes. He grunted and smiled. Those two blue pools that held such mystery and intrigue. He wanted to dive into those pools and see what was at the bottom, hiding from view. For he could sense there was a good deal more to Emma Bradshaw than what floated on the surface.

He thought about Sarah's dream and scoffed. How could this be the woman for him? She was no doubt from a rich East Coast family, used to luxury and money and comfort. Women liked that didn't last long on the Front Range—unless they were willing to change and adapt. And few were. And many that tried, failed.

Somehow, though, he sensed Miss Bradshaw had a tough spirit underneath her skittery appearance. A bit like her horse.

A twinge of guilt ran through his heart, thinking about Alice. He could never expect to find the kind of love he'd had with her. And he had to admit—the thought of allowing another woman into his heart frightened him a mite. But he knew Alice wouldn't want him to mope over her the rest of his life. She'd want him to remarry, knowing how much love he had to give. He would just have to push past the guilt and take a chance. But he had no intention of working all that hard to make an impression on any woman.

After what he'd been through in life, he'd learned there was no place for either posturing or trying hard to impress anyone. Life ran a hard track over your back, and the best course was to deal honestly with others and to show respect when possible. He had little tolerance for anyone who mistreated another—be it an animal or a person. He regretted he had practically scolded her for her reckless behavior, but a fierce protectiveness had come over him when he flashed back to seeing her being thrown from her horse. He'd needed to pound home how dangerous the prairie could be.

He then wondered what had compelled her to ride out alone along the Platte. She didn't seem all that happy about going back home, maybe fearful of what repercussions she'd face there. Well, maybe when he went into Greeley tomorrow, he'd pay her a courteous visit—just to see how she was feeling. And maybe he'd learn a little more about the evocative Emma Bradshaw.

Emma listened distractedly to Sarah talk about the unpredictable weather on the Front Range as she searched the streets near her home for signs of anyone about that might notice her. She'd asked Sarah to drive the buggy down the back alley that lined the row of houses on her street. Hopefully, she could sneak into the house without anyone noticing. Another batch of dark clouds simmered overhead, threatening more rain. The weather sure did change here from moment to moment. That was something she wouldn't forget anytime soon.

"If you could let me off here, this would be fine."

Sarah drew up the reins and the horse stopped. "Are you sure? Which house is yours?"

Emma pointed to the third house down the narrow dirt alleyway. She turned to Sarah, who seemed like she understood Emma's intention.

"Lucas'll bring your horse back in a few days. I s'pose you'll have some explaining to do." She nodded at the house that seemed to be waiting in judgment for her arrival.

Emma nodded and carefully stepped down from the buckboard bench, gathering up her torn and muddied skirts. Well, this dress had seen its last. Served her right for wearing one of her favorite dresses in a hailstorm on the back of a skittish horse.

She thanked Sarah once more, then stood to the side and watched until the horse and buggy exited the alleyway and veered left out of town. She blew out a breath, noticing that no one was around and the block seemed quiet in the lazy summer afternoon.

All she needed to do was slip quietly in through the back door and tiptoe to her room. Hopefully her mother was busy somewhere else in the house—instructing Josephine or one of the "borrowed" servants what to scrub next.

To her dismay, she found the back door locked. Locked? Her heart began to pound hard in her chest. That meant she had to go around to the front—where anyone and everyone might see her. But what choice did she have? She certainly couldn't knock and announce her shameful presence.

At that moment, however, she didn't have to face that humiliation. The back door was thrown open wide. To Emma's horror, not just her mother stood there with a cross look on her face but her father as well. His look bespoke fury as his eyes studied the sorry state of her clothing and hair. Her mother seemed about to swoon.

Emma gulped hard, realizing if her father was home in the middle of the day, it meant her mother had been so hysterical over her vanishing act that she'd gone and fetched him.

Her mother visibly trembled, although Emma couldn't tell if it was from relief or anger. A heavy, portentous silence hung heavy between them until her father spoke. She'd never heard him this angry.

Through clenched teeth he said, "You are in a lot of trouble, young lady. Get into the house."

Chapter 9

AS PUNISHMENT, HER PARENTS FORBADE her to step foot from the house unescorted for a week, but thankfully the next day was Sunday, which meant they would all go to church together. And that would give Emma a chance to speak with Randall—or so she presumed. There were a dozen or more churches in Greeley, but her parents intended on joining the one Mr. Turnbull attended, which was only six blocks from their house.

As Emma got ready, with Josephine's help, she hoped her parents would be in a more gracious, forgiving mood—considering that this was the Lord's Day. Her father had gone on a tirade once she entered the house, and Emma couldn't fault him. She could have died somewhere out on the prairie, and they wouldn't have been the wiser. When they heard how a cowboy had saved her and taken her to an Indian's ranch, her mother nearly had apoplexy. No amount of reassurance could convince her parents that Mr. Rawlings was a decent, kind man who had behaved perfectly gentlemanly toward her. If her mother had her way, she wouldn't let Emma ever go outside alone. And her father made it clear she was not allowed for any reason whatsoever to step outside the fenced perimeter of the town. Ever.

Emma understood their concerns and acquiesced to their wishes. She had no interest in venturing again out into the wild anytime soon, anyway. She could content herself to exploring the town and finding a quiet place in a field to draw and paint. And hopefully Randall would make time in his busy schedule to court her. At least that was what she hoped.

Thinking she might see him at church made her flustered, and she hurried Josephine to finish up with her hair. When finally ready, Emma studied herself in the full-length mirror standing in the corner of her room. Her indigo dress complemented her eyes, and her many taffeta skirts swished as she turned one way, then another. Fortunately she'd been spared visible scratches and bruises from her fall, although her legs and back ached in spurts. Walking would do her some good to work out the stiffness, she surmised. She patted her hair to make sure all the pins were in place, and was pleased at how much nicer she looked than yesterday. She hoped Randall would notice her.

She thought about her mare and hoped she was recovering quickly. Which made her think of Lucas Rawlings and how gentle he'd been with her horse—and with her. Thinking about the way he'd gazed at her with his emerald eyes, and that warm, confident smile . . .

She pushed aside her fanciful thoughts. No doubt she thought him attractive because of all the adventurous Wild West stories she and Randall used to read. Mr. Rawlings reminded her of those dashing, brave heroes who rode across the plains on their mustangs and saved the poor settlers from Indian attacks.

She grinned. Her "hero" seemed more likely to team up with the Indians to fight the settlers. A frown creased her face. She didn't understand why so many people hated the Indians. They'd been living here in the West first, and it seemed to her it was the white man who disrupted their way of life and killed them and forced them to relocate to Indian reservations. She then thought about Sarah, and what she had told her as they rode back together to town. How her grandfather had been killed in some massacre. And how her grandmother had decided to leave, and go with her tribe to Oklahoma. Emma could tell, as Sarah talked, that there was much unspoken pain and sorrow in her past. Emma wondered if Sarah often encountered people who treated her with contempt due to her heritage. She hoped not.

But people formed opinions, and often from ignorance. All she had to do was look at her parents, who claimed to be open-minded and fair.

Her thoughts were interrupted by her mother's shrill call to hurry, and she went to join her parents.

As they walked down the street with a soft, crisp breeze buffeting them, they noticed many other couples and families, dressed in their Sunday finest, heading to the various churches sprinkled throughout the town. People courteously nodded and greeted them as they passed, and Emma felt excited that she would finally meet some other people. Maybe even some girls her age.

Her hopes were realized when they arrived at the steps of the pretty whitewashed church with a bell tower above the entry. Emma spotted two girls who looked near her age. Her father waved over a man who was standing with one of them, and a woman and two boys, who appeared to be identical twins about ten years old, followed behind him. The girl smiled when she caught sight of Emma, and Emma felt a genuine kindness in her greeting.

Her father introduced them as the Edwardses. Mr. Edwards introduced the two boys—Henry and Tom—and his daughter, Violet. Emma noted her happy round face held a welcoming expression, and although Violet filled out her dress a bit, especially at the waist, she was pretty in a simple way. She didn't have the airs of someone who had been raised with a lot of money. She seemed easygoing and genuine, and Emma immediately liked her.

After they exchanged greetings, her father said, "Mr. Edwards designed our home—and many others in Greeley. They've been here since the founding of the town."

Emma's mother immediately began gushing her praises of their house, and then engaged Mrs. Edwards in a lively conversation, allowing Emma to spend some time chatting with Violet. She learned Violet was a year older than she, and her personality was as sweet as her simple looks. Emma wouldn't call her beautiful, but Violet had a sincere, friendly nature and liked to laugh. She seemed to find almost everything Emma said funny.

"Do you have any hobbies?" Violet asked. "I'm studying music, and want to someday play in an orchestra."

Emma was surprised. "What instrument do you play?"

"The flute. I'll play for you sometime. Do you play an instrument?"

Emma shrugged. "I took piano lessons for years, but I lack talent. But I love to draw and paint and hope to one day publish my artwork."

Violet's eyes grew big. "I'd love to see your drawings! I can't even draw a straight line."

Emma's attention was distracted by boys' loud voices. Mr. Edwards had grabbed the arms of both his sons and was scolding them, but Emma couldn't hear what was being said. Violet laughed and shook her head. "My brothers are wild and get into a lot of trouble. All they do is play cowboys and talk about hunting buffalo."

She leaned in close to Emma and rolled her eyes. "They drive me batty. But at least now that they've got ponies to ride, they don't bother me so much anymore when I'm trying to practice. And Lucas is teaching them to rope and ride properly, which keeps them plenty busy—"

"Lucas. Do you mean Lucas Rawlings? The veterinarian?"

Violet nodded. "He's the vet we use for our horses."

Emma could picture Mr. Rawlings spending time patiently teaching a couple of wild boys. He seemed to have a well of patience. How sweet of him to take those two boys under his wing. No doubt their father was very busy with his work and probably didn't have the time—or know-how—to teach his sons such skills. *Maybe Violet would know if Mr. Rawlings has a wife and children.* But she could never ask such a nosy question. And what would Violet think? She chided herself for even thinking such thoughts.

Violet pulled back in surprise. "So, have you met him?"

Emma nodded, but before she could say more, the church bell rang and clanged out a sonorous tone that filled the air around them.

"Time to go inside," Violet said, taking her arm. She shot Emma a genuine smile. "I'm so glad to meet you! There's one other girl near our age—Lily—that goes to our church, but she's . . . well, you'll have to see for yourself. I do hope, though, we'll become fast friends."

Emma smiled back, grateful to have finally made a friend. "I'm sure we will."

She glanced around to see if Randall had come, but she saw neither him nor his father. Maybe they were already inside the church. Thinking about his sweet face made her smile. She had wanted to invite him and his father to dinner, but after her fiasco yesterday, she didn't dare mention it to her mother. She would have to hope she could sway Randall to show her around the town sometime this week. *Since I'm not allowed anywhere without an escort*, she reminded herself with annoyance.

Emma sat with her family alongside the Edwardses near the middle of the church. As they were singing the opening hymn, Emma caught movement in the back of the church. Randall and his father slipped in and sat in one of the last pews.

Emma breathed a sigh of relief, and her pulse quickened. Her quick glance showed Randall handsomely dressed in his Sunday best, and when he spotted her looking back, he sent her a smile and a nod. With hot cheeks, she turned to the front and focused on singing from her hymnal. The shame and regret of yesterday flitted away like clouds breaking apart in a brisk wind, leaving her with a shiver of excitement, knowing she would finally get to speak with Randall—the first time since the day they'd arrived on the train.

Under her lashes, Emma caught sight of Randall walking her way. She felt her cheeks heat up as he approached, looking very handsome and rested. Much more at ease than when she last saw him.

"Emma," he said, taking her gloved hand and gallantly kissing it. Emma felt her cheeks heat another notch. He threw her a smile that sent her heart racing, and she fumbled for words. Why was she so befuddled around him—the boy she used to chase around the yard? *Because the little boy has grown up to be a fine, charming man.*

"Hello, Randall. I'm so pleased to see you. How have you been settling into your new job?"

A shadow passed across his eyes for just a moment, but Randall quickly sported a smile. "Very well. Father has been putting my schooling to the test. My desk is piled high with his books and receipts, but I'm wading through them." He lowered his voice and leaned a little closer, which made the hairs on the nape of her neck stand on end. "I learned he'd been trying to sort it all out himself for a while, without an accountant. He may be a shrewd businessman, but he's not the most organized. It may take years for me to put everything right."

Randall glanced to the left, and Emma caught sight of his father speaking with hers. She noticed visible relief on Randall's face.

"Well," she said, "I'm sure you are up to the task." His expression, though, showed he worried if that were so.

Churchgoers milled around the front lawn, and Emma and Randall walked to stand under the swaying branches of a willow that filtered out most of the hot noon sun.

"Have you been introduced to anyone yet?"

Emma nodded her head toward Violet and her family, who stood on the front steps of the church speaking to the pastor. "Violet is sweet. I think we'll become good friends."

Randall nodded. "My father introduced me to Mr. Edwards earlier. He built my father's house—and yours, I understand." He tipped his head toward a finely dressed couple coming down the steps of the church, followed by a young woman wearing a very fashionable dress and hat. She looked every bit the fashion model out of Godey's Lady's Book. Even held her chin up, which accentuated a pert turned-up nose.

"And who is that?" Emma asked.

Randall let out a quiet chuckle. "The Wilkersons and their daughter, Lily."

Oh, Emma thought, *that must be the Lily Violet was speaking about earlier.* She wondered at Randall's amusement until she saw Lily walk right up to a young man standing alone on the lawn. Even from where Emma stood, she could tell Lily was flirting—quite unabashedly. Emma knew her type. And apparently so did Randall.

"The Wilkersons have a produce shipping business here in Greeley. Mr. Wilkerson owns numerous warehouses back in New Jersey. He has a large facility at the north end of town. Some of the residents sell their produce out of town via his shipping company. I hear he wants to get into potatoes."

Emma turned back to look at Randall, having watched enough of Lily and her ministrations to the poor young man who appeared a bit flustered by her forwardness.

Randall asked suddenly, "Would you like to take a walk—see more of the town? We could have a light lunch at the hotel. They're open on Sundays."

Emma smiled, pleased at the offer and knowing her father shouldn't have any objection to her being out with Randall. The idea of spending the afternoon out of her house and away from her parents appealed to her greatly. She wasn't sure she'd heard the last of their chastisement for her recent escapade.

"Let's go ask my parents," she said.

As they walked over, Randall looped her arm through his. Emma sucked in a gasp. That was quite forward of him, to do so in public, at church. Which made Emma wonder about his intentions. For surely he was announcing to all his interest in her.

Emma tried to calm her breathing as she came up to her father. "Randall has expressed interest in showing me more of the town. Would that be all right, Father?"

"Why, of course," her father said, giving Randall a look of approval. Her mother stopped talking to Mrs. Edwards and looked over. A beatific smile rose on her face upon seeing Randall with Emma.

"Oh, dear Randall. How nice you look. Very stylish."

Emma cringed. Her mother always commented on what others wore. But Randall politely returned the compliment, remarking on her mother's lovely sea-green dress and matching bonnet.

Emma stifled a smile. Having four older sisters surely had taught him to compliment a woman on her attire. She could only imagine what it had been like for him growing up in a house surrounded by teenage girls all concerned over their appearance.

"Well, shall we go?" she said, eager to be off and not get entangled in any lengthy introductions of more of her neighbors. It seemed her parents were introducing themselves to everyone, and she was aware of many sets of eyes upon her, perhaps wondering who she was and who this man was with her. Did they think she and Randall were engaged? She caught Lily looking over at her. *Hopefully she will think so, and leave Randall alone.* Lily was a true beauty, perhaps only a year or two older than she, and she would turn any man's head. Emma wondered why she wasn't married already. But maybe she was more interested in the pursuit than the catch.

Randall led her down the walkway toward the street, where Emma caught sight of Violet, with her brothers in tow. The two boys seemed quite happy to be dragged away from the church.

"Hello," Violet said cheerily, coming toward them. She smiled at Randall, but Emma could tell it was sincere and unpretentious. "Who's this?" she asked Emma.

"This . . . is Randall Turnbull. He and I grew up together, and he's also just moved out here, to work with his father."

"Pleased to make your acquaintance," Violet said with a curtsey.

"And yours," Randall replied with a tip of his bowler hat.

"Turnbull. Ah, I know your father. From when my father was building his house."

If Violet had any negative feelings for Mr. Turnbull, she hid them. But perhaps Randall's father was all charm and gentility to those who didn't know him well.

Violet's two brothers tugged hard on her arms. One of them whined, "Vi, let's go!"

Violet scolded him with a severe look. "Thomas, mind your manners, or I won't take you."

The boys instantly stopped wiggling and shut their mouths.

"Papa's given me some money for ice cream. Do you want to come along?" Violet asked Emma, then questioned Randall with her eyes.

Before Randall could answer, Emma spoke. "Randall's going to show me around town, and then we're having lunch."

"Oh, that sounds lovely! Well," she said, rolling her eyes. "I better go before my arms get ripped from their sockets." She called back to Emma as she hurried down the road, "Maybe I'll come by tomorrow to see you."

"I'd love that," Emma called back, chuckling at the sight of her new friend being dragged down the street.

"Would you like to show me your office?" Emma asked.

Randall's jaw tightened. "Not today. I'd rather forget about work for a while."

As if he heard his son, Mr. Turnbull was suddenly alongside them. Emma hadn't seen him come up.

Randall stopped abruptly, and Emma heard him suck in a breath.

"Where are you going?" Mr. Turnbull asked, a bit demanding. She noted he didn't even bother to say hello to her.

"I'm taking Emma on a walk—to show her some of the town. She hasn't had a chance to see it yet." Randall reached up to his throat and fiddled with his shirt collar.

Mr. Turnbull gave Emma a hasty glance, then returned his scrutinizing gaze to his son. "I see. Well, that's a fine idea," he conceded.

Emma heard Randall let out a long breath as he stood stiffly beside her. Why did Randall bristle so easily around his father? He seemed practically terrified.

She gave Mr. Turnbull a sweet smile as she patted Randall's arm. "I do hope we can have you and Randall over for dinner sometime. Perhaps next Sunday, after church? Mother and I were discussing having you over."

Mr. Turnbull smiled in a way that gave him the appearance of a squirrel with acorns stuffed in its cheeks. "Why, that would be lovely, Miss Bradshaw." He then turned to look Randall in the eyes. Emma could almost feel the coldness emanate from his gaze.

"Don't forget I must have the totals for last month's expenditures first thing in the morning."

"I haven't forgotten," Randall said evenly. He stood there unmoving—like a frightened horse, Emma thought—until Mr. Turnbull said good day, tipped his hat at her, and returned to the church.

Randall bit his lip. She waited, unsure what to say. He resumed walking, looking off somewhere in the distance. Emma kept pace by his side.

"Does that mean you have to work today?" When Randall nodded, she said, "But it's Sunday—"

"Tell that to my father. Sunday is just like any other day to him. A day to make money."

Emma grew thoughtful. It was wrong to work on Sunday, the Lord's Day. Why couldn't Randall just tell his father no? What was the rush to have those records done by Monday morning? What difference would a few hours make?

But Emma said nothing. She just walked in silence alongside Randall while he fumed, his mind preoccupied, hardly noticing she was there.

Lucas pushed open the door of the mercantile with his shoulder while balancing the load in his arms. He'd put off getting the rest of the supplies he needed to start stringing the new fencing, and Sarah had asked him to pick up "a few things"—although her list filled nearly a full page. Since he attended church in town, he assured her it was no bother. But he knew to bring the wagon instead of riding Ransom. At least his horse would get a Sunday rest, even if he didn't.

As he carried the first load—which included a fifty-pound sack of flour—out to the street, he thought about the sermon he'd listened to this morning. About how husbands should treat their wives, and how wives should respect their husbands. His mind had drifted to happy memories of his short years with Alice. Three years married, and now three years without her. How the time fled by. Would he get old and crotchety before he ever found someone to marry? Who would want him then?

Lucas shook his head as he flopped the heavy sack down on the wagon's flat bed situated behind the buckboard. He arranged the sacks and went back into the store for the rest of his load. He'd been trying to forget—or at least ignore—that vision Sarah'd had of the blue pools. When she saw Emma Bradshaw open her eyes that morning, it was clear from her expression she believed this was the woman for him. A rich, fancy young woman from a big city who knew nothing about surviving the hardships of the Front Range. A woman who was used to ease and comfort. He doubted she would last long out here.

He chortled as he pushed the door back open and skipped down the steps to the street. What did Sarah know, anyway? A lot about herbs and healing, and plenty about horses. But he didn't fancy her being a matchmaker or fortune-teller. He'd pick his own wife, in his own good time.

A glance down the street stopped him in his tracks. He straightened and watched as Emma Bradshaw came out of a shop—accompanied by a man who seemed quite familiar with her. Lucas knew he shouldn't stare, but he couldn't take his eyes off her. She was maybe fifty feet from him, but facing the street and not looking his way. She was dressed in a stunning blue skirt and stark white buttoned blouse that shimmered in the afternoon sunlight. Her black hair was swept up on her head and topped with a simple bonnet that tied under her chin. She was quite a different sight than the muddy mess he'd tended to on the bank of the South Platte.

Lucas climbed up onto the bench seat and picked up the reins, but he couldn't get himself to cluck at the horse. The young man who had Emma's arm wrapped around his exuded wealth and class. Lucas hadn't seen him around, but he didn't know everyone. It was evident the man had affection for Miss Bradshaw.

His throat tightened as he watched her laugh at something the man said, throwing back her head and exposing her creamy neck. Lucas's chest filled with a fierce longing, which both surprised and annoyed him. Clearly this woman with the two blue pools already had her sights set on another man. Besides, who was he—a cowboy veterinarian—to even consider courting a woman of her means and upbringing? Sure, he'd been raised in a family with money and class for a time—before the war ripped it all away and forced him into years of hard labor under the Confederate flag. But that was past. He had nothing now. Nothing but his skills and his haunting memories.

Nothing to offer a lady like Emma Bradshaw.

Emma touched the man's cheek, and Lucas flinched. He swallowed and pushed his hat down over his forehead. He then pushed thoughts of Emma's sweet face and soft skin out of his mind and drove the wagon straight out of town, past the couple strolling happily down the boardwalk, resisting the urge to look back.

When he turned onto the wide road leaving town, he urged the horse into a fast trot. He couldn't get back to the ranch soon enough.

Chapter 10

JOSEPHINE CAME OUT ONTO THE front porch with a tray of lemonade and two tall glasses. Emma got up from the long wooden settee, fighting a wave of dizziness. "Oh, thank you so much, Josephine," she said, taking the tray from her.

"Anything else you and your friend need, Miss Emma?" She smiled at Violet.

"No, this is wonderful. I'm still full from breakfast," Emma said, pouring a glass for Violet and handing it to her. She was glad her mother was busy instructing the new maid that a placement agency in Denver had found for her. Hopefully that would help reduce her mother's tendency toward hysteria—and her determination to put Emma to work.

She sat back down next to Violet and wiped her brow with her handkerchief. This was the hottest day yet. Already sweltering and not halfway to noon. Violet had come over an hour ago, and Emma had shown her some of the drawings in her portfolio. They spent some time talking in her room, but the house felt stifling, and so they chatted on the porch, fanning themselves, although all it did was move the hot air around. Emma was glad she wore a simple dress today, and a less constricting corset. She felt about to wilt.

"So tell me about the Fourth of July celebration next week in that park."

"Island Grove Park," Violet said.

"Well, what events do they feature, and who comes?"

Violet sipped her lemonade and let out a sigh of joy. "This is delicious. Um, they hold horse races, and a pie-eating contest—which my brothers always participate in even though they never win. But they don't care. They love pie."

Emma laughed and took a long drink of her lemonade, relishing the cool liquid down her hot throat.

"And there are lots of other things. Contests and competitions. Hundreds, maybe thousands, of people attend."

"That is a big event."

Violet nodded. "Just think about next year—the centennial. The town committee has already come up with a name for it: The Greeley One Hundred Grand. People will come from all over the state, or so my mother says. She's on the committee."

Violet set down her glass and threw Emma a sly look. "Sooooo . . . tell me about Randall Turnbull."

Emma felt suddenly self-conscious. She'd had such a nice afternoon with Randall yesterday, and he'd been the perfect gentleman, regaling her with his wry sense of humor. But he seemed a bit distant, and it made Emma wonder yet again just how serious his interest was in her. Did he just consider her a friend, or did he feel more than that? She couldn't tell, and not knowing was plaguing her waking hours and disrupting her sleep. Surely he knew she cared for him. But she could never be forward with him, or tell him how she felt.

She thought about Lily Wilkerson and the way she threw herself at men. No, she wanted Randall to love her, without pushing him in any way. But did she love him?

Her feelings confused her. She was certainly attracted to him, and they'd known each other so long, how could they not grow to love each other with ease? Who else could she ever feel this comfortable with? It seemed an obvious match, and she could do much worse.

"Well," she said, shaking off her unsettling mood, "Randall and I grew up near each other and played together for years. Then his family moved away, oh, back when we were about ten. We only just reconnected on the train coming out here."

"Oh, Emma, he's such a dream. You really have found a wonderful man. Has he proposed to you yet?"

"Violet!" Emma flushed and raised her eyebrows. "We . . . we're only now getting to know each other again . . ."

"He's perfect," Violet said with an emphatic nod of her head. "Don't let him slip away." She giggled. "Or Lily might get her clutches into him."

"Heaven forbid," Emma joked. She finished her lemonade and set the glass down on the tray. "He is a very sweet man. But he didn't want to come out here, and his father is . . . difficult. I think he'd like to go back East, to finish college."

"But now that you're here, he'll want to stay." Violet pursed her lips as if challenging Emma to refute her.

"We'll see," Emma said, allowing a chuckle. It felt good to sit and gossip with a girlfriend. She was so glad Violet had come by. And hopefully, soon, her father would lift her prison sentence and allow her to go visit over at Violet's. At least her parents approved of her new friend.

"Who's that?" Violet said, pointing down the street.

Emma's mouth dropped open. "Oh. It's my brother, Walter, and his wife, Lynette." How surprising to see them out on such a hot day. But Lynette actually looked well. She had color in her cheeks, and she was smiling as she walked alongside Walter carrying a parasol. She hadn't seen Lynette since the day they arrived in Greeley, but her brother had been over a few times and had reported on Lynette's health.

She jumped up and went over to greet them.

"What a wonderful surprise. Did Mother know you were coming over? She didn't say anything to me."

Lynette answered, "No, we didn't want to trouble her. I felt like taking a walk, and Walter was working at home today, so he's indulging me." She gave Emma a warm smile.

"I heard about your little misadventure the other day," Walter said to Emma with a bit of a cynical scowl. Emma ignored his remark. Just like him to say something like that—and without even first saying hello. Lynette, as usual, pretended she didn't hear him.

She took Lynette's hands and studied her face. She did look much healthier, with a glow about her. "Let me get you both some lemonade." She turned to present her friend. "This is Violet Edwards. You know her father—he designed and built our houses."

Her brother's face lit up in recognition. "Oh, yes. Pleased to make your acquaintance."

Lynette said hello as they all followed Emma into the house.

Emma called out, "Mother, look who's here."

Emma's mother came from around the corner into the front entry. When she saw Walter and Lynette, she hurried over, sputtering in delight and asking questions one after another. Emma excused herself and went to inquire of Josephine about more lemonade. Violet came with her.

Violet whispered, "Your mother likes to talk."

Emma rolled her eyes. The two exchanged knowing looks and then erupted into laughter. After she found Josephine in the pantry, she said to Violet, "Let's go back outside. It'll be too noisy in the house. And I don't think Walter and Lynette will stay long."

"What are your plans for this week?" Violet asked her. "I have to help my mother with organizing some of the events at the celebration next Saturday. I've been elected to the decoration committee, although I'd much rather be the taste-tester for the cake contest."

Emma grinned. She so enjoyed Violet's enthusiasm and sense of humor. Such a refreshing change from the usual seriousness expressed by her family. "I'm hoping to spend a lot of time drawing. There are so many wildflowers and native plants I've never seen before—"

Emma's words dried up and blew away like chaff as she stared down the street. Coming her way was a cowboy riding a mustang—and leading her mare, Shahayla.

"Why, that's Lucas Rawlings," Violet said, waving at him from the porch.

Emma's breath hitched at the sight of the veterinarian on his horse, at home in the saddle as if he'd been born in it. She watched the easy sway of his body as he trotted up the road, the mustang swishing his head back and forth, responding to his rider's confident control. Once again Emma sensed his intuitive connection with horses, as she noted Shahayla behaving downright meek and mild. No one had ever been able to pony her like that. But Lucas Rawlings somehow seemed to have managed it.

Mr. Rawlings waved back, tipping his wide-brimmed hat in greeting as he came up in front of the house and stopped. Emma watched him as he swung his leg over and dismounted, and his gaze snagged hers for a brief moment. There was something about his eyes that made it hard for Emma to pull back from. A sincerity, a genuineness that she rarely saw? Whatever it was, it sent a shudder through her body.

She followed Violet down the front steps to the street, her thoughts muddled. She felt a smile rise up on her face, but she hoped he didn't misinterpret it to mean she was excited to see him.

"You've brought back my horse. Thank you so much, Mr. Rawlings."

She noticed something pass briefly across his face, almost as if he were blushing.

Violet spoke up. "You two know each other?"

Emma said under her breath, "I'll explain later." Violet's eyes widened in curiosity, but she nodded and didn't ask any more questions.

"Please, just call me Lucas, Miss Bradshaw." He gave her a crooked smile that made her even hotter than she already felt. Perspiration beaded on her forehead, and she dabbed at it with the handkerchief she kept in the little pocket in her skirt. "Using 'mister' sounds so formal." He chuckled. "And makes me feel old."

"All right . . . Lucas," Emma said, liking the feel of his name on her tongue.

Violet chided him. "Lucas, you're not old. Why, I bet you're not even thirty."

He nodded with a grin. "No, not even. But getting there, Miss Edwards."

"Well," Violet said, feigning irritation, "how come we get to call you by your first name, but you call us Miss Bradshaw and Miss Edwards?"

Lucas frowned but his eyes danced. Emma was unable to utter a word as she watched their friendly banter. "Well, Miss Edwards, my mother taught me to have good manners, and it wouldn't be proper to address such fine ladies so familiarly."

Violet shook her head with an amused grin on her face. "So, my brothers want to know when you're going to take them out buffalo hunting."

Lucas threw his head back and laughed. "Those boys. I bet your father is ruing the day he took them to that Wild West show." He walked around his horse and untied Shahayla's lead rope from the saddle strings, then brought Emma's mare to her.

Emma's hand accidentally brushed his as he handed her the lead. Her face pinpricked with heat. She noticed his muscular arms from under her lashes and thought how wonderful it would feel to be held by such strong arms. A woman would surely feel safe ensconced in them.

Trying to hide her telltale embarrassment, she bent down and looked at the fine stitching that ran along her mare's leg. "You've done a wonderful job on her," Emma offered, sliding her hand down the length of the mare's flank. She stood and found herself up close to his face. He smelled of earth and dust and peppermint soap. Now she knew she was blushing.

She fanned her face as she stood. "Oh my, I think this heat is getting to me. But at least the air out here in Colorado is so dry."

Violet came over and stroked her mare's neck. "She's a beautiful horse, Emma."

"Yes," Emma said. "But, I've been told she's not fit for the West and all its dangers." She cast a nod in Lucas's direction. "That I should purchase a mustang"—she raised her eyebrows in a teasing question to Lucas—"or perhaps a mule would suit me better?"

Lucas cocked his head and gave her a smile that dazzled. "A mule's not a bad idea. They're the more practical and surefooted beast of burden. Although they can be mighty stubborn."

Somehow Emma sensed he directed that last word at her, albeit playfully. Maybe she did seem a bit stubborn to him, the way she resisted his suggestion to get a more practical horse. But then again, she imagined he didn't want a repeat performance of having to rescue her from her own foolishness. *Although, who wouldn't want to be rescued by such a handsome, strong cowboy like Lucas Rawlings?*

He added, "But maybe a mule's not glamorous enough for you?"

Emma frowned. What was he implying—that she was stuck up? How dare he?

"I'd ride a mule," she said in her defense, "so long as it obeyed my commands." A twinge of discomfort lodged in her stomach as Lucas studied her face. He then shook his head and chuckled.

"Does that say something about the kind of man you hope to marry?"

Emma's jaw dropped in shock. Violet, though, laughed, then prodded Emma with her elbow.

"He's just teasing you. He does that with everyone." She turned to Lucas. "Now look—you've embarrassed her."

Lucas bit his lip and took a step toward Emma. He swept his hat off his head, revealing his tawny brown hair that fell to his shoulders, and gave a little bow. "My apologies, Miss Bradshaw." Emma blushed.

"What are you apologizing for?"

Emma turned abruptly at the sound of her brother's voice. Walter stood in the doorway, a scowl on his face.

"And who are you?" he added, stomping down the front steps and coming up to Lucas, who stood a few inches taller than her brother.

Lucas put his hat back on his head and stood there with a calm expression while Walter scrutinized him.

"Walter," Emma said, horrified at her brother's rudeness. "This is Mr. Rawlings. He's the one who . . . helped me the other day. He's a veterinarian, and he stitched the gash in Shahayla's leg. He's just returning my horse."

Her stomach roiled at her brother's behavior. She hated how overprotective—and quick to judge—Walter was. Why did he have such a short temper and irritable personality? He'd always been bossy toward her, and seemed to think he knew what was best for her. But she wasn't a child anymore. She didn't need his protection.

"Well," Walter said to her, calming down measurably. "You can understand my reaction, seeing this stranger standing so close to you and not knowing his intentions."

"I assure you I have no intentions other than to return Miss Bradshaw's horse to her," Lucas answered with polite control. Emma admired the way his manner diffused her brother's anger.

Lucas walked back over to his horse and laid a hand on the saddle.

Emma, flustered by this uncomfortable confrontation, said, "Mr. Rawlings, please wait a moment. You need to be paid for your services."

Lucas held up his hand and shook his head, his eyes on Walter, who stood with his hands on his hips, as if she were an impenetrable stone wall. "No need. I'm glad I was there to help."

Emma thought her brother should have been glad as well, since he'd obviously heard what had happened to her and how Lucas had saved her. He should be thanking the cowboy, not glaring at him and accusing of him of some impropriety.

Emma went over to Lucas as he mounted his horse and took up the reins. She said in a quiet tone so Walter couldn't hear her, keeping a respectable distance, although she wanted badly to touch his hand in apology for her brother's bad behavior. "I'm very grateful for all you've done . . . Lucas."

When she said his name, she saw a flare of emotion streak his face. He met her gaze only briefly, but in those few seconds she saw that same look she'd seen the other day, as if she could see deep into his soul and sense some kind of pain in there. Somehow she knew he had a story to tell, but would he tell her?

She pulled back. *My thoughts are running wild. The heat has surely addled my brain.*

Lucas straightened in the saddle and said a polite good day to Violet and Walter, then turned back to Emma and merely touched the rim of his hat and said in a near whisper, "You take care, Miss Bradshaw."

Emma watched him turn his horse and head down the road. She picked up her horse's lead rope lying over the handrail of the steps leading up to the porch, and without looking at her brother, she said to Violet, "Do you want to come with me? Shahayla's stall is over there." She pointed down the street.

Violet skipped down the steps and came alongside her. As they walked down the lane, she blew out a breath. "Well, that was uncomfortable."

"Please ignore my brother. He can be rude sometimes."

"I'll say." She then burst out laughing. "So can my brothers. Brothers are a big pain—no matter how old they are, I guess."

Emma felt the tension in her body ease. She realized, as she opened the door to the barn and put her horse in her stall, that it wasn't just Walter's behavior that had her stomach tied in knots. It was the way Lucas had looked at her, and how his nearness had made her heart hammer in her chest.

She let out a breath as she grabbed a flake of hay from the wooden pallet just outside the stall. Why did Lucas Rawlings make her feel so strange? She couldn't get his emerald eyes and kind smile out of her mind.

Violet held the door open as Emma tossed the hay over to Shahayla. She patted her horse on the neck and whispered to her, "I can tell you like him too."

Her horse tucked into the hay and snorted. Emma chuckled and turned to Violet. "Seeing her eat makes me hungry. Should we see what's for lunch?"

Violet nodded and smacked her lips. "Yes. let's go eat. I'm always hungry."

Chapter 11

EMMA STOOD AND STRETCHED, ROLLING her neck to get out the kinks. Bees and flies buzzed in a cloud around her head in the warm, lazy afternoon as she looked across to the wide expanse of crops growing in the irrigated fields. It was hard to believe these hundreds of acres, once inhospitable desert, were watered by way of a twenty-mile-long system of waterways and flumes that wended through the cactus and up hills, carrying snowmelt from the South Platte River. Mr. Turnbull had bragged about this great feat of engineering when they'd gotten off the train.

And it truly was an impressive achievement, brought about by determined East Coast transplants to the Front Range. They had made the desert bloom like a paradise, albeit through much sweat and hard work. However, it served to remind her—as she looked with wonder upon the waving golden wheat stalks and thick fields of sun-ripened corn—that a person only need envision a dream, and then take hold of it. Colorado seemed to embody the idea of promise. Would it prove true for her? She wondered.

Emma stepped back and looked at the drawing clipped to her easel. She'd been drawing for hours, and although she felt stiff and desirous of a nap in a cool, dark room, finally getting out in the open fields and using her inks had been thrilling.

She was just completing her third drawing of some of the wildflowers that were sprinkled across the prairie. Although she wasn't sure of their names, she hoped later to research them in her botanical books. She was glad she had found some magazines back in New York on the flora of the West, although they weren't very extensive. Which renewed her hope that maybe she'd be the first artist to document much of the flora of the Front Range. She hoped her detailed studies—of plants, seeds, flowers, and roots—would provide ample information to any university she might submit them to. Her first choice, of course, would be Vassar. She would not give up hope that one day she could attend there. She allowed herself a fanciful thought: *Or maybe even teach botany, or botanical drawing.*

From where she sat on her blanket in her stocking feet, her sketchpad propped up on her small portable easel, she could look over at the town, with its neat streets and buildings laid out in rows. The stately Rocky Mountains rising to her left had been distracting her as she drew her fine lines on the expensive linen paper. She had never imagined what an impressive presence they cast upon the flat land that rolled out like a carpet before such regality. The only mountains she'd been in were not really mountains at all. Molehills compared to these towering peaks. Maybe one day she would take a trip into their heights and find herself peering down on her town plopped alongside the confluence of two rivers. How small it would look.

She returned to her easel, dipping her pen nib in the jar of black ink and working in crosshatched detail of the flowers' stamens. Perhaps tomorrow she'd add all the color, knowing she would hardly forget the vibrant shades of gold, buttery yellow, and soft lavender she'd been looking at for hours.

She imagined showing Randall her latest work, picturing his approving smile, with him saying words that validated and admired her talent. She chided herself for wanting to impress him in some way. But she did want him to see she'd grown into a woman with talents and aspirations. And she knew he would wholly support anything she'd want to do. That was reason enough to consider him for a husband. She could never marry anyone who would want to squelch her creativity, or expect her to merely be an ornament on a man's arm.

She let out a breath as she finished the last strokes, then stepped back, pleased at the work she'd done. This last drawing was her best by far. Maybe it was due to the breathtaking scenery and the fresh air that tickled her neck. She couldn't remember ever feeling so alive and invigorated like this back in New York.

Thinking of the crowded city with its tall buildings crammed down rows of streets made her appreciate this wide-open space before her. The openness and unspoiled beauty truly made her heart soar. She could really learn to love this land, she realized with a start. Although, her mind quickly filled up with certain comforts she missed. Like the Metropolitan Museum of Art, and the huge rooms full of books at the public library. But each place had its blessings and drawbacks.

While the ink was drying, she got up and decided to collect some of the wild herbs she spotted growing all around. Clumps of pennyroyal with their dull leaves and dusty purple heads perfumed the air with its minty fragrance. Her mother especially loved mint tea. She'd also spotted fennel, mullein, yarrow, and clusters of rose hips that she could also add to the tea.

As she collected armloads of plants to stuff into the roomy satchel that she'd carried her art supplies in, she felt a rumble under her feet. She stopped and listened, identifying the faint sound of pounding hooves. When she swiveled around and faced the mountain range, she saw three horses with riders heading her way on a narrow deer track that ran along the north edge of the town. Well, one was a horse. The other two following him were much smaller. Ponies, certainly. And their riders were smaller than the man on the mustang. A shaggy dog ran after them, barking intermittently. It then dawned on her who the man was. She could tell not just by the horse and the smooth gait but by the comportment of the rider, and the shape of his hat.

Lucas Rawlings.

Her throat became dry as she stood there, the plants draped across her arms, watching. The sight of his masculine physique on his strong, graceful horse against the backdrop of the Rockies painted an iconic picture of the West. He was like a painting in a magazine, symbolizing the spirit of freedom and wildness. Man one with nature. She felt as if she should memorize this vision before her, and it not only humbled her but filled her with awe.

She now understood a little why this man intrigued her. He embodied the freedom she one day hoped she'd feel and know. The freedom to be herself and live the life she wanted to lead, uncaring what anyone else thought. For a woman, such thinking to most men was rebellious and improper, evidenced by the continual opposition to the women's suffrage movement. But watching Lucas Rawlings canter across the open range caused her heart to pound in rhythm with his horse's hooves. She'd never met a man who seemed so comfortable with himself, knowing who he was and what he wanted.

But what does he really want? Hoping not to arouse suspicion or overdue curiosity, Emma had summoned the nerve to ask Violet about this cowboy vet. Violet was happy to fill her in on everything she knew about him—which included that he was not married, but had been at one time. When Emma had asked what happened to his wife, she shrugged. She didn't know, and it surely would be impolite to ask.

But Emma had a sense that the deep longing or pain she'd noticed in his eyes indicated some terrible loss. She hated to think so, but what else could be the reason for his current unmarried state? For living by himself at Sarah's ranch instead of in town? Either his wife had left him or had died. She wondered which, and how long ago it had happened. But of course she wouldn't ask. She wondered why she wanted to know anyway. It wasn't any of her business.

To her surprise, Lucas and his two diminutive followers veered off the track and headed toward her. He'd spotted her. But did he recognize her from that far off? Well, she had recognized him, so perhaps he had.

And of course! The two boys with him were Violet's brothers. Emma chuckled as Lucas and his companions rode up to her, slowing to a walk—no doubt to avoid burying her in dust. She guessed they'd been out searching for buffalo. Her eyes dropped to the rifle tied to the pack behind his saddle. Had he meant to shoot one, if he found one?

Lucas came to a stop about twenty feet from her and slid off his horse. He threw the reins over his gelding's head and turned to the boys, who were dismounting.

"Say hello to Miss Bradshaw," he instructed.

The boys suddenly noticed her, then tipped their hats and muttered hello.

Lucas nodded, satisfied. "Now, you can let them graze a little, but walk them a bit to cool them down."

In unison they answered him, "Yes sir." He handed one of the twins his own horse's reins. "Take Ransom too. He'll behave for you." The boy's eyes widened, as if he felt honored at this directive. He took the reins from Lucas, and the two boys began walking their charges. Mostly tugging on them, Emma noted, amused. Clearly those ponies meant to get as much grass into their mouths as possible. The dog nipped playfully at their heels.

Lucas turned back to her and tipped his hat. He threw her a warm, easy smile that made her tingle all over. "Miss Bradshaw."

"Hello, Lucas. Shoot any buffalo?"

He laughed. "No, but not for lack of trying."

His eyes swam with mirth, and Emma felt suddenly flustered. She set down the armload of plants as she stood on the blanket. She should have put her shoes on, for heaven's sake. Lucas came over and studied the drawing drying on her easel. He then cocked his head and chewed his lip.

"You have quite a talent there," he said. He smiled at her, and her face grew hot. He took a moment to look over the details she had rendered. "Your technique is excellent. Just as good as any I've seen."

Emma didn't know what to say. She fussed with her pots of ink and pens, putting them in their cases and then into her satchel. She glanced toward the north and saw the boys busy carrying out their orders.

"Have you . . . seen many botanical illustrations?" She knew it was a strange thing to ask, but she couldn't seem to put a coherent sentence together. Why did she get so disconcerted every time he stood next to her? He was so close she could feel his body heat and smell his fresh earthy scent mixed with horse, practically intoxicating.

He turned and looked at her. "I've done my share of studying flora and fauna. In vet school back in Philadelphia." He gestured at her drawing. "Lupinus arboreus. Considered invasive in some places. A bit toxic, but if you soak the seeds in a salt solution, they're edible. Some of the Indian tribes eat them. Horses usually ignore lupins."

Emma stared at him. She'd hardly expected to hear this kind of scholarly speech come from a cowboy's mouth. And he spoke so matter-of-factly—not in an attempt to show off his knowledge, the way so many of her rich upper-class acquaintances back in New York did, to impress others. Rather, his tone suggested he was intrigued by plants—the way she was.

He glanced down at her pile of herbs and flowers, and a serious look came over his features. "Are you planning on taking those home with you, to draw them later?"

"Actually, no," Emma said, covering her now-dry illustration with a sheet of tissue paper. "I plan to dry most of them and use them for teas. And for sachets." Would he know what a sachet was? Of course he would, if he'd been married before. Surely his wife would have had them to freshen up her undergarments. Emma's mind flitted to an image of Lucas holding a woman close, smelling her skin and the lavender scent of her silk chemise. A shudder went through her chest at the thought of those arms no longer able to wrap around a woman he loved.

She lowered her gaze, hoping Lucas didn't see the look on her face as she fussed with closing the sketchbook cover and setting the pad inside her satchel. She would put her shoes on and lace them up, but imagined how difficult it would be to appear ladylike while doing so. Better to wait until he left, and then she'd head home. But right now, she had no interest in hurrying home. She wanted to know more how much he knew about these wild plants. Maybe he could tell her the names of some of these flowers growing in this field, which would help her to properly label her drawings.

She was about to ask him about the little clumps of pinks at her feet, when he began pulling out some of the plants from her bundle. He narrowed his eyes at her, and his look took her aback.

"Do you know what this is?" he asked, making sure he'd collected all from her pile.

"Yes, those are wild carrots. I thought they'd be a nice addition to dinner."

To her surprise, he threw them to the ground. "Nice, if you wanted to kill everyone in your family."

She gasped. "What?"

"Poison Hemlock. Corium maculatum. Not Daucus carota."

"I . . . I . . ." Emma felt not only foolish but horrified. Was he playing a joke on her? No, his look was serious, and full of concern. Not at all smug, although it was clear he knew well what he was talking about. He lived here; she was the newcomer. And he would have to know about poisonous plants as a vet. He no doubt had treated animals that had ingested poison. She bit her lip, unable to utter a word. There was a lot more depth to this cowboy than what she first presumed.

"See," he said, picking up one stalk and coming up close to her face. She sucked in a breath and held it as his smile rested upon her, just the way he'd looked when he'd spoken to her horse and calmed her when he stitched her up. "Notice the smooth stem? The chalky residue? Take a whiff."

He held the plant up to her nose, and she made a sour face. "Hemlock has an unpleasant odor," he said, "whereas wild carrots smell very much like carrots. They have fuzzy stems and tighter flowers."

He stepped back and dropped the stalk of hemlock. "But it's easy to see why the two get confused. The leaves look almost identical. Unfortunately, many unsuspecting folks have died due to their lack of proper knowledge."

And so would have my family. Emma cringed thinking of how stupid she was. She picked up the remainder of her plants, wondering what other deathly dishes she might be about to give her family. "Wh-what about these?"

He fingered through her bouquet as she held it in her arms, then said, "You've made good choices with the rest of them." He shot her a sweet look. "It's an honest mistake you made."

Emma let out a trembling breath. "If you hadn't come when you had—"

"But I guess the good Lord saw fit that I did. And I'm glad." His eyes sparkled as he smiled, his lips curled in a crooked smile. "I'd hate to think of anything else bad happening to you. Only been here a couple of weeks, and looks like the Wild West is already out to get you." He let out a good-natured laugh. "But I sense you're up to the challenge."

Emma shook her head, still trying to recover from the shock of this discovery. "Once again, kind sir, I'm grateful to you. You've saved me twice from my foolishness."

"My pleasure," he said, and she could tell he meant it. "As much as I enjoy rescuing you, I hope I'll have other opportunities to engage your delightful company without the elements of danger and potential death."

Emma tried to laugh along with him as the two boys came over leading the three horses.

"We're starving," one of them said. The other nodded vigorously.

Lucas ruffled their heads, a glint of mischief in his eyes. Emma enjoyed watching his affectionate treatment of these boys. *He must really love children. He'd make a wonderful father.* How sad he never got to have any. She thought about her own father—how distant and unaffectionate he was. She would never be that way with her own children. And she would want a husband . . . like Lucas, she acknowledged. One who would play with his children and let them know how loved they were.

She then thought of Randall, wondering if he too liked children. He hadn't said anything to her about wanting them. Or even wanting to marry, for that matter. The thought brought a frown to her face.

"Well," Lucas said to the boys, "I'm starving too. All that buffalo hunting sure creates a fierce appetite in a man." He threw a humored glance over at Emma, but his words sounded hungry for more than food. Or was she imagining that?

She hurried to gather up her things, then became aware of her shoeless feet. Before she could think of what to say, Lucas tipped his hat at her and mounted his horse. The boys followed suit.

"Be careful walking back through the tall grass, Miss Bradshaw. There're often rattlesnakes around."

Emma sucked in a breath, horrified.

"You usually hear them before you step on them." He locked a smile onto her. Now she knew he was playing with her. "So you might want to walk to the path over yonder." He pointed back to the deer track he and the boys had ridden down. "Safer."

He let his eyes scan the dry plains, blue with mirage lakes in the shimmering heat and backed by the sweep of mountains. "You also need to be careful with all that Opuntia polyacantha. I don't know if you have much cactus out where you're from, but if you get some of those prickly pear needles in your tender soles"—he gestured his head at her feet—"they can cause a lot of swelling and pain." He threw her a smile, but Emma felt chastised nonetheless.

"Thank you, Mr. Rawlings." At that moment she couldn't bring herself to call him by his first name. She felt so utterly foolish and naïve. Here she was, in a place abounding in danger, and she sat drawing as if she were sitting on a bench in Central Park. Maybe the West was a bit too wild for her. She never had to worry about snakes and hailstones and poison hemlock before.

"Would you like us to escort you back?" At that the boys let out groans of complaint.

"That won't be necessary, I'm sure," Emma said. "Besides, you've got two hungry boys in tow."

"Yes, Miss Bradshaw, I do." He paused, then added. "Have you thought about what I said? About getting a proper horse to ride? I think Sarah has a couple in mind for you, ones she thinks would suit you just fine."

Emma pushed past her feelings of foolishness and said, "I have been considering your suggestion." She thought about her incident by the river. She was tired of making unwise decisions. Maybe it was time she listened to the advice of those who'd been out on the Front Range awhile. If anyone could pick a good horse for her, Sarah could. She had no doubt.

"I'll speak to my father. Maybe he'll be willing to come out to the ranch with me to look at some of the horses. He owns a lot of racehorses back East."

Lucas grinned, but his look told her that far from impressed him. "I think that's a fine plan, Miss Bradshaw. He nudged his horse around to face town. "Good day."

Before Emma could utter another word, he rode off, the two hungry boys and a shaggy dog on his tail.

Lucas led his mustang along the road, his heart almost as heavy as his stomach. He'd thoroughly enjoyed a huge feast of food at Miz Edwards's table; she knew how much he appreciated her fine cooking—especially her sweet fruit pies bursting out of their crusts. But the whole time he ate, his thoughts were distracted from the friendly banter around the table. He couldn't get Emma Bradshaw out of his mind. Her piercing blue eyes, her soft skin and full lips. The way she tipped her head and blushed at his words.

He'd thought her haughty and stubborn the day they'd met — she seemed like so many young women he'd encountered from rich, upper-class families, come out west all high-minded and thinking they could tame the wilderness as easily as picking out a hat from a rack. But the more time he spent with her, the more he realized she was anything but haughty. She had the kind of zest for life and learning as had Alice. Just looking at her botanical illustrations affirmed not just her tremendous talent but a passion and curiosity for God's creation. And just as Sarah had said — a fire burned under that blue ice. Maybe fire hot enough to melt the ice around his heart.

But it was clear she had a beau. He'd seen the way she looked at that young man, their arms entwined. Both of them dressed up in their rich East Coast finery. One quick look had told him the man exuded wealth and class. It would be wrong to interfere with someone else's courting. Maybe they were even engaged — he didn't know. And he certainly wasn't going to ask.

Lucas scowled and kicked at Ransom's flanks, urging him into a run. The sinking sun bled deep colors of red and orange across the horizon, and the wind bit at his face as his horse's legs chewed up the last mile of road south of Sarah's ranch. His emotions felt as raw as his cheeks by the time he veered into the lane leading up to the large ranch house. Ransom breathed hard as Lucas slid off and unbuckled the cinch.

He thought about that dandy young man who had been walking with Emma. Soft, well-mannered. He was probably well-educated — and maybe he could even speak Latin. And maybe that would impress a woman like Emma Bradshaw. But would he know how to protect a woman from the dangers in Colorado Territory? Did he know how to shoot a gun? Did he have the backbone to defend his woman from ruffians and outlaws who had nothing but evil intent in their hearts?

Lucas grunted. He could hardly imagine such a man out in a blizzard hauling in firewood or repairing a wagon's axle that had broken and lay mired in a muddy sinkhole. Such a man wouldn't deign to get his hands and fine clothes dirty. And you had to be willing to get dirty out on the Front Range. Life out here was dirt and more dirt. Dust, snakes, tumbleweeds and cactus. Blizzards, tornadoes, dust storms. It wasn't a picnic. You had to have not just physical strength but a strength of heart to weather it all. To beat the elements and the hard knocks life threw at you.

He'd surely faced more than his share in his twenty-eight years of life. He doubted that proper gentleman from the East had ever had to get his hands dirty, let alone risk his life to protect the ones he loved. And Emma needed a man who was not just willing but able. She deserved such a man.

Lucas let his thoughts rumble as he brushed down his horse and turned him out in the pasture with Sarah's other horses. By the time he stomped the dirt off his boots and swung open the front door, night had fallen like a shroud over the land. A few early stars peeked through the blackness overhead, and ground owls punctured the night with their haunting cries.

He wasn't expecting the scene he saw when he walked into the kitchen. Eli was sitting at the table, his face bruised and bloody. He leaned on one arm while Sarah dabbed something on the back of his head. LeRoy stood near the ice box, his arms folded across his chest, and a brooding scowl on his face.

Eli winced and swore under his breath.

It was clear they'd been having an argument, but when Lucas walked in, they hushed up. Sarah shot him a look that told the half of it. Lucas could guess the other half.

Maybe he should have had that talk with Eli, Lucas realized with regret. But he and Sarah both knew Eli hardly took heed of anyone's counsel other than his own.

Eli looked up at Lucas with one eye black and so swollen he could barely open it. Which made Lucas wonder what Eli's attackers looked like once Eli had finished with them.

"Anything broken?" Lucas asked, still standing at the threshold of the door, wondering how safe it was to step further into this morass. "Do you want me to take a look?"

Sarah shook her head. "His nose is busted. I cleaned and packed it."

Lucas could tell she'd done a good job. She often helped him doctor up horses when they'd gotten hurt, and he imagined she'd learned plenty while growing up with her people on how to tend to human ailments and injuries. He doubted he'd do much better with Eli's nose.

Eli complained through his obvious pain. "Lucas, you need to talk some sense into her." He jerked his head toward his mother.

Seems like you're the one who needs the talking-to. But considering the frayed and touchy tempers in the room, he said, "What about?"

"Dunnigan and his buddies are determined to force us off our ranch. He says if Ma doesn't take Chisholm's offer, she'll be sorry. They think if they spew a lot of threats, we'll just run away with our tails atwixt our legs. Well, that's not gonna happen."

"So, what do you want her to do?"

Eli's agitation had him squirming. "She wants to let the sheriff handle it. Like that lazy son of a snake is going to do a thing about it? Everyone knows how he feels about Indians. He's probably egging those men on."

Sarah threw the blood-drenched cloth into a tin basin filled with water. "And you're not? Fighting and yelling will only make them more determined. The ranch is legally mine. No one can run us off or take it away. The law's on our side."

Eli made a noise of disgust. LeRoy remained unmoving, unblinking, listening but not contributing his opinion. He'd learned long ago to stay out of the viper pit when his mother and brother went at it.

"The law?" Eli was practically yelling now. "Ma, how many treaties has the US government broken with Indian nations over the last hundred years? The law? You really think any white men care about the law when it comes to Indians? The law is what they decide it is. And Dunnigan and his cronies have their own idea of law—which you dang well know. Whatever they want, they take. They've shot men over cattle. You think they value the life of an Indian more? Huh?"

Sarah shook her head and crossed her arms. "And what do you think will happen if I take the law into my hands? Where do you think I'll end up—and this ranch? You're only adding wood to the fire. Making things worse." She then grumbled something in her Indian tongue, and Lucas was glad he couldn't translate it.

But Lucas saw Eli's point. And Sarah's too. He knew Sarah had spoken to Sheriff Weyburn a number of times about the threats over the last year. Yet, there wasn't much the sheriff could do—if he did care to deal with it—other than tell Dunnigan and the other cattle ranchers to lay off. It wasn't his jurisdiction; and the marshall over in Evans stayed out of conflicts like this—more interested in pandering votes. The important question was, Just how far would Dunnigan take this? Would he resort to violence? How badly did he want Sarah's choice land?

He'd considered talking to Dunnigan himself, but what could he say, really? If the cattleman was determined to force Sarah out one way or another, Lucas would hardly be able to reason with him. But one thing was for certain—if those men's threats turned ugly, Lucas would do whatever he could to stand alongside Sarah and her sons, regardless of the danger.

He'd been forced to kill men in the war, as much as he hated doing it. He had a high regard for life. But just like in the war—if he had to defend himself and those standing with him, he'd do it without a second thought. Whatever the consequences. He decided to change the subject and hopefully diffuse some of the rage ricocheting around the room.

"You still planning on entering the races next week at the park?" Lucas asked Eli.

Eli's eyes simmered with fierce determination. "Yes. Broken nose or not."

Lucas knew Eli meant to do more than show his prowess at riding. All the cattlemen, ranchers, farmers, and townspeople would be at the big Fourth of July celebration. Every year he and LeRoy won most of the ribbons, but Lucas had a feeling this year winning meant more than a few token awards and impressing the girls watching from the stands. In past years, some arguments and fights had broken out—mostly due to unruly men who'd been drinking whiskey and found themselves restless and bored. But these were minor incidents quickly squelched by the sheriff and his temperance committee.

However, Lucas had a strong feeling things might get out of hand this year—especially if Eli didn't get his rage under control. Since there was no way Sarah would be able to talk Eli out of participating in the events, someone would have to keep a close eye on Eli.

Lucas chewed on his lip as he watched Eli get up and storm out of the room and LeRoy shake his head.

Lucas usually didn't carry his Colt when he went to the annual celebration. Folks came from all over to enjoy the food and festivities and have a great time with their families. Hardly an event that required carrying a gun. But this year he would.

Chapter 12

EMMA WAS ASTOUNDED BY THE huge crowds at the park. As her family's carriage pulled up to the entrance fronted by large plots of colorful pansies and chrysanthemums, she noticed hundreds of people, dressed in a variety of garb, milling around, talking, and carrying baskets of food. Through the hordes of people she could make out a large riding arena in the back, surrounded by wooden stands, already filled to crowding with spectators. From the loud cheering, she guessed a race was in progress. She had hoped to find Violet upon arriving, but this would be no easy task. However, Emma knew her brothers would be entering some of the pony races for youngsters, so maybe she could locate her somewhere in the stands.

Her father nodded at the attendant who took the reins of their horse. With his head high, Charles Bradshaw took his wife's arm and smiled. "This way," he said, leading them to a side gate marked "Private," away from the long lines waiting to enter.

"Emma," her mother said, pulling her attention away from the sights of all the ladies dressed in their summer fashions and sun bonnets walking with their children in tow. "Pay attention and stay close." Her mother frowned with disapproval at the sight of a group of shabbily dressed men who appeared to be ranch hands or laborers—and who were eying Emma up and down with a lecherous look. One whiff as they walked by told Emma they'd been drinking—and hadn't bathed in a long while. Emma's mother made an audible noise of disapproval as she pulled on Emma's arm to steer her wide of the loitering men, who seemed to have nothing better to do than look at the young women as they entered the park. One of the reasons her father had chosen Greeley was the strict no-alcohol laws, but that didn't prevent visitors from outside the town limits from drinking.

"Where are we going?" Emma asked.

"Mr. Turnbull has reserved a special table for us near the arena. And he has a private seating section for us to watch the races." Her mother fluttered the fan in her hand, trying to cool her face in the already-hot morning. Emma thought she was overdressed, but her mother always had to look her best and make an impression. Emma opted for comfort.

She followed her parents closely, noting the wide assortment of people attending the event. Clearly most of the people were not from Greeley. Few were dressed in fine clothing such as they were. Most were in simple dress, many of them cowboys and farmers in their denim pants and overalls. There were groups of Chinese families and others she guessed were Mexican, with their picnic baskets and colorful outfits. Groups of men stood around laughing or playing games on the dirt. They threw horseshoes, and even knives, letting out bursts of laughter as well as profanity. Emma's ears heated at some of the coarse language. She glanced at her mother, who kept her eyes narrowed and focused ahead, as if fording a dangerous creek and aiming at the far shore for safety.

Emma glanced around for Violet or anyone else she recognized from town and their church. Only when they arrived at the shady picnic area filled with long wooden tables did she spot their pastor and his wife, and the Wilkersons and their daughter, Lily. Emma had no interest in talking to Lily, though, and hoped that Violet's family would soon arrive.

Already sitting at one of the tables was Lynette and Walter. Emma was greatly cheered at seeing her sister-in-law looking so pretty with a grin on her face. Dozens of weeping willows had been planted in rows, and their sweeping boughs created a nice shade cover that dispelled much of the heat. On two long tables covered in pale yellow lace-trimmed tablecloths were platters of food and large glass tureens of something to drink. Emma presumed it was lemonade, and the large blocks of ice floating in it made her suddenly thirsty.

As her parents walked over to speak to some of the families seated at the tables, many already eating their lunches, Emma poured herself a glass of lemonade and said hello to the ladies setting out more food. Dishes filled nearly every inch of the tables, and there were huge fruit and vegetable salads, meats of all kinds, roasted ears of corn, and delectable-looking desserts. Clouds of insects swarmed around everyone's heads, but most people ignored them. Regardless of the buzzing gnats and flies, it was a feast for the eyes, and no doubt for the stomach as well. Emma couldn't wait to taste everything.

With her drink in hand, she went over and visited with Lynette and Walter. She finally had a little time to sit and chat with her sister-in-law. All the while, Walter seemed morose and distracted, eyeing the crowds and watching the goings-on. But Emma couldn't quite tell his mood. If she didn't know better, she would think he'd been drinking. His eyes were a bit glassy and dazed, and he moved unsteadily when he walked to the table to get a plate of food. Emma knew her brother enjoyed his fine scotch in the evenings, but she'd never seen him inebriated in public. Had his drinking gotten worse due to Lynette's continual health issues? If Lynette was upset by his behavior, she showed no sign, but she was never one to reveal much of what she felt, always keeping composed and collected. Sometimes Emma wished she could be more like her.

Emma was grateful for the huge grassy lawns in the park. So much of Greeley was dirt, and dust coated everything. But with the park situated right alongside the Cache la Poudre River, the grounds were well-watered by irrigation ditches that ran in long narrow canals, and large flowerbeds added a soothing fragrance to the dry air. Still, the heat penetrated through the boughs overhead, and Emma was glad she'd worn a lightweight cotton dress with just two taffeta petticoats.

She knew Mr. Turnbull was actively involved in putting on this annual event. Randall had told her after church on Sunday that he would be busy in the park office for most of the day, but he promised to watch some of the races with her in the afternoon. Emma looked forward to spending time with him in a relaxed social setting such as this. And she'd heard there would be a dance in the evening. That was what she looked forward to the most. Hopefully Randall would dance with her, take her hand in his, and together they would speak in quiet voices and dance to romantic music.

She envisioned his arm around her waist, his eyes gazing into hers. She wanted so badly for him to open up and tell how he felt about her. She wanted him to fall in love with her, and to see that look of adoration in his eyes. Surely he cared for her. And he must have some intentions. Would he make them known tonight, under a full moon amid the beautiful setting of the park, with the river gently flowing behind them?

Emma let out a breath and finally spotted Violet. With a wave, she caught her friend's attention. Violet hurried over, and Emma gave her a hug.

"Hurry, Thomas and Henry are entered in the next race. Will you come watch with me?"

Emma nodded and turned to Lynette. After she introduced them to each other, she asked Lynette, "If my mother asks about me, would you tell her I'm with Violet? We'll be sure to come back after we watch some of the races." Emma was thrilled Violet had come to fetch her. She'd much rather sit with Violet than with stuffy Mr. Turnbull—even if that meant Randall wouldn't be sitting with her. She frowned thinking of how Randall acted around his father. He seemed so bullied and afraid of him. Did he ever dare speak his mind or disagree with his father?

Violet threaded through the crush of the crowd, holding tight to Emma's hand. They climbed the steps of the stands partway to where the Edwardses were sitting. Mrs. Edwards gave Emma a big welcoming smile. Mr. Edwards said hello to Emma and scooted down to make room for the girls.

"Why, Emma, I'm so glad Violet found you. Come, sit with us. The boys are about to race."

"What is this event?" Emma asked, looking down at the row of about a dozen boys on their ponies positioned at one end of the arena, waiting tensely for the race to begin. They each held the reins in one hand and something shiny in their other.

Violet answered, "It's the egg race. They have to keep the egg on the spoon, gallop to the end, spin around, and run back. The first back across the line with their egg still on his spoon wins."

Emma shook her head. "That doesn't seem all that easy."

Violet laughed. "It's not. Usually the boys try to run too fast. Most make it to the turnaround, but they lose their egg when they swing their pony to head back. It's fun to watch though."

Violet was right. The boys took off when the gunshot rang out, and Thomas and Henry did real well until the turnaround, where they both dropped their eggs. Even from where they were sitting, Emma could tell the frustration and disappointment on all the boys' faces as eggs dropped one after another on the dirt. However, quite a few boys galloped home with their arm outstretched and their egg balancing on their spoon. The crowd cheered the winner, who tossed his egg up in the air after he crossed the finish line. Emma could tell Violet's brothers looked dejected.

"Oh well," Mrs. Edwards said. "Balancing eggs isn't their strongest talent. I'm sure they'll do better in the keyhole competition."

"How many races are they participating in?"

Violet said, "There are about six or seven events for the kids. The cutest you missed: the mutton-buster."

Emma laughed. "Mutton-buster? What's that?"

"The tiny kids, under five, ride big, fat sheep. There's a strap cinched around the sheep's belly so they have something to hold on to. You should see them when they let them out of the chute. The kids bounce along as the sheep trots down the arena, and slowly they slip to the side until they just fall off and land on the ground."

"Sounds adorable."

"They have to stay on at least ten seconds. But few ever make it that long." Violet's eyes twinkled.

Over the next hour they watched the rest of the children's events, and Emma was surprised to see some young girls competing. They rode astride, wearing trousers just like the boys—to Emma's astonishment. She wondered what kind of parents would let their little girls dress and ride like boys.

Then, to her surprise, when they announced the adult events, Emma spotted Lucas Rawlings on his mustang trotting out into the arena. Violet saw him too.

"Oh, there's Lucas." She nudged her mother. "Do you think he'll win the reining competition again this year?"

"I've no doubt," Mrs. Edwards said. "If he's still riding Ransom."

Emma's eyes widened at their talk. She knew Lucas could ride a horse, but win competitions? He surely was full of surprises.

"What do they have to do in this event?" she asked.

"Oh, lots of things," Violet answered, as about a dozen horses and riders warmed up by circling the arena in a slow lope. "They have to execute perfect circles, using flying lead changes. Then they have to do a run-down and flying stop, then back the horse up ten feet—oh, you'll see. It takes a lot of control, and shows off both the horse and rider's ability."

The horses then circled back to one end of the arena, and one by one their numbers and names were called. Emma was amazed at the agility of the riders, but when Lucas's name was called and he pulled Ransom out into the arena for his turn, Emma held her breath. She watched in awe as he maneuvered his mustang, smooth as glass, looking relaxed and confident. The other riders were good, but Lucas excelled far beyond their adequate riding skills. It was as if he and Ransom were of one mind, joined at the hip. He finished to a wildly cheering crowd, and no one—not even Emma—was surprised when he was announced as the winner at the end of the event. He rode up to the judge's stand and swept his hat off his head and nodded at the crowd. He then took his trophy and rode out of the arena.

Emma blew out a trembling breath. She had been greatly impressed by his performance. He rode as if it were the most natural thing in the world, as if it were a dance. She'd never seen such grace and poise and control, and it implied he'd spent many hours training Ransom to respond to his subtle cues.

Emma smirked, feeling that familiar stirring in her chest. She could imagine how a woman would respond to such gentleness and patience under his guiding hand. She blushed at the thought, realizing her imagination was leading her to picture an intimacy she had no business dwelling on. But she couldn't get the thought of what those strong arms would feel like around her waist. She'd never felt such fervent desire as she did in this moment. Not even being close to Randall gave her such stirrings of passion.

This was wrong. She was wrong to allow herself to fantasize such things. Lucas was not her type. He belonged to the wild, untamed West—a place he felt wholly at home and fit into, like a hand in a glove. He was made of the stuff that thrived in such a harsh, challenging environment, and she was not. He'd made that clear when he showed her how naïve and fragile she was. Even if she learned to love living out here, she could never look at the West the way Lucas did. She needed a safe, comfortable life, in a proper home, with a husband who could provide for her in the style in which she'd been accustomed. A man with class, culture, and fine upbringing. Someone with whom she could discuss news and books, someone with education and experience in the world at large.

Randall could provide all that for her. He would support her desire to be an artist and maybe would encourage her to attend college, even become a botanist, if that's what she wanted. Maybe once they married, they'd move back to New York. She knew if she asked Randall, he'd say yes. He didn't want to be out here any more than she did. He would have to stand up to his father, though, and Emma knew what would happen if he did. He'd be cut out of his family, and from his father's money. But Randall had talent and ability. He could easily get a job with a firm back East. Emma had no doubt that even if Mr. Turnbull disowned his son, Randall could succeed in business and provide comfortably for her. Even if they had to scale down their lifestyle, Emma would be willing—if it meant Randall would be free of his father's chains.

The thought of marrying Randall and moving back to New York stirred Emma with impatience. She needed to put this cowboy out of her mind—he only represented childish dreams and romantic notions from adventure stories. She was attracted to the idea of him because he represented the freedom she wanted. But she knew she could never thrive in a life in the West. Just like her crape myrtle. She had carted it all the way from New York, determined to make it adapt and learn to "bloom where it was planted," as Mrs. Turner had said. But Emma figured if she planted her tree in Colorado, forcing it to endure the harsh elements and deficient soil, it would probably die. She could water and feed it all she wanted, but some plants required certain conditions in order to survive. And so did some people. She should accept the truth about herself before she made a grave mistake.

Violet tugged on Emma's sleeve. "Emma, did you hear me? They're about to start the really exciting events. The roping competitions."

Emma listened absentmindedly while Violet explained all the upcoming events. Her heart felt heavy thinking and worrying over Randall and wondering just what he felt for her. She knew she should get back to the picnic area, where he might already be waiting for her, but she told Violet she'd stay a little while longer.

The next events were exciting, and to Emma's surprise, she heard the names of Sarah's sons announced. They were entered in all the next events, which included individual and team roping, barrel racing, pole bending, and a trail class. Emma was riveted by the speed and agility of the riders, and especially amazed at how quickly the cowboys shot out of the gates and had the calves lassoed and tied off in a matter of seconds. She'd never seen anything like it in her life.

Caught up in the excitement, she found herself cheering and clapping at the impressive performances of all the riders. Eli and LeRoy Banks, though, made off with a large number of ribbons, and she smiled as they whooped and hollered upon collecting their awards. Even though they didn't look much like Indians, they seemed to act the part—maybe to entertain the crowd. Eli—the one she hadn't met yet—even wore a feathered headdress, and his horse was decorated with paint and sported a colorful Indian blanket. Emma wondered if anyone in the crowd would be upset by that, but she had seen some people around the park dressed in Indian garb. She supposed there were some Indians still around—people like Sarah who owned and ran businesses and didn't pose a threat to the settlers.

Realizing hours must have passed, Emma turned to Violet. "I should get back to my parents. And I'm starving. Can you come with me?"

Mrs. Edwards nodded. "I'm off to the pie and cake competition. I'm one of the judges."

"Does that mean you get to taste them all?" Emma asked.

"Yes, and believe me—it's hard to pick a winner. But we have three judges and we use a score card. Do you like to bake?"

"Heavens, no," Emma said. "I've never baked a thing in my life." She had rarely ever stepped foot in a kitchen.

Mrs. Edwards laughed, and Emma wondered what she was thinking. Did she think Emma stuck-up? She hoped she didn't give that impression.

Emma added, somewhat awkwardly, "I suppose I should learn someday." Although she really had no interest in learning how to cook or bake. She was content to have others cook for her.

Mr. Edwards spoke—for the first time. He was one of the quietest men she'd ever met. With a sly grin he said, "It's a mighty fine skill for a young woman to have. You know what they say—the way to a man's heart . . ."

Emma chuckled, wondering if Mr. Edwards had married his wife mostly for her cooking. Emma imagined she was a wonderful cook, and wouldn't fault him if he had done so.

"Well, I'll walk you girls back," Mrs. Edwards said. "Ed needs to go find the boys, and I don't want you two young ladies wandering unchaperoned. There are all kinds of disagreeable characters loitering around. And as the day goes on, the more drunk some of them get—even though liquor is prohibited in the park. It's not safe."

The girls nodded, and after saying good-bye to Mr. Edwards they walked back over to the picnic area, where Emma found her parents, and Walter and Lynette, sitting with Randall and his father. At least a dozen other families were seated at the tables, and Emma recognized most from church.

Randall's eyes lit up when he saw her, and he quickly took her hand and led her to sit beside him. Violet joined them, and soon they were all eating and drinking lemonade in the sultry heat of the late afternoon. Mr. Turnbull commanded the table, speaking loudly about various topics, forcing everyone to listen to his opinions. The families seemed to be enjoying their meal and chatting with neighbors. The atmosphere was lively, and crowds of people wandered through the park around them, heading to the races and other games, or to the food tables.

Emma wished she could go someplace quiet with Randall to talk, but he seemed perfectly content to sit at the table and listen to his father and the other men discussing politics and the proposal to make Colorado a state. Emma filtered out the conversation, feeling mostly ignored. Why didn't Randall want to talk to her? Was he sitting there out of polite obligation?

She turned to him, about to suggest they maybe go for a walk along the river, when Mr. Turnbull mumbled something under his breath. Emma turned and saw his face redden with a scowl.

"Those blasted Indians. What are *they* doing here?" His voice was loud enough to carry across the picnic area.

Shocked by his pronouncement, Emma turned to see who he was looking at. The blood drained from her cheeks.

Coming toward the tables from the direction of the arena was Sarah and her two sons, their faces happy and flushed from the heat. And Lucas Rawlings was walking with them.

Chapter 13

"I DON'T KNOW WHY ANY savages are still here on the Front Range. We moved them all out years ago." Ernest Turnbull stood stiffly at the end of the picnic table, his eyes narrowed on Sarah and her sons. "They're vile and deceitful—the whole lot of them."

Emma could hardly breathe. How could Randall's father be so mean and prejudiced? Her hands shook as anger welled up in her stomach. A glance around the tables showed most of the picnickers felt uncomfortable with Mr. Turnbull's pronouncements, but no one seemed to be offended enough—or brave enough—to speak up. Well, she wouldn't stand to listen to such talk, if he meant to continue hurling insults at Sarah.

Emma watched as Sarah, her sons, and Lucas Rawlings helped themselves to food from the long tables, which Emma understood had been set out for anyone wanting to feast. The whole point of the picnic was to show generosity to all. Many of the less fortunate from Greeley's outlying communities had been coming over and filling their plates, their gratitude expressed for such kindness. The town's churches organized this event, which Emma felt was the perfect example of Christian charity.

Apparently, though, Mr. Turnbull's Christian charity had its restrictions.

One man with big moustaches and thick eyebrows waggled a finger at Mr. Turnbull, when he had an opening to speak. "There're plenty of peaceful redskins. We've lived here much longer than you have, Mr. Turnbull. And we still do trades with Indians who bring us buffalo hides even now. For years, they were our biggest suppliers. Before the settlers came to the territory, the trappers and Indians got along just fine—"

"Hogwash!" Mr. Turnbull said, craning his red neck and squinting his eyes at the man. "When we began laying out the railroad line for Union Pacific, the savages attacked settlers, burned their homes along one hundred and fifty miles of trail. And they'd still be plotting their vicious attacks against peaceable citizens if they hadn't been carted off to Oklahoma—where they can be watched and controlled."

Emma had hoped Sarah and her sons would take their food to eat elsewhere, but they seemed impervious to the heated discussion going on and took seats at a nearby empty table. Surely they heard every word being spoken, but from their faces, she couldn't tell. Maybe they'd heard such talk so often that it didn't bother them. But it bothered her—greatly.

Lucas seemed to be whispering something to one of Sarah's sons—the younger one. She guessed Lucas was trying to calm him down, for the young man started getting agitated. And when Emma saw him throw a look at Mr. Turnbull, Emma cringed, fearing something terrible might happen. Would a fight break out?

Emma turned back to look at Randall, who had his head down and was eating his food in quiet concentration. He kept a blank expression on his face, and Emma wondered just what he was thinking about his father's tirade. Did he share the same opinions? How could he? Yet, he didn't say a word, or give a hint of reaction as the argument around them grew in volume.

A few of the men had joined in the heated discussion over the evils of the red man. Emma's parents listened with interest, and at one point her father even grinned. She felt incensed at him too. This was not a theoretical discussion; they were making sweeping statements about a race of people who had been forced off their land and herded onto reservations far away from where they'd be living. But Mr. Turnbull did not see any evil in that. All he seemed to care about was the railroad paving the way for good Christian families to settle out West following the mandate of manifest destiny.

Emma pushed her plate away, unable to eat another bite. The food soured in her stomach. It grieved her to see so few defending the oppressed. And to see the cruel remarks being made in public—in front of Sarah and her sons. No one in their social circles back in New York would ever dare show such rude behavior—at least not in public.

Emma stood and turned to the table where Lucas sat with Sarah's family. Lucas caught her eye, his look questioning her. She felt as if she were in a raging river, trapped between rocks, the current pulling her in different directions. But when Sarah smiled at her, a smile full of gentleness and wholly lacking in malice or anger, Emma could no longer tolerate a moment longer at her table. Randall looked up at her and touched her arm.

"What are you doing?" he asked in a quiet tone. Fear danced in his eyes.

Suddenly Randall disgusted her. He had spent his life trying to be invisible, hiding from his father's wrath, and here he was—still doing the same thing. He avoided confrontation at all costs. And she understood why. But at some point avoidance became cowardice. And a man who couldn't stand up for right and decency was hardly a man at all.

Emma pulled away from Randall and walked resolutely over to Sarah's table. Her sons eyed her curiously, but said polite hellos as she nodded and smiled.

"Hello, Sarah," she said, her nerves on edge, sensing dozens of eyes on her back. She looked at Lucas, and his smile warmed her all over. "Do you mind if I join you and your family?"

Sarah scooted over and patted the bench. "How nice of you to come sit with us." Emma thought she looked pretty, with her hair done up in a bun and wearing a new calico-print dress with pearl buttons. If Sarah paid any mind to the mean comments, she didn't show it.

"Boys, say hello to Miss Bradshaw. I think you met LeRoy at the ranch," Sarah said. Her sons tipped their hats at her—a gesture Emma had come to understand was the Colorado equivalent of "hello."

Emma nodded at Sarah's older son, who resembled her quite a bit with his dark eyes and hair. And he had her smile.

"This is Eli," she added, nudging her son sitting beside her. He gave Emma more of a grunt than a hello, then turned all his attention on the plate of food in front of him. She wondered if the bandage across his nose was the result of his competing in the roping events.

Emma told him, "I watched you and your brother in the horse show. You're both excellent riders. Very impressive."

Eli grunted again, but LeRoy thanked her for the compliment. He picked up his fork and waited for her to say more.

"Please, don't let me interrupt your meal. I've already eaten." She blew out a trembling breath, feeling very self-conscious and wondering if coming over here was akin to declaring war. From under her lashes, she looked back at her family and saw stern looks on their faces. Her mother was back to fanning herself, waving her hand in a frantic flutter. Lynette kept a polite reserved expression on her face, but Walter's glare held nothing back. Well, what did he care about where she sat and with whom she spoke? Her father was now engaged in some heated discussion, but Emma could tell they'd changed topics and were talking about some town ordinances, much to Emma's relief.

Lucas, sitting across from her, pulled her attention back. He picked up a roasted ear of corn and bit into it. She couldn't get over the enormous amount of food piled on the men's plates. But then again, she hadn't spent the afternoon competing in horse races. "So, Miss Bradshaw. What brings you over here to the Indian camp?"

Emma's throat constricted. She didn't know how to answer. He seemed to be teasing her, and she didn't find any of this funny.

But he then lowered his voice, and his tone was kind. "There will always be people like him," he said, motioning with his head toward Mr. Turnbull. "Fear causes folks to close their hearts. To distrust others. But in a few more years most folks will have forgotten that Indians had ever been dangerous or that the buffalo and antelope had once freely roamed the plains." He looked around the park as if seeing past it all, seeing into the future. "You are a witness to the last of the true West, Miss Bradshaw. Take a good look before it vanishes forever."

Emma let Lucas's wistful words soak in. He of all people would be able to grasp such a bigger, encompassing vision of their country. So much was changing. Her life had changed drastically. But she could see how the whole nation was undergoing change, like a woman in labor. A civil war had nearly ripped apart the country, and soon it would be the twentieth century. Maybe for someone as brave and competent as Lucas Rawlings, the future was promising, and exciting. But Emma understood why many were fearful. Change was often frightening.

She looked over at Randall's father and frowned. *But that is no excuse to treat other people unjustly.*

"Lucas tells me you're thinking of getting a good, sturdy horse," Sarah said, breaking Emma's thoughtful mood. "I think I might have just the horse for you."

"Which one, Ma?" Eli asked between bites of chicken. "That slowpoke paint you've been working with?"

Sarah answered him, but her eyes were on Emma. "No, I'm thinking Emma would do better with a more spirited horse. *Hoonevasane.*"

Eli's eyes widened in surprise, but Lucas nodded his approval.

"Protector." Lucas turned to Emma. "That's what his name means. Sure, he's spirited, but he's as loyal and attentive as Hoesta."

"Who's Hoesta?" she asked Lucas. She brushed a stray strand of hair from her face as the wind began to pick up, then retied her bonnet's strings. It was always so windy on the Front Range. She would have to figure out something to make her hair behave better.

"Ma's dog," LeRoy said with a chuckle. "Although he's pretty much adopted Lucas. Follows him everywhere—even in five feet of snow."

Emma nodded. "I think I saw him the other day—when you were out with the Edwards boys."

Lucas finished off the ear of corn and started in on a piece of cornbread drenched in honey. "Yep. His name means fireball. When he was a pup, he tripped and fell into a campfire. We had to roll him around to put the fire out. He was none the worse for wear, although most of his fur had fizzled off."

Eli laughed. "He sure looked ugly for a time."

Emma chuckled but said, "Poor dog."

Lucas shook his head, amused. "Anyway, Sarah knows her horses. And she can always tell which one will suit a particular rider, even if the buyer disagrees. They would all do well to take her advice."

"Thank you, Sarah. I haven't yet discussed it with my father, but I would like to come over and see your horses. I'm sure they're all fine quality."

Sarah nodded and slathered a piece of cornbread with butter. "Some are a bit wild and feisty. But a mustang's surefooted and doesn't spook easily. Why, Ransom—Lucas's horse—takes delight in stomping on rattlesnakes. It's a favorite hobby of his."

Emma felt the blood drain from her face. But Lucas threw his head back and laughed.

"She's pulling your leg. But truthfully, he has been known to step on a snake or two because he hates those pesky creatures. I don't think he delights in it though."

Emma felt some of the afternoon's tension drain from her limbs. She chatted with Sarah as the men around her ate, and soon they were sharing stories with her about horses and roping. Emma asked Lucas about the reining event he'd won, and he talked a bit about the skills horses needed to learn to work with cattle, a gleam in his eyes. Emma listened, enrapt by his passion and respect for these animals that seemed to be his whole life.

Sarah explained how, ten years ago, her husband had been thrown by a horse he was trying to break, and his neck had snapped when he hit the fence post. After his death, she and her then-teenage sons ran the ranch. Emma was astounded to hear of Sarah's fortitude and determination to keep the ranch afloat, even though the workload was often overwhelming. Having Lucas come join them three years ago, to Sarah, was a godsend.

Sarah then told Emma a bit about her parents and grandparents, and how her father, a buffalo trader, had met her mother, a Cheyenne daughter of her tribe's medicine woman.

Emma had so many questions about Sarah's Indian heritage, and Sarah willingly answered. She was especially fascinated hearing about the many plants that could be harvested on the plains, and their many medicinal uses.

"I would love to learn more about all these plants. My dream is to paint and catalog as many native plants as I can."

Lucas nodded enthusiastically while wielding a chicken leg in his hand. "Emma's a fine artist. You should see her drawings. They're as good as any I've seen in medical texts."

"That so?" Sarah said, her eyes dancing at Lucas's words. A funny look passed between Sarah and Lucas, making Emma feel as though they'd been talking about her.

Sarah then said to Emma, "Come to the ranch some morning. I'll take you out on a river walk and show you some plants that can be made into salves, or prepared and eaten. Ever eaten a cattail?"

"A what?" Emma's horrified look had Sarah's sons roaring in laughter.

Lucas tipped his head coyly and questioned her with a smirk. "You do know what cattails are, right?"

"I . . . I suppose I don't. At least, I don't think you mean tails belonging to cats."

That set off more laughing. Lucas chuckled. "Cattails grow in marshy areas. They look like brown sausages on a stick. The rhizomes are edible."

"And mighty tasty," LeRoy added.

"You can make flour from the starch, and from that make cattail bread," Sarah added.

Emma shook her head. When she looked out at the dry, vast plains to the east, all she saw was dirt and cactus and danger. Now she was beginning to understand how the prairie would appear wholly different to those who lived off it for survival. What she thought was a land of desolation and emptiness was really one rich in food and sustenance. Now more than ever she felt excitement stir inside, thinking of all the wonderful facts she would learn about these plants she planned to draw and detail. In addition to the drawings, she could write about the many uses the native peoples had for these plants, with instructions on how to prepare the foods and medicines. Her original idea of sketching plants had now blossomed into a project that would require years of learning — an education she could never get at Vassar.

"Sarah, I would be so grateful if you'd teach me about the plants on the Front Range." She shot Lucas a smile, her heart overflowing with excitement. "I would even be willing to try some of that cattail bread."

Lucas studied her face as if really seeing her for the first time. His shimmering green eyes sent her heart racing.

He leaned across to her and said so quietly she could barely hear him, "Don't you think your beau might be missing you?" He tipped his head toward where Randall was sitting behind her. She didn't want to look back to see anyone at that table. It would only spoil her happy mood.

What should she tell him? She didn't even know if Randall was her "beau." And right now, she wasn't at all happy with him.

Before she could answer, though, a young cowboy with scuffed-up clothes and boots, his hat askew, came stumbling over to their table.

"Howdy, Lucas . . . so, who do we have here?" The man nearly tripped and banged into the table. Emma could smell the liquor on his breath, and his acrid stench told her he hadn't bathed in a very long time. She winced and drew back.

Sarah jumped up and moved out of the man's way as he leaned across the table.

"Gus Woodson, you've been drinking," Sarah scolded sternly. She crossed her arms over her chest. "Get on home."

Lucas also stood, but Sarah's sons sat and glared at the man, who had a hard time staying upright. Eli fumed and tried to stand, but LeRoy yanked his arm. Emma wondered at the undercurrents of anger coming from Sarah's sons. Who was this man?

Lucas took Gus's arm, none too lightly. The man swatted at him, then turned his full inebriated attention on Emma.

"Well, looks like you've caught yerself a purdy one, Lucas. Whas her name? Whass yer name, you purdy thing—"

To Emma's horror, the man grabbed the back of her head and pulled her close to his face. Emma winced and tried to pull back, but the man pulled harder, pursing his lips as if he planned to kiss her. A squeal slipped from her throat.

"That's quite enough," Lucas warned, pulling harder on Gus's arm but failing to wrench him away from the table.

To Emma's horror, the drunken cowboy pawed at her blouse, getting his fingers stuck in the fabric. As he pulled back, the first few buttons popped off and her blouse ripped open, revealing more skin than Emma would ever show in public. Even her chemise underneath was torn. She gasped and cried out as she covered her exposed chest with her arm.

"Jes one little biddy kiss . . ." Gus crooned, pawing at her again.

Somehow Emma managed to wriggle up from the table, with Sarah's arm around her in a protective manner.

Gus swung around, throwing a wide arcing blow at Lucas's face, but Lucas dodged the blow adeptly and tightened his grip on Gus's wrist. He then twisted the man's hand until he yelped. Gus began spewing curses at Lucas. And not only at Lucas, but saying awful things about Sarah and her sons.

"That does it, you bumptious rogue!" Eli wrested his arm away from LeRoy and jumped to his feet. "You're a good-for-nothing piece of buffalo hide. I'm tired of your disrespect." He lunged at Gus and punched him hard in the gut. Gus groaned and crumpled, but then came at Eli like a bull.

Now Lucas had two unruly men to get under control. LeRoy leaped from the bench and helped him, and Emma couldn't tell whose arms were swinging. But someone then clipped Lucas in the eye, and he pulled back in pain. Emma wanted to rush to him, but she knew she'd only get hurt. How could she help anyway?

Sarah calmly and quickly extricated her younger son from the foray, missing the wild swings of his arm—showing she'd perhaps had practice at this. Eli seemed to have a volatile temper—as evidenced by the way his mother and brother reacted almost instinctively to his sudden outburst. Lucas, rubbing his eye with one hand and collaring Gus with the other, finally managed to calm the drunken cowboy down.

"Gus, rattle your hooks on home, before you regret this more than you already do," Lucas hissed at him, looking sternly at the drunk and shaking him for good measure.

Gus lowered his head, looked around as if trying to figure out where he was, and stumbled off toward the entrance of the park.

Lucas blew out a breath and smoothed his shirt, tucking it back in. He looked over at Emma, noting the damage to her clothes. Emma could tell her face was bright red. She stood by the table, shaking and embarrassed. Sarah pulled a woolen shawl from a cloth bag she had on the bench and draped it around Emma's shoulders.

Emma thanked her and noticed her family had suddenly gathered around the table. Her father was livid.

"What on earth is going on over here? Emma, what happened to your clothes?"

Her mother nearly screeched. "Your blouse is torn! Who did this to you?"

Walter didn't wait for an answer. He marched up to Lucas and grabbed him by his shirt collar. "How dare you, cowboy." Lucas stood, unruffled, not saying a word or moving an inch. "I'll show you not to treat my sister like a whore—"

"Walter!" Emma yelled, shocked at both his language and behavior. "Lucas didn't touch me. It was that drunken cowboy." She pointed through the crowd, but her assailant had left the park—thank God.

Walter stared Lucas down, then released his grip in a sudden push. Lucas stepped back and rubbed his eye. Emma now could clearly tell Walter had been drinking. Surely her father must have noticed. What would he think? Her father had strict views regarding where and when a man could drink liquor.

Emma's father shook his head. "Emma, get your things. We're leaving. I can't have you looking like this in public."

"That's what happens when you associate with Indians," Walter said, to Emma's shock. "Why did you go over and sit with them?" His berating tone did not ask for an answer.

"I'm thoroughly upset with your behavior, young lady," her father said between clenched teeth, aware of the group of people watching their conversation and eyeing Sarah and her sons suspiciously.

"*My* beha—" Emma couldn't even finish the word; she was shocked he would accuse her of causing this altercation.

Violet pushed through the crowd and came over to Emma. "Are you all right?"

Emma nodded, but her entire body trembled. She didn't know if it was due to that man's attack or her anger at her father.

"I'll go back home with you," Violet offered.

Emma's mother firmly pushed Violet back. "Emma doesn't need company right now. Come, Emma, let's go."

All Emma could do was apologize to Violet with her eyes.

Her father looked at Walter and snapped, "Get the carriage ready."

Walter nodded and headed toward the entrance to the park, leaving Lynette behind with a befuddled look on her face.

Emma felt tears pressing the backs of her eyes. She had been having such a wonderful time—until that cowboy ruined it all. But thankfully Lucas stepped in when he had. She shuddered thinking what more the drunken man would have done had Lucas not gotten him off her. She grimaced at the realization that he had saved her yet again.

And where had Randall been this whole time? As she stood there waiting for her family to say their hasty good-byes and gather up their things, she finally spotted him standing beside his father.

Emma's mouth dropped open, but she quickly closed it. Randall's face was blank and emotionless. But not his father's.

Mr. Turnbull stood next to Randall, like a judge presiding over court, scowling at Sarah and shaking his head in judgment. No doubt he blamed her and her "savage Indian" sons for the altercation and disruption of the picnic. Emma wanted to run up to him and set him straight, but what would that do? Only prove she was an Indian sympathizer. And no doubt he'd have words for her as well. She forced down the bitter taste in her throat. She'd suffered enough embarrassment for one afternoon.

She looked back at Randall. He finally met her gaze, and she saw concern in his eyes. Had he seen what transpired? Or was he unaware of what had happened? Why wouldn't he come over and talk to her?

She gritted her teeth. She knew the answer. His father had made him stay out of the fray. He wouldn't allow his son to get into a fistfight and muss up his expensive clothes. Not even for the woman he loved. Or maybe didn't love. Either way, he should have done something. What would he do if, once they were married, some man tried to attack her? Would he still stand back and do nothing, afraid of getting hurt or ruining his clothes? Afraid his father would be ashamed of him? Worried he wouldn't do the proper thing?

Emma closed her eyes in disappointment. Tears streamed down her cheeks, but she didn't care. At that moment she knew she would never be able to love Randall. How could she love a man who didn't run to her aid when she was threatened? Who didn't put a woman's safety ahead of his own?

Emma felt someone touch her arm. She opened her eyes and through her tears saw a blurry Lucas. Over his shoulder she saw her parents glare at him, their expression casting blame on him for what had happened. It was so unfair.

Her father stormed over—no doubt intending to get another dangerous cowboy away from her.

She whispered quickly, "Thank you, Lucas. I'm grateful to you—once again."

He stepped back when he saw her father approach. "I'd do it again, Miss Bradshaw." He whispered as he tipped his hat and gave her a reassuring smile, "I'm growing fond of rescuing you."

A rush of gratitude coursed her body. His words were like soothing water in a barren wasteland.

Emma's father grabbed her arm and put on a show of being incensed. She threw Lucas a look of apology as her father nearly dragged her toward the entrance of the park, pressing through the crowds at such a hurried pace she kept tripping over her feet. She hadn't even had an opportunity to thank Sarah or her sons. Well, she still had Sarah's shawl wrapped around her shoulders. She'd have to find a way to get out to the ranch and return it to her.

Emma glanced behind her. Her mother and Lynette were making their way to the entrance, and Emma noticed Lucas following. Perhaps he wanted to see her off safely, worried that drunken cowboy might still be around. She noticed him scanning the crowds as he kept up with her pace. To her chagrin, Randall was nowhere in sight.

Emma tightened the shawl around her shoulders, reliving the fear she'd felt at the man's groping hands and his whiskey breath. Once again she realized how much she needed protection in this dangerous place. A man who could—and would—loving defend her and keep her safe. A rescuer—that's what she wanted.

A man like Lucas Rawlings.

If only Randall were more like him, she thought with bitterness.

Chapter 14

WHILE WALKING ACROSS THE PARK, Lucas fumed. He was incensed at the way Emma's family was treating her, shuffling her off as if she were a criminal, instead of comforting her after her frightening ordeal. He could only imagine how a proper young woman such as Emma would be terror-stricken having a drunk, pawing cattle-prodder like Gus Woodson ripping at her clothes.

Lucas's anger boiled in his chest, and he knew if he didn't work hard at pushing down, it might erupt. He clenched his jaw thinking about how he'd deal with Woodson later. But he had greater concerns at the moment.

From where he stood, he could see Emma's brother. He had gone to fetch the horse and buggy her family had arrived in, which had been housed in the park's livery stables, where all the many buggies, carriages, and horses were kept while the picnickers were enjoying the festivities. But someone had stopped him on the way out. And now—Lucas noted with narrowed eyes—both Rusty Dunnigan and Caleb Dixon—those vile cattle ranchers—had waylaid him and were talking to him in a conspiratorial manner. And Walter was paying rapt attention.

Lucas scowled. He'd spotted those men near the picnic area right before Woodson had stumbled over and terrorized Emma. He wouldn't put it past those two to have steered Woodson in Emma's direction, planting lewd suggestions in his addled, drunken mind. It wouldn't take much smarts for someone like Dunnigan to figure out that Walter was Emma's brother—and note how disapproving he was of his sister "cohorting with Indians" at the July Fourth picnic. Dunnigan was nothing if not shrewd and calculating. But Lucas planned to stay one step ahead of him.

Lucas watched as Emma's brother led the horse pulling the carriage over to the curb so his family could hurry away from the park, and get Emma away from drunken cowboys and dirty Indians. Lucas shook his head. As angry as that Mr. Turnbull had made him by his bigoted, cruel remarks, what upset Lucas even more was seeing how Emma's "beau" had done absolutely nothing to help her. Lucas had glared at the young man, shocked—more like flabbergasted—wondering just what kind of man would stand back and watch the woman he loved get mauled by some drunken cowboy. It was shameful enough the man didn't speak out against his father for the mean things he was saying about Indians. But Lucas could not tolerate a man who would let any woman be mistreated.

A sin of omission was just as bad—and sometimes worse—than a committed sin. And to stand back and watch a woman be accosted and not do a thing was akin to the priest and rabbi that crossed the street when they saw the poor Israelite beat up and left for dead. The Good Book gave that story of the Good Samaritan for a reason, and the Lord made it clear folks couldn't turn a blind eye if they wanted to be a proper neighbor.

This was the man Emma Bradshaw loved? Lucas ground his teeth so hard his jaw ached. Well, if that was her idea of the ideal husband, then she could have him. He just didn't understand how she could want a man like that, though. He wasn't a man; he was a worm. How could a man with such soft hands and a lack of gumption ever protect a woman like Emma? The man probably never faced a day of danger—or hard work—in his life. And if he wouldn't even stand up and defend her against a harmless drunk, what would he do when a *real* danger came along?

He couldn't stand the idea of Emma Bradshaw marrying a man like that. Did she love him because he was rich and had a fancy education? Lucas grunted bitterly. Well, he'd come from a rich family too, and had as good if not better an education than that pansy from the East. But he wasn't going to go around flaunting that fact. That's not how you won a woman's heart. And if that's all a woman wanted, she wasn't the kind of woman for Lucas Rawlings. He wanted a woman to love him for who he was, not what he had.

He kicked at the dirt, fighting the feelings that burned like a hot iron. It was as if her name was being branded into the very flesh of his heart, and he couldn't do a thing about it. He lassoed the fierce need running loose inside him and pulled it tight, hoping to strangle it. But the pain of the truth wriggled its way out from his grasp, slippery than any frisky calf.

He had to face the truth—he was hopelessly, undeniably crazy in love with Emma Bradshaw. He wanted nothing more than to scoop her up into his arms and kiss her. Kiss her until she melted into him and they joined hearts, never to be severed. He longed to hear her whisper his name, to unpin her beautiful black hair and watch it cascade down her back. He envisioned running his hand along her neck, caressing her soft skin and hearing her words of love for him. Losing himself in those deep pools of blue that were her eyes.

Every nerve in his body ached at the thought of her in his arms, and as much as he needed to, he couldn't stop the avalanche of images tumbling in his mind. His eyes were so thirsty for her, he could hardly breathe as he watched her, standing beside her mother, waiting to get in the carriage.

He took a few more steps, as if being pulled into her orbit against his will. He just had to get close to her again, even if she wasn't aware he was there. She was so close, but she may as well been as far away as the moon. Knowing how much he wanted her and could never have her was a terrible pain. Was he destined to suffer over women his entire life?

Lucas's attention was jerked away when Emma's brother pulled the Cleveland Bay carriage horse to the curb, and the horse suddenly reared and screeched. Without hesitation, Lucas pushed past the people in front of him, hurrying to the carriage. Out of the corner of his eye, he saw Emma and her mother jump back, but another woman—the one he took to be Walter's wife—got her feet tripped up, and she began to stumble toward the spooked horse. One quick assessment made it clear what had happened.

Walter was struggling with the reins as the horse squealed again, rearing up and back and tossing its head, trying to break free of its breeching. The buggy jounced up and down, and by the time Lucas got to the horse, Walter was screaming at it. Lucas could tell Walter had been drinking and was paying no mind that his wife was about to be kicked. No one seemed to notice her; all eyes were on the rearing horse.

Then, to Lucas's horror, Walter took the whip he held in his other hand and began lashing out at the Bay. He smashed the whip cruelly on the horse's face and neck, making it even more hysterical.

And as the horse cried more, Walter hit it harder and harder, screaming for the horse to shut up and behave.

Lucas's mounting anger finally exploded.

In front of a gathering crowd, he yanked the whip from Walter's hand and pushed him away from the horse. He threw a glance over at the woman, who was trying to find her balance, her hand over her stomach. He had to get the horse to calm down, to back him up, before that woman got trampled. Why didn't Walter see his wife was in danger? How could he be such an arrogant chucklehead as to think beating a horse getting stung by yellow jackets would calm it down?

Even from where he stood, he could see the horse's ankles swelling. Lucas struggled with Walter, who kept a tight hold of the reins and tried to push Lucas away.

"Get out of here, Cowboy! What are you doing?" Walter snarled at him and swung a fist in his general direction.

Then Walter raised his hand this time to beat the horse. The last thread of Lucas's patience snapped.

Lucas smashed Walter's nose with his fist. He had no time to engage in a gentlemanly discussion. He swung again and punched him in the gut, knowing his own rage was getting the best of him. Before he could do too much damage, he reined himself in. But he had accomplished what he'd set out to do, wishing he hadn't needed to resort to violence. But this man was endangering everyone around him. And he needed to be taught a lesson.

Lucas would not tolerate cruelty. And especially not to a helpless, defenseless animal.

Walter covered his nose with his hands, relinquishing the reins. He stumbled back from the carriage. Lucas quickly stepped alongside the horse and laid a calming hand on its neck. He spoke quietly to it as the horse stomped its feet, no doubt feeling the pain of the stings. He had some salve in his medical bag over at the arena that would greatly soothe the poor beast. But right now he knew the horse was more agitated over the beating than the bee stings. The Bay needed to know it was safe and out of danger.

In a few moments, Lucas had the horse under control. He raised his eyes and saw the crowd watching, riveted, as the mayhem of the last few minutes dissipated into calm. Lucas kept uttering words of sympathy to the horse, stroking its flank, careful not to touch its ankles. The Bay nickered in distress, as if telling Lucas all its troubles. "I know, fella, I know," Lucas said. "I won't let him hurt you again."

When he spotted LeRoy a few feet back, Lucas gestured him over. LeRoy hurried to his side and took the reins, studying Walter as if memorizing his face. Good, now that things were under control, Lucas needed to have a few words with the insolent younger Mr. Bradshaw.

Before Lucas could say anything, Walter stomped toward him and stuck a finger in his face. "How dare you? How dare you hit me, you . . . Indian lover? You're just as savage as they are," he said, scowling and looking over at LeRoy, who stood unmoving, holding the reins and keeping his face expressionless. Lucas smirked. That was why he'd called LeRoy over. That man could keep a straight face even if the hounds of hell were breaking down his door. And Lucas needed to diffuse all the anger raging around him—especially his own.

Lucas was aware of Emma's eyes on his. Not just hers, though, but also her father's, and her mother's. But he didn't care. Wrong was wrong. It couldn't be swept under the rug like a pile of dirt.

Lucas pushed Walter's finger out of his face and grabbed his arm hard. Walter winced and yelped, trying to pull away, but Lucas held tight, just the way he'd handle a cow about to get itself tangled in barbed wire.

"Don't you *ever* lift your arm in anger toward any defenseless animal. Do you hear me? If I *ever* again see you beat a horse, I'll take that whip and beat you to an inch of your life. And I mean it."

He tipped his head toward Walter's wife. "Your reckless behavior almost got your wife killed. You should have been paying more attention to her instead of the horse. Here she is pregnant with your child and in harm's way. And all you could think about was making that horse mind you."

Walter's jaw dropped, but not a word came out.

Lucas glanced over and saw a look of shock on Emma's face. He figured she was appalled at what he was doing, but he didn't care. If she disapproved of his actions and words, then she deserved this family—and her beau, who was conveniently nowhere around. Lucas was about as fed up as he could be. But his anger was finally seeping out.

He looked at Walter again. "The poor horse stepped in a yellow-jacket nest." He added as he wiped his hands on his pants and pushed his hair from his face, "I'd like to see how you'd react if your legs got all stung like that. You'd probably squeal and dance a bit too."

Lucas didn't wait for an apology. He highly doubted one would come even if he stood there until the first winter snow fell. He looked over at Emma's father, whose cold, stern face was hard to read. Lucas couldn't tell who the man was angrier at—his own son or the cowboy who had just humiliated his son in front of about fifty onlookers.

He blew out a breath and made sure Emma's father knew he was speaking to him. He met the man's cold eyes with his own frosty ones. "I'm going over to the arena to get my medical bag. Don't move this horse or carriage. I'll treat the stings, and in a little while this Bay should be able to take you folks back home. And I'll send some salve home with you. Make sure you wash his legs with cool water and put more salve on tonight. That should do the trick. In fact, if you can lead him over to one of the irrigation ditches and let him stand in the cool water for a spell, that would be even better."

Mr. Bradshaw nodded but said nothing. Emma had mentioned her father owned race horses. He hoped that meant her father cared for an animal's well-being and would tend to this horse, although having money to buy expensive horses didn't necessarily equate with kindness.

Mr. Bradshaw then walked over and took the reins from LeRoy, who left to stand beside Lucas. They watched a scowling Walter go over to his wife and take her arm, then lead her away from the crowd. Lucas couldn't make out the expression on the poor woman's face, but he hoped Walter wouldn't take his humiliation out on such a delicate woman. It had been obvious to him immediately that she was frail and not having an easy pregnancy. He figured her about four or five months along, but she appeared a bit anemic. He shook his head in annoyance. You'd think a man with a wife in that condition would be watching out for her welfare. And not getting drunk.

Once Lucas assessed the fiasco was over and saw that the horse, although still fidgety, was reasonably calm, he looked over at Emma, who had tears glistening in her eyes. He tried to muster a smile, but just couldn't. Clearly she was disappointed in him and how he'd treated her brother. Why, he'd practically embarrassed her whole family in front of the entire town of Greeley. He doubted if she or anyone in her family would ever say two words to him ever again.

But it couldn't have been helped. Given the choice, he'd handle it exactly the same way again.

"Come on," he said to LeRoy, not even trying to mask the bitterness in his voice. "Let's go."

Emma stood as if invisible as her family spoke in harsh undertones to one another, their voices like a murmuring, agitated sea around her, their eyes watchful of those around them who might overhear, or worse—mishear.

It was clear to Emma what her parents—and Walter—had thought of Lucas's spate of anger, but she didn't blame him at all. In fact, she was proud that he had stood up to her brother's horrid behavior. And now knowing Lynette was pregnant—clearly as much to her parents' surprise as to her own—she would gladly voice her support of his actions. For, it was highly probable Lucas had saved Lynette's life by his bold and unhesitant actions, doing what was necessary to get Walter and his whip away from the poor frightened horse.

Emma's heart was still racing as she looked over at Lynette, who was now sitting and fanning herself under the broad shade of a weeping willow. Now that she knew her sister-in-law's condition, she could detect her pregnancy, although it was mostly hidden by the many petticoats under her dress. But Lynette, being as slight as she was, probably wouldn't show greatly until her later months. If she made it through unscathed. No wonder she had been so sick on the train.

Clearly that worry was on everyone's mind at present. But Lynette had only had a scare, nothing worse, thank God. Emma didn't recall how far along Lynette had been when she'd lost the other babies, but she didn't think it was more than two or three months. She hoped Lynette was out of danger so she and Walter might truly become parents, finally.

Emma hoped with all her heart this would prove true. A baby would make everyone happy—especially her father. Maybe Walter's drinking had much to do with Lynette's precarious health and this pregnancy. He'd kept this secret well, she noted. He'd wisely learned from Lynette's miscarriages not to make joyful pronouncements of an impending birth. Emma breathed out a sigh of hope. Maybe this would also distract her father enough so that he would discontinue his efforts to marry her off.

More tears pressed her eyes as she thought about Randall. How she had hoped he'd grown into the man she'd want to marry. But what a great disappointment he was to her. Surely he'd always be her friend; they shared a past she could never dismiss. But she doubted in her heart of hearts she could ever marry a man like him.

She turned her head toward the east, away from her family, hoping no one would see her tears.

She lost track of the time as she wept silently, ruing the day she boarded the train to Colorado Territory. How would she ever be happy living in Greeley? What hope would she ever have in finding love and getting married? Her heart felt as hard and unfeeling as a stone, lodged tightly in her chest, making it hard for her to breathe.

A nudge to her shoulder made her hastily wipe at her face and turn around. Relieved to find Violet beside her, she felt comforted somewhat by her friendly smile.

Violet led her over to a table far enough away that they could speak without being overheard. The crowd that had gathered to watch the incident with the carriage had long dissipated, with picnickers off to watch more horse races, or prepare for the dance. From where they sat, Emma could see the elevated stage, festooned with colorful streamers and tiny American flags. A few musicians carried their instruments and positioned them on the stage. How she had looked forward to the dance. Although it was possible she could go home, change clothes, and return, she doubted her father—after the afternoon's humiliation—would allow it. And who would she dance with anyway? she mused despondently.

"I didn't see what happened," Violet said, nodding toward the street, "but I heard." She patted Emma's arm and looked at the shawl Emma kept wrapped tight across her chest. "Frankly, I would have died if some drunken cowboy ripped at my dress. How frightened you must have been." Violet make a clucking sound. "But I heard what Lucas did. And how he punched your brother. Oh boy."

Emma waited for her to continue, but to her surprise, Violet began to laugh. "I bet your brother is steaming mad. To be put in his place like that — in front of everyone." Her laugh trailed off. "But poor Lucas. I know he did the right thing, but I have a feeling he'll never be welcome at your house."

"Not likely," Emma replied, working hard at keeping the emotion out of her voice. She wanted to be polite to Violet, but she wished to be left alone in her misery.

"But how come your sweetheart didn't come over when that cowboy made improper advances? And why weren't you sitting with him at lunch?"

Emma could no longer hold back the deluge of tears. A great sob burst from her throat and she cried, feeling utterly embarrassed.

"Oh, I've upset you — " Violet said.

"No," Emma choked out, "no, it's not you. I . . . I . . . oh, Violet, I'm so unhappy."

Emma buried her head in her hands, wishing her friend wasn't witness to her silly bout of emotion. But she hurt all over, as if this disappointment she felt was a pain emanating from every pore in her skin. What could she say to Violet? Nothing. She could never tell anyone how she felt.

Emma was grateful Violet didn't press the point. A true friend, Violet just sat beside her with her arm around Emma's shoulder, quiet and supportive. Emma figured she'd learned such kindness from her mother. Emma wished her own mother was as sweet and affectionate as Violet's. She wished she was anyone else but herself at this moment.

Finally the stream of tears dried to a trickle, then stopped altogether. Violet handed Emma a handkerchief, and when she blew her nose, making a loud unladylike snort, the two girls both erupted in laughter, Emma grateful for the release and the friend at her side. As she stuffed the crumpled, wet handkerchief in her skirt pocket, she looked up to see her father marching toward her. Emma sucked in a breath and felt Violet stiffen beside her.

"Come, Emma. The carriage is ready and we're leaving." He gave a cursory glance at Violet but said nothing to her.

Emma's father turned away in a brisk huff and began walking back to the street. Emma turned to Violet.

"Thank you—for being my friend," she said.

Violet hugged her and nodded. "I'll come by and visit soon."

Emma didn't think she would want any company for a long while, but she smiled and told Violet to enjoy the rest of the celebration.

"I'll tell you all about it," Violet replied. "I'm especially curious to see who Lily sinks her clutches into tonight." She raised her eyebrows in an attempt to make Emma laugh, but Emma could only force a smile.

She hurried after her father, dread descending upon her as quickly as a Colorado hailstorm. And like hail, she expected hard words to strike her. If not tonight, soon. Somehow she knew that whatever anger her parents felt from the afternoon's incidents, it would be directed at her.

Chapter 15

W EEKS WENT BY, BUT EMMA hardly noticed, other than indications that summer was slipping into fall. The fields around had turned brown, and the wind hotter and drier. Most of the crops had been harvested, leaving fallowed rows of dirt that blew in dusty whirlwinds around the town. For the first week after the picnic, she'd hardly left her room. Josephine brought meals to her, but Emma had no appetite. She told her mother she was sick with a stomach ailment, and that worked to quell the nagging. But when her clothes began hanging on her, her mother's distress turned into constant fretting.

Finally, a local doctor had been called in to see Emma, a kindly rotund old Boston man who had been in Colorado for decades. As he examined her, he regaled her with stories of the early days on the frontier, and as he chatted on, he looked at her nose and throat and made sounds like *aha* and *ahum*, studying her with squinty eyes through thick bifocal lenses.

"Well, my pretty little lady," the doctor finally said that late hot August morning he'd paid a visit, "I don't think you are suffering from any fatal disease." He lowered his voice, and with a knowing grin said, "I'm not a stranger to the likes of what ails you. Seen many a young maid wistfully waste away from unrequited love." He abruptly stepped back and stuffed his stethoscope into his bag. "But I won't say a word." He put a finger to his lips and wiggled his eyebrows. "The parents will want some cure, of which there is none but the usual—marriage. However, I will supply you with this formula." He pulled a dark corked bottle from his bag and handed it to her. "It's harmless, really," he confided, "but if you can plaster a smile on that pretty little face of yours from time to time, your parents will be appeased."

He closed the clasp of his bag with a loud click and tipped his bowler hat at her. "In time you'll get over him. Find another young man worthy of your affections. Good day, Miss Bradshaw."

Emma stood speechless, unsure whether to gasp or guffaw. She looked suspiciously at the unlabeled bottle in her hand, imagining the good doctor made his fortune from selling his patients sugar water. How many women, Emma wondered, were suffering from unrequited love? If only that were her problem. Would this tincture cure disappointment? It wasn't just that she was unhappy with Randall; her whole life had been forced into an unexpected direction. What cure was there for that?

She went over and looked out the window. The barn that had been halfway done when they'd first come to Greeley had been completed, and Shahayla now cropped at the few bits of mostly dead grass in the paddock only feet from where she stood. It comforted her to have her horse nearby, and she spent hours sitting in her chair mindlessly watching her, her heart numb and as hard as a rock in her chest.

Violet had been by to see her a few times, but Emma hadn't been much company. Her friend's visits had tapered off, and now Emma only saw her on Sundays at church. As much as she protested she was not well and didn't want to go out, her parents insisted she at least go to church, where she had no choice but to be polite and speak to Randall. He had sent inquiries after her following the picnic—asking if he could call on her—but Emma sent back word that she was feeling poorly and was not up to entertaining visitors. At church his eyes questioned her distant mood, but his words were polite and merely friendly. Had his father warned him away from her? Told her she was a no-good Indian lover?

Her own father had lectured her quite harshly those first few days after the fiasco at the park, forbidding her to do this and that or speak to such people or go to such places. He was ever more determined to keep her safe from the perils of the West by shrinking her world to a few blocks.

But what had he been thinking when he decided to tear his family away from their established life in New York and hauled them out to a dangerous frontier? Clearly life was much harder here than he'd expected. She had discovered quickly that many Easterners had come out to Greeley with an idyllic concept of a paradise, but had been rudely awakened to the truth. Her mother, even after these many weeks, had not at all "acclimated" to her new life in the dirt and dust. The hardship of living with only a few servants—and ones not nearly as capable as their former ones—caused her mother much distress, and she voiced this distress loudly and often. Without her charities and social clubs, she had too much idle time on her hands, and Emma suspected she must be very lonely.

As a consequence, her mother's fainting spells had increased—as had her ingestion of laudanum. Often Emma would find her sound asleep on top of her bedcovers in the middle of the day, the thin blue bottle on her nightstand. Emma wondered if her father knew about her mother's "medicine"—or perhaps he was the one who had procured it for her, hoping it would calm her unending waves of hysterics.

With her father and Walter spending long hours each day downtown at their office, running Father's many businesses long-distance, Emma at least didn't have to talk to or see him much. And other than her mother pressuring her to eat every now and then, Emma was mostly left alone to her thoughts, which were anything but welcome company. No one seemed to pay much attention to her comings and goings, so she often took to walking the back roads of the town, staying within the miles of straight-wire fencing erected around the acres of farmland.

At least Lynette's pregnancy and overall health was improving, which encouraged Emma greatly. She truly wanted Lynette to have a healthy baby and enjoy motherhood. Perhaps becoming a father would change Walter, erase his continual scowl and curt tone he took with her whenever she saw him.

Emma had been stunned at hearing Lucas's words to Walter at the picnic. How had he known Lynette was pregnant—when even she had no idea? But, she reminded herself, Lucas had gone through medical training—albeit veterinary school—where he must have honed his powers of observation in order to be a good diagnostician. But regardless of whether he'd learned this skill or came by it naturally, she'd come to know he was a man of keen observation. He paid attention to detail. He certainly noticed little things about her when he was around. He seemed to detect her moods—even her innermost thoughts. Was she so easy to read, or was he able to read everyone like that? In a way, it discomfited her, and made her feel as if under sharp scrutiny. But in another way, it came across as thoughtful and caring.

Someone taking the time and bother to know her and how she felt. And that was something she so longed for—and wished Randall would express more often to her.

Over the past weeks Emma suffered through the family Sunday dinners, forcing herself to eat a bite here and there while she listened to her brother and father talk about the goings-on in Greeley. She noted they never spoke of Randall or Lucas or Indians, or mentioned Emma's possible marital prospects, which in the past had often been the topic of the hour. Instead, she'd learned more than she wanted to about tanning buffalo hides and the price of exporting and refining the leather to make into coats for the wealthy customers back East. Her father's newest venture was to ship the soft, supple buffalo hides that had been transformed into what he termed "serviceable leather," which was then fashioned into belts, vests, and even upholstery material and textured wall paneling, her father claiming it "more flexible and more elastic than cowhide." His intent was to cash in on the buffalo market before he lost his chance. Apparently the beasts, which had once overrun the plains, were dwindling in number—no doubt due to the excessive hunting carried on in recent years.

She turned from the window and decided to work on some of her drawings. She'd put together more than a dozen completed illustrations, inked and colored. But she hadn't yet taken up Sarah's offer to walk with her and teach her all about the native plants of the Front Range. As much as Emma wanted to do so, she couldn't bear the thought of seeing Lucas at the ranch.

Just thinking about him brought an onrush of uncomfortable feelings, most of which she didn't understand. She was embarrassed by her naivety and ignorance of so many things, although she knew Lucas wasn't trying to embarrass her. Yet somehow, around him, she ended up saying and doing foolish things—or finding herself needing his help. His words kept replaying in her head—how he'd come to enjoy rescuing her.

But she didn't want to keep appearing like a helpless woman who couldn't stand on her own. She needed to feel competent and resilient, without relying on any man's help. That's why she had wanted more than anything to go to college. To become strong in her independence. She hoped to find a husband who would both respect and help her to become so. But Randall didn't seem to have the backbone to be that man. Or was she being too hard on him? Maybe she had misunderstood his actions that day at the park. Guilt welled up and made her regret her harsh judgment of her long-time friend. She at least owed it to him to explain, didn't she? Oh, this was all so confusing.

If only she could board the next train out of Greeley and return to New York. She couldn't imagine feeling any more lonely and alone than she did here, with the wide open sky above her and the endless miles of flat empty land spreading out around her under the shadow of such imposing mountains, which only emphasized her insignificance and vulnerability.

As she picked up her pen and dipped it in the ink, studying the half-completed illustration before her, she knew returning to New York was not an option. Her father would never allow it, and without his financial support, she would be destitute. She would have to somehow find that resilience and inner strength out here, in the middle of the untamed West. But how?

Staring at the details of the Lupinus arboreus, she thought of Sarah—the strongest, most resilient woman she'd ever met. No doubt Sarah had spent a lifetime overcoming tremendous obstacles, and felt entirely at home and at peace on the Front Range. And she had offered to teach Emma about the plants of the plains. But now Emma realized Sarah could teach her something much more valuable than the medicinal uses of flowers.

Sarah could teach her how to make Colorado her home.

Tomorrow, despite any consequences, she would pay Sarah a visit.

Lucas pushed Ransom hard as the surefooted horse navigated his way through the jagged rocky outcroppings. The evening air swirled warm around his sweaty head, and he pulled off his hat and wiped his brow as he approached the crawling creek up ahead, not much more than a rivulet carved into smooth rock. But this was the only water source around for his horse, so he gave Ransom his head as he came to a stop, then slid off and stretched, listening to his horse slurp the cool water bubbling out of the spring. He then took a swig of springwater from his canteen, grateful for the refreshing liquid slipping down his dusty, parched throat.

Shortly after Lucas had come down from the mountains to live and work at Sarah's ranch, he had discovered this place of solitude. Even though the open plains afforded him privacy enough, what helped him work through his grief was a long, hard ride across the prairie, followed by a climb up into the foothills to this secluded outcropping of rock, where he could look far down upon the world and watch the evening descend on the Front Range.

He took his usual seat on a smooth gray rocky promontory sticking out of the cliff, overhanging the endless valley below. A pair of ospreys circled overhead, claiming their territory and crying out their sharp chirps, sounding like hen chicks. Lucas watched them in their graceful flight, winging on the updraft, their distinct black-and-white markings on their wings and underside glinting in the light of the setting sun. Down below, spread out before him, the grasses of the Front Range undulated like a golden sea, drenched in the colors of the evening sun, speckled with clumps of dusty green sagebrush and prickly pear cactus.

He used to think the land ugly, after a childhood spent in the lush bluegrass-carpeted hills of Kentucky and then the breathtaking panoramas of the Rockies' ranges towering outside his windows in

Leadville. But in recent months he'd come to appreciate a different kind of beauty offered by the wide expanse of prairie—a starkness and raw simplicity foreign to the jagged sweep of mountains behind him. Nothing could lay hidden on the open range.

In the mountains, a man could hide his past, his fears, his secrets, his dreams. Here, there was no place to hide. If he ran from his troubles, they straggled behind him. Like a flat, undisturbed reflection shown on the surface of a pristine lake, the flat, barren landscape allowed for no distortion of a man's soul. Whatever a man was, he had to face.

Lucas had resisted looking into that soul he had dragged with him out of the confines and shadows of the Rockies. But gradually he had been forced to face that reflection. Only recently he had been able to come up here and sit and experience a measure of peace. He had hardly shaken off the horrors of the war when he'd lost Alice. She had been the balm for his soul. Her touch had slowly erased the painful memories of those years of death and horror. And he had come to believe that in time, under her spell, he would forget the past—that it would fade like a troubled dream upon awakening. And it almost had.

And now? Whatever gains he had made in finding peace in his heart he'd now lost. All because of those two blue pools.

He watched the evening light trickle away and thought how hope was like that. At first a bright light that shone like a beacon, guiding folks through life. But then just like the onset of night, it quickly slipped away, leaving only darkness and despair.

He had hoped Sarah was right about Emma Bradshaw, and maybe she was. Maybe Emma was the woman for him. But she seemed as inaccessible as the stars beginning to pierce the canopy of sky. Part of him wanted to give up and concede that she was lost to him. It wasn't in his nature to chase down a woman or coerce her into loving him. What kind of love would that be?

Alice had been so right for him, and he for her. From the moment they met, they'd had an easy discourse, as if they'd known each other all their lives. He'd never once had to prove anything to her to make her love him. To win her heart. From the moment he'd met her over the back of her horse at his blacksmith's shop in Leadville, he knew she was special, unlike any woman he'd ever known. She made him feel keenly alive when he was around her, as if colors flared into brilliance when she walked or spoke. With her, the universe righted itself; everything clicked into place, like a key turning in a tumbler.

He had that same feeling around Emma. But apparently she didn't feel similarly. Yet Sarah had seen Emma in her vision. Emma, with the fire beneath the ice that could melt the frost in his heart.

What if he told Emma how he felt? The thought shook him to his boots. But what did he have to lose? At worst, she might laugh at him. Or maybe even slap his face. But he could deal with that. Maybe she'd never speak to him again. But how would that be worse than what he was going through now? Already this intoxicating woman from the East Coast disrupted his sleep and consumed many of his waking hours. Something had to be done to quell the restlessness he felt.

He hadn't seen her for weeks, heard she was staying in town. He'd gotten Violet Edwards to tell him how Emma fared, although Violet eyed him curiously when he asked that day he showed up to take her brothers for a ride out toward the foothills. Hearing Emma had been ill had made him want to run over and see her, but how could he just show up at her house? He imagined her father would slam the door in his face. But she couldn't still be unwell—unless it was something serious. And that thought had been one of the many that had stolen his sense of peace. That, and wondering if Emma Bradshaw was of yet engaged to be married. Surely Violet would have mentioned it in all her talking, as she was fond of telling him all the news she picked up on any given day.

There's still time. Lucas snorted at the admonishment in his head. Time for what? He knew the answer but didn't want to admit it. Time to tell her how he felt. Confess his love, come hell or high water her response. Whether or not he had a chance at winning her love, he knew he couldn't carry this unbearable burden much longer. At least if he told her, got it off his chest, he could be satisfied. He could walk away knowing he'd been honest, although why he'd want to open himself up to a world of hurt was beyond understanding. Maybe it was because he entertained a tiny glimmer—as tiny as each of the twinkling lights above him—that maybe she did feel something for him.

He would never get in the way of anyone's courtship, but he knew that man she cared for was not the right man for her. He slapped his hands on the rock in frustration. No, Emma was too spirited, too . . . special for an ordinary man like him. Whether or not she knew it, Emma was made for the West. Underneath her East Coast prim-and-proper exterior was an adventurous woman who delighted in learning and exploring the world around her. Under the right conditions, with the right nurturing, Emma Bradshaw would bloom like a desert rose.

With the right man.

And Lucas knew he alone was that man.

He had always fought for the things he believed in and the people he loved. But how could he fight for Emma? Men who beat horses into submission only earned their fear. He needed to earn her love. And he had no idea how to do it. He had just about every practical skill to ensure his survival in the harsh elements of the West, but felt completely empty-handed and stupid when it came to figuring out how to woo Emma Bradshaw's heart.

Regardless, he understood now he was no longer at a crossroads. There was only one path open to him—the path of honest truth.

He would have to find a way, and the proper time and place, to pour out his heart. He only hoped Emma Bradshaw wouldn't trample it down like a raging buffalo. As he stood and brushed off his pants, listening for his horse somewhere in the scrubby sagebrush, he supposed he'd just have to take his chances and see her reaction. He just hoped he wasn't too late.

Chapter 16

A FEW DAYS PASSED BEFORE Emma felt she could slip away without being noticed. Her mother had left early to attend some women's club meeting—a new activity that had her all excited and seemed to pull her out of her nervous moods. Maybe her mother just lacked purpose, Emma thought. Having projects to do for the community would occupy her thoughts and her hands, giving Emma a reprieve from the continual drama in their home.

She hadn't taken Shahayla out beyond the boundaries of town since that terrible day of the hailstorm, but she didn't expect to encounter any disasters as she kept her horse to a walk and stayed on the wide dirt road leading north to the river. One glance at the sky told her the weather would cooperate—at least for a while. She'd well learned not to trust her eyes. And this time she'd worn a proper riding habit and not an expensive flowing dress that could get caught up in her horse's legs. This skirt was tailored especially for riding sidesaddle, and she sat comfortably and confident with her right leg draped over the leaping horn and her hair tightly pinned up under her bonnet.

She took the time to enjoy the beautiful September day. Already some of the shrubby trees were turning colors. And even from where she walked her horse, she could see streaks of fall color ribboning through the foothills of the Rockies. The road hugging the town running north-south was the main "thoroughfare" that led all the way to Cheyenne, and as she left Greeley behind her, she relaxed, seeing numerous travelers coming and going in their wagons and on horseback, all giving her a friendly greeting on this cool morning.

As she rode with the river glistening in the east under the rarified morning air blowing down from the mountains, her heart pounded a little hard in her chest. Would Lucas be at the ranch when she got there? She hadn't seen him in weeks, although Violet had said he'd been by a few times to take her brothers out riding. And, she'd confided, he'd asked about her, and expressed concern upon hearing she'd been ill.

Emma admitted to herself that he could have been asking out of politeness—the way he'd ask about anyone he knew. Still, it warmed her to think of his inquiring about her, and now, knowing she might see him after all this time, she had to admit she was feeling anxious, nervous. But why? Her feelings for him still confused her. He was constantly coming into her thoughts, and she often found herself daydreaming about him—sometimes inappropriately. But what woman wouldn't think about Lucas Rawlings? He was ruggedly handsome, strong and muscular, yet gentle and soft-spoken. With his education and talents, he would be a catch for any girl. But did he even want "any girl"?

She knew one of the reasons she just had to see Sarah was to glean more about this intriguing cowboy who worked at the ranch.

But how would she ask questions without rousing undue curiosity? Emma had the feeling Sarah and Lucas spoke familiarly with each other, and it would not do to have Sarah suspect Emma had any special feelings toward her employee and lodger.

As she spotted the wide dirt road leading off to Sarah's ranch, she marveled at the beauty of the location. She hadn't paid any mind to it that day Sarah had taken her back home—so distraught she'd been over her accident. But now she saw the river valley with new eyes. Sarah's ranch was situated at a confluence of waters. Whether these were two distinct rivers, she wasn't sure. But she knew the wide, flat river to her right was the South Platte. And here a lively tributary joined to it from further north, as the river winded around west and north.

Flocks of birds flitted over the water, swooping and diving, their chatter puncturing the morning quiet. Two gray deer with large mule-like ears drank from the stream on the opposite bank, lifting their heads momentarily, then ignoring her as they continued drinking. Wide swaths of grasses bordered the water the entire length of the river, in a rich range of hues—from dusty pale sage to dark shiny green the color of moss. Sprinkled in among the grasses were bits of flowers that still bloomed this late in the year. Emma imagined springtime was a riot of color along the river, once the snows melted. Would her eyes be longing for color by then, after a long, harsh white winter?

Barking erupted as Emma trotted along the drive to the entry of Sarah's ranch house. She recognized the shaggy black-and-white dog—Hoesta, Lucas had called him. *Fireball.* She smiled recalling the story behind his name. His bark, however, probably wouldn't scare anyone away, but it did alert his owner—for Sarah promptly came out the front door in a brown calico dress, wiping her hands on a plaid-patterned apron tied around her waist.

"Well, what a pleasant surprise," Sarah said with a genuine smile after hushing the dog and coming over to take her horse's reins. "You've picked a right fine morning to visit. And your mare seems a good deal more at ease than the last time she was here." Sarah said something to her horse in a soft tone, and Emma couldn't miss the affection in her smile. Clearly she loved horses—maybe as much as Lucas did. As Emma slid down from her horse, Sarah added, "Why don't I put her out in the pasture? Do you want some coffee? Got some made fresh."

Emma stepped back as Sarah pulled the reins over Shahayla's head and led the mare over to the field next to the large barn she'd awoken in after her nasty fall. "She'll be fine out here with the brood mares," she said as she unlatched the gate.

Emma watched as Sarah removed the horse's headstall and saddle, setting them over the railing of the wood fence. She then patted the mare gently on the rump, sending her out into a fenced field. The other mares nickered at her, but Shahayla was more interested in cropping the fresh grass than making friends.

"Now, how 'bout that coffee?" Sarah asked as she came back to Emma's side.

Emma didn't particularly want any coffee, but Sarah seemed intent on serving her some, so she followed her into her kitchen, noticing how the golden wood beams and floors made the spacious area inviting and homey. Nothing like the high white plastered walls of her home, with the elegant décor and furnishings her mother had specially ordered from the finest furniture suppliers back East. Sarah's kitchen looked orderly and lived-in. And to her relief—but also a bit to her disappointment—she didn't see Lucas anywhere.

As if reading her mind, Sarah said. "You missed Lucas and the boys. They're off stringing barbed wire on the west perimeter of the property. Although, it's likely they'll come tromping in around noon. If you have the whole day free, I'd recommend we pack a lunch and eat along the river. There're plenty of plants to search for and collect, even this late in the season. Although, many have long lost their blooms. But I'll just have to describe 'em for you, all right?"

"I'd be entirely grateful to you," Emma said. "I don't want to impose upon your time, though—if you have other things planned to do today."

Sarah's eyes crinkled as she chuckled. "Emma, there are always too many chores to do on any given day and not enough hours in a day to do 'em. So it won't hurt anything to put a few off for tomorrow—so long as the horses are fed—and the men. And the latter can fend for themselves, if they don't have the patience to wait for someone to fix 'em a meal."

Emma laughed, enjoying the warm feeling she had sitting at Sarah's kitchen table and sipping an exceptionally delicious cup of coffee. She asked Sarah, who was putting food from her ice box into a large leather pouch, "Is there something in this coffee? I'm tasting . . ."

"Chicory root. And a dash of nutmeg. Gives it a nice nutty flavor."

Emma licked her lips. "It does. It's delicious."

Sarah gave Emma a gleaming smile. "Then I'll be sure to send you home with a pouchful."

"Is that something you learned from . . . your Indian heritage?"

Sarah laughed. "Oh heavens no. Lucas is the one who introduced me to it—learned about it from a miner who came from New Orleans. He said he'd drunk coffee spiced that way up in the mountains, where he used to live."

Emma asked evenly, hoping her tone didn't betray her great curiosity, "And where was that?"

"Up in Leadville." Sarah cast her a glance before packing more food into the pouch. It seemed like she was preparing for a long week's trip, with the amount of food she was stuffing inside. "That's where he lived for a time. Moved there after the gold rush up in those parts fizzled out. A lot of cheap property to buy back then." Her face grew thoughtful. "But when his wife and baby died, he came down here. Hoping to heal, to find a way to move on."

Sarah grew quiet, and Emma was glad she busied herself filling a water jug from the kitchen pump and didn't look her way. She felt at a loss for words, wanting to know what happened but knowing it would be impolite to ask. Her heart ached for Lucas. He had not only lost a wife in death—but also a baby? She couldn't conceive of the grief he must have endured. It wouldn't surprise her if he never wanted to marry again.

"We don't have to go far to find some plants commonly used by the Cheyenne. My grandmother was a medicine woman in our tribe, so she taught me a lot. I used to tag along with her, collecting and preparing plants." She slung the pouch over her shoulder and walked to the door. As she opened it, she gestured to Emma to follow her out. "Nearly every plant on the Front Range has some practical use. Food, medicine, spiritual power."

As she followed Sarah, Emma lifted her skirts while walking around deep ruts in the road. Sarah kept on talking, explaining to her how the Plains Indians had thrived in Colorado, following the innumerable herds of buffalo, mostly living undisturbed in peace with the white trappers and settlers until the railroad companies started coming. She spoke a bit about her husband, whom she'd clearly loved and greatly missed—a quiet, industrious man with a large heart and wry sense of humor. "Lucas reminds me of him sometimes," she said thoughtfully, although it was clear to Emma that Sarah only felt a kind of motherly affection for the cowboy. "He's a good influence on my sons too. And Eli especially needs some steering straight. Sometimes I just want to kick that boy into the day after tomorrow." She said those words with a good-natured smile, but Emma heard the bite in her tone.

Emma asked her polite questions about Eli and LeRoy, and Sarah was glad to indulge her in numerous tales of her boys and the many troubles they'd gotten into while growing up. Before long, she and Sarah had come to a sandy narrow path wending close to the banks of the river. *Not far from where I took my fall*, Emma recalled with some embarrassment. If Sarah thought her a fool for having ridden so carelessly that day, she never betrayed such a sentiment. She spoke kindly, and Emma relished how welcome and accepted Sarah made her feel. So different from the way her parents treated her.

"I brought along some paper. I hope you won't mind if I write down what you tell me about the various plants. I'll never remember it all."

"Why, that's a fine idea. We can pick some plants for you to press, and if you want to sketch, we're in no hurry. Although, if I'm not back by dinnertime, the horses will make a fuss."

It struck Emma how Sarah seemed such a part of the landscape; she had no need to hurry to get somewhere or accomplish something. Certainly she had a ranch to run and horses to tend to, but Emma had never met anyone so free of ambition or the need to make an impression. It made Emma realize how disconnected she felt with her world—the whole world, in a way. No doubt Sarah had a serious respect for nature and its forces, as life in the wilderness presented countless dangers and challenges. But she seemed so at peace with her place amid nature, and her pace was unhurried and unfettered by trivial cares. Emma hoped Sarah could help her find a similar peace out here in Colorado. She would need it, whether she ever married or not.

"Well, this cheery plant's a good one to start with. Have you seen these around?"

Emma nodded at the large bushy shrub with bright yellow daisy-like flowers.

"Take a whiff." Sarah nodded at the plant.

"It smells . . . like menthol." She winced. "That's pretty strong."

"The Cheyenne call it *hitunehisse-eyo* or bark medicine. You make a tea by boiling the leaves, roots, and stems. Let the steam cover your face to get rid of a headache. The settlers named it arrowleaf balsamroot—see how the leaves are pointed like arrows?" She broke off a flower stem and handed it to Emma. "Here's a good sample to press. You can also chew the root for a sore throat or headache."

Emma held the flower close and studied the petals. "There are plenty of these behind my house, so I can sketch those," she said, thinking of how versatile this one plant was. She never imagined something that looked like a daisy could have so many medicinal uses. She reached into her satchel and pulled out a sheet of paper and her pencil. Sarah wandered around studying marks on the ground while Emma wrote.

"A cat's been through here in the last day or so," Sarah said without looking up. Emma supposed she did not mean a common house cat. The thought of something bigger and more aggressive caused her to tense. She glanced around, half-expecting to see a mountain lion crouching in wait for her.

"Are there many around?" she asked.

Sarah straightened and looked across the river. "Some. They range about forty miles and keep to themselves. So long as they have plenty of deer at hand, they rarely come close to the ranch. They're shy around people."

"Thank goodness," Emma muttered.

"And now that the buffalo have been overhunted and rarely pass through here, we don't see the large packs of wolves roaming the plains in the early summer."

Emma cringed even more at the thought of wolves searching the open fields for prey. She finished writing her notes and put her paper and pencil back in her satchel, still giving a glance around to make sure they weren't in any danger. With Sarah's casual listing of predators and Lucas's litany of dangerous plants, Emma felt even more unsure she could ever feel comfortable living in the West. She'd heard people at church talking about the droughts in recent years and how, when the irrigation ditches ran out of water, well, there was just no water at all for the town. What did people drink? How did they bathe? It was hard enough to stay clean with the constant wind whipping up grit and dust, even with plenty of water coming through the pipes into the house. She'd hate to have to go without bathing.

Sarah walked on once she saw Emma was ready. They took their time examining the foliage along the river. In less than an hour Sarah pointed out at least a dozen various common-looking plants and described their uses. Some, like mint, Emma might have concluded correctly, but others, like the tiny fuzzy blue-flowered silverleaf, she would never have figured out. The silverleaf with it shiny leaves was in the pea family and useful for calming cramps. Sarah also explained how some plants had spiritual uses to her tribe, such as the everlasting prairie flower. Its blue powder, rubbed on fighters and horses alike, was thought to provide protection in battle, making them light and quick in movement

She so enjoyed Sarah's "tour" she hardly noticed the time passing, and her respect for Sarah's knowledge of the land grew in great measure. As the sun rose above them, a cool breeze kicked up from the river, and Emma pulled a shawl from her satchel and wrapped it around her shoulders. The drop in temperature didn't seem to bother Sarah though, who found a wide, flat rock for them to sit on not far from the riverbank.

The South Platte had been low at the start of summer, but now it was more like a wide mudflat. Bird and deer footprints littered a strip along the bank, and Sarah pointed out other footprints—of raccoon, skunk, opossum, and prairie dog—that had come down to drink in the last day. Emma looked around and saw only herds of black cattle grazing—hundreds of them speckling the flat prairie, occasionally lowing to one another.

"Do you ever have problems with wild animals attacking your horses?" Emma asked.

Sarah bit her lip and looked out at the cattle. "On occasion we've had a mountain lion come around. But we have much more trouble with the two-legged variety of varmint than the four-legged."

Emma pulled her knees up to her chest to get warmer. A glance to the west showed roiling clouds. Was another hailstorm on its way—or perhaps even early snow? She turned back to Sarah. "Do you mean thieves? Men try to steal your horses?"

"Oh, there are plenty of rustlers around, but I tag all my horses." She pulled on her ear and gestured to the cows. "Just like the cattle ranchers brand their herds, to be able to tell which ones are theirs, I ink my ranch brand inside each horse's ear. No, I'm not worried about anyone stealing a horse."

But Emma could tell she was troubled about something. Was Sarah in danger? After hearing the way certain people spoke about the Indians at the July Fourth picnic, Emma wondered if Sarah occasionally—or more than occasionally—met with threats of some sort. But it was one thing to verbally slander someone; it was another thing altogether to act on a threat. She imagined, however, that some people wouldn't feel safe unless every last Indian was removed from their sight. Yet, how could anyone consider Sarah a threat?

Sarah pulled some bread and cheese and dried fruit of some sort from her bag and laid it down on a checkered towel on the rock. Together they ate without speaking, Emma respecting Sarah's shift to silence. Emma thought about the half-dozen sketches she'd made this morning using her special lead pencils with the glued-on rubber erasers. They lacked detail, but Emma had gotten enough down on paper to be able to identify the plants again. More importantly, she'd taken the time to write extensive notes about each plant—notes she hoped to use for the book she planned to compile. Her heart welled with gratitude for Sarah's willingness to share her knowledge and time.

"Maybe when we get back to the ranch, I'll introduce you to Protector—the paint gelding I think would make a good choice for you," Sarah said, putting away the leftover bits of food now that they'd finished eating.

"Oh, I'd like that very much. I'd love to see all your horses. I didn't get the chance . . . the last time I was here."

Sarah chuckled. "You were a bit indisposed at the time." She cocked her head and looked at Emma with a curious expression— the way someone might study a bird. "Good thing Lucas heard you that day and came to your aid." She shook her head slowly. "I believe he was meant to find you."

Emma's heart jolted in her chest. "What do you mean?"

Sarah grew thoughtful, as if considering whether or not to answer. "Your paths were meant to cross." She closed her mouth and said no more.

Emma didn't know what to say. Thinking about Lucas made her warm all over, and suddenly she imagined him sitting here, beside her, with his strong arm around her shoulder, pulling her close to him to keep away the chilly breeze, his body radiating comforting heat. She felt her face grow hot at the thought.

Sarah made a soft grunting noise. "He feels that way about you too," she said.

"What way?" Emma said defensively before she could catch herself. She wasn't sure what stunned her more—Sarah's boldness to speak so freely or her declaration that Lucas felt anything for her at all. But her words ricocheted in her head. Did Lucas truly have feelings for her? How could that be? He was polite to her and teased her, but he treated Violet—and even Violet's brothers—the same way. Had Sarah seen something in Lucas's behavior to warrant this belief? Her pulsed raced as another thought came to her—maybe Lucas had confided his feelings to Sarah? Emma longed to know what he might have said, but she would never deign to ask.

Sarah looked back across the rangeland, allowing Emma to simmer in her questions. Then she said, "A truer man you would never find. True, and honest. I'd rather a man outspoken and direct than one who wields fancy words to impress. Some don't abide by such directness, but with Lucas there is never any guile or unkind intention. He speaks his mind, but he's well-mannered." She smiled in approval.

Emma nodded politely, hoping to steer the conversation in another direction. She felt utterly flustered thinking about Lucas and listening to Sarah speak of him with such high praise, as if trying to convince Emma he was the man for her.

But as much as she tried to force herself to change the subject, she found herself asking, "Does he talk about me—to you? I mean . . . I just don't see—"

Sarah laid a hand on Emma's wrist, and Emma closed her mouth, feeling foolish. It was hardly proper for her to be asking questions about Sarah's employee. But Sarah said in a reassuring voice, "When two people are meant for each other, their hearts will sing together. The sky will embrace them, and the stars will shine ever brighter."

She gave Emma a wide knowing smile. Emma's thoughts tumbled. Maybe Sarah was a regular matchmaker, and felt Lucas was lonely and needed to remarry. That didn't mean Emma and he were destined for each other. Emma didn't believe in destiny or fate. You had to make your own decisions—and your own future. Otherwise other people would make it for you. She could only pray God would direct her to the right man to marry and give her the wisdom to know who that might be.

Couldn't it also have been meant for Emma to reunite with Randall after all these years? Didn't she owe it to him to allow him time to adjust to living in Colorado and working for his father? Yes, he'd acted insensitive to her at the picnic, but she knew he was struggling to adjust to an uncomfortable new life, as was she. And having to work in such close proximity with his father. Her own actions since moving out here had not shown the greatest wisdom or discernment either, so didn't she owe him time to find his feet? He held such a special place in her heart; she wasn't ready yet to dismiss that or the bond they'd built over all those years growing up.

She suddenly felt bad for turning down his requests to see her. What must he think? Guilt stabbed her for her selfish, inconsiderate behavior toward him. Randall hardly knew anyone in Greeley either. She might possibly be the only true friend he had, and she'd been pushing him away. Well, she would see what she could do to remedy that.

As Sarah stood and brushed off her skirt, Emma noticed a small dark cloud across the river. She got to her feet and said, "That's odd. That cloud is so low. And it's moving fast—"

Sarah sucked in a breath, which made Emma swivel to look at her. Sarah's face had paled and her eyes widened.

"That's not a cloud. Come, we need to hurry back to the ranch." She didn't wait for Emma but started off in a trot down along the river path.

"If it's not a cloud," Emma said, feeling trepidation trickle down her spine as she hurried after her, "then what is it?"

Without turning around, Sarah said in an obviously distressed tone, "Locusts."

Chapter 17

BY THE TIME THEY'D REACHED the front door, the sky was thick with grasshoppers, which, Sarah told her, were also called locusts. Emma had seen a few here and there on the ground around town. But she never imagined anything as frightening as this—insects in a swarm of biblical proportion.

She'd started to scream by the time they arrived at the kitchen door, with the hopping, flying insects landing all over her—in her hair, on her clothes, smacking her face. She promptly stopped screaming, though, when a few of the wriggling invaders rammed the insides of her throat and she coughed them out. Horrified, she ducked her head under her shawl, barely able to open her eyes to see through the hurtling bodies and wings.

Sarah hurried her inside and slammed shut the door, leaving most of the grasshoppers outside in a brooding, foreboding dark sky. They had nearly blocked out the sun by their sheer numbers!

A dozen or more of the insects careened around the small room, landing on shelves and in the sink and floor.

Still squirming in fright as more of the creatures hopped off her clothes, Emma danced around in place until she could no longer see any others on her person.

"I'm glad I shut that window before we left." Sarah pointed a finger at the window in the kitchen. "I expected a storm, but not of that type."

Emma's heart finally slowed to normal, and she blew out a breath. A few grasshoppers still hopped aimlessly around the kitchen, but Sarah deftly scooped them all up into a clay jug and corked them.

Sarah shook her head, dismayed. "That late wheat crop won't ever get harvested now. But it's a good thing these critters came late this year. At least most of the early crops, and the corn, have been harvested in town. By nightfall there won't be even a shred of a wheat stalk growing out of the ground."

"Do these . . . locusts attack every year?" Emma asked, shivering at the thought. Wasn't it enough to have to deal with dust, drought, and blizzards? She was glad her family didn't depend on farming for their livelihood. But many of the families in Greeley did. Her heart went out to these hardworking farmers trying to eke out a living from the ground.

"No, not even. But in '73, we had an awful stretch. First, the coldest, longest winter in years. Then the locusts, smack in the middle of summer"—Sarah paused to calmly pull a grasshopper out of her tangled strands of hair—"cleaned the fields as if nothing had ever been planted before. Followed by a mild winter with little snow. Which portends drought the following year. This was the first year most of the farmers felt they were back in business. And now . . ."

She blew out a breath and went over to the water pump connected to the big ceramic sink. After filling the metal kettle with water, she blew on the embers in her cast-iron stove and added some pieces of wood. "I'll make us some tea while we wait this out."

Emma stiffened. "How long . . . will it take before they . . . finish and leave?"

Sarah grunted and shook her head as she pulled down two mugs from a shelf and opened a tin. "Can't rightly say. But once the critters find food, they'll stay on it until every last bit is gone. So, I'm thinking in a few hours you should be able to head back to town, at least without getting overrun—"

Just then the front door blew open. Emma let out a little squeal as a whirlwind of grasshoppers blew in, followed by men in long coats. Emma sucked in a breath, embarrassed by her fright, as Sarah's two sons—followed by Lucas Rawlings—tromped in, all noise and bluster.

Eli laughed, pulled off his hat, and shook his shoulder-length hair. A few grasshoppers came flying out and landed near her feet. She jumped back. Eli looked at her and narrowed his eyes in a friendly chastisement.

"You're not scared of a few little bugs, are you, Miss Bradshaw?"

"Eli, where're your manners?" Sarah asked, cuffing him on the side of his head. Eli grumbled an apology.

Emma glanced over at Lucas and LeRoy, who were clearly stifling a laugh. Lucas tipped his hat at her and coughed politely— no doubt to keep from chuckling. She knew she must be a sight and once again felt that familiar embarrassment in front of Lucas.

Why did they have to come into the kitchen right then? She hadn't even had time to neaten up after the brisk run she and Sarah had made back to the ranch. And with all her waving and dancing around to shake off the grasshoppers, her hairpins had loosened and most of her hair had fallen in a heap to her shoulders. Mud crusted her shoes and the hem of her dress. She hated to think what she looked like. If her father saw her now . . .

She wanted to ask Sarah if she could use some other room to neaten up, but froze where she stood. Suddenly she felt overwhelmed by the last few moments' events—hurrying while under attack, feeling frightened and flustered, and now—being in Lucas's company in such disarray . . . again. What must he think of her? And Sarah's words swarmed her like other pesky insects, reminding her Lucas had feelings of some sort for her. All told, she felt completely befuddled and unable to do anything other than fall into one of the chairs at the kitchen table.

Lucas rushed over to her. She felt strong arms cupping her shoulders, helping ease her to the seat. Her head spun, but she willed herself not to faint. She would not succumb to drama like her mother, she told herself. But she did feel awfully lightheaded, and her corset pinched her waist tight, constricting her breathing. Instantly a cup of hot tea was placed before her. Emma smiled her thanks at Sarah, who sat down across from her with her own steaming mug.

"Are you all right, Miss Bradshaw?"

Against her will, she got snared in those emerald-green eyes. Sarah might be wrong about Lucas having feelings for her, but by the way he was studying her, there was no doubt of his genuine concern—at the very least. That could just be his nature. *He takes a kind interest in the well-being of all—people and animals alike. Maybe Sarah was misinterpreting what she saw.* But not for the first time did she see something in the depth of his eyes—that smoldering look of desire that almost reached out to her in yearning.

She wrenched her gaze away and stared at the steam rising from her mug. The room felt suddenly overly warm and stuffy.

LeRoy hung his coat up on a peg by the door and said, "We were starting on the line of fencing behind the hay barn when they hit—"

Eli interrupted, waving his arms enthusiastically. "LeRoy didn't see them coming, but by the time I got three words out of my mouth, they'd swarmed us. LeRoy was in the middle of saying something, and ended up with a mouthful of 'hopper." He opened the ice box door and took out something that looked like a haunch of smoked meat. He then went to the bread box and took out a small loaf of dark bread. He threw Emma a skewed smile. "You can eat 'em, you know? Right tasty." He smacked his lips, and Sarah promptly sideswiped his head again.

"You're going to make Miss Bradshaw faint with all your talking," she said.

Sarah then chuckled, fished a dead insect out of the sink, and plopped it on the counter. Emma could see hundreds—if not thousands—of the insects winging past the window. The loud droning sent a shudder across her neck. She leaned over the minty tea and breathed deep. A long-pent-up sign escaped her throat.

"That's the little mint plant I showed you earlier," she said, nodding at her cup of tea. "That, and a sprig of chamomile."

"Thank you. It's very soothing," Emma said, grateful they hadn't gone far from the ranch in their foray for plants. What if she had been riding back to Greeley . . . ? Shahayla!

"My horse—" Emma said with alarm, pushing her tea back and rising from her chair.

Lucas, who was still at her side—perhaps making sure she didn't plan to faint dead away anytime soon—laid his hand on her shoulder. His touch sent a shudder through her, and reminded her of her earlier thoughts of him holding her in the wind. She lowered her face, hoping he wouldn't try to meet her eyes, for she knew she had to be blushing. Why did his simple touch affect her so strongly?

When Randall took her hand or her arm, she felt nothing like this . . . frisson of electricity. It was puzzling and disturbing.

"Don't worry about your mare. The other horses have been through this before. They'll have run into the barn, where they're probably happily eating some hay. The grasshoppers won't bother them. They're only interested in finding their next meal—and a good thing it isn't horse." He gave her a crooked, reassuring smile. "Or pretty young ladies."

But despite his attempt to ease her mind, her unsettled feeling grew to agitation. Where was her mother right now? What if she had been walking back home after her women's club meeting when the grasshoppers swarmed into town? She gasped imagining her mother overtaken by thousands of these winged attackers. And then pictured her mother arriving home, worried sick when she discovered Emma gone.

Emma wilted. She had told no one where she'd gone. Her parents—once again—would be frantic, wondering where she was. And she'd be punished yet again.

She jumped to her feet, but the sight of the swarm outside the window reminded her she could not dare leave until they were gone. And there was no way she would be able to ride her horse back. She imagined how terrified Shahayla must be right now, despite being with other horses in the barn.

"Please," she said to Lucas, trying to avoid getting caught in his gaze again, "I really must get home. My mother will be terribly worried—" No more words could escape through her choked-up throat. Tears pushed out the corners of her eyes, despite her efforts to tell herself not to cry. How in the world could she get home though? Every minute she delayed was agony, knowing how her mother's imagination would terrorize her with visions of Emma dead somewhere, thrown off her horse. No doubt her father had hurried home, worried over her mother. And together they'd discover that Shahayla was not in her stall. Could things get any worse?

Sarah said, "Best you just stay here awhile, until the locusts clear out." She came over and took her arm, then led her into the adjoining room, which had comfortable-looking worn sofas and overstuffed chairs positioned before a large stone fireplace. No fire presently burned in the hearth, but Emma imagined during the winter Sarah and her sons—and no doubt Lucas—spent many hours in here in front of a blazing fire, watching snow fall and pile in drifts outside the windows.

Eli and LeRoy were now sitting at the table eating a hearty lunch—apparently not very distressed by the insect attack, as evidenced by their untroubled appetite. But they had lived here all their lives. Emma supposed they'd lived through many locust swarms. And since they didn't grow any food crops, she guessed the appearance of so many insects was merely a momentary annoyance.

As she fought back her tears, the loud thrumming and banging against the wood siding of the ranch house lessened. Through the window she could tell the swarm had greatly thinned. But was this just a momentary lull? Were more swarms coming? She had no idea how such insects behaved, but she was thankful they didn't bite. At least that was some consolation. Maybe she could walk alongside her horse back to town. It would take her an hour or more, but that was better than getting thrown—and having to be rescued yet again by Lucas Rawlings.

As if reading her mind, he came over and knelt before her, so his face was level with hers. Even though he kept a polite distance, his nearness felt intimate, and she smelled his earthy mountain smell—the scent of hay and soil and damp cotton. A manly scent, but one that practically intoxicated her this close. She looked into his utterly handsome face—so calm and sweet, gentle and yet mildly chiseled by the weather and years of working under a hot sun. Yet the lines in his face only made him look mature and rugged in a raw attractive way.

And when he smiled, it literally took her breath away. His smile was like an angel's—if angels could be cowboys. But she couldn't imagine a more reassuring and loving smile on any man's face. Not even Randall's came close to comparing.

She once again felt terribly self-conscious, knowing what a mess she must look. She found her voice after some effort. "I fear you must think I'm not much of a lady, Mr. Rawlings. Seeing as you often find me in a sorry state of disarray. I hope I haven't given you the impression that I care little for my appearance." She hoped her voice sounded dignified, to make up for her disheveled condition.

In a quiet tone so no one else could hear, he said, "Miss Bradshaw, you could be dressed in sackcloth with ashes streaked across your face and I don't think there'd be a more beautiful woman in all the earth."

Emma's breath caught in her throat. If any other man said such words, she'd presume he was toying with her, trying to win her favor through flattery—as she had heard similar lines from unscrupulous would-be suitors before. But one look at Lucas's face told Emma that Sarah had spoken the honest truth about this man. He was direct and spoke his mind—or in this case, his heart. She detected not a hint of cynicism and saw he was wholly sincere. And this realization set her trembling.

The tears she had barely held back now streamed down her face. Why was she crying? It made no sense. Her emotions were in a tangle, and she wished she could run and hide.

Lucas pulled back, a frown on his face. "I didn't mean to upset you, Miss Bradshaw. Please forgive me if I said anything untoward—"

"No, please," Emma said, hastily wiping her face with the back of her hand. "Your words are a kindness, I understand. I am just a bit overwrought by the day's events, and worried over my mother, who is given to much hysteria over the smallest inconveniences."

He reached into a pocket of his loose leather vest and pulled out a handkerchief. She thought it odd he'd carry such an item on him. But she sat there, unable to move or speak, as he gently wiped her cheeks, smiling for all the world as if he couldn't think of anything he'd rather be doing at this very moment than dry up her tears. His tender touch sent more shudders through her, and her heart pounded as if trying to beat out of her chest.

She fought back the urge to throw her arms around him and weep. The months of living out here, away from her familiar life back East, trying hard to make friends and adjust to the different and often frightening life in such a wild, rugged place as Colorado Territory, all seemed to crash down upon her like an avalanche of rocks careening down the side of a steep mountain. As if sensing her need, still kneeling before her, he pulled her head lightly to his chest and smoothed her hair as he comforted her.

She could no longer hold back. The tears fell and soaked his shirt, yet he never flinched or pulled back. He just stayed right there, stroking her head and murmuring words of comfort, the way he had comforted her horse the day he stitched her up.

"There, there," he said, resting his chin on the top of her head as she sniffed and tried to stop crying. "It's all right. Just go ahead and cry and let it all out. No one's going to mind."

She knew she should feel even more embarrassed for her unrestrained show of emotion, but Lucas's words drained her of shame, and instead she felt the anxiety and worry fade away; the storm of fear and tears that had come upon her as suddenly as the locust attack dwindled to nothing, leaving her exhausted but strangely calm. When she lifted her head and gazed out the kitchen window, she saw that only a few insects now swirled in the air.

"I'll take you home," Lucas said softly, standing and relinquishing his hand from her head. She saw her tears had left a large wet stain on his vest, but he didn't pay it any mind. His eyes were on hers, and he searched her face. She could still feel his soothing hands stroking her hair, and now that he had pulled away, she felt chilled and empty.

"I think it best if you ride with me on Ransom. He won't mind the extra weight if I put you up in front—being that you're so light. But I wouldn't advise riding your mare, seeing as there's no way to know how she'll act if another swarm of grasshoppers come through while we're on the road. We can pony her. If that's all right with you." He added, surely in an attempt to make her laugh, "Ransom isn't bothered by the hoppers; he just chews 'em up and spits 'em out."

Emma nodded and giggled. Then she frowned. What would her mother think if she saw her daughter riding into town sitting with Lucas behind her and his arms around her waist? Yet, it was worth the scolding if it meant she could get home quickly and safely. And, she had to admit, the thought of riding with Lucas tucked up behind her made her heart pound faster. She would get to feel his strong, comforting arms holding her all the way back to town . . .

She then wondered why Sarah didn't offer to take her back in the buggy like she'd done before. But maybe Sarah had already wasted too much of her day. And it would take time to rig up the horse and breeching. Then again, looking at Sarah's expression as she watched their quiet conversation from the kitchen, Emma wondered again if Sarah was playing matchmaker, and encouraging these "romantic notions" she seemed to believe Lucas had for Emma.

Well, at this moment, all that mattered was getting home as quickly and safely as possible, and Lucas's suggestion made the most sense. Shahayla would hardly spook at anything if Ransom remained calm. Emma smirked at the thought that their horses were a lot like their owners. While in Lucas's company and under his protection, she had little to fear. She trusted him and knew he would keep her safe. She had never felt this trusting toward any man—not even Randall. But Lucas was in his element; the open range was his world. She doubted he'd feel at all in control in the hustle and bustle of New York, where a man could hardly turn around without knocking something over. She imagined Lucas would feel just as out of place there as she felt here.

"Do you want to . . . freshen up before we go?"

Emma imagined he also pictured how her mother might react seeing her in such a state. "Oh yes, I would. So long as I don't have to go outside just yet."

Lucas shot Sarah a look, as if they had an unspoken language between them. "Emma could use your help," he said, without being specific. Sarah got up and came over to them. He then looked back at Emma. "I'll go fetch the horses, and when you're ready, you can meet me outside." He added, "You don't need to be afraid, Miss Bradshaw; I'll get you safely home."

Emma laid her hand on his, and his face brightened. "I know you will," she said. "And please, call me Emma." She felt her face flush again, knowing allowing such familiarity was crossing a line of impropriety. But she couldn't bear hearing him keep addressing her so formally. "Now that I've cried all over your shirt, I think we're past formalities."

Lucas chuckled, and the warmth of the sound rushed all the way to her toes. She smiled for the first time in hours. "All right," he said, ". . . Emma."

Her name coming from his lips had the solemnity of a prayer. It brushed over her like a feather.

Emma watched as he walked out in his easy, confident gait, unable to take her eyes off him.

Sarah finally broke the spell. "Come," she said, gesturing to a far room, "let's get you tidied up so Lucas can take you home." She said the words evenly, but Emma detected a noticeable twinkling in her eyes.

Chapter 18

THEY RODE MOSTLY IN SILENCE the three miles back to town. Emma feared the grasshoppers would descend once more, as they had when she and Sarah had run back to the ranch, but only a few stray ones flitted past them now and then. Emma wasn't sure if Lucas had been wholly honest with her when he insisted she stay put on his horse, just in case a swarm blew in and her horse spooked. Although she knew he was primarily concerned about her safety, part of her hoped he'd kept her on his horse because he wanted to be close to her.

She had to admit, at this moment, she couldn't think of anyplace she'd rather be than perched on Lucas's saddle in front of him, with his comforting arms draped around the sides of her body as he lightly held the reins. Ransom was so responsive to Lucas's subtle signals and shift in body posture that he hardly had to move at all. At one point, where the empty road leveled out, Lucas asked if she'd like to lope, promising he'd hold on to her so she didn't slip off—since she was sitting sidesaddle on what he called "an ordinary Mexican saddle." Seeing that Shahayla was prancing with nervous energy from the day's earlier commotion, she turned her head and gave Lucas a nod and smile, a bubble of joy welling up in her heart.

Despite the fright she'd had that morning, the brisk fall air and thrill of riding ensconced in a cowboy's arms couldn't be more romantic. Well, she could think of other things that would make it more so, but she did not allow her mind to wander off in that direction. Emma was surprised by Ransom's perfectly smooth gait; she hardly bounced at all—although Lucas's arms pressed in close and held her secure. By the time they'd slowed to a walk, with both horses breathing hard, Emma found herself hardly taking a breath at all. Her heart pounded in a way that made her feel more alive than she'd ever felt. She chalked it up to the stunning fall day and the relief that the swarm of grasshoppers had dissipated. But her heart argued that there was a different reason for such deep-seated joy.

The smooth half-hour ride passed before she knew it, and all too soon they were turning onto her street. Without suggesting it, he'd gone north past the main entrance to town, by the railroad depot, and turned in closer to her house. No doubt to avoid curious onlookers who might come to wrong conclusions—even though he told her if the grasshoppers were in town, they'd be engulfing the crop fields right now. His route kept them as far from the fields as possible.

Stormy clouds had gathered overhead, threatening rain. The temperature had dropped as well, and Emma pulled her shawl tighter around her shoulders. No one was on the street, and an eerie calm draped the neighborhood. Dozens of grasshoppers winged on the wind around them, appearing aimless. Emma wondered if they'd already eaten every plant in town and were engorged and sated.

Lucas stopped the horses and looked around. He shook his head. "Some of the farmers have their methods for trying to kill the 'hoppers, like using nets or kerosene or setting traps, but nothing really works. I hope most got their crops in before now. Although the barley and corn farmers have lost everything, no doubt."

She glanced down the street to Mrs. Turner's house, and even from this distance she could tell the insects had made short work of her lavish flower garden. Everything had been eaten down to the nub.

"I didn't know they ate flowers," she said, shaking her head sadly, knowing how much her neighbor prided herself on her garden. She imagined how upset the old woman would be. But at least she could replant; nothing was truly lost. Emma was glad she kept her pathetic little crape myrtle in the sunny anteroom at the back of the house. She had brought it inside when the weather had turned cold at night, unsure if it could survive.

"Flowers, tree bark, lichen, weeds, even other grasshoppers— if they're hungry enough." Lucas swiveled in the saddle, taking in the town. "They eat their weight in food each day. The best defense is chickens; they love the bugs. But you'd need an awful lot of them to make any dent in a swarm like the one we saw today. I've heard some swarms get up to a mile wide and long."

Lucas dismounted, then reached up and helped Emma slide off his horse, his hands gently gripping her waist. They were halfway down her block, but she supposed he didn't want to take the chance of her mother seeing her on his horse with his arms around her. She doubted her mother was outside though—now that it was evident the grasshoppers had come through this part of town. Emma imagined her cowering in her bedroom or hiding under the coverlet of her bed. But she appreciated his discretion.

At their first encounter, Emma expected this cowboy to be rough around the edges, but one thing she'd learned about Lucas

Rawlings was that he was as mannered and considerate as any well-bred East Coast man raised in a proper home. She wondered what kind of home and family he had been raised in.

She walked around Ransom and untied her mare's lead rope from the saddle strings, giving her a pat on her neck. Lucas had strapped her horse's bridle to her saddle and put a halter on the mare instead for the trip back to town. Emma made to remove the halter, but Lucas laid his hand on her wrist. His touch once more sent a shudder through her.

"Keep it for now. No sense putting her bridle on when you're only taking her over to her paddock. You can return it to me later."

Emma thanked him and wondered if he said this in order to have an excuse to see her again. But now that they were close to her home, she felt suddenly self-conscious and awkward. Had anyone seen them riding together? Just what would people think, and would they tell her parents? Maybe this hadn't been a wise idea. She could have ridden Shahayla without incident. As much as she'd enjoyed the intimacy of riding with Lucas, it was an improper indulgence — on both their parts.

She didn't think he was taking advantage of her — not at all. But could she trust him to keep his own passions in check? She hardly knew him, and she'd been taught quite pointedly not to put herself in a compromising position in which a man might not be able to control himself. Riding in his arms the way she did would surely fit that description, yet Lucas had been the perfect gentleman. If he truly did feel anything for her — emotionally or physically — he didn't reveal as much. Which made her wonder what went on in his mind; so often she could tell he was thinking about something, but he held back from speaking. He was mostly a mystery to her — an intriguing, compelling mystery.

So she could only guess what might have gone through his mind as he rode to town with her pressed so close. Surely her nearness brought back memories of his wife. Maybe he hadn't had a woman in his arms, this close to him, since his wife died.

Emma then thought of how she'd cried at Sarah's and how he cradled her close and soothed her with his words and hands. Had he done that with his wife? While she lay dying?

Maybe her riding back with him had stirred up painful memories, and that was why he was now so quiet and thoughtful, looking down toward town, a slight frown on his face. She wanted to say something but found she couldn't think of anything that wouldn't sound forced or trite. They stood in the middle of the street, unspeaking. Then Lucas suddenly turned back to her, and she noticed his eyes glistening with tears.

"Is something the matter?" she asked quietly, glancing around as the nipping wind kicked up and dust swirled in small whirlwinds around them. He looked like he was struggling to find a way to answer her.

Fat raindrops now splattered on her head and around her feet. Shahayla pawed the ground restlessly as if wanting to go to her sheltered stall and be fed. For once, Emma didn't care that her hair was coming undone. She didn't care if anyone saw them at that moment. Seeing Lucas's face etched with such emotion tugged hard at her heart. She'd never met a man with such an honest, vulnerable expression. He did nothing to hide his emotions, which was something men just didn't do—at least not other men Emma knew. And his expression spoke of grief and loss.

He reached over and gently pushed a strand of wayward hair behind her ear. This simple touch of his hand caused her to tremble. He moved closer, dropping his hand to the side of her head, slowly pulling her toward him. Her heart beat hard as she realized he meant to kiss her. Her breath caught in her throat.

The poignant magic of the moment was shattered, though, by a loud, deep shout coming from down the street.

"Emma, what are you doing? Who is that with you?"

Emma turned and became horror-struck at the sight of her father—dressed in one of his fine three-piece suits—barreling down from their front porch and into the street. He stretched out his arms, his face scrunched and red, as if ready to grab her, as if she were in some kind of mortal danger. But she knew why he had such an expression. She quickly took a step back from Lucas, but to her surprise, he made no defensive move at all. His face showed no concern or remorse—nothing to indicate shame or embarrassment over what could only appear to her father as a moment of high indiscretion.

She touched a hand to her neck as a coldness washed over her. Suddenly the air seemed biting and unforgiving.

Emma flashed on how Lucas had practically ordered her father to take care of the carriage horse at the picnic, and not in a kindly tone. But she didn't fault Lucas at all for his anger and harsh words that day. His actions may have saved Lynette's life—although she doubted Walter would ever forgive the way Lucas had humiliated him in front of the crowd. And by humiliating her brother, Lucas had, by association, humiliated her father. No doubt her father was not happy to see her with Lucas. Especially not in such an intimate pose.

She swallowed hard, wondering just how her father would punish her this time. She squelched the knot of anger forming in her gut.

He strode up to Lucas, his face splotched red, as if he'd been recently arguing. Emma bit her lip to keep from saying a word. She knew there was nothing she could say in her defense—or in Lucas's.

"Mr. Rawlings, I don't know what you are up to," he said, practically seething as he pushed his face into Lucas's. "But I want you to stay away from my daughter—"

"Father!" Emma couldn't just stand there and listen to her father yell at Lucas, who'd done nothing wrong. Before she could say more, he spun and faced her, his finger pointed close to her eyes.

"Not another word from you." He blew out a hard breath and turned back to Lucas, his face hardened with deep wrinkled lines. "Where were you two? Did you arrange to meet her secretly somewhere?"

Emma withheld a gasp. Lucas waited—no doubt to make sure her father was willing to let him answer. A moment passed, with Lucas still standing calmly and unruffled, and then he spoke in a quiet tone. Emma smirked despondently. He'd have little success using his talents at calming horses on her father.

"Mr. Bradshaw, your daughter came over to visit Sarah Banks, the owner of the ranch where I live. I believe you've made her acquaintance." When her father said nothing, his face still as tight as a drum, Lucas continued calmly, leaning up against Ransom and holding the reins loosely in his hand. "When the grasshoppers appeared, I'd been laying fencing with her sons. We ducked inside the house to wait out the swarm, and that's where I encountered Miss Bradshaw. She was frightened, so I offered to escort her back to town. After her last incident with her horse, I was . . . concerned about her returning home safely." He added evenly, "And here she is."

To Emma's surprise, he summarily dismissed her father by tipping his hat and swiftly mounting his horse. He pulled lightly on the reins, forcing Ransom to back away a few steps. Without even a quick glance at Emma or offering any farewell, he met her father's burning gaze without a flinch, then adeptly spun his horse around in one smooth move—like she'd seen in the horse competition at the picnic—and took off down the road, first at a trot, then at a full canter.

Emma realized she had been holding her breath, and she let it out in a sigh. Her father stood there unmoving a few long moments. Then he turned to face her. She could tell he was working hard to contain his rage.

"We'll discuss this later, young lady. For now, your mother needs you." He headed back toward their house, and Emma hurried after him, her heart in her throat.

"Is Mother all right? Did something happen?"

He didn't answer her, leaving her with an awful feeling of dread.

When she stepped inside, she heard talking and footsteps on the wood flooring. She was surprised to see dozens of grasshoppers bouncing around the rooms and hallway,   smacking into the walls and windows. Perhaps they had blown in and now that the windows were closed could find no way out. Why were none of the servants catching them? Emma thought this very odd, and the house too quiet. Where was her mother?

She stepped carefully, trying to avoid the insects—which now hardly frightened her. Her thoughts were on her mother, imagining the worst. She noticed her father had gone into his study, and as she walked by she saw him standing at the window, staring out, deep in thought. At least he wasn't yelling at her, although she thought that might be better than his anger-choked silence.

Would her father forbid her from going to Sarah's now? From speaking to Lucas? Just the thought made her stomach clench. She was tired of being a prisoner in her home, under her father's thumb. But what could she do? *Nothing. I can do nothing but obey. And hope someday I will find a way out.* Yet the only way out, from what she could conclude, was marriage. And the only man she knew her parents would approve of was Randall.

But maybe . . . maybe he might be her lifeline. She did so adore him. If only she really knew how he felt. Oh, she was so confused.

She knew Randall had his faults. But no one was perfect, and maybe she was just being foolish to hope for someone dashing and fearless to sweep her off her feet. Maybe she had read too many of those adventure stories with Randall when they were young.

Just then, as she walked toward her parents' room, hoping to find her mother, she saw Josephine stride toward her—dressed in a traveling outfit and carrying two suitcases.

She stopped before Emma, a look of resignation on her face. Emma's jaw dropped as she realized what Josephine was doing. The older woman pressed her mouth into a tight line, and Emma noticed her eyes filling with tears.

"Josephine," Emma practically whispered. "You're leaving us . . ."

"I was content to come out here upon the missus' request," she told Emma in a forlorn but firm tone, "and I could tolerate the dust and hard work; I'd grown up with worse." She visibly shuddered. "But those . . . bugs! The house was full of 'em, Miss Emma, and I've never had such a fright in my life. Nor do I intend to live in a town where such things swoop in like the plague of Moses." A grasshopper flew by her face, and she paled and screeched, waving her hands. "I-I'm sorry," she said, flustered beyond reason.

Emma gently took hold of her hands, bringing them down to Josephine's sides. "It's all right. I understand."

Josephine's eyes darted around, on the alert for another attack. She shook her head spastically. "I'm sorry, Miss Emma. I have to go. I'm catching the three o'clock train to Denver. I'll go back to New York and find another position, spend some time with my nieces and nephews. Your father was gracious enough to write me a commendation."

"My mother? Is she all right?"

Josephine chewed her lip. "She's . . . lying down. The evil things practically attacked her while she was taking her bath. The tub is still half-filled with 'em. She slipped and fell trying to get out before I could go help her. I heard her scream, but there were so many . . ."

Josephine's eyes were seared with terror. Emma patted her arm.

"You've had quite a scare. But they're mostly gone now. Are you sure you're not being too hasty — ?"

The maid who had worked for their family all Emma's life straightened and held her chin high. "I've made my decision." Then her face softened. "I wish you well, Miss Emma." In a quieter voice she added, "I hope you marry that fine young man who sat with you on the train. He'll take good care of you. Then you can have your own home and . . ." She let the words trail off.

Josephine didn't need to finish her sentence for Emma to understand the implications. Emma wondered if it was more her mother's hysterics and drama these past few months that had pushed Josephine out the door than the grasshoppers. Although she was sure the invasion of those pests was the last straw for her.

Emma frowned and threw her arms around Josephine. She'd hardly ever touched her in all these years; it was highly inappropriate. But Emma felt such affection and respect for this stalwart woman who had served her family well.

Josephine was a bit taken aback by the unexpected show of affection, but she smiled, and the tears in her eyes fell upon her cheeks.

Emma said, "Please write to me and tell me how you are. I only wish the best for you. I hope my father gave you some traveling money in addition to your wages."

"Oh yes, he was more than generous."

Good. Josephine deserves every penny. "Well, I don't mean to keep you waiting. Is no one else here — no other servants?"

Josephine shook her head. "The cook should be here shortly, to start dinner. I feel terrible —"

"Don't," Emma said firmly. "You have your own life to live. You have to choose the right course for yourself, not for anyone else."

As Josephine nodded and turned to go out the door, Emma knew she had said those words more for her own benefit than for Josephine's.

She watched their long-time servant march down the front steps to the street. Then she turned and headed toward her mother's bedroom—not at all happy to see what she'd find.

Chapter 19

THE GRASSHOPPERS DID INDEED EAT every bit of vegetation before that week was out, Lucas noted as he sat his horse at the far northern town boundary, next to Irrigation Ditch #2. This late in the year, the ditch was practically dry. *But now that doesn't matter—with the fall crops destroyed.* He let his gaze pan the hundreds of acres of corn and barley that had been devoured to the nub, the grasshoppers now long gone, although millions of eggs had been deposited in the soil and would hatch next spring. Where they went, Lucas had no idea. The brown fallow fields looked forlorn in the askant autumn light—mirroring his mood.

He felt bad for the farmers who'd had to endure yet another disaster. But they were a tough, determined lot. Lucas knew many of the families, as they had draft horses that pulled their plows, and Lucas had treated, wormed, and vaccinated many of them over the last few years. It seemed whenever they experienced such a setback, the farmers just set their jaws and dug in, working harder than ever, remaining hopeful and anticipating a better harvest next year.

I could learn a lesson or two from them. Lucas's thoughts slipped back to Emma, as they tended to just about every minute of every waking hour. She had even made inroads into his dreams. Whereas once he'd only dreamed of Alice, now he awoke some nights with Emma's soft skin and faint perfume scent of lavender and violets drifting in and out of his head. His ache for her was almost a physical pain—one he worked hard to alleviate by immersing himself in chores and treating the many animals that needed his care. This week especially seemed replete with horse injuries and ailments, as well as some emergency stitching caused by range cattle straying into barbed wire.

Lucas knew the local cattle ranchers were not happy about the barbed wire. The railroad had strung line along both sides of the tracks, and the townspeople of Greeley were completing stringing fifty miles of wire around their fields. Just one more thing to rile the likes of Rusty Dunnigan and his Indian-hater pals. Lucas had gone into the lumberyard in Evans yesterday, to pick up a dozen sheets of wood siding needed in replacing one side of the barn that had rotted away last winter, and when he'd gone into Myer's Saloon to refill his canteen with water before heading home, he was more than surprised by who he saw sitting with the ranchers. None other than Emma Bradshaw's brother. And from the looks of him, he'd been drinking—heavily.

Which made Lucas wonder. Not so much about the drinking, since Greeley was a teetotalist town where liquor was strictly forbidden—although he imagined plenty of men dipped into their brandy in the privacy of their homes. The nearest town that had a saloon was Evans, five miles south. No, what piqued his curiosity was why Walter Bradshaw—a refined, rich young man with a pregnant high-society wife—would socialize with the likes of such men. Men who were unscrupulous, unmannered, and scheming. Did Walter find companionship in their kind, or was he getting involved in some shady business dealings? One thing was for sure, Lucas presumed Walter's father had no idea whom his son was associating with. And even if he did, he had no idea of the harm these evil men could inflict.

It was no secret to those who'd been living awhile on the Front Range that some who had crossed Dunnigan and his "gang" of irate, mean ranchers who cared for nothing but profit had not lived to tell about it. Although Sheriff Weyburn had never been able to prove these ranchers responsible for the handful of mysterious deaths, it was understood all those men had at one point exchanged words — and often fists — with these local ranchers. *Just like Eli had.* And Lucas knew it was only a matter of time before things would come to a head with Rusty and Eli. And Sarah.

Lucas didn't believe Sarah should buckle under such threats and sell her ranch, but he also worried for her. Sure, she could shoot a gun and pop the head feathers off a raven without even skimming the scalp, but she was one woman against many armed and dangerous men. And as much as Eli and LeRoy protested they could handle any trouble that might come their way, Lucas seriously doubted they could hold back Morgan Chisholm — the richest rancher north of Denver who wanted her choice riverfront property — should he have a mind to cross the line and just take what he felt should be his — using Dunnigan and his pals as his own "law" enforcers. And he'd made it plenty clear he planned to acquire the Banks Ranch one way or another.

Lucas clucked his tongue, the presentiment of disaster looming around his head like a roiling storm cloud. As he spun Ransom around and galloped back to the ranch, he could smell snow in the air. The peaks of the Rockies to the west were half hidden in dense dark clouds. The foothills were ablaze in fall color. Winter would soon be upon them, descending in a shroud of bitterly cold wind, bringing one heavy snowstorm after another and burying the landscape in thick white drifts.

Lucas shivered as a blast of cold air coming down from the mountains whipped his hair and bit through his clothes, feeling like chilly fingers pawing through his heavy coat and pants.

He hadn't seen Emma in weeks. Not since that morning he'd ridden back with her to Greeley and her father had threatened him. As he rode into town this morning, he considered paying a call on Emma—under the auspices of intending to speak with Mr. Bradshaw about Walter's association with the ranchers. He felt the father should know Walter was treading on dangerous ground. But then he reminded himself it was none of his business, and he figured Emma's father would only become enraged by his interfering. And Lucas didn't want to do anything else to stir the man's ire.

He closed his eyes as he slowed Ransom down to a walk at the edge of Sarah's property, Hoesta running from somewhere far afield toward him, barking his squeaky bark. Without wanting to, Lucas let his mind wander back to the morning when he'd wrapped his arms around Emma's waist as they rode to town, the act only feeding his longing so that by the time he'd dismounted and helped her down, he could barely contain his great need. He would have kissed her; in that moment he knew his love for her was undeniable. And it seemed to him she'd wanted that kiss.

And then . . .

Lucas clenched his jaw and slid off Ransom, the sky now dark and pregnant with snow above him. With Hoesta playfully nipping at his heels, he walked his horse to the barn and methodically, mindlessly, took off his saddle and bridle, brushed Ransom down, then let him out in the pasture. He checked to make sure the barn doors leading to the paddocks were latched open so when the snow blew, the horses could all get cover and stay warm. Already most had grown their winter coats—which told Lucas they were in for an early and long winter. And it was only the first week of October.

He needed to see Emma again. He'd heard nothing about her lately and wondered if she still had eyes for that East Coast dandy. He knew he was letting her slip away by not pressing his suit for her. But he didn't see how he could make inroads into her heart with her family standing guard at the entrance. Sarah had advised him to attend the Harvest Dance; surely she'd be there. The dance was a gay affair, with music and dancing and tables full of food, held at the large Grange Hall. All the young men and women attended, hoping to find love. Lucas had gone the last three years with Eli and LeRoy and had watched, amused, as the unmarried women—young and old—giggled and batted their eyelashes as they chatted and danced with them. Although his heart was buried in a cold grave up in Leadville, he'd good-naturedly indulged the young girls in a dance or two, letting himself partake of the fun and gaiety in the hopes of fending off the impending sadness he knew would engulf him once winter set in. Somehow the cold and starkness, however sublime, magnified his loneliness and grief. He did not look forward to another hard winter, but he'd get through it, as he always did.

If he knew Emma Bradshaw had feelings for him, he'd get through it a lot easier, he told himself as he stomped the mud from his boots and the cold from his body and entered into the welcoming warmth of the kitchen. As if Sarah knew just when he'd come back, a hot mug of spiced coffee sat on the warmer plate of the wood stove. His mug. But Sarah was nowhere in sight. He glanced out the window and saw fat flakes of snow whipping in the wind.

His limbs tingled as the chill in his bones was dispelled by the heat. He stripped off his coat, took off his hat, and plopped down in a chair, grateful for a simple thing like a nice hot cup of coffee. Sarah had assured him last night by the crackling fire in the hearth that Emma Bradshaw was in love with him—she just didn't know it yet.

Lucas had let out an amused laugh. "You just have to help her realize it," she'd told him. When he asked her pointedly just how he would be able to get around her brother and father, Sarah had shaken her head and given him a look that said he was as dense as a water-soaked board.

"Don't try to get around them. Find a way to win them over."

But how? And even if he did, that didn't guarantee she felt what he felt. He chuckled thinking about Sarah's pronouncement. *"She's in love with you. She just doesn't know it yet."*

It was up to him to win her heart. And for some reason he felt the Harvest Dance would be his last chance. So he would attend this year. But this year he wouldn't go to be amused by the festivities. He would go with the intention of winning a certain young lady's heart.

"Come closer, Emma dear." Emma's mother closed her puffy eyes and gestured weakly with her hand.

For once Emma didn't think her mother was overdramatizing; she appeared terribly ill. Or perhaps all her hysteria and worry since moving here had weakened her health. But whatever the cause, Emma's heartstrings were pulled taut seeing her lovely mother so frail and bedridden. Her mother had always been filled with vim, dashing about to social circles in New York and attending charity balls and galas. Contrary to the advice Mrs. Turner had said was embraced by the founders of Greeley, her mother had not bloomed where she'd been planted. She looked altogether withered.

Emma eyed the nearly empty blue bottle sitting conspicuously on the nightstand beside her bed. She picked it up and showed it to her mother. "How much of this do you take each day?" She didn't attempt to mask the stern tone of her inquiry.

Her mother opened her eyes, saw what Emma was holding up, and gave out a long sigh. "It helps with my heart palpitations." She quickly patted her chest and swallowed. She leaned forward, her auburn hair in disarray and falling around her face. A look of panic washed over her features. "Oh, Emma. What are we ever to do without Josephine?" She looked out the window as if seeing doom riding up to their doorstep. Then she whipped her head around. "You must find us some help. Your father says he's exhausted all possibilities, but there surely must be *some* properly trained servants in this godforsaken wilderness—"

"I'm sure there are, Mother," Emma said, doing her best to calm her mother's rising anxiety. "Why, I know the Wilkersons have a full staff." Or so Violet had informed her. "And there must be other placement agencies—if not in Denver then in some other larger cities. If need be we can place an advertisement for help."

Her father had told Emma she must do all she can to help her mother get well. And Emma knew her mother could not function without servants. At very least a lady's maid, cook, and housemaid or two. The house wasn't all that large; and the work was not as intensive as a larger estate would demand. Surely she would be able to find suitable help, and her father would pay whatever it cost—of that Emma had no doubt.

After she spoke reassuringly with her mother for some time, answering her questions about trivial things and assuring her the grasshoppers would not be back, her mother took her hands in her own and said in a raspy voice, "Emma, my sweet darling girl, you must stop wandering off. You are giving your father grief and making me sick with worry. It's time you married. And Randall is the perfect choice—"

"But, Mother. I don't know. He hasn't—"

At this, her mother smiled—a knowing, mischievous smile. One that never failed to send Emma's stomach into twists. *Here it comes—the lecture.* But she didn't have the heart to argue with her mother in such a weak state. She must do her best to cheer her mother up.

"A young woman like you needs a husband. Someone to care for her and keep her safe. Especially here, in such a dangerous place. So many dangers . . ." Her mother's voice trailed off, and her eyelids closed heavily.

"Yes, Mother," Emma said, knowing compliancy was the best course. She'd wanted to tell her that Randall had not made any such intentions known to her, but she could see her mother was drifting off to sleep. She set the bottle back down on the table, certain this "medicine" was doing her mother more harm than good. Maybe she could ask Lucas about laudanum. Would he know of its dangers, if there were any?

Thinking about Lucas brought a rush of conflicted feelings into her heart. She could almost feel the warmth of his arms around her waist. And she would never forget how he'd looked at her with such need, pulling her close, about to kiss her.

She closed her eyes and imagined that kiss, feeling his soft, warm lips teasing hers, his hand running through her hair. A kiss that set her whole body on fire.

Footsteps shook her abruptly from her reverie. She jumped to her feet, shaky and weak-kneed.

"Emma," her father said quietly, noting his wife asleep. He gestured her to come out into the hall.

"Randall Turnbull has sent word that he will be calling on you at three."

"Today? What time is it now?" A flutter of panic struck her. She'd only seen him briefly all these months, turning down his requests to pay her a visit. The thought of him visiting her stirred a long-slumbering excitement. Hadn't she decided she'd been unkind to him, ignoring him, when he was practically the only true friend she had? Even if he didn't love her or want to marry her, he was still her friend, and she missed him.

"It's quarter to two. You have plenty of time to get ready."

It was so much harder to dress and do her hair without Josephine's help, but she would manage. She'd been learning to manage without many things since moving to Colorado. At least Randall wouldn't scrutinize her hairstyle or dress the way some men might. Suddenly she recalled what Lucas had said to her that morning: *"Miss Bradshaw, you could be dressed in sackcloth with ashes streaked across your face, and I don't think there'd be a more beautiful woman in all the earth."*

The words sent a shiver across her neck. Randall had never said anything so romantic to her. *Give him a chance*, she chided herself. Randall, for all his gregariousness, had a streak of shyness. She thought of his playful smile and gentle manner. She was fond of him. She smiled, about to run off to her room to wash and prepare for his visit.

"Emma," her father said, standing sternly in the middle of the hall.

She stopped, the tone of his voice making her freeze.

"I've been patient with you, knowing that moving out here has been . . . an adjustment. However, I will only tolerate so much unruly behavior—"

Emma raised a hand impulsively, about to protest, but her father's severe look made her shut tight her mouth.

"It is highly improper for you to go gallivanting out of town. Why, you were thrown from your horse and could have died. And you are spending too much time outside the safety of this community. There are dangers out on the range—and not just natural ones. You are young and attractive, and there are men out there without scruples, dangerous men . . ." He cleared his throat and looked off at nothing, thoughtful. "There is plenty to do in

Greeley, and fine young churchgoing women for you to associate with." He turned back to her. "And I do not want you anywhere around that veterinarian. Do you hear me?"

Emma must have made a noise, because her father grabbed her wrist forcefully and glared at her. Emma trembled at his rising fury. He seethed the words, "I mean it, Emaline. The man's trouble and uncouth. I've learned that he'd fought in the war—in the *Confederacy*. Do you know what this means? He killed Union soldiers. Maybe even someone we knew, one of our neighbors, our friends."

Emma pulled away from her father's grip. Who cared what side he fought on in the war? That was ten years ago. She didn't know how old Lucas was, but he must have been young when he joined up. A teenager. She thought of the hundreds of thousands of lives lost in the war, and although she had been a child during those horrible years of bloodshed and devastation, she did know that those on both sides had thought their cause was just. And she imagined Lucas would never willingly kill anyone—not unless he was forced to.

Emma looked at her father, at a loss for words. He stepped back and looked down his nose at her. "Your suitor will be here shortly. I suggest you be grateful there is a refined, educated man who is interested in your hand in marriage—"

"What?" Emma's stomach twisted in knots again. Had her father been talking to Randall—or worse—to Randall's father? Was this some sort of a scheme on their part? She knew her father had something to do with Randall's accompanying her on the train, but marriage? Was Randall involved in this plan? Or had he come to her father to ask her hand in marriage? It was possible, but hardly likely. They'd barely spoken more than a few sentences over the last few months. And why now? What would prompt Randall to suddenly think to propose to her?

She could only think of one reason—his father. Her life was barreling out of control, like a runaway horse.

"Just go get ready," her father said in his no-nonsense tone.

Emma's feet felt glued to the floorboards. None of the protests she meant to utter could get past the huge rock lodged in her throat. She stood unmoving as her father spun around and headed into the bedroom where her mother lay half-conscious. The door shutting in her face seemed like an exclamation mark at the end of a sentence.

Her mind went numb and quiet. So much had gone on in these last days, and her emotions were in turmoil. She couldn't think a clear thought. Then she heard her parents' loud whispering—the words seeping under the door to her ears.

It was clear they were arguing about her. She caught snatches of sentences that were reiterations of her father's disapproval of Emma's behavior and her need to marry. A pause ensued, followed by her mother saying, "But will he agree?"

"He already has," her father answered succinctly. "It's all been arranged."

"And what about Lynette? Any word from the doctor?"

"Only that she must stay in bed. There is still hope." His voice grew dark and solemn.

She gasped. *Still hope? Hope for what?* Emma pondered. *Oh no—he can't mean the baby, can he?*

A horrible sick feeling filled Emma's stomach, making her suddenly queasy. Could Lynette lose the baby this late in her pregnancy? She then heard her father.

"All the more reason to hurry this engagement. The sooner Emma marries . . ."

Emma couldn't make out the rest of his words; he began walking across the floor and the clacking of his shoes muddled the sound. And her mother continually moaning, "Oh dear, oh dear," didn't make it any easier to hear. Emma's chest constricted, and she had trouble drawing a breath.

I should get to my room and change. Oh, what will I say to Randall? The last thing she felt up to doing was entertaining company. And there was no one here yet to prepare tea or offer him any food. The temporary cook her father had hired wouldn't be here until five o'clock to prepare their dinner. But she couldn't concern herself with such trivial things right now. Perhaps they could take a walk. Maybe even stop in and visit Lynette. But would she be up to visitors? Why hadn't anyone told Emma about Lynette's condition? Once again, it was clear no one was telling her anything. It was as if she wasn't even a part of this family, with her life being arranged neatly for her without her consent.

She fumed as she hurried to her room to wash up and change her clothes. But all the while, as she readied herself and brushed out her long hair, she thought about Lynette and the baby. About how awful it would be if she lost this one too. She couldn't imagine how Lynette could bear it. Or what her brother or father would think.

No wonder her father was pushing marriage on her once more.

Chapter 20

E MMA FELT SO FLUSTERED WHEN the front doorbell rang that
she nearly tripped over her feet to answer the door. She could
hardly focus with her emotions in such turmoil—anger at her father,
disgust at her mother, worry over Lynette, annoyance at her
brother. And underneath it all was an unbearable ache that made
her want a man's strong arms wrapped around her. A man to take
her away from all this anguish and fear and make her feel safe and
loved.

When she threw open the door, she found Randall standing on
the stoop with a bouquet of beautiful red roses in one hand and a
bulky wrapped package in the other. He was dressed in a smart
three-piece wool suit and looked as dashing as always. He tipped
his hat at her, revealing an unusual nervousness in his demeanor.
His smile was a welcoming shoal of warmth in this utterly dreary,
depressing day. The heavy weight lifted from her heart upon seeing

his sweet smile looking upon her with adoration. How had she forgotten what a comfort he was to her?

"Oh, Randall. I'm so glad you're here. Come in," she said, ushering him inside. In a whisper, she confided, "I think it best if we took a walk." She tipped her head to the back of the house, and even though she could hear nothing from where they stood, Randall immediately understood the gist of her comment. How many times had they snuck out of his house when they'd been children, to get away from the scrutiny of adults?

"There's a park nearby. We can talk there," he said, his comforting tone washing over her like warm sunshine.

She set the roses down on the hutch and grabbed her long woolen coat from the entry closet and put it on. Then she picked up her bonnet and tied the strings under her chin. Randall waited with the patience of a man who'd grown up with four fashion-conscious sisters, and his eyes told her he was in no hurry. She was grateful for his calm, gentle spirit after the aggravation of the last few hours.

Once she was ready, he took her arm and they went out into the brisk afternoon, a steady wind blowing around them as they walked. Emma tucked her head into her warm collar, wondering if the park would be too cold to enjoy. But when they'd walked the few blocks to the small corner park with the whitewashed gazebo in the center, the wind abated, and sunlight streaked through breaks in the clouds.

"Oh, it's so good to get out of the house," she said, the breeze helping to whisk away her sour mood. She breathed deeply, relishing the fresh mountain air, so different from New York's muggy, thick air. Summer had vanished overnight, and it appeared fall might as well. She smelled snow on the air.

Randall sat her down on one of the ornate scrolled ironwork benches and took both her hands in his and rubbed them together to warm them. She flushed at his forwardness, for his touch seemed so intimate for some reason. He then handed her the package he'd been carrying.

She gave him a big smile. "What is this? It's not my birthday—"

"I know," he said sweetly. "It's something I ordered for you a while back. It only just came in on the train yesterday."

Puzzled, Emma took the nicely wrapped package festooned with blue satin ribbons and set it in her lap. It had an odd shape to it, and was about as large as a bread box. She shot Randall a glance expressing her suspicion. What might he have ordered that would have taken so long to get here—and from where?

"Go ahead," he urged, his childlike excitement spilling over. Suddenly she was back in the playroom at his house, looking at the pile of presents he had just gotten under the Christmas tree. She was aware of how easy it was to sit with him, to laugh and share her innermost feelings without worrying what kind of impression she might make.

Randall—she hadn't seen him in all those years, yet she felt as if they'd never lived apart. She knew him so well, and he her. How could she ever feel this comfortable with any other man?

Why had she forgotten this when she came out to Colorado? She had presumed he had changed, now that he was living and working with his father. But he hadn't—not at all. One look told her he was the same kind, sweet boy she'd spent many a summer with. And his expression showed how much he cared for her. Was he merely shy about his feelings? Maybe he just needed time to say just what he felt. All this time she'd thought he didn't really care for her, but now she realized how wrong she was. And how badly she had treated him by practically ignoring all his advances. And being so unforgiving about his lack of help at the picnic. Maybe he hadn't really seen that cowboy paw at her.

She carefully untied the ribbons, then worked at peeling back the tape binding the package.

He laughed at her slow, meticulous method of opening his present. "Oh, just rip it open," he said with a chuckle.

She showed mock scorn in her frown. "Now, that's an improper way to unwrap a package. Besides, I want to keep this lovely wrapping. It's so pretty. I can't imagine you bought it anywhere in Greeley."

A flush of red tinted his ears. "No, it's from France, actually . . ."

Her brows lifted. *France?* She finally got the stubborn bits of tape to cooperate and unwrapped his gift. She gave out a little gasp at seeing the beautiful French handmade paper—a whole block of it—and a set of very expensive inks. His gift had cost a small fortune, and although she knew it probably did not set him back financially in any way, the fact that he had taken time to special-order these wonderful drawing supplies all the way from Europe touched her greatly.

"So you can create the finest botanical drawings this side of the Mississippi," he said, his smile full of joy, but at the same time a bit self-conscious and worried. "Do you like them? I mean, did I buy the right kind of paper? The merchant I wrote to suggested this for the kind of fine detail you do—"

Emma's heart soared. No one had given her such a thoughtful, useful gift. She leaned over and gave Randall a kiss on his cheek, which made his face turn bright red. She had never kissed him before, and a girlish giggle came out of her mouth.

"Oh, Randall, it's perfect! You have made my day." She ran her hand over the lovely texture of the pressed paper. "I'll be able to create wonderful illustrations with this paper. And the ink! This is the finest ink in the world." She looked into his molasses-brown eyes and lost herself in their depths. "Thank you so much. You don't know how much this means to me."

Randall seemed completely flustered at her words, as if he wanted to throw his arms around her. But they were adults now, and such playful affection had to be curtailed. He once more took her hands in his, and as the sun baked the grass around them, the intoxicating scent of mowed lawn ushered a sense of peace into her heart.

There was hope, she thought. Hope that in the midst of this new, challenging, and frightening life in the wilderness she could find a rock to sit on, to give her perspective. Randall seemed in that moment to be just the refuge she truly needed. He accepted her for who she was, and encouraged her dreams. Maybe, together, they could make a life here—or better yet, in New York, as she had earlier hoped.

She dared ask him the question that had been prodding her mind all these months. "Have you considered moving back to New York? I mean, after you get your father's books in order? Surely he could hire an accountant to do what you do?"

"I have. It's what I want more than anything." He took a look around him. "I'm not cut out for the Wild West. I . . . feel so out of place here." He shook his head. "But, I can't see any way to leave. My father would never allow it."

"I don't understand." And she didn't. His father could afford to hire the best accountant in the country. Randall didn't answer her. He gazed off into space, a frown deeply etched on his face.

A sense of disappointment welled up inside her. "What if you just . . . leave? What could he do? You're a capable man. Surely you—"

"Emma," he said, his tone cutting her to the quick. "Please." He blew out a long breath. "It's . . . complicated. For now, I must stay. Maybe one day—"

"You could go back to school. Finish your schooling and get your degree. You said you wanted to go into publishing—"

He turned and met her eyes, and his pained look confused her. Why was this such an unattainable dream? Why would he be so willing to give up? Just what power did his father wield over him? She couldn't imagine Randall giving in to his father over the issue of inheritance.

"That was just a fanciful dream. I'm sure in time I'll adjust to life out here. Look at all these people." He gestured to the houses on the street, although no one was outside at the moment. Most were busy at work—in their stores or in the fields. "They've made huge adjustments in their lives. They've found their place here."

But his look told her he imagined he never truly would. He was a city man, and he hadn't come out here on his own volition. He had been forced. Just as she had been. So why should either of them stay? This was not their dream.

He lifted his chin, shaking off his glum mood. He smiled at her, but his smile did not reach his eyes. "So, I've decided to make this life work for me. And I believe I could truly be happy here"—he once more met her gaze, but this time he seemed filled with longing—"if I had you by my side, making a life with me."

Emma sucked in a breath. Even though her father had implied Randall meant to propose to her, she hardly believed he would. Is that what he was doing? Proposing?

Before she could say a word, Randall reached into his vest pocket and pulled out a small box. Even more stunned, Emma watched him drop to one knee and open the box inches from her face. A shiny gold band with a row of sparkling diamonds rested on a velvet cushion.

"Emma Bradshaw," he said, his voice trembling and cracking, "I would like to ask your hand in marriage."

His words hung heavily on the air, and Emma stared at him in equal parts of astonishment and confusion. She heard her father's words in her head: *It's all been arranged. The sooner she marries . . .*

"I . . . I . . ." Emma willed herself to be calm. But coils of anger and irritation wrapped around her heart. She couldn't help blurt out the words, "But do you love me?"

Randall was taken aback at her question. No doubt he expected her to give him an answer. What was he thinking? He hadn't even courted her. Did he think that because they'd been childhood friends, that meant he truly knew her heart, her needs?

Oh why was she thinking these thoughts? He had just proposed to her, and now she was asking him intimidating questions. But she had to know. Did he truly love her? She couldn't imagine marrying anyone who didn't. *But do you even love him? Isn't that just as important?*

Randall pulled back, awkwardly holding the ring in his hand. His face filled with worry and exasperation. "Emma, I adore you. You must know that. Anyone can speak words of love. But . . . a man shows his love by his actions. By his honor, and the respect he shows his wife. I would be a faithful, loving husband to you. Do you doubt it?" he asked.

She sensed a panic in his tone, and she did so want to reassure him. She knew how hard this must be for him. But she wasn't ready for this. As much as she wanted to marry—and she felt no one could be a kinder, sweeter husband than he—upon hearing his actual proposal, she felt a rush of doubt. Did she love him? Could she grow to love him in time? Did it matter?

Maybe she was just expecting something unattainable. The romance she fantasized about—that all young women dreamed of—how real was that? Wasn't it more important to be practical and think of things like security and companionship? How could she marry anyone more suitable than Randall? She had to admit it—she couldn't.

So what if her father had perhaps suggested to Randall to propose? What if he had even bribed him in some way—with some monetary offer? She couldn't imagine Randall being swayed by an offer of money; that made no sense. And even if her father — or his — had pressured him to propose, would he really do so if he didn't want to?

As soon as that question came into her mind, her body washed cold. She knew the answer. She didn't doubt he would do so if his father had demanded it. So she had to ask; she just had to.

"Randall," she said, trying to sound as kind and gentle as she could. She even took his hand and gave it a little squeeze. "Is this really what *you* want?" She let out a trembling sigh, and her next words came out on paper-thin breath. "Do you really want to marry me?"

The tiny hesitation that flitted in his eyes before he spoke told all. Her heart sank.

"Of course I do, Emma. I truly believe we were meant for each other. I promise I'll do everything I can to make you happy — "

"Even move back to New York?"

He shut his mouth, and she could tell he fumbled for an answer. "If I can find a way to do so, I will. If that's what you really want. It might take some time . . ."

She bit her lip and looked out at the towering mountains sitting like silent sentinels in judgment of her. As if they were mocking her, challenging her to listen to her heart.

She looked down at the ring resting in his open palm. This offering of his. She should be happy. And he deserved happiness too. But could she make him happy?

Without meaning to, Lucas came to her mind. He'd married once, and she imagined he had been happy and in love. Looking forward to his baby, to being a father. And then, his wife died and he lost everything. *He'd lost everything he loved. I saw the pain in his eyes — his loss. And his need.*

She blew out a shaky breath upon realizing how much Lucas Rawlings might need *her*. Want her. There was no denying it; she'd seen it clearly in his eyes as he made to kiss her. He longed for her, and just the thought set a fierce longing loose inside her.

She closed her eyes, then opened them to gaze into Randall's questioning ones. She saw no need there. No fiery longing that cried out to her. All she saw was a sweet, kind friend who was probably asking to marry her because he'd been told to.

She felt suddenly tired and sad. Even if Lucas truly did love her, as Sarah had implied, her family would never approve of him. If she married him, she would ruin their lives, tear her family apart. And right now her family was teetering on the edge of disintegration—with her mother barely keeping her sanity and her brother drinking and Lynette ill and possibly about to lose her baby . . . No, she had to be sensible, practical. Find ways to bring peace and healing to her family. If she meant to live here in Greeley for the indeterminate future, she had to please her parents, and make life as easy on everyone as possible. If only for Lynette's sake. Maybe, once the baby was born, she could think about what she really wanted in life. She could pursue her dreams.

She looked down at the gifts Randall had given her, sitting beside her on the bench. Randall wanted her to pursue those dreams. He could give her a comfortable life, and she knew he would treat her lovingly and tenderly. Was it wrong to expect more than that?

"I'm sorry I've been so quiet, and I haven't answered your question," she said, her tone deeply apologetic. "I don't mean to hurt you, Randall. It is just so . . . sudden." She smiled at him, hoping to dispel his obvious distress. "Would you let me think about this awhile? Before I give you my answer?"

"Of course," he said, looking every bit the refined gentleman he was. "I realize it is a bit sudden . . ." He seemed to want to say more, but a silence grew between them, and he looked down at his feet. He slipped the ring back into his pocket without a word.

"Why don't we head back to my house?" she suggested. "I can certainly boil water, and a cup of tea sounds wonderful right now."

Randall nodded, seemingly appeased for the moment, and perhaps a bit relieved, Emma noted. Maybe he was hoping she'd say no. But how could she think that? He did look utterly crestfallen by her answer. But she hadn't said no. She would take some time and ponder his proposal. Although maybe it was silly to wait.

As he took her arm and led her down the street, she thought about Violet's gushing words and how she'd urged Emma to marry him. *"He's perfect. Don't let him slip away."* He did feel so right, next to her. And he was so handsome and educated. She could imagine his arms around her, his mouth on hers . . .

A flicker of hope danced in her heart. She imagined children with his deep-brown eyes and rusty-colored hair. She could picture him reading them books, telling adventurous stories with an embellished tone, the way he used to read to her when they were children. Randall Turnbull was a kind man with a tender heart. Surely she could grow to love him, in time—in the way a wife was meant to love her husband.

And if she married him, it would get her out of her house and out from under her father's harsh authority.

With that reassuring thought, she hugged her new drawing paper close and walked with Randall down the dirt road toward her home.

Chapter 21

EMMA'S FATHER BROUGHT THE HORSE and buggy to a stop in front of the Turnbull estate. Well, for Greeley it seemed like an estate, Emma thought, with the stone walkway lined with weeping willows, and a wraparound porch hugging the colonial-style house. It wasn't a palatial country mansion, but much bigger and elegant than any other house around—other than the Meekers' impressive two-story adobe home near the center of town. Even in the dim light of the lit lanterns hanging on posts down both sides of the walkway, Emma could tell Mr. Turnbull must employ a full-time gardener to maintain the elaborate hedgerows and perennial beds. So shortly after the grasshoppers had devastated most of the flora in the town, his yard appeared unscathed. But Emma concluded all she saw around her must have been newly planted—aside from the trees, which were bare this time of year anyway.

Emma had seen the Turnbull house from the street, but this was the first time she'd been invited inside. When Randall had sent an invitation to her whole family to come to dinner, a feeling of trepidation had washed over her. And now, as she climbed the steps in her most lovely silk gown and wearing her pearls and long lace gloves, an even greater sense of dread filled her. She stepped into the ornate entry, where the butler took her wrap and hat, then realized this was no small affair but rather a party populated by a dozen or more of the wealthiest citizens of Greeley.

Her mother, just behind her, let out a small cry of delight. "Oh, Emma," she said, hurrying to remove her coat and thrusting it at the butler, who stood at attention with his arms outstretched to take her things, "what a lovely, lovely home!"

Of course her mother would be impressed; the house oozed wealth. Emma noted Mr. Turnbull had spared no expense in crafting and furnishing his spacious home. From the intricate mahogany crown molding to the crystal chandeliers and sconces, his house was every bit the ostentatious home he had in New York. Emma imagined the party was due to Mrs. Turnbull's recent arrival in town, come to take in the "quaint festive holiday season" on the wild frontier—as her mother had put it. Emma had been told Randall's mother had managed to tear herself away from all her social obligations in Albany in order to pay her husband and son a visit.

How odd that his parents lived apart, Emma thought, as her mother practically dragged her into the parlor, where a dozen or more elegantly dressed guests mingled and spoke in animated voices. But, she recalled, for many years Randall's father traveled due to his dealings with the railroads and had hardly ever been home. They'd be used to living separate lives.

Her parents walked off to speak with the pastor and his wife, who were sitting on a settee across the room, and she blew out a breath of relief. Ever since Randall had proposed to her, her father had been stern and impatient with her. No doubt he'd hoped she would have given Randall an immediate answer. And during the last week, her mother acted as if the "engagement" was settled, trying to get Emma to talk about wedding plans, much to her dismay. She noted, grimly, that her mother had instantly perked up after hearing of Randall's proposal. Although, the news that Emma had found a placement agency in Omaha with just the right servants they required had greatly relieved her mother. Whether any would last long after arriving was another matter altogether.

A servant handed Emma a flute of champagne, and another offered her canapés from a silver platter. Spice-scented candles burned brightly along the sideboard loaded with hors d'oeuvres. A quick glance told her Randall was not in the room yet, but she spotted her brother and Lynette, and she could tell from the strain on Lynette's face that she was unwell. Was it wise for her to be out—and attending a party, no less? Emma imagined the doctor would have warned her if it posed a danger. So perhaps Lynette was better. The thought sent a wave of relief coursing through her. She would make it a point sometime this evening to talk with her. But for now, she wanted to visit with Violet, whom she spotted standing alongside her parents, who were engaged in deep conversation with the Wilkersons. She noted the wild twins were absent—no doubt home with a sitter. A wise decision, Emma thought with a smirk. She imagined their parents wouldn't have a moment to enjoy the party, trying to keep them from misbehaving.

Lily stood next to her mother, looking entirely bored, dressed in a gorgeous green silk gown, with her hair done up perfectly and adorned with a web of pearls. She truly was a beauty, Emma noted, wondering again why she hadn't yet married. Emma had hardly said more than a few words to Lily, she realized with guilt. She should make an effort to get to know her. Lily was a few years older than she, but there were so few young ladies close to Emma's age. Did Lily resent living out here, so far from the social life of high society? How did she spend her time?

As Emma made her way through the crowd of guests, she said polite hellos and nodded her head. She knew most from church. Aside from the Wilkersons and Edwardses, the elderly Mitchells, from Poughkeepsie, New York, and the Baxters—wheat farmers— were here in attendance. A few others were strangers to her, but she could tell by the dress and manners that they came from high society. Just before she reached Violet, though, a familiar booming voice erupted from a room off the parlor.

"Welcome, my dear friends," Ernest Turnbull said. "We're delighted you have come."

Emma turned and saw Randall's father, impeccably dressed with his wife clinging to his arm, entering the room. Mrs. Turnbull glittered with jewels on her arms and around her neck, looking every bit like a strutting pigeon, her large chest jutting out and her chin high.

They made their way around the room, welcoming their guests. Violet waved at Emma and Emma smiled back, holding back a chuckle as Violet made a funny face that was clearly an imitation of Mrs. Turnbull's manner. Then she felt a hand on her arm.

She spun and found Randall at her side. "Oh," she said, happy at seeing him, "I didn't see you come in."

He took her hand and squeezed it. With a kindly look he said, "I'm so glad to finally have you over to the house. Although, I've never been comfortable at such affairs. But now that you're here with me . . ."

His smile set her at ease. He added, "I suppose I should greet all the guests as well. And I need to reacquaint you with Mother. Will you join me?"

Emma nodded, allowing him to loop her arm around his. Beset by a case of nerves, she wondered whether Randall's mother would remember her after all these years. And she had hoped to avoid speaking to Mr. Turnbull, if at all possible. She couldn't imagine he thought all that highly of her, having seen her sitting with Sarah and her sons at the picnic. It puzzled her to think he would approve of Randall marrying her, but seeing her father now in close discourse with him, exchanging hearty laughs and knowing smiles, only reinforced Emma's suspicions that both fathers were somehow in collusion regarding Randall's proposal of marriage. The thought once more set Emma's anger churning, making her feel a pawn in their game of life.

Pushing these thoughts from her mind, she pasted on a smile and allowed Randall to make their rounds in the room. By the time they'd said hello to all the guests, a servant came into the parlor and rang the dinner bell. Randall led Emma to the dining room.

The table was beautifully set, with places for sixteen, which all the guests and their hosts filled. It had been months since Emma had had such an elegant repast, with so many courses of finely prepared food, served by three footmen serving dishes and clearing away plates. Mr. Turnbull, of course, had the finest china and silver, and it was clear he meant to impress his guests.

During dinner, Emma said little, allowing the light, friendly banter to flow over her while her restlessness and discomfort grew. Although she felt quite comfortable with the formality of the meal, she noticed both her father's and Mr. Turnbull's eyes often upon her, watching her warily. Randall seemed to take no notice of her mood, smiling gaily and behaving as expected — as the dutiful, well-mannered son of a wealthy railroad baron. Although he sat beside her, he seemed miles away, only occasionally throwing her a friendly smile. Violet was far down at the end of the table, sitting across from Lily, the two girls chatting amiably.

Despite all the company surrounding her and trying to engage her in conversation, Emma felt strangely empty and alone. She had a sudden wish to be out riding her horse across the open range, breathing in the refreshing mountain air, free from the scrutinizing gazes of the townspeople sitting around the table. She'd never felt this stifled and constricted in New York, even with all those people and the crowded streets. Here, she was under a magnifying glass; nothing she did went unnoticed.

Was she slowly becoming acclimated to living in the West? The thought struck her forcefully. Gradually over the months she had been setting down roots deep into the Colorado soil, and she realized now how she was coming to love the wide open space—not just loving it but also needing it. The stark beauty of the endless rolling land, the slow-moving wide river, and the majestic mountains changing color each day invigorated her spirit in a way she'd never experienced before. The Front Range spoke to her soul, but up until now she barely heard its whisperings. For the first time since moving here she wondered if she really would be happier back in New York.

And at the thought of leaving here to return to the East, a picture of Lucas Rawlings invaded her mind and made her heart ache with another, different kind of emptiness. Why did this cowboy unravel her so? Just picturing his rugged, handsome face and easy smile set her heart racing. And always she felt his strong arms around her waist, holding her gently but with a tenacity, as if he never wanted to let her go. And when she recalled the way he'd leaned toward her to kiss her, with his emerald eyes smoldering with desire . . .

She clenched her eyes shut, wanting to erase this night, this room, these people. She longed to be standing alongside the silvery Platte River, with the bowl of stars twinkling overhead, Lucas's arms drawing her close to his broad chest, his hands running through her hair, pulling her face to his, his tender lips hot on hers.

She could feel that kiss as if he'd already kissed her, as if his hands belonged on her body, caressing her skin, cradling her face. Her body washed hot, a fire surging through her limbs. Suddenly the room was too hot, the others around her too close. She couldn't seem to catch her breath.

As she reached for her glass of water with a shaky hand, nearly frantic to excuse herself and get out in the cold night air, Mr. Turnbull suddenly tapped his crystal glass and stood.

"Friends," he said boisterously, casting a glance at all his guests, "it pleases me to share with you some wonderful news. You all know my son, Randall"—he then gestured to Randall to stand—"who is here with the lovely Miss Emma Bradshaw."

Emma was stricken at his words and felt the blood rush from her face as all eyes turned her way. What was he doing? Why did he say that in front of everyone?

She looked to Randall, whose flushed face and puzzled expression showed he was also at a loss for understanding what his father was doing. He reached for her hand under the table and gripped it, then reluctantly stood, nodding politely to all the guests.

Emma looked first at her father, then her mother, then at Mrs. Turnbull. Each had a strange smug expression on their faces. Her throat constricted so tightly she could hardly draw in a breath. She gripped her napkin in her hands and kneaded it.

Without ever casting a glance her way, Mr. Turnbull continued his oratory. "So it is with great joy and delight that I have brought you all here tonight to announce the engagement of our son to the daughter of Mr. and Mrs. Charles Bradshaw—our long-time friends who have recently moved out here from New York."

A shock of horror shuddered through Emma. *What did he just say?* She shook her head as if she were underwater. Noises, words, sounds battered her as all the guests around the table began talking at once, smiling and laughing and reaching over to touch her arm, pat her on the shoulder. She heard "congratulations" and "we're so happy for you" and other similar sentiments, but the words sounded foreign and confusing, and all she could think of was to run, to leave this place and get far away.

And then her befuddlement turned to fury. Yet she could do nothing but force a smile and nod her head and act for all the world as if she was happy. As if she had truly agreed to marry Randall. She could hardly speak out in denial and contradict Mr. Turnbull. Not in his own home, and not in front of a roomful of honored guests. Guests that were her neighbors in this small town, with whom she had to live and face day after day.

She dared not look at Randall's father. Or her own. She knew what she would see on their faces—the threat they would silently give her should she dare speak out in dissent. How could they? How dare they? She had been led into a trap, and the door had been sprung. There would be no escape. Not unless she ran away. And she could hardly do that, without a penny to her name and no place to run to. No, her father had planned this well, just as he had done in the planning of their move to Colorado.

"Ah, the dessert." Mr. Turnbull gestured to the tall iced layer cake the footman brought in and set down on the sideboard, acting for all the world as if he'd done nothing offensive. Emma sat frozen in her seat, her fury now seeping away. Numbness set in, and her mind grew quiet. As cake and coffee were served and life went on as if nothing untoward had occurred, Randall leaned over and whispered in her ear.

"I am so sorry, Emma. I had no idea he would do that." He gave her cheek a little kiss, as if that would make it all better and she would overlook his father's presumption. Or her father's complicity. As if it had never mattered what answer she ultimately would have given Randall. As if it mattered not at all what she wanted.

Yet, she had no choice but to comply. She would marry Randall.

Chapter 22

THE FINE POWDER OF SNOW blanketed the streets, although by midmorning it had mostly melted, leaving the roads a muddy slush. Hoesta jogged alongside the flat bed as the draft horse snorted frosty steam out his nose, Lucas noting the dog delighting in the small drifts of snow, bounding along in a joyful mood—the first real snow of the season. It was only the first week of November, but the temperature had been unseasonably cold—usually the harbinger of blizzards in winter. Lucas as well felt an encroaching storm building in his heart, wondering if it would bury him. What would he do if he couldn't win Emma's heart? How could he face yet another long, miserable, lonely winter in his small cabin? Perhaps he would have been better off if he'd never met her.

He hadn't seen her in weeks—not since that day he'd dropped her at her house and her father yelled at him. Since then he'd buried himself in work, helping Eli and LeRoy finish stringing the last lines of barbed wire and replacing the barn siding and fixing latches to prepare for the eventuality of fifty-five head of horses needing shelter from the winter storms soon to beset the open range. He'd inoculated the horses and mules in town and on the outlying farms, and treated various infections and illnesses, and in all his meanderings around town had not seen the lovely Miss Emma Bradshaw. With the Edwards twins in school and the inclement weather keeping the boys from riding, Lucas had little excuse to glean from Violet any gossip about Emma, which he so desperately longed to hear.

Lately he'd been hearing packs of wolves and coyotes howling mournfully throughout the night, across the rivers. They echoed the sentiments in his soul, often keeping him up and robbing him of sleep. As a result, today, hauling the dozen bales of straw over to the Grange in preparation for the big harvest festival, he rode wearily, the chill only adding to his misery and the low-hanging dark clouds pregnant with snow adding to his gloomy mood.

Yet, he held out a glimmer of hope that he'd finally see Emma — as Mrs. Edwards had told him the Grange hall would be a flurry of activity today, with all the young ladies helping decorate for the annual affair. The last few years Lucas had helped with the fire pit outside, where a huge bonfire would be lit for those wanting to come outside and take a break from the dancing and festivities. His task this morning was to unload and position all the straw bales around the rock-lined circle, then go back to the ranch and load up the pile of firewood needed to last the night of the event.

When he pulled up in front of the Grange, he noticed two women dressed in heavy coats and hats trying to drag something large and unwieldy out the front doors. Bounding up the stairs with Hoesta yipping at his heels, he recognized Mrs. Wilkerson and one of the ladies that worked at the mercantile, Mrs. Prouel.

"Here, ladies, let me help you with that." Lucas reached down to assist with their large bulky item, unsure just what they were hauling out of the Grange.

The two women looked up from their struggle with a start.

"Oh, dear Mr. Rawlings, God bless you. Thank you." Mrs. Wilkerson patted what looked like a straw-stuffed man, righting the felt hat on its head. Lucas wondered why she was dressed in such fancy clothes for such an activity, but she always seemed to present a high-society appearance in every instance in which he'd seen her—as did her daughter, Lily. Perhaps in time, like so many other women who'd come out from the big cities to the Front Range, they'd come to see that more practical attire was in order.

Mrs. Prouel, a somewhat heavy-set lady lacking any airs, panted and wiped her hand across her brow. "We're fixing to set this fine gentleman on the lawn right outside the doors." She fiddled with the corncob pipe attached to his cloth mouth. The life-size straw man wore a farmer's overalls and red checkered shirt. "He's a dandy, doncha think?" she asked Lucas.

He nodded and hefted the manikin carefully, noting bits of straw falling out the sleeves. He tried to stuff them back in as the two women propped the double doors open.

"Oh, don't mind that," Mrs. Wilkerson said, waving her hand in dismissal. "We'll finish stuffing him once he's properly placed."

Lucas grinned. "Just point me in the right direction."

Once he had the straw man set up to welcome all at the entrance of the Grange, the ladies ushered him inside, eager to warm him up with hot cider and revitalize his waning energy with warm molasses cookies. He knew saying no would offend them, and accepting their invitation would give him the chance to come inside and see if Emma was there. So he stepped inside the spacious hall—which was still a bit cold although he saw a blazing fire in the stone hearth at the back of the room—and scanned across the faces of the dozen or so women busily working on crafts projects at the many long tables until his eyes lit upon Emma.

She had her back to him, and instead of her hair being coiled up in a bun and tucked under a bonnet, the long black locks spilled down over her shoulders. She wore a simple rose-colored skirt that flared out around her, the ruffles of her petticoats sweeping the tops of her shoes. An elegant white blouse hugged the curve of her waist. Lucas sucked in a breath, hardly able to move.

He took off his hat and slid off his sheepskin-lined coat, then draped it over his arm. The two ladies he had helped led him over to a table against the wall, to make sure he got his deserved refreshments. Mrs. Prouel continued talking at him, explaining all the projects they were constructing and where everything would go. He heard almost nothing she said; only smiled and nodded as he caught glances of Emma.

"Look," Violet said, spotting him, "there's Lucas. Lucas! Come see what we're making," she called out to him, waving him over.

Emma spun around, as did Lily Wilkerson, who stood at Emma's side. Even from where he stood, twenty feet away, he saw color rush to Emma's cheeks. He politely thanked Mrs. Prouel, who stuffed a hot mug of cider into one hand and three cookies in the other, then made his way over the young ladies at their table.

He kept a polite distance, although he wanted nothing more than to gather Emma up in his arms and kiss her. *Bide your time; the dance is only hours away.* This surely wasn't the place to let his emotions show, so he worked hard to keep a polite smile on his face, avoiding falling into those two deep blue pools belonging to the woman he loved.

He looked at Violet and asked, "So what are you busy ladies up to here?"

Although Violet eagerly answered in a long explanation, he didn't hear a word she said. He nodded at what he deemed were the right times, then, feeling about ready to jump out of his boots, tried to excuse himself. It was torture to stand so close to Emma without being able to touch her.

A glance across the room showed Emma's mother glaring at him with narrowed eyes. He could only imagine how she felt about him, with both her husband and her son taking such a dislike to him. But when she caught him looking at her, she hastily turned her head and began talking to Mrs. Edwards, who was busily attaching large cutout paper pumpkins to the walls. He then noticed Emma's sister-in-law sitting in a nearby chair, knitting. He was glad to see her looking so well, and she was now quite far along in her pregnancy.

"I'm so glad you're here," Lily Wilkerson said, drawing Lucas's attention. "I need to get some supplies out of the back closet, and they're up quite high."

Lucas didn't know Miss Wilkerson all that well. He'd spoken to her on occasion at her house and at the stables, when treating her horse—a fine Selle Francais jumper—but from just those few encounters, he felt uneasy around her. He'd met women like her before but none so forward in their flirtations. Granted, it was hard to take his eyes off her; she was stunning. But he sensed much of her beauty was superficial, only skin deep. And he found her brazen advances uncomfortable; he didn't want to hurt the young woman's feelings, but hoped not to encourage them either. Was she hunting for a husband? If so, why hadn't she married yet? Someone as beautiful and cultured as she was could surely land a husband of fine breeding with little effort.

So, after setting down his hat and coat, he followed her into the back room with trepidation, not wanting to leave Emma's side. But he was the only man around, and he wouldn't want to appear unwilling to help any lady requiring his assistance. Yet, all he could think about was Emma and the many words he needed to say to her.

Lily stopped at the entrance to the long, dark closet at the back of the room. A wide, high shelf ran the length of the closet on both sides, and boxes were piled up to the ceiling. She pointed to a ladder resting against the back wall.

"I hope it won't be any bother, Lucas," she said, her voice silky and inviting. "I need all these down." She pointed at a stack of boxes directly above her. "These six."

"All right," Lucas said, feeling a bit claustrophobic and uncomfortable in the small space with her. She was wearing an intoxicating perfume, which wafted around him as he moved the ladder into position and climbed up the rungs to reach the boxes.

"You can hand them down to me, one at a time," she said sweetly.

Lucas felt her eyes keenly on him as he maneuvered the towering stack carefully to take down the top one without toppling the rest. As he gave her the first box, her hand brushed against his. The rickety ladder wiggled unsteadily, and as he sought to regain his balance, Lily hurried to set the box down, then wrapped her hands around his calves.

"Steady there, Lucas." She stood there with her hands on him for a long time, and Lucas felt the sweat trickle down the back of his neck.

"I'm fine, Miss Wilkerson—"

She let go and huffed. "Please, call me Lily. I can't bear to hear you speak so formally to me."

All Lucas could do was nod. He hurried to retrieve the rest of the boxes, anxious to get out of this confining space and back to Emma's side. The minutes dragged as he handed one box after another to Lily. Finally, he climbed down and set the ladder back where he'd found it.

"You are coming to the dance tomorrow, Lucas? I'd be so disappointed if you weren't there."

Lucas swallowed and weighed his words. "I plan to be there . . ." He was about to say "Miss Wilkerson" but expected he'd get another scolding.

Lily took two of the boxes in her arms and started back to the hall. "Oh, you have heard the news, haven't you?"

Lucas followed behind her carrying two of the heaviest boxes. As they came close to the table where Emma worked alongside Violet, arranging dried flowers into some sort of bouquets, Lily announced in a particularly loud voice, "Emma is engaged to be married. To Randall Turnbull." She spun around to catch his reaction. "Isn't that just wonderful?" She tipped her head to Emma and said to her, "Although, you two haven't set a date, right?"

Lucas nearly dropped the boxes. An icy coldness washed over him, and he was sure the stricken look on his face was as plain as day. His heart seemed to stop beating, and his hands grew sweaty. *Engaged? Then I'm too late.*

He chanced looking at Emma's face. She gave him an odd look—perhaps she was puzzled by his shocked reaction.

Oblivious to the sickly feeling washing over him, Violet spoke up cheerily. "I'm sure it will be so grand! And, Emma, Randall is so wonderful." She turned to Lucas and said, "Have you met Emma's fiancé? Surely you know his father, Mr. Turnbull?"

Lucas shook his head. He forced the words out of his mouth past the huge rock lodged in his throat. "No, I . . . haven't had the pleasure . . ."

It took all his resolve not to run. But he knew he had to congratulate Emma on her news, although to him the engagement was as dour a tiding as a funeral announcement. And a part of him did die in that moment, along with all hope of ever holding her in his arms again. A pain streaked through his heart as if he'd been stabbed.

"Are you unwell?" Lily asked him, leaning close and taking his arm.

He fought the urge to shake her off. Instead, he pulled back and willed his heart to stop pounding so hard. After blowing out a shaky breath he hoped no one detected, he turned to Emma and with as kind a voice as he could muster, said, "Well, Miss Bradshaw, my congratulations. I . . . wish you all the happiness in the world." No truer words could he speak, although he'd hoped that happiness would have been with him, not with that East Coast dandy. He kept his head tipped respectfully, not wanting her to see his face.

Get out, before you make a fool of yourself and say something you'll regret. You had your chance and you lost it.

"Thank you, Lucas," Emma said.

Although Lucas didn't want to meet her eyes, something in her voice snagged him. He took a chance and looked at her. Instead of the happiness over such a joyous prospect as marriage, a heavy sadness marred her face. It was as if he could see through her eyes to the bottom of those blue pools and deep into her heart. It was clear—at least to him—that underneath the smile she wore was a world of hurt and pain. Why and how he knew this, he was uncertain. But her heart spoke to his without words, in a speech all its own.

Her unhappiness shook him. Just what was going on in Emma Bradshaw's life? Why would she marry this man if she didn't love him? He couldn't imagine anyone—not even her hard-handed father—forcing her into a marriage she didn't want. But this was hardly the time or place to ask her questions.

His head swam in confusion, and his heart hurt almost more than he could bear. He excused himself in a mumble and collected his coat and hat. Then, with a polite nod to the three young ladies at the table, he hurried outside and down the steps to his wagon.

A cold blast of wind cut through his clothes and chilled him to his core. He put on his coat and buttoned it up, knowing it would do little to chase the chill now settling in his bones. Sarah had remarked on the ice that encased his heart, after she had seen the blue pools in her vision. Emma was to be the one to melt that ice. Lucas chortled bitterly. There was no chance it would melt now.

She's fleeing one cage only to be locked up in another. She'll never be free to bloom and grow, married to a man like that. She'll be trapped in a small house in Greeley, confined to the expectations of society and her stuffy husband. A woman like Emma needed the wide open spaces of the West in order to breathe. In order to be truly happy. She needed a man who could set her free from her cage.

But he'd had his chance to declare his love. And now that chance was lost to him. And so was she.

Numb and defeated, Lucas climbed up onto the bench seat of the buckboard and swung the horse around to the fire pit. He stepped down and began unloading the straw bales with the grappling hook, throwing them to the ground. He worked efficiently to move the bales into place, finishing quickly in order to leave the Grange as soon as he could. He couldn't foster the thought of being there another moment—on the off chance that Emma might come outside to speak with him.

Out of the corner of his eye, he saw someone come down the front steps. His pulse quickened and his body froze up, until he saw that it wasn't Emma. It was her sister-in-law, taking careful steps down to the ground. He looked around but didn't see anyone else outside. Where was she going?

To his surprise, she came over to him.

"Ah, I'm glad to find you still here, Mr. Rawlings," she said in a friendly tone. She was dressed in a warm long woolen coat and hat, and rested one hand on her abdomen.

Lucas blew out a breath, trying to chase away the tumultuous emotions that held him sway. He set down the hook and tipped his hat at her.

"Miz Bradshaw, it's good to see you well. You look rested and hale."

She gave him a genuine smile. "I am. Thank you." She rested a gloved hand on his wrist as if steadying herself.

"Here, please sit down." He led her over to one of the straw bales and she sat, a bit out of breath. "Do you need my help—?"

"Oh no; I came out to speak with you."

Lucas's eyebrows raised, and he felt a rush of discomfort. He felt awkward talking to this woman whom he'd never properly met—and whose husband loathed him.

He cleared his throat. "I suppose I should apologize for my behavior that day, at the park—"

"Nonsense. It is I, Mr. Rawlings, who should be apologizing to you. I am entirely grateful to you for what you did. I have no doubt you saved my life that day, and I've been remiss about thanking you properly."

"Ma'am, you don't need to thank me. I'm just glad I'd been there to help. Your husband . . . he didn't . . . he wasn't aware that the horse had been stung—"

"It was a brave thing you did, and you put yourself in harm's way for me. And for my baby." She smiled and once more laid her hand over the child in her womb.

Just then the doors to the Grange swung open. Emma's mother stepped out, and upon spotting her daughter-in-law, waved her hand in a frantic motion. She called out, "Lynette, you'll catch your death of cold out there. Come back inside."

Lynette merely waved and nodded, then turned her attention back to Lucas. The older woman hesitated, then headed back inside, the doors closing behind her.

"Are you cold, Miz Bradshaw? Perhaps I should help you —" He stood before her, offering his arm.

But she shook her head and smiled once more, her cheeks rosy from the biting wind. "I feel better than I have in years. I actually enjoy this refreshing cold. The summer heat was nearly my undoing. And then I was confined to bed rest for nearly two months. But the doctor assures me I'm out of danger." She added, her tone joyful, "And the baby is healthy and strong, praise God."

Lucas nodded, truly happy for her, although every time he saw a woman so pregnant, his mind flitted back to Alice and how happy she was before she gave birth. And how she'd had no indication that anything would go wrong when she went into labor.

Lucas shoved those painful memories down forcefully. *Lord*, he prayed with his eyes closed, *don't let this be the fate of this gentle woman. Bless her with an easy delivery and full recovery.*

He opened his eyes, feeling a welcoming sense of calm blanket him. "When are you due?" he asked her.

"The end of the year. A Christmas baby," she said, excitement in her eyes.

"I'm happy for you." He added, "That was right nice of you to come out here to speak with me, Miz Bradshaw. And what about your husband? Is he happy about the baby?"

He asked this in curiosity, knowing he was probably overstepping. But after having witnessed her husband's rude, inconsiderate behavior — not to mention his associating with those detestable ranchers — he wondered if the man was treating his wife properly.

Lynette's eyes flashed with apprehension. "He is." She drew in a shaky breath and looked across the open expanse of snow covering the yard. "But I'm concerned."

It wasn't his place to pry, or to warn her about her husband's risky activities, but maybe she had no one to talk to. He sat down at the end of the straw bale and faced her, waiting to see if she would say more.

She finally turned and looked at him, worry in her face. "He drinks—as I'm sure you've seen. Which is of great concern and a source of distress to both myself and his parents. You can imagine . . . since the Bradshaws chose to move to Greeley mostly due to the temperance philosophy. I sometimes wonder if my father-in-law pushed to move here in an attempt to get Walter to stop drinking."

"So, his drinking isn't anything new?"

She let out a sad sigh. "No, not by any means, Mr. Rawlings. He started drinking heavily after I lost the first baby . . ." She turned to him once more. "I lost three, and after each loss, he drank more. I'm hoping . . . well, you can see why I'm so glad I'm finally going to have a baby. Walter wants so badly to have children, as do I . . ."

Lucas's heart went out to her. He of all people knew what it felt like to lose a baby. His gut wrenched as memories of holding his dead infant son in his arms flooded into his mind. He shook his head and stood.

"Then, I'm sure once the baby is born, things will . . . get better." He reached for her arm, wishing he could warn her somehow about the unscrupulous ranchers her husband had been seen with. But he couldn't burden her with this. He could only hope that her husband would realize what danger he was in, before it was too late. And that once their baby was born, he'd stay home more and stop drinking.

But Lucas suspected it would take more than the arrival of a baby to get a man like Walter Bradshaw to shape up for his wife and child. That man had a mean side, and if Lucas had ever seen a more arrogant, self-absorbed man this side of the Mississippi, he couldn't think of one. In a way, he felt sorry for Lynette. She deserved a better man.

So does Emma, he thought, the pain of his loss once again emptying him, leaving him with an unquenchable, unbearable thirst deep in his soul.

He walked in silence, lost in his thoughts, leading Lynette to the entrance and up the stairs to the doors.

"Thank you for listening to me," she told him. "I . . . don't really have anyone to talk to, and I know so few people here in town."

"My pleasure, ma'am," Lucas said, tipping his hat to her and retreating down the stairs. He turned back and said, "You take care, now, Miz Bradshaw. I look forward to saying hello to that baby of yours soon."

She gave him another warm smile and went inside.

Lucas then strode over to the wagon, hopped up to the seat, and headed out of town, knowing the way home but feeling utterly lost.

Chapter 23

As Randall helped Emma out of the carriage, she leaned close to him, allowing him to link his arm in hers. The dark night was cold and moonless, but the cheery lights shining through the Grange Hall windows beckoned with warmth and shelter, and a fire blazed in the fire pit nearby.

Drifts of snow lay piled along the edges, and more snow had been forecasted. Emma imagined her cheeks must be red from the biting wind, but thankfully they would be inside soon. Randall turned to look at her as they walked carefully up the icy walkway.

"How are you managing?" he asked.

She smiled to reassure him, knowing he meant the ice, but the question reached her heart with deeper meaning. She'd thought she had finally accepted the fact that she was to be Randall's wife, knowing it was a wise and practical decision. But ever since she saw Lucas yesterday morning in the hall, doubts assailed her. And along with those doubts seeped in a malaise of disappointment and the feeling that she was settling for something less than what she wanted. Not that she could truly fault Randall in any way. He was everything a woman of her background and breeding should desire. So why did she feel so unsure? Was she just being haughty, expecting something she didn't deserve—or that wasn't possible?

Her mother's words railed at her, over and over. How women were meant to be a support to their husbands. That in being a wife and mother, she would find her true fulfillment and joy. She just had to submit and give it time. And she wanted to believe this was true. Yet, last evening, while her mother rambled on excitedly about a spring wedding for her, and all the many things they must do to prepare, Emma could not stir up any enthusiasm. She just sat and listened, working on a sketch, while her mother went on and on, more cheerful than Emma had seen her in months.

With Lynette's baby soon to come, and now her own engagement to Randall, Mother has practically recovered from her melancholy. And it was good to see her mother so well. So Emma felt guilty having any doubts about the engagement, even though she had been tricked into it. She knew she could have done worse—much worse. Her father could have arranged to marry her off to someone wholly detestable, and then what would she have done? No, she told herself as Randall escorted her into the brightly lit and cheerily decorated hall, she should be happy. And grateful to Randall. She had no doubt he would be a kind, attentive husband. That's what she wanted most of all, wasn't it?

She allowed him to take her coat and hat as she looked around the crowded, noisy room. Already it seemed as if most of the town was here, all dressed in their finest holiday outfits and happily eating, drinking, and talking. Lively music played from the back of the hall, and Emma spotted the musicians in the far corner next to the roaring hearth. A rousing bit of fiddling soared across the overly warm room.

She turned to Randall, who had also taken off his overcoat and given it to the woman who had greeted them at the door. She studied Randall's face, knowing how uncomfortable he was in large crowds.

"Why, you seem awfully flushed," she told him.

He fanned his hand at the perspiration gathered on his brow. He hesitated before speaking. "I . . . I do feel a bit hot."

She took his arm again. "Well, let's get you something to drink. There's punch over there." She led him to a long table that held a huge glass punchbowl and glasses. Platters of cookies, cakes, and other sweets filled the table. Emma was glad she'd eaten a substantial dinner before coming, as these treats looked delectable. The new cook her father had gotten from Omaha was wonderful — an older Irish woman with a serious personality and a talent for spicing her dishes. The Irish lamb stew they'd had tonight had been delicious. And met with her parents' approval — which was all that mattered. Her mother couldn't stop praising the cook's talent.

"This is quite the celebration," Randall said, wiping his forehead with his handkerchief and looking around. Emma saw his eyes rest on a gathering of men at a table near the back. She spotted his father standing and speaking, as usual, to a number of men who were listening attentively — her father and brother among them. *Mr. Turnbull seems to always need an audience.*

Emma couldn't help feeling anger toward her father and Randall's for the way they'd arranged this marriage without her consent. But there was nothing to be done for it now, she kept reminding herself. She had to make the best of it, hoping in time she could find it in her heart to forgive them both. But for the moment, she let her ire simmer. Well, she would have a good time tonight. There were so few dances held in Greeley, and she hadn't danced in ages.

She looked over at the many couples on the dance floor in front of the band. They all seemed merry and gay, and her foot started tapping to the music. She was unfamiliar with the dance they were doing, but it looked fun, and she was eager to join in. Her eyes located Violet and a few other young women from church, dancing with older men as their partners. Even from where Emma stood, she could tell Violet was laughing.

"Come," she said to Randall, "let's go join Violet and dance."

Randall's face turned ashen. "I am not a good dancer," he confessed. "I'm afraid I'll make a fool of myself—and of you, when I step on your feet."

"Nonsense," she said, tugging playfully on his arm. "It doesn't look all that difficult."

He conceded with a nod, and they threaded through the crowd until they arrived at Violet's side, just as a song concluded. Violet's cheeks were cherry red, and she picked up her fan from a nearby chair and fanned herself, then turned toward her dance partner.

"Thank you for the dance, Mr. Fields."

Emma hadn't seen this man before; he looked old enough to be Violet's father, but she didn't seem to care a bit. He gave a polite tip of his head while twirling his moustache, then trotted off to the refreshment table in his old-fashioned suit and two-toned shoes.

"Oh, hello!" Violet said to Emma and Randall, plopping down in the chair, still winded from her exertion.

"Who was that?" Emma asked.

"Oh, Mr. Fields. He's one of my neighbors. He and his wife are wheat farmers. He just loves to dance, and his wife has terrible bursitis. That's her over there." Violet gave a little wave to a portly lady sitting against the wall with a plate of desserts resting in her lap. The woman gave a little wave back while stuffing something in her mouth.

Emma chuckled. "No young eligible bachelors around for you to dance with?" Emma asked. Randall smiled at her side, politely saying nothing on the topic. She scanned those around them, recognizing a few townspeople. She also noted Lily now standing alone against the wall, eyeing the front door.

Emma whispered to Violet, "I wonder who she is waiting for."

Violet chuckled and wiggled her eyebrows. "I guess we'll see."

Emma laughed, then turned to Randall. "Shall we try to dance this next . . . jig . . . or whatever it is?"

"They're called reels," Violet offered. "A Scottish dance. Lots of fun, and a lot of spinning and twirling. If you watch a few, you'll catch on."

"I think watching's a splendid idea," Randall said, looking every bit relieved to put off dancing for a bit. He sat suddenly in a chair, and Emma saw a distressed look come over his features.

"Are you unwell, Randall?" He did look more and more pale by the minute. "Perhaps I should get you some more punch." She noticed he had drunk his entire glass already.

"Please, you don't need bother—"

She laid a hand on his shoulder and felt him tremble under her touch. She then pressed her hand against his forehead.

"Why, you're hot."

He nodded, and his breath came out in shallow spurts.

"I mean, you're feverish. You should be in bed," she said, worry welling up inside her. She looked around for Randall's mother, then spotted her huddled in the midst of a group of the wealthy women of the town—not surprisingly. Her own mother was busy chatting with the pastor's wife next to the refreshments, but cast a curious glance her way.

"We should get you home, right away," Emma said. "Wait here."

Randall hung his head, and Violet sat down beside him, her face full of worry as well.

Emma made her way to Mrs. Turnbull, who looked with alarm at her son, then instructed Emma where to find their driver, who she could instruct to take Randall home.

When she returned to Randall's side, he looked even worse. "Come," she said, "I'll help you get into the carriage." She exchanged a look with Violet, saying, "I'll be back shortly."

"My parents' driver is here," he barely muttered, allowing Emma to take his arm and lead him toward the door. She caught her mother's questioning face but ignored it.

"I should ride back with you. To make sure you get into bed and have all you need."

Randall shook his head. "The servants . . . will help. I'm sure once I get a good night's sleep I'll be fine."

Emma appreciated his effort to reassure her, but she could tell he wouldn't be fine—at least not that soon. Did he have influenza? She hadn't heard of anyone in town coming down with it. She pushed aside the twinge of worry. She'd so hoped they'd have a nice time tonight.

"I'll find your doctor, and make sure he calls on you in the morning." She wasn't sure she could trust his parents to do so.

All Randall could do at this point was nod weakly and force a smile to his face. Emma retrieved his coat and hat; led him outside, where she dressed him warmly; and told him to wait. She then found his driver, who was over warming himself by the fire and drinking something steaming hot—where Randall's mother had told her he'd be. After helping him into the carriage and saying a wistful good-bye, she stood and watched the carriage drive away, hoping the doctor would have some medicine that would help him.

Sad and disappointed, she climbed back up the stairs and went inside. But she wouldn't allow her worry over Randall ruin her evening. She'd looked forward to this night for a long time, and who knew when she'd have the chance to socialize and enjoy such sprightly music? With all the heaviness and family drama in her life lately, she deserved a night of fun.

She pushed her gloomy mood away and decided to make her way back to Violet's side. But as she turned from the fire to head to the steps, she nearly bumped into Lucas.

He stood at the base of the stairs, dressed in a knee-length woolen coat, with his trademark felt hat on his head. Emma instantly felt her cheeks warm. She hadn't been this close to him since that day he'd ridden to town with her, which sent her mind promptly back to the moment he'd almost kissed her.

Her words tangled in her throat. His stunning eyes searched hers, and she was struck by his rugged handsomeness and manly stature, but his expression puzzled her. She couldn't tell if he was pleased to see her or not, and his look was troubled.

The frosty wind whipped around her and cut through her clothes.

"Emma," he said, nearly breathless. He glanced down at her clothing. "You should get inside; you're cold."

Her teeth chattered as she wrapped her arms around herself, but she didn't feel so cold as much as self-conscious. She suddenly didn't want to go inside, where all the noise and frivolity would sweep her away. All she wanted in this moment was to be near Lucas. *How can you think that?* she chided herself. *You're engaged to be married. You shouldn't even be talking to him.*

But she squelched the voice in her head and said, "I think I'll warm up by the fire—it looks so inviting. Would you join me?"

He hesitated, then looked up toward the front doors to the Grange, as if expecting someone to come looking for him. *Or maybe he's worried my father might come out looking for me.*

But he then nodded and followed her over to the fire pit. She was glad no one else was outside at present, for she wanted badly to talk to him. She worried he would be upset with her, for not having told him about her engagement herself, although she'd assumed he'd known, the way news spread around Greeley. She felt she owed him an explanation, at least. But what would she tell him? Would he even care?

The blazing fire was wonderfully warming. She held up her gloved hands to the heat and let the flames seep warmth into her face and body. After closing her eyes for a moment, she turned to Lucas. His piercing gaze once more unsettled her.

"Is your fiancé ill?" he asked, sounding genuinely concerned.

"Yes," she answered. "He's feverish. But I hope a good night's sleep will help."

Lucas nodded. "I wish him a speedy recovery." After a moment he said, "I want to apologize for . . . that day, when I took you home. I overstepped, and it roused your father's anger. It was entirely my fault. And I didn't know at the time that you were engaged—"

"I wasn't," she retorted. "At least I wasn't then."

"But you are now," he said evenly. He drew in a breath and added, "But you're not happy. Why?"

Emma was taken aback by his forwardness, but he made no apology. How did he know her heart?

As if reading her mind, he said quietly, "Yesterday, in the hall, when I congratulated you. I saw it in your face." He frowned. "Is your father making you marry him? Is this what you truly want for yourself?"

When she didn't answer and looked away, he reached over and took her chin in his hand, then gently turned her to face him.

"Emma, do you love him?" he asked simply, in a soft tone.

The question hit her like the hard edge of a cold iron. She hadn't wanted to ask herself this, always denying her feelings and pushing away her internal arguments. Love wasn't the important thing, her mother kept telling her. But Lucas's question made her realize it was. It was the *only* thing that mattered.

Her throat closed up, and tears spilled from her eyes. Something burst inside her, releasing a torrent of pain and sadness. He reached out and put his hands on her arms and rubbed them. Then she heard the doors open, and he dropped his arms and stepped back. A few couples skipped down the stairs and came over to the fire. Emma brushed the tears from her face and turned so no one could see her. Why had she cried like that? It was as if Lucas had a magic key to unlocking her inner feelings—feelings she didn't even know she had.

Lucas took her arm. "Let's get you inside, Miss Bradshaw," he said, then tipped his hat at the merry partygoers chatting in front of the fire. Thankfully she knew none of them.

They walked in silence, Emma sniffling back the tears that pressed against her eyes and lodged in her throat. When they got to the top step, he said, "Maybe you should go inside alone. In case your father spots me. I don't think he'd take too kindly to seeing you with me."

At this moment, Emma didn't care what her father would think. It took all her strength to not throw herself into Lucas's strong arms—the only place she felt right. But she had to fight this yearning, as much as it pained her. Why couldn't she feel this way with Randall? What had this cowboy done to her heart? It was if he'd claimed it for himself and branded it with his own mark.

He nodded for her to go inside, a slight smile on his face. She wished she knew what he was feeling, if he truly felt what she felt. *Sarah believes it*, she told herself, recalling her words to her. *"When two people are meant for each other, their hearts will sing together. The sky will embrace them, and the stars will shine ever brighter."*

She looked up at the bowlful of twinkling stars overhead. Were they meant for each other? How could they be? They were as different as the day was from the night.

An unbearable ache grew in her heart as she stood on the stoop, oblivious to the cold and wind. And then the front doors to the Grange opened, shaking her out of her reverie.

Chapter 24

VIOLET STUCK HER HEAD OUT. "Oh, there you are. Oh, Lucas, you're finally here! Come inside." She grabbed Emma's arm and dragged her through the doors.

Out of the corner of her eye, Emma saw Lucas follow. Violet said, "You're so cold. Did you get Randall off home all right? I hope he'll be better soon."

"I did. Thank you for your concern," Emma told her, noting Lucas didn't seem at all worried about her father spotting them together. Well, Lucas had just as much right to enjoy the harvest celebration as anyone else.

"I'm sorry he's sick, but you may as well have some fun while you're here," Violet declared. "The musicians are about to start up again." Her eyes widened in excitement. "We're going to do a Virginia reel."

"What's that?" Emma asked, letting Violet pull her along through the crush of people.

"You'll see." She looked past Emma and called out, "You know how to do a reel, don't you, Lucas?"

Emma swiveled her head and saw Lucas was right behind her. "I sure do," he said. "It's my favorite dance."

"Well then, I'm nabbing you as my partner. I'm tired of dancing with these stodgy old men. They can't keep up with me." She gave an exaggerated pout.

Emma couldn't help but laugh at Violet's lighthearted banter.

"All right, Miss Edwards, I'll happily oblige you." Lucas threw Emma a smile, but it held sadness in it. She couldn't help feeling he had more to say to her, but could she bear hearing it? She pushed aside her tumultuous emotions and decided to allow herself to take Violet's advice and have some harmless fun.

When they arrived on the dance floor, couples were pairing off, and the fiddler was telling everyone to get into position. Emma stood off to the side as Violet skipped out to the dance floor, dragging Lucas by his sleeve. Emma grinned at her friend's antics, but couldn't take her eyes off Lucas. They joined the other couples in a long line, the ladies facing the men.

"Now greet your partners and dosey-doe . . ." the fiddler sang. And the dance began.

Emma watched, fascinated by all the instructions the fiddler called out to the dancers, who did as they were told, all in time to the quick-paced music. The other musicians strummed on a guitar and a large upright bass, with another one banging on a drum. The dancers kicked up their feet, twirled around, and stepped lively to the beat. One and all looked to be having wonderful fun, and Emma couldn't wait for her chance to try this reel. It was certainly like no dance she'd ever seen before. The dances she knew were waltzes and polkas, and no one ever laughed or swung their partner so gaily. But who would she dance with?

When the dance ended, Violet came rushing back over, but Lucas walked over to stand near the musicians, where most of the other men waited. "You see how easy that is? You can do it. Now all we have to do is find you a partner. Maybe Lucas—"

Emma saw Violet's countenance drop. A frown draped her face. "Oh. Lily."

Emma saw Lily make a beeline across the dance floor, weaving through the men who stood waiting for the next reel to be announced, straight to Lucas. Emma couldn't hear her from where she stood, but when Lily took Lucas's hand, she leaned in close to him and whispered something in his ear. Emma could tell Lucas looked embarrassed, and he backed away a bit from Lily.

However, Lily was not at all deterred by Lucas's resistance. She led him out to the dance floor just as the fiddler called the tune. Violet huffed beside Emma. She whispered to her, "Ever since she dragged him into the back room yesterday, she's been acting strange. That whole time he was there, when we were making the decorations? She didn't take her eye off him for one second." She rolled her eyes. "As if someone like Lucas would ever give her the time of day."

As Lucas bowed to Lily, following the instructions the caller gave, Emma noted Lucas being ever the polite gentleman. But when he had to pull Lily into his arms and swing her around, a pang of envy shot through Emma's heart. She watched him laugh and his eyes sparked. It was obvious he was enjoying the dance, and Lily looked gorgeous as usual. How could any man resist her beauty and charms?

Emma tried to look away, but her eyes were glued on Lucas— on the way he moved his body, swaying to the beat, his muscular legs pounding the floor. With his strong arms he swung Lily again and again, and she laughed and leaned close to his face, her smile coy and inviting. Lucas smiled back at her, and Emma's heart sank. She could watch no more, her whole body aching to be pulled into his arms. And she couldn't bear to see Lucas looking so longingly at Lily. So as the song ended, she told Violet she needed something to drink.

"Oh no you don't," Violet said, tugging on Emma's blouse. "It's your turn."

"But, I have no partner —"

"Yes you do." Lucas strode up to her, his face glistening with perspiration. He swiped his wavy hair from his eyes and pinned her with his gaze. Lily stood behind him, a frown on her face. Emma's heart raced.

Lucas held out both arms and raised his eyebrows. "You East Coast belles need to know what real dancing is all about. None of that stuffy waltzing around allowed here."

Emma's mouth went dry as he took her hands and led her out to the dance floor. Flustered, she said, "I don't know what to do."

He cocked his head and gave her that crooked grin that took her breath away. "It's easy, Miss Bradshaw." His emerald eyes dove into hers. "Just do what the caller says. And follow my lead." He added almost under his breath, close to her ear, "I won't let you down." His hot breath sent shudders through her limbs.

Emma could only nod. She swallowed past the lump in her throat, and the music started up. Lucas stood tall and calm across from her, and Emma had the sense that time had stopped. Suddenly the sounds around her grew muffled in her head, and the people blurred into a blend of colors, faceless and nameless. All she could see was Lucas inches in front of her, looking for all the world as if she was the most beautiful thing he'd ever seen. She thought her heart would beat right out of her chest.

In a daze, the music swept her away. Without thinking, her feet moved to the rhythm, and she found herself intoxicated by the fiddling and by Lucas's gentle grip as he swung her first one way and then the next. His hand on her waist was hot, and her face flushed as if on fire. He got so close at times his cheek brushed against hers, and his breath tickled her ears. She felt dizzy and for a moment closed her eyes, but when she opened them, Lucas was gazing deep, as if searching for her, that same look of longing spilling over.

After what felt like hours—although she knew it had only been minutes—the reel ended with the men bowing, followed by the women curtseying. Emma felt so lightheaded and strange at this point, she could barely walk. Her legs shook as she turned from Lucas and made her way to the side of the dance floor, where Violet awaited her, bright-eyed and clapping her hands.

"You're a natural," her friend told her. "Isn't this so much fun?"

Emma nodded, then drew in a deep breath, trying to dispel the dizziness. Her thoughts wandered lost, and she couldn't focus on what Violet was saying. Her entire body buzzed as if jolted with electricity. Out of the corner of her eye, she saw Lucas by the hearth, wiping his brow and casting a glance her way. Even from this distance, she felt that compelling connection to him. He seemed about to come over to her, but then two men came up and started talking to him. She didn't recognize them, but they were well-dressed; obviously men of some means. Emma figured they were some of the rich businessmen of Greeley, and from Lucas's expression, she didn't think he liked them very much.

Curious. She wished she knew what they were discussing.

"Are you ready for another dance?" Violet asked her, tugging on Emma's blouse.

Emma turned her attention to her friend. "Oh, maybe in a while. I'm going to get some punch. But you go on without me. You seem to be enjoying this so much."

"All right," Violet said, scanning the gathering of men across the dance floor, no doubt determining who her next partner should be. Emma noted Lily had moved closer to the hearth, only a few feet from Lucas, but he hadn't noticed her. He was now deep in conversation with the two men.

Then one gestured to a table—where Mr. Turnbull, Walter, and her father sat. *Oh dear, this can't be good. What do these men want with Lucas?* She noted Lucas nod and accompany the men, who were smiling but didn't seem at all friendly. When they got to the table, where at least a dozen men from Greeley crowded, all dressed in expensive clothing and engaged in serious discussion, the two men sat, but Lucas kept standing, his arms crossed over his chest, a contrast in his denim jeans and checkered flannel shirt.

This can't be about me, she thought. Her father would never summon Lucas over to humiliate or accuse him in public. But what about Mr. Turnbull? She noted none of the men seemed upset, and they acknowledged Lucas with polite nods and greetings. Puzzling. They must have wanted his opinion on something. He was a veterinarian—maybe they had concerns about their livestock or horses. That would make sense.

Emma, still shaky from dancing with Lucas, made her way to the refreshment table and poured herself a glass of punch. Her thoughts flitted briefly to Randall, hoping he wasn't too ill and was getting some sleep. However much she felt guilty about having a good time without him—and even guiltier about the feelings she was allowing herself to indulge in about Lucas—she couldn't muster up much remorse. She was so tired of trying to do what was right, to please everyone else. Was it so wrong to want to live her own life, free to choose her destiny, and unfettered from unwanted obligations?

The months—and yes, years—of trying to be the dutiful daughter and the perfect society woman suddenly felt like a heavy sack resting on her shoulders. A sack she wished to toss aside so she could run free and unburdened. She had thought going to college would provide her that freedom. So once she moved out here to Colorado with her family and was forced to give up the dream, the burden was still there. Marriage seemed the only way out. And now? Now thinking about marrying Randall, even though she adored him, felt like she was replacing one unbearable burden for another.

She heard Lucas's words in her head. *"But do you love him?"* She understood why he'd asked that question, why it was the most important question she could ask herself—because only love would lift that burden. Lucas somehow saw the heavy weight she was carrying. How trapped she felt. How cramped her life was in this all-too-small container. She would never bloom and grow unless she married a man she loved.

The sharp pang of this realization cut her to the quick, causing tears to spring to her eyes. She had been telling herself over and over that in time she would grow to love Randall, and that she needed to be patient. But now she knew, in her heart of hearts, that even though she could love him for the man he was, she would never be *in love* with him. It wasn't something you could talk yourself into, or force yourself to feel. It wasn't a matter of the will, as her mother implied. It was a matter of the heart. And it mattered.

Emma pressed her back against the wall next to the table, as people talked in animated voices and dancers danced reels and the musicians played their lively tunes. Sadness and loneliness filled every pore in her body, but she could see no escape from her misery.

I should be happy. I should be grateful to have such a fine man for a fiancé. Why can't I be happy?

Men's voices caught her attention, and she swung her head to look to the back of the hall, where Lucas was still standing and talking to the other men seated around the table. But now it sounded more like arguing than civil discussion. Lucas had his hands on his hips, and a few of the men had gotten to their feet. One man who Emma didn't know leaned right into Lucas's face accusingly and wagged a finger at him.

It may well be a man's discussion, but there's no law that says a woman can't listen in. As she walked over to the table, she wondered why none of the women in the room seemed perturbed by the agitated discourse taking place. Perhaps the loud music and conversation prevented many from hearing. Or maybe the women couldn't be bothered with the conversations of their men. And normally Emma didn't care. But it concerned her that Lucas was being singled out, and noting Walter scowling at him made her feet move even faster. If they were accusing Lucas of something, then she wanted to hear what it was. And if it had something to do with Sarah and her sons, she would give those men a piece of her mind — whether they wanted it or not.

The men were so embroiled in their heated banter that they paid her no mind as she came near and stopped a few feet away. Her father and brother both saw her but ignored her—no doubt assuming she'd get bored and find someone to gossip with. She realized neither truly knew her at all. When had her father or brother ever asked her opinion on anything?

Lucas was turned away from her so he didn't see her, but she could hear the men clearly. They were discussing the war. She listened for a minute as they argued over economic policies and Lincoln's cabinet and General Lee's strategies. Many of the men voiced strong opinions with haughty attitudes, and it took little time from Emma to realize they were trying to bait Lucas. She knew why—he had served on the side of the Confederacy. Why were men still railing over the war when it had ended a decade ago? Couldn't they let go of the past and move on?

It seemed many couldn't, for they began to pound Lucas with criticisms for the nefarious actions of the South, as if the Confederates were the only ones that had killed and ravaged their opponents. It riled her to hear their arrogant complaints.

Lucas finally seemed fed up. He waved his hands briskly to shut them all up. "Let me tell you something about that war." He looked into the faces of the men glaring at him. "While you were in your warm, comfortable homes, far from the fighting, enjoying your five-course meals and imported cigars, hundreds of thousands of *boys* killed each other in the mud and muck. You look at war as an intellectual exercise. I lived it for four years, in the midst of the blood and horror—"

"Are you calling us cowards?" one gaunt man with large moustaches said, his eyes narrowed in challenge.

"No," Lucas answered evenly. "I'm saying war is ugly and cruel. When you see the bodies of young men lying in pieces under a cold sky, bloated and infested with flies, it's a picture you don't easily forget. One you can never erase from your mind. You want me to defend the South so you can argue why the North was right. Well, I won't. I didn't join up. I was fourteen. The man who cared for me was a veterinarian, a fine Englishman who volunteered to help in the war effort to take care of the horses conscripted by the armies. You may not know that an estimated million and a half horses died in the war. They suffered brutality along with the men who rode them. I stayed by this man's side and helped him. It didn't matter to me which side I helped. I did what I could to ease the suffering of man and beast alike."

Lucas shook his head, and Emma could see how enraged he was. "I saw more death than a man should ever see in a lifetime, and then some. I served God and man as best I could, and when the war was over, I didn't care which side won." He gave each man a severe look. "In my eyes, everyone lost."

Emma looked at her father, who was listening with rapt attention. To her surprise, he nodded in agreement. Walter's face still presented the pasted-on scowl he'd had all night. Others made angry noises and waved their hands around. Another round of argument broke out, led by none other than Randall's father, but Lucas would have no more of it. He spun around and strode away from the group, wiping his hand across his brow. He brushed by Emma without a glance, then crossed the long hall, stopped to retrieve his hat and coat at the cloakroom, and went out the front doors.

Emma sucked in a breath. She'd never thought Lucas could ever get that riled up. But the things he said made sense. She could only imagine the horrors he must have witnessed on the battlefields in the South. She'd heard horrific stories, and so many lives had been lost. And he'd been so young to have to witness such evil.

Was Lucas leaving? Going back to Sarah's ranch? Without thinking, she hurried to the doors, hoping no one would detect the urgency she felt. She just had to talk to him—tonight. The things he said to her . . . the way he looked at her . . . She needed him to tell her if she was wrong to marry Randall. If she was throwing her life away.

She threw open the doors, and a cold blast hit her that chafed her face. She should go back inside and get her coat, but she feared Lucas might leave if she did. A few fat flakes of snow landed on her eyelashes and cheeks as she stood at the top of the landing and looked for Lucas. A crowd stood close to the bonfire, chatting merrily, but Lucas wasn't among them.

Then she spotted him down the street. She could make out his form at the corner, a dim light from a lamp in the closest house illuminating his figure. Steam puffed from his mouth in the biting cold as he stared off into the sky, looking as lost and lonely as she felt.

She ducked her head down, wrapping her arms around herself to try to stay warm, but the cold enveloped her like a shawl, gnawing into her skin. Walking briskly, she passed the partygoers, who were too busy laughing and teasing one another to notice her. As she approached Lucas, he turned and watched her, questions swimming in his eyes.

"You shouldn't be out here," he said. He stood and stared at her, a puzzled expression on his face. Soft light from the lamp caught in the lines on his face and shone on his wavy hair that tickled his collar.

He let the words hang in the frigid air. She didn't know if he was worried she'd catch her death of cold or that she'd get in trouble for talking to him. But whichever it was, she didn't care.

When he realized she wasn't going to leave, he pulled off his long woolen coat and draped it around her shoulders. The warmth from his body and the manly scent of his skin wafted up to her face, and she clutched the coat tightly around her, her heart pounding in her throat.

"Thank you," she said, almost afraid to look at him for fear of drowning in his eyes once more. "But you're going to freeze."

"I'll be fine," he said, then studied her face. "You heard the men talking in there."

She nodded as he chewed his lip thoughtfully. She watched the puffs of steam come out his open mouth, waiting for him to say more. He seemed so far away, and she yearned to find a way across this chasm to him.

"What are you thinking about?" she dared ask him.

He tipped his head, and a sorrowful look came over him. "My mother." He pressed his lips together and looked away. "I haven't thought of her in a long while."

"Where is she now?" Emma asked.

He shrugged and blew out a breath. "Dead, probably. When the war was over, I went back home, to Lexington. I hadn't heard from her in over a year by then. I was eighteen, ready to take care of her—the war had made me a man, in more ways than I'd wanted. When I left to serve, she was still living in our home on the ranch, close to my aunt and uncle and their children. I missed them all so much . . ."

Emma waited while Lucas wandered in his memories. Then he spoke again, but this time his words came out shaky, full of emotion. "When I got there, they were gone. The house was a pile of cinders. Nothing to salvage, no one to tell me what happened, if they escaped, who had done this horrific deed . . ."

Emma's heart wrenched at Lucas's pain. His life seemed a book full of suffering. And yet he still found a way to live a fulfilled life each day. He'd kept his sanity—and his humanity—through all the loss and pain. She doubted many men could come through what he had so unscathed. Her admiration and awe of this cowboy deepened.

"I'm so sorry," she said, noticing him shaking—but whether it was from his memories or from the cold, she couldn't tell.

He blew out a hard breath, then turned to look at her. "I ran from my past, Emma, hoping to forget the horror and pain and loss. I had nothing—no possessions, no money, no work . . . no family. I wanted to get as far from the bloody battlefields as possible. I'd heard gold had been discovered in Colorado Territory—way up in the mountains, where thick forests grew and mighty rivers roared. It sounded like the perfect place to run to. But I'd vowed to myself that after the war I'd get a proper degree so I could practice veterinary medicine. So after two years of college in Pennsylvania, I went west."

He kicked at some rocks and rubbed his arms to keep warm. Emma wanted to suggest they go back inside, but she didn't want him to stop talking. He seemed to need to open up, and she was glad he felt he could share his most intimate feelings with her. She'd never known a man to let his emotions out so freely. Was that because the pain couldn't help but seep out of him? Or that he'd lost whatever pretensions he'd had long ago?

"I know Sarah told you about my wife." He met her gaze, and once more the pain flared in his face. "I met her up in Leadville, where I worked as a farrier and blacksmith." He gave a weak chuckle. "I was too late to cash in on the gold rush, but I was able to put all my training to use and made a name and living for myself. After meeting Alice I thought . . . I thought all the pain would fade away. I was finally happy, so happy . . ."

He wiped a tear from his eye and choked back a sob. Emma waited, feeling uncomfortable and helpless. What could she say to take away his hurt? Nothing. Words were useless. Her heart ached for him, for his loss.

When more tears slid down his cheeks, she reached for his hand. He took it like grabbing for a lifeline, and his skin was cool against her hot palm. He stared hard at the sky, the tears glistening on his face like pearls. He spoke softly, to the night. "The folks that come out here, out west—they're all running from something. Just like I was." He suddenly turned to her and snagged her with his intense gaze. "They think they'll find something out here that will heal them, that will make them forget the pain of the past. But the open range doesn't do that for you. The wide open land only mirrors back to you what you're afraid to see, what's inside yourself. The trick is to run *to* something. To accept what you're shown, and embrace it no matter how wild, how uncomfortable. Only then can you finally find peace. Find your place in this big, wide world." He shook his head, gazing deeper and deeper into her eyes, like falling into a pool of water. Emma started to shake all over, but she didn't know why.

Lucas faced her, only inches away. His warm breath blew like a caress onto her face. She trembled as he tightened his grip on her hand. "Some people," he now whispered, "are afraid to see inside. They don't want to look. Eventually they leave, go back where they came from. I've seen it happen again and again. But then there's those who face the truth, and see what they must do to realize their dreams."

He reached up and put one hand on the side of her head, then caressed her cheek. Emma's heart fluttered at his touch. Her head screamed for her to back away, telling herself this was wrong, dangerous. But her feet were frozen to the ground. The quiet of the night muffled her thoughts, and she stood mesmerized by Lucas's gentle strokes.

"Oh, Emma, Emma . . ." The words came from deep in his throat, filled with longing. She sensed the strength of his desire for her, and it sparked an insatiable need to fling herself into his arms.

He pressed his lips to her forehead, then planted butterfly kisses on her cheeks, her throat. She moaned, her mouth dropping open. "The moment I met you, I knew you. It was . . . as if my spirit called out to yours." He sighed, his smile a caress all its own.

She gulped, sucking air as if drowning in his passion. "Lucas, I—"

He put a finger to her lips. "I know what you're going to say. But I know your heart. It's like our hearts sing the same song."

Sarah's words floated back into her mind. *Their hearts will sing together . . .*

He stroked her cheek, his touch like the flutter of wings. Her limbs caught fire, and her breath hitched. Tears still filled his eyes.

"I thought I'd never love again after Alice. I didn't want to open my heart up to pain ever again. And then you came—as if you were sent to me. An angel to bring peace to my soul. I knew then what I had to do. The open prairie showed me the truth, how much I need you."

He cupped her chin in his hands. "How much I love you, Emma Bradshaw. And I'm gonna marry you."

At those words it was if her heart did start to sing, resonating with his, like two plucked strings in perfect harmony. She now saw the truth staring at her, plain as day. The truth in her heart that she'd refused to see. That not only did Lucas Rawlings love her—she loved him. Terribly so.

"Oh, Lucas," she said, her breath wavering with emotion. "Oh, how I love you too. I do."

Before she could utter another word, he pulled her close and pressed his lips on hers. As his hot mouth opened and his tongue ran over her lips, he wiggled his arms under the coat to embrace her, then pushed his hard body against hers, her breasts swelling against him.

Emma moaned at his passion, as her mouth eagerly joined with his and her body flamed with need. His cool arms soon warmed under the heat of his coat, and his hands stroked her back as he pressed into her. She felt the muscles ripple in his arms against her skin, her thin blouse no barrier to his tender touch. Her hands held his head, her fingers running through his thick hair, electrified at the touch.

On and on he kissed her, moving his lips from her mouth to her neck, to her ear, his fingers exploring her face, tangling up in her hair. He kissed her like a man thirsting for water after wandering the desert, and she was swept into his fervor as if she'd fallen in a wild river that pulled her along at breakneck speed. Yet not against her will, for she drowned gladly in his arms, coming up for air again and again, not drowning but feeling rescued, delivered from some danger and brought to a place of refuge. That place of peace he spoke of.

Exquisite joy and boundless love—this was what she'd been missing, what she'd been searching for—the safe place in his arms. The cherished place in his heart. She felt his love pour into her like liquid moonlight, filling the empty place in her soul to the brim, until the love flowed over the lip and spilled around her.

He nuzzled her neck, and she threw her head back and gasped. If he wasn't holding her tight, she would have collapsed. Her knees buckled, but he held her and kept her from falling. But all she wanted to do was fall and fall and fall, wanting never to hit solid ground.

"Oh, Emma," he said once more, kissing her lips again as if he couldn't get enough of her. And she couldn't get enough of him. His tongue reached out to hers, and their mouths locked in a sea of heat. Emma closed her eyes as she shut out the world, her life, her cares. Her arms roamed down his sides, along his back, and his taut muscles and trim body quivered in response. She yearned for him to be closer still, to merge his body with her, to unite so that they were one body, one soul.

The long pent-up dam of love in her heart burst. This was the answer to her question—the one she meant to ask him. Whether she should marry a man she didn't love.

She now knew the answer. She couldn't bear to think of any man other than Lucas holding and kissing her. This is where she belonged. Lucas made the stars shine brighter and the wide open sky embrace her.

Finally he pulled back and drew in a shaky breath. His eyes flitted across her face, as if memorizing her. As if making sure this was not a dream. She would think it a dream as well, but here she was, wrapped in his arms, in his love. His.

Suddenly she fell backward, pulled from her feet. Before she could suck in a breath, she landed on the hard ground. An arm reached across her, and she saw it swing. Someone stepped in front of her, between her and Lucas. She stifled a cry.

Then she heard a loud thump, and a groan. In the semidarkness she identified the figure of the man who hunched in front of her. Even from the back, she knew it was Walter.

He punched Lucas again and again. Lucas fell but scurried back up. Emma could tell he was trying to grab Walter's hands, to stop him from pummeling him. Yet, he didn't hit back. He pulled Walter off to the side of the street, away from where she sat.

She struggled to her feet, her head reeling. "Walter, stop! Stop!"

But he kept swinging. Lucas ducked and sidestepped Walter, then managed to get a grip on Walter's forearm. Lucas twisted and swung Walter around, pulling his arm in a wrench behind his back. That stopped Walter in his tracks.

Emma's heart pounded in dread. "What are you doing?" she yelled at her brother.

He sneered at her and spit out, "I should be asking you that question. You're a tramp! Out here kissing this cowboy—when the man you are engaged to be married to is home, sick in bed. You're a filthy, disgusting whore—"

Lucas backhanded Walter so hard, Walter's head jerked back. It sounded like Lucas had cracked her brother's cheekbone. "Don't you ever speak to your sister like that. Or to any woman, for that matter—"

Walter spit blood of out his mouth. Lucas still had him in an arm lock even though Walter struggled hard to get free. Her brother was bigger and heavier than Lucas, but Lucas had him pinned just like a roped calf. Walter wasn't going anywhere, and Lucas had a grip on Walter's free wrist, to keep him from hitting him back.

"I knew you were trouble from the first moment I laid eyes on you," Walter said to Lucas, his words a hiss through his clenched teeth. "You've been after my sister all this time. And I thought you were told to stay away from her."

He thrashed his body from side to side, trying once more to get free, but Lucas held him fast. Emma's mind raced with fearful thoughts—what Walter would say to their father. To their mother. What Randall would do when he heard. *Oh, poor Randall.* Guilt assailed her, and a sharp pain stabbed her gut. Oh, what had she done? What would she do now?

She looked at Lucas and felt overwhelmed by the love squeezing out of her. She couldn't bear it if anything kept them apart—not now, not ever. Somehow, some way, they would have to be together. Even if her family disowned her and never spoke to her again. It didn't matter. If Lucas truly loved her, they would make a way.

As if reading her thoughts, Lucas turned and caught her with his eyes. He tipped his head toward the Grange Hall. "Emma, go. Go back inside." His eyes were full of promise, and it hurt to think of leaving his side. She shook her head, but he frowned. "Emma, go."

Tears streamed down her cheeks, but she did nothing to stop them. She slipped off his coat and set it on the ground. Her brother kept his narrowed eyes on her, his face as hateful as she'd ever seen.

"If you tell Father—" she began.

"You'll what?" he answered with a bitter, nasty laugh. "What can you do to *me?*"

Emma fumed. She could threaten to tell her father about Walter's drinking, but then, her father already well knew about that. And she didn't want to say anything that might cause trouble for Lynette. Especially not now, when she was so close to having her baby.

No, there was nothing she could do. Walter would happily tell their father how he'd caught Emma and Lucas in an indecent and wanton indiscretion. Her father would then do everything he could to prevent Emma from ever seeing Lucas again. She should just run away. That was her only option. If her father didn't kick her out first.

She shivered from the cold and the shock of realizing her life had just shattered into a million pieces. And like a broken mirror, there was no salvaging it. She'd only get cut and bleed. She glared at Walter, whose victorious smile rested upon her as she stumbled her way back to the hall.

She cast a look back at Lucas and watched as he released Walter and pushed him away. Then, with Walter staring him down, he walked down the street, away from the Grange, leaving her and the broken pieces of her life behind.

Chapter 25

THE DREADED MOMENT HAD COME, but Emma steeled her resolve, knowing she was about to lose everything—and perhaps everyone—she loved. She had no doubt Walter had told her father what he'd seen last night outside the Grange Hall because her mother had left for church early this morning even before Emma had awakened. Anna, the new lady's maid, had told her she'd seen her mother leave, while helping Emma dress and brushing her hair. And had warned her that her father was pacing in his study, anxious to speak with her.

She stood looking out the window at the steady fall of snow turning the ugly muddy streets a pristine white, then composed her nerve as she strode down the hall to face her father. The chill in the house mirrored the cold pain lodged in her stomach, and she clutched her wool wrap tighter around her shoulders. Although she'd often longed to defy her father, up until now she had never done more than voice a weak complaint. But this was different from all the other times her father overrode her desires with his authority. This decision affected the rest of her life. It was hers to make, not his.

When she entered into his study, her father glanced up from his desk. His look was stern but reserved. Without a word, he gestured to her to sit down in the chair opposite him. Emma sat and waited, but refused to give him any satisfaction by cowering in fear or proffering an apology for her behavior. He studied her with narrowed eyes, then gave a sigh.

"I don't even know where to begin," he said, his tone now revealing the anger he kept in check. "What is wrong with you, Emaline? You are an engaged woman. I told you to stay away from that cowboy. I told you—"

Emma wanted to stop up her ears. "Yes, you have *told* me and *told* me, over and over. Told me how to live my life. Who to date. Where to live. How to live. And now, who to marry—"

He jumped to his feet, his eyes warning her that she was on dangerous ground. "Yes, that is precisely so. Because you are my child, my charge and responsibility, and you must be obedient to me. I have raised you and provided everything for you—given you a life of comfort and privilege, and because of that, you owe me and your mother—"

Emma could not stand him glaring down on her, making her feel small and humiliated. She stood, pulled her shoulders back, and lifted her chin. "Yes, I do owe you, and I'm grateful to you. But you do not *own* me. Or have a right to control my life. I'm almost of age, and although I am still in your house and under your authority, I have my own life to live. My own dreams and wishes for my future." Her throat tightened, and she swallowed to avoid choking on her words. "You're trying to squelch my dreams. To destroy every chance I have for happiness and fulfillment—"

Her father slammed his hand on his desk, making Emma wince. She stepped back. "Destroy your happiness? You're about to be married to perhaps the wealthiest, most eligible bachelor for miles around. A man you admire and respect. A man who adores you. How is that destroying your life?"

"You didn't even ask me if I wanted to marry him," Emma said, seething. She leaned toward her father and placed her palms on his desk. "And apparently no one bothered to ask Randall either—to see if he had any interest at all in marrying me! A fine arrangement you and Mr. Turnbull came up with—to suit your own needs and protect your own interests."

Emma scowled and sucked in a breath. Her heart beat so hard, blood thumped in her ears. "I won't have it, Father. I won't be used any longer as a pawn in your game of life. And I'm sure Randall resents your presumption as much as I do."

Emma's father let out a guttural noise and raised his hand as if to strike her. But instead of flinging herself out of his way, she stood without flinching, staring him in the eye. Her chest shook, and then her hands, as she watched her father lower his hand and clench his teeth.

He just didn't understand. Or maybe he didn't care. Whichever, Emma felt a door had just slammed shut. Her life as it had been up to this moment was over. Yet, instead of feeling bitter or hateful, a surge of sadness washed over her, and she grew calm. She knew she could just walk away and not look back. Did she have a choice? No. Even if she wanted, she couldn't go back to being the dutiful, submissive daughter she had been. Not since Lucas had kissed her. His kiss was the key that locked that door.

"Emma, Emma," her father said, shaking his head slowly from side to side. His look told her he couldn't be more disappointed in her. But she felt a strange distance from him, as if he were standing on a far shore, with an ocean between them, unable to reach over and touch her. Her life was drifting away from his, and as much as it hurt, it was irreversible and inevitable.

"Father," she said, her heart aching—for him, for Lucas. "I won't marry Randall. I don't love him." She drew in a shaky breath. "I love Lucas. And he loves me—"

"Oh, for—" He threw his arms in the air and crossed the room. Emma could hear his labored breathing as he stared out the window, the snow falling and falling.

He spun around to face her. "We'll discuss this later. You should go to church; you're already late."

"No. And there's nothing to discuss. I've made my decision, regardless of the consequences—"

He scowled and wagged a finger in her face. "Oh, there *will* be consequences, young lady, if you insist on this course of action. Believe me."

"Oh, I believe you," Emma said, pursing her lips together. She could only imagine what punishments her father had in store for her. But what could he do, really? Even if he denounced and disowned her, he couldn't prevent her from marrying Lucas. He couldn't force her to get on a train and go back to New York. He could make all the threats he wanted, but they would do no good.

She shook her head, and tears filled her eyes. Her words came out barely a whisper. "Don't you want me to be happy, Father? Why is it so wrong for me to be in love with Lucas Rawlings? He's an honorable man. He has a respectable job, and is educated and intelligent—"

He pressed his back against the wall and folded his arms across his chest. "That's not the point—"

"Then what *is* the point? Father, what is the point?"

He frowned, and anger seared his face. "The point is I'm your father, and I know what's best for you. What will make you happiest in the long run."

Emma almost laughed. "No. You don't. You truly don't."

He stomped his foot. "This discussion is over—for now."

She scoffed and marched to the door, then turned and faced him. "This discussion was over before it started."

She then walked to the front door, put on her coat and hat, and headed into the snow. She needed to go to church, knowing she had a lot of praying to do. She hoped God would forgive her for her impertinence with her father, and help her find a way to keep his love. But she knew she had to stand up for herself, for her love for Lucas. Maybe in time her father would come to see what a good man he was, and how right he was for her. *God, that will take a miracle from you.*

And as much as she needed a miracle, she knew better than to expect one.

For three weeks, the snow fell. But nearly every afternoon the sun pushed the clouds away, and a dry warm breeze melted the scant inches. The town's roads became muddy ponds with deep ruts, and even the boardwalks in front of the stores were slippery and filthy. Emma decided to ride Shahayla to the train depot instead of walk, hoping to avoid muddying up her clothes too much.

She felt trepidation over seeing Randall, knowing it was wrong of her to not tell him truthfully the matters of her heart. After she had kissed Lucas and knew she could never marry Randall, she'd planned on confessing all to Randall right away. He deserved to know, regardless of how hurt and humiliated he might — *would*, she corrected herself—feel. And she did not want him to find out about her love for Lucas from some other source—namely her brother. From what she could tell, though, from Randall's innocent and sweet treatment of her, he had no idea she was in love with Lucas Rawlings.

Each day she told herself to confess to him. But as the days turned into weeks, she just couldn't get up the nerve to tell him. There never seemed to be an appropriate time—if there truly could be one—with only seeing him at church. His father was keeping him so busy, he hardly had time to eat, he explained apologetically. And now, he and his father were about to leave for Denver on business for three weeks, scheduled to return the day before Christmas. So how could she tell him today, as he was leaving? Yet, if she didn't tell him, she was being unfair. And she would never confess in a letter; she could think of nothing more cruel.

Guilt racked her as she rode through the town, navigating the least muddy streets. When she got to the depot, she dismounted at the hitching post and tied her mare alongside two other horses. The waiting train belched steam, and a few passengers waited next to the tracks to embark. A weak sun shone overhead, and the day was cool.

Even as she stood there, looking around for Randall, her heart cried out for Lucas. She hadn't seen him since that night he kissed her and confessed his love. His absence was a torment, but she had sent word to him through Violet two days later, in a sealed note, to stay away for now, knowing Lucas was to come over to give the twins their riding lessons. She assured him of her eternal love, hoping he'd believe her. Violet, thankfully, had assumed it was a payment for veterinary services, so she didn't ask awkward questions. But her friend's enthusiastic rambling over Emma's engagement to Randall had welled up more guilt inside Emma. She wished she could tell her only friend the truth; she so longed to talk about this anguish in her heart. But she didn't dare speak out for fear she would make everything even worse than it was. And she couldn't bear to think of Violet upset and ashamed of her. What would Violet think? What would everyone in town think once they learned she planned to break her engagement to Randall?

Knowing Lucas, he would not wait long before coming to her house and confessing his love for her to her parents and his desire to marry her. He was not a man to hold back from standing up for what he believed or what he wanted. Yet, he'd expressed concern over her relationship with her family. When he rode with her back to Greeley, the day the grasshoppers had invaded, he told her to cherish her family. They were the most important thing she had in life, and even though she felt at odds with them, they loved her. She hadn't known at the time that Lucas had lost everyone he'd ever loved. His father, his mother. His aunt, uncle, cousins. His wife and baby. He of all people knew how precious family was, and how easily lost.

So as much as Lucas might want to gallop to town and whisk her away from her stifling life under her father's harsh authority, she knew he would do all he could to prevent her from losing her family's love and respect. She had to keep faith in his love, and be patient.

Yet, if he was hoping somehow to win her family over before he married her, he would have to wait until the stars fell from the sky. Better if they planned to elope and get married in Denver or someplace far away. Even though she wasn't of age, surely they could find someone to marry them without her father's approval. And if not, they could marry each other under the eyes of God, who had fashioned marriage for the purpose of bringing a man and woman together in loving union. She would be content to live in Lucas's little cabin on Sarah's ranch, with little in the way of comfort and material possessions. The only thing she needed was Lucas and his loving arms around her, holding and cherishing her. Nothing more. Oh, how she missed him and longed to feel his soft lips on hers.

"Emma!"

Emma spun around and saw Randall walking toward her from the street, his father at his side. He held out a large bouquet of flowers—roses and daffodils and irises.

"Oh, Randall. They're beautiful," she said, taking them from him. "Where did you get flowers like these this time of year?" she asked, pushing her guilt down once more. He looked as handsome as ever, but his careworn face showed he'd had little sleep. And that he wasn't at all happy to be going on this trip with his father.

She politely said hello to Mr. Turnbull, who tipped his hat at her and excused himself to go inside the depot. His eyes held little warmth. When he was out of earshot, Randall took her arm and leaned close to her. Emma's face grew hot, thinking how cruel she was being to lead him on. She had to tell him. She must.

"Emma," he whispered, not looking at her. "I'm sorry to be going. I'm sorry I haven't spent any time with you these past weeks. My father works me mercilessly . . ." His voice trailed off. He then turned to her. "He is working with a group of investors in Denver to develop a northern railway line into the northwest territory above Oregon and into Canada. Why he needs me there, I don't know." He sighed. "He's managed fine without me all these years building these railroads." He chewed his lip, and looked back toward the depot, as if to watch for his father.

"When I get back, we will have to talk," he said, his tone sounding defeated and unhappy. It hurt Emma's heart to see him like this. But what did this portend? Was it possible he meant to call off the marriage? She wanted to encourage him but not give him false hope. She would never lie to him, but wasn't her omission of truth as much a lie? Yet, it would be better to let him tell her what he needed first. Maybe he had decided to move back to New York after all, and wanted her to come with him. That was the most likely scenario.

New York. For months she had thought all her happiness lay there, back where she'd left her dreams of college and becoming a botanical illustrator. Now she couldn't imagine ever going back. *Colorado has become my home*, she realized. Truly her home.

Somehow, with Lucas's help she had begun to bloom here in this new place in which she'd been planted against her will.

She looked out across the vast plains to the majestic Rocky Mountains snow-capped and glistening. Lucas was right. The open prairie was a mirror, revealing who you were and showing you your greatest fears and deepest desires. You could either run away from what you saw, or you could face it and embrace the stark truth. He'd told her you had to run *to* the dream that beckoned you, the promise that Colorado offered you. No matter how difficult or uncertain.

She took Randall's hand and squeezed it, trying to assure him of how much she cared for him. "Yes, we'll talk when you get back. At Christmas." She caught a glimpse of his father coming back over to them. "Have a safe trip and send me a letter or two." She was careful not to say anything that would hurt him later. It struck her that he had never told her he loved her, and she had never told him either. Yet the deep regard they had for each other would endure—this she knew. Even if he did become hurt and angry when she broke off their engagement. But she had to hope he'd eventually forgive her. She truly wanted him to be happy—but not at the expense of her own happiness.

The train's shrill whistle blew, and porters scurried to the load luggage sitting on the platform. Mr. Turnbull looked at Randall and said curtly, "It's time to board, Randall. Say your good-byes." He nodded at Emma. "Miss Bradshaw, do take care of yourself."

"I wish you a safe journey, Mr. Turnbull." She smiled and allowed him to kiss her gloved hand, which he did in a perfunctory manner.

Randall then leaned over and kissed Emma on her cheek. His eyes reflected a deep sadness and regret, although she guessed it had more to do with his upcoming travels with his father than about leaving her.

"I'll see you in a few weeks," he said, mustering a smile.

Emma nodded and watched as they boarded, then waited until the train pulled out of the station, chugging and rumbling down the tracks.

Once the train was out of sight, she looked to the north end of town, imagining Lucas at Sarah's ranch, working in the barn or riding Ransom through the drifts of snow. She wished she could run to him now and throw herself in his arms. Her father was at work, and her mother at her women's guild meeting. If she hurried, she could ride to the ranch, see Lucas, and be back before no one was the wiser.

But the snow had begun falling again—this time in fat, heavy flakes that lighted wet and cold on her shoulders and face. If a blizzard was coming, she could get stranded on the road or at the ranch, and then what? She'd heard stories from Violet of townspeople who had gotten caught unawares in a sudden snowstorm and had died of exposure, unable to find their way to shelter. She looked at the beautiful bouquet of flowers in her hand. It could bring shame upon Randall if anyone saw her, even if she gave some excuse of needing to go to Sarah's ranch.

No, while Randall was gone, it would be wholly inappropriate for her to be seen with Lucas. She needed to first talk to Randall, to break her engagement with him properly. It was the right thing to do. So she would wait. She was willing to wait for years if it meant she and Lucas would be together. Sarah was right—they were meant for each other. And if that was true, nothing on heaven or on earth could keep them separate for long.

She held on to that promise, a wistful smile on her face. *I love you, Lucas. Soon . . . soon . . .*

Chapter 26

LUCAS KNEW SOMETHING WAS WRONG the moment he stepped into the kitchen. The strong aroma of sage and cedar and something sweet wafted around him, and although his stomach was grumbling for breakfast, he looked through the house for Sarah. He found her on the back porch, standing, unmoving, and looking out at the mountains, the air strangely sparkling. The hazy cold winter morning promised a dry, clear day, which normally would set Sarah in a good mood. But one look at her told him she was greatly troubled.

She said without turning, "Eli and LeRoy got back late last night. They were down in Evans."

"What happened?" Lucas asked. It must be serious since she didn't have a mug of hot coffee in her hand. Now he knew why he'd sensed something off when he came inside; he was always met with the strong aroma of coffee. But not this morning.

Sarah turned and cocked her head. "I don't know yet. But we will soon find out." She listened for a moment, and sure enough, footsteps pounded from the far end of the house, where her sons' bedrooms were.

Lucas gently took her arm. "Come, I'll make you coffee, and breakfast."

She shook her head, which worried him even more. A shiver danced across his neck. If she wasn't eating or drinking right now, he wouldn't either.

Lucas followed her to the sitting room, where the leftover embers from last night's fire faintly glowed. On the small table in front of the sofa was a flat stone with a tied-up bundle of herbs lying on it. She picked up the herbs and poked it into the charred wood. When the end started smoldering, she turned and stood before him and waved it up and down in front of him. She'd never done this before, but he didn't want to break her concentration to ask why she was doing this. He stood there and waited until she was finished circling his body and muttering words in Cheyenne under her breath.

Just then Eli and LeRoy tromped into the room and stopped abruptly.

Whatever trouble Sarah had sensed was written all over their faces. But they appeared unharmed, so they hadn't been in a tussle. Yet, their faces were brimming with emotion.

"Sit," Sarah said evenly, setting the bundle of smoldering herbs on the dish. Her boys complied, exchanging a nervous glance as they lowered down onto the long sofa. They waited for further instructions.

Sarah ignored them and came over to Lucas, who stood by the hearth. "The Cheyenne use sage to drive away bad spirits, bad thoughts. The cedar smoke rises to the heavens in prayer, to protect those in danger. And the sweetgrass welcomes in the good spirits.

Helps to keep a clear, level head." She threw Eli a look that Lucas couldn't decipher.

"Let's hear it," she said to LeRoy, her hands on her hips.

LeRoy got up and paced, his face in a scowl. "Now, Ma, just listen. We didn't get into any trouble." Eli nodded vigorously, and Sarah pursed her lips together, as if she didn't believe LeRoy. "Just hear me out," he insisted.

Sarah sat in the big stuffed chair next to Lucas. Her face was calm and unexpressive as she scrutinized LeRoy. When she laid her hands in her lap and blew out a breath, LeRoy continued.

"After we got done delivering those horses to the Caldwells, we headed over to the saloon for a drink. You know—Old Myer's place. Thought we'd git warm a spell and then head home. But when we came near the alleyway behind the building, we heard voices, arguing."

Eli cut in. "It was Gus Woodson—drunk as all get out and blathering about somethin'."

"Let LeRoy tell it," Sarah told him.

It rattled Lucas to see LeRoy this agitated.

"All right," LeRoy said, coming to a halt in front of his mother. "It's like this. We leaned close to listen, to get a look-see, but I swear no one saw us. But we heard what they said just fine." He looked at Eli, who nodded again. "Rusty Dunnigan sounded mean and threatening, and I think Gus got punched a few times by the grunts and groans we heard. Rusty said something like, 'You and your big mouth. You had to tell him about that Indian kid, didn't you? Just had to brag about dumping his body in the river.'" He looked at Lucas. "You heard about that, right? It's been in the paper—this kid had been working at the mill down in LaSalle. Got into some scrap with Caleb Dixon, with plenty o' witnesses. Then—he disappeared. No one's heard from him. That's who Rusty was talking about."

Sarah's face tightened but she said nothing. She looked at the fireless hearth and waited. Lucas gritted his teeth, thinking about that poor kid and the fatal mistake he'd made. Something had to be done once and for all to rein in these ranchers.

"So," LeRoy continued. "Gus belly-ached, saying, 'So what? He ain't got no reason to tell anyone. And who'd believe him anyway? He's a drunk too.' And then Rusty says, 'and now he knows what we're planning. You idiot,' Rusty screamed at him, 'that fancy-pants is going to tell his sister, and she'll tell those Indians and that cowboy. She's *friendly* with them. And their pappy's rich and knows the sheriff.'"

Lucas stiffened. They were talking about Walter. He clenched his fists and set his jaw. Walter was a dead man—no doubt about it. LeRoy looked at him.

"They mentioned Walter's name. That's him—right? Your sweetheart's brother? The one I saw at the picnic."

Lucas nodded, his gut turning sour. He looked at Sarah, who nodded back. She sure had a nose for danger. And Lucas could hardly think of a more dangerous situation—especially for Emma's brother. Lucas regretted not having said anything to Emma's father before now. He'd hoped all Walter was doing was socializing with those vile men, maybe buying them drinks and just listening to their complaints. But it was clear now that Walter was in over his head, and had nary a clue. Lucas had to warn him and Mr. Bradshaw, now, regardless of how they regarded him. Emma's whole family might be in danger.

His feet got twitchy, and he wanted to bolt out of the room. But he needed to know more.

He asked LeRoy, "Did they say anything else about this plan?"

Eli couldn't hobble his lips any longer. "Do they have to? You know whatever plan they're scheming, it means they're coming here at some point to do some damage. But before they get a chance—"

Sarah laid a hand on Eli's arm, but she said nothing, and her look was thoughtful, not angry. He threw himself back against the sofa cushions. She got up and fetched the small box from the shelf, and pulled out a leather pouch.

She felt around inside and pulled out a small glass jar. LeRoy said, "Ma, they said something about a party in Fort Collins. Woodson told Dunnigan that Walter and his family would be there today. It's clear what they mean to do."

Lucas's blood raced in his ears. *Fort Collins is fifteen miles away. A lot of open, desolate road . . .*

"I'll head over to Greeley. See if I can catch the Bradshaws before they head out," he said, glancing out at the bright, clear morning. "It's about a three-hour ride by carriage to Fort Collins. What's this party?"

Sarah turned to him, a small bottle in her hand. She pulled the cork out and went over to him. "The town holds it every year at the community center. A charity auction to raise money for the needy. It's an all-day affair, so . . . it's likely they're already on their way."

"Then I'll catch up to them." He wondered why Walter would be going to this event. With his pregnant wife? He supposed he might, if his father wanted the whole family together. Not too harrowing a journey so long as the road is clear and dry. But there was no counting on the weather—ever—on the Front Range.

"Ma," Eli protested, "we're not going to just sit here like ducks and wait until those men decide to attack us."

"No." Sarah dipped her finger into the small jar of blue powder and then streaked a line down one of Lucas's cheeks. She streaked the other cheek, and then his forehead.

She walked up to Eli, who jumped to his feet. "I know," she said, performing the same actions on Eli's face. He responded with a smile and narrowed eyes. "I want you two to be careful. Watch and listen. I won't abide by any unnecessary violence." She fixed her gaze on Eli. "But do what you have to." She added, "This thing's come to a head, and the time for talk is over."

"You got that right," Eli mumbled with a scowl under his breath.

When she was done with Eli, she did the same procedure on LeRoy; although, the blue powder just turned clear once rubbed into the skin. Lucas guessed they'd had this done to them before, but Sarah saw he looked for an explanation.

"This is made from a little flower called everlasting. The Cheyenne believe the powder helps the warrior become invisible. It keeps the honorable one safe, makes him quick in battle, and protects him from evil."

Lucas gulped. He'd never seen Sarah like this—so strangely calm, instructing her sons in this manner. He imagined a tribe of Cheyenne readying for battle, wondering how many times Sarah had witnessed such preparations when a child among her people.

Eli and LeRoy came and stood in front of Sarah and closed their eyes. Sarah closed hers, and waving her hands slowly as she circled them, she sang—or chanted—words in an undertone, in the Cheyenne language. Lucas didn't understand a word of it, but he felt tingling all over his body and an odd surge of energy fill the room.

When she finished chanting, she hugged LeRoy, then Eli, without saying another word.

They tipped their hats at her, and headed for the door. LeRoy threw a glance at Lucas that showed him calm, confident, and determined. Sarah went over and relit her herb stick. The moment the door closed, Lucas rushed to his cabin and grabbed his gun belt and strapped it around his waist. He checked over his Colt, made sure it was fully loaded. He then picked up his Henry .44 rifle and two boxes of ammunition and tucked them under his arm. When he got back into the sitting room, Sarah was sitting before the stone plate, burning more of the sagey-sweet herbs and mumbling in Cheyenne.

As he grabbed his coat off the wall hook, she said to him, "Fear slumbers beneath the rocks, like a bear in hibernation. And when disturbed, it roars. But do not be afraid of the bear. It cannot stay in the den forever; it must face the light."

She came over to the door, put her hands on his shoulders, and looked him in the eye. "Don't be afraid to face your fear. For if you stare down the bear, it will turn and lumber away, never to bother you again. Only then will you be free of it."

What fear? Lucas's heart pounded mercilessly in his chest. Sweat broke out on his forehead, but he drew in a long breath and calmed his nerve. Emma. His greatest fear was losing her. Was he going to lose her? The thought made him yearn to bolt, chase her down, and wrap her in his arms. But Sarah kept her hands on him, and he felt power and heat seep from her palms into his shoulders. His legs shook.

"She is on the other side of your fear. Once you go through it, you will find her there, waiting." Her smile was reassuring.

Lucas gulped and searched her face for the answers he so desperately needed. But she said nothing more. She broke her enchantment with a light chuckle and patted his hat down on his head.

"Go. Do what is needed. May your horse be swift and your heart strong."

A crushing weight of worry pressed down on him, fueling his sense of urgency. He thanked Sarah, found his warm gloves and thick wool scarf by the door, and filled up a canteen. He wanted to tell her to be watchful, and to be careful, but he knew she would. But she would now be here alone and no match for a gang of ruffians. He grunted. He hated to think what Eli and LeRoy might do, and hoped they could stop whatever those men had planned without anyone dying. But somehow he knew death was never too far away from the likes of men like Rusty Dunnigan and Caleb Dixon.

Sarah was right, he thought sadly, the time for talk was over. A man — or woman — had to protect their own, if they had no one else to do the protecting for them.

Lucas hurried out, the morning growing late and the sun arcing the sky. Not a cloud marred the blue pool overhead, and the dry air was as still as death. Lucas shuddered. *The calm before the storm?* He saddled up, tying his rifle and supplies behind the cantel, and then mounted Ransom.

"Let's go, pal," he said, swinging his horse around and kicking hard. A rock lodged in his gut as he tore off down the dirt road. "I hope to God I'm not too late.

The ride to Fort Collins was long and tiring, with little to see other than flat desert, cactus, and scrub brush, reminding Emma once more how vast and lonely this high desert was. Leftover snowdrifts dotted the landscape, and only the clumps of cottonwoods growing along the Platte some distance away broke up the expansive horizon.

The rhythmic rocking of the spacious carriage had put her mother to sleep beside her, her head bobbing against the wall of the carriage.

Walter sat across from them, with his arm linked through Lynette's, looking bored.

Emma's father was outside on the bench seat, driving the team of Cleveland Bays — Mr. Turnbull's rig and horses he'd kindly offered to them to use while he and Randall were in Denver. The leather seats were cold, but between them all they had plenty of warm blankets. Her father had a heavy buffalo hide to keep his legs warm, but Emma imagined he must be quite cold, having been exposed to the elements for the last few hours.

But it was clear they were coming into a town—finally. Fort Collins looked bigger than Greeley, and the storefronts older. The trees lining the streets were taller than those in Greeley as well. She'd learned there had been a fort here not all that long ago, but once the Indians had been relocated and the threats of skirmishes ended, settlers flooded in and agriculture boomed along the Cache la Poudre River. There was even an agriculture college there, which piqued Emma's curiosity. Unfortunately they wouldn't have time to explore the town much, if at all. She'd promised her mother she'd help with the auction, and with Lynette, who had insisted on coming.

"It's my last chance to get out of town and see the land before the baby comes and winter sets in," her sister-in-law had told her when they left this morning. Emma could imagine how restless and impatient Lynette was to have her baby—although she still had a full month to go. Emma couldn't imagine how Lynette could get much bigger though. She looked over at Lynette's waist. *She must be so uncomfortable.*

As if hearing her thoughts, Lynette let out a little moan. Walter looked at her with concern.

"It's just my back," she told him, patting his hand reassuringly. "It's been aching all day. And this carriage ride, although quite comfortable, is not helping much."

He tipped his head to get a good look out the window. "Well, we seem to have arrived. I'll take you for a short walk around the town," he said, sounding eager himself to get out of the carriage. "Some fresh air will do us both good."

Although he'd been polite to Emma, Walter had hardly said three words to her in recent weeks. If they'd been alone, she could only imagine what he'd say to her. And what she'd say to him. It took tremendous control to restrain her anger at him for how he treated Lucas, but she tried to understand his viewpoint. He had seen his engaged sister kissing another man. Could she fault him for being protective and angry? She heaved a sigh, wondering if she and Walter would ever become friends. She so looked forward to being an aunt, and hoped she would be welcomed at their house and allowed to help with the baby. It behooved her to try to get on Walter's good side — if that was even possible.

Emma was pleased to see Walter showing so much concern over Lynette. And he was sober, for a change. Although, it *was* morning. However, his face looked bright and his eyes clear. Perhaps he'd stopped drinking recently, now with the baby's impending birth. *Or maybe he knows Father would be furious if he detected any liquor on his breath.* It was clear there was tension between father and son, but maybe today's outing would help bring them all together as a family. *Although I would rather be spending it with Lucas.*

Thoughts of him and his kisses had plagued her the whole ride, and she'd closed her eyes and replayed the way his lips had hungrily tasted hers, and his hands had explored her body. She ached with longing for him, and the pain of their separation was unbearable. She had been counting the days until Randall would be back, so she could do what must be done.

She'd mulled over and over what might happen when Randall returned. How he would react to her calling off their engagement. What her father would do and say when he learned she planned to marry Lucas Rawlings. Her mother would faint dead away, no doubt. Maybe they'd throw Emma out on the street. She hoped they would understand, see how much she and Lucas loved each other. Maybe in time they would accept him as their son-in-law. But if not, that was the price she was willing to pay for love. She would make no compromises. Or give any excuses.

The carriage slowed to a stop. Emma looked out and saw they were at a large, long pale-yellow block building. To her surprise, dozens of people milled around out on the lawn, dressed in warm winter clothes and boots. When she opened the carriage door and stepped down, a cool breeze soothed her face, chasing away the tiredness and the tightness in her limbs. Her mother, awake now, came out and set about business right away, giving Emma a litany of all the things they needed to do for the auction. Apparently the Greeley women's charity group had been given the assignment to lay out all the auction items with the proper bidding sheets and decorations.

Her father helped Lynette out of the carriage, with Walter supporting her back from behind. "I'll take the horses to the carriage house," he said, pointing to an adjoining structure already quite filled with similar carriages and buggies.

Her mother nodded and took Emma's arm, practically dragging her inside. Walter and Lynette strolled down the gravel path near the street, Lynette waddling like a duck. Emma smiled at the thought of a baby, imagining children with Lucas's wavy hair and deep-green eyes. A pang hit her as she remembered his lost son. Would he want children after what he'd suffered? She hoped so. Surely they would bring joy and comfort to his soul, chase away his loss. Although Emma knew he would never forget the baby he lost—or Alice. And she would never expect him to. She prayed they would have many full and happy years together—and many children.

With a smile lighting up her face at that thought, she went inside, taking in the warmth and gaiety and joy of the season. The hall was decorated with Christmas cheer from floor to ceiling, the draped pine boughs giving off a heady scent. She had a lot to be grateful for, she mused, as she followed her mother across the hall full of chatter and music. She loved a wonderful man—and had found him here in Colorado Territory—a place she least expected to find one. And she was coming to love the Front Range, also much to her surprise.

She scanned the room, looking for a familiar face but not expecting any. Violet's family had planned to come, but then relatives had paid a surprise visit from St. Louis, so they were staying in Greeley. Emma was sad Violet wasn't there to make her laugh and take her mind off Lucas.

She sucked in a breath. Standing against the wall were two young men she recognized—even from this far away. Just by his stance Emma could tell the one with the light-brown hair and dark hat was Eli, Sarah's son. And LeRoy stood beside him. They were studying the crowd as if looking for someone. *If they're here, maybe Sarah is too. And that could mean Lucas might . . .*

She looked over everyone in the large hall, but saw neither Sarah nor Lucas. She had to find out if Lucas was here—or coming. But as she hurried over to them, they spotted her, and both their faces formed a frown. Emma slowed and swallowed her worry. They weren't angry, not at her, but the look on their faces concerned her.

"Hello, Eli. LeRoy," she said, her voice quiet. "Is something the matter?"

LeRoy answered in a serious tone. "Is your brother here?" Eli was still searching the crowd, with an even more agitated look on his face.

Emma's stomach twisted. "My brother. Why are you asking?"

"Is he *here*?" LeRoy repeated, clearly trying not to be rude, but insistent.

"Yes. He's taking a walk with Lynette. Why do—?"

"Which way did they go?"

"Um . . . to the right, once you head out the front doors. But I don't understand—"

LeRoy nudged Eli, who nodded and hurried out.

LeRoy looked at Emma, with Sarah's charcoal eyes and prominent mouth. He seemed to have streaks of blue, barely noticeable, on his cheeks. "I can't say anything right now. I'll let Lucas explain."

"Lucas! Is he here?" Her heart fluttered at the thought of seeing him, now, here. The ache grew inside her, igniting her longing. She glanced around the crowded room.

"Not yet," LeRoy told her. "He'll be here soon." He seemed to spot someone by the door, but Emma couldn't tell who he was looking at. "I have to go," he said.

"But . . . what about Walter? Is he all right? Has something happened?"

LeRoy tipped his head, the brim of his hat shadowing his brooding eyes. "Not yet. And we're fixin' to keep it that way."

LeRoy strode away from her, leaving his words hanging ominously in the air.

Emma's head spun, and she drew in short breaths. *Oh, Walter, what have you done?*

Chapter 27

LUCAS KEPT RANSOM AT A steady pace, glad the road to Fort Collins was dry and the weather cooperating. Although, his bones told him snow was somewhere near. The way the air slightly warmed and the currents shifted made him uneasy. Even while riding at a fast clip, he could sense this—something he'd learned from all his years in Colorado Territory. *The weather here is more fickle than a comely gal with too many suitors.* The two spiring tops of Longs Peak to the south were smothered in black clouds, the sky pewter and darkening by the minute. But that was about sixty miles away. Lucas grunted. The way storms blew in, it could be six miles just as easily.

He'd figured Emma and her family would be gone by the time he made it to their house, and when the servant who'd answered the door told him when they'd left, Lucas knew Sarah had been right —

they were probably already in Fort Collins—if they made it there without incident. *Please, Lord, let it be so.*

Few travelers were out on the one lone road between Greeley and Fort Collins. Farms were well spaced and secluded—mostly wheat farmers, with their farmhouses set way back and their fields now plowed under and fallow for winter. He'd passed a few people driving buckboard wagons, hauling things like potatoes and feed. He'd seen no sign of Rusty and his ilk as he galloped Ransom hard, but he didn't expect he would. If they meant to waylay Walter Bradshaw, they'd wait until they could get him alone, and that meant in town. Which also meant they'd have to show up at the community center—or somewhere close to it. Or plan an ambush against Emma's whole family under the shroud of night. That thought send a ripple of unease across his skin.

Hopefully Eli and LeRoy had gotten there in time. Time to stop—or at least delay—whatever it was Dunnigan planned to do to Walter.

At that thought, Lucas ground his teeth and leaned into Ransom's neck. His skin was numb from the brisk air scratching his face, and even his gloved hands were stiff with cold. He couldn't be more than a half hour behind Sarah's sons. He patted Ransom on the neck, grateful for the mustang blood that made his horse love to run for hours on end. Lucas chuckled. Emma's horse would probably outlast Ransom by a few hundred miles, being an Arabian. If only the breed wasn't so skittish and hot-blooded; they'd come in handy covering these long stretches between towns.

Finally, he rode into the outskirts of Fort Collins. He'd made good time, although every minute agonized him. His thoughts kept drifting to Emma, knowing he'd see her, relishing the sight of her. Yet, as much as he longed to pull her away from the folks at the auction, gather her in his arms and smother her with kisses, he had vital business to take care of first. Maybe later—if all turned out well. But still, as he slowed to a trot coming to the main part of town, it would take all he had in him not to run to her and draw her into his loving arms. It hurt to think about her, about how much he needed her. His love burned like hot coals. That ice Sarah talked about, encasing his heart — it had truly melted away, freeing him.

He let his love for Emma strengthen his heart, and push away the nagging worry Sarah's other pronouncement had inspired. He had to face his greatest fear. What had she seen — or sensed? It irked him when she said mysterious things like that, then didn't explain. He shook his head and slid off his horse. He looked across the lawn at all the folks outside enjoying a mild winter day, the weak sun dangling above. Then he walked over to the hitching post, where he caught sight of Eli's and LeRoy's horses.

He spun around, checking for them, but they weren't anywhere nearby. Maybe they were inside. If Dunnigan was looking for Walter, he wouldn't be waiting inside, nor dare make a shady move with so many people around. But that's where he'd find Walter — Lucas hoped.

He switched out Ransom's bridle with a halter, then tied him off. After sticking the bridle behind his saddle, he felt for the Colt pistol at his side, making sure his coat covered his gun belt. He'd raise suspicion marching into a fancy fundraising event showing his sidearm.

Rather than make a public appearance at the entrance, he went around back and found a door that led into the big kitchen. He tipped his hat at the group of ladies busily preparing the food as he entered. They took little notice of him, and he kept his hat down over his face. If anyone recognized him, he'd feel obliged to say hello, and he didn't want to be rude. Hopefully few of Greeley's citizens would be here today. It was a far stretch to ride, even on a warm summer's day. And most of the founding families of Greeley tended not to stray too far from home, keeping to themselves to prevent the unwanted evils of the world from contaminating them.

When he came to the end of the long hall, his heart careened to a stop.

There she was. Lucas gulped at the sight of Emma standing and talking to her sister-in-law over by the auction table. He slapped away the yearning rising and scanned the room some more. It was hard wrenching his eyes from Emma, but he had to. Where was Walter?

There! He was sitting with Emma's father, chatting with some other men. Lucas blew out a breath. Dunnigan and his buddies were nowhere in sight. Walter would be safe in here—if he stayed here. But at some point he'd have to go home. *But not without an escort.*

Lucas's eyes widened as a man turned his head—the burly one sitting across from Emma's father. *Why, this is fortuitous. The sheriff.* Lucas wondered what he was doing here, but from the look on his face it was clear Mitch Weyburn knew nothing about the danger Walter was in. He was laughing hard, no doubt telling one of his sappy jokes he'd picked up back in Texas.

Lucas stood back out of sight, assessing the room. Where were Eli and LeRoy? If they knew Walter was in the room—and sitting with the sheriff, of all people—then they were probably outside, keeping an eye out for Dunnigan. He wasn't sure if LeRoy or Eli would recognize the ranchers' horses, and Lucas figured if those murderers meant to cause trouble here, they'd ride ones no one would associate with them.

Well, Lucas thought, now was as good a time as any.

He sucked in a long breath and blew it out, shaking his head. He hoped Emma wouldn't spot him right away. He needed to talk to Walter—and to the father. And it wouldn't hurt it all to have the sheriff there too. He only hoped Weyburn would take this threat seriously. There was no telling with this sheriff.

Emma's father stopped talking in midsentence when he saw Lucas approaching the table. The look on his face alerted Walter, who craned his neck around. Walter's cheeks blazed red, and Lucas glimpsed the elder Bradshaw gripping his son's wrist, keeping him in check.

The sheriff, unaware of the tension at the table, let out a cheerful greeting and invited Lucas to join him. "Mr. Rawlings, this is a pleasant surprise. What brings you here? Donating some of your fine veterinary services for the auction?"

Lucas made to speak, but Mr. Bradshaw beat him to it. His voice was terse. "Mr. Rawlings, I don't suppose you have someplace else you'd rather be right now? Far away from my daughter?"

Lucas reeled inside at the man's unmasked threat. Even the sheriff, who was one card short of a full house, picked up on Bradshaw's tone. He cast a puzzled look at the man, then pushed his chair back amused, waiting to see what might transpire next.

Lucas ignored him and glowered at Bradshaw. Walter sat with clenched teeth and fists, also waiting, but not doing a very good job. Lucas made sure to stay out of Walter's swinging range. He needed to get some things said first. He had little doubt fisticuffs would shortly follow.

"I'm not here to see Emma, sir. I came here to talk to you . . . about your son."

Mr. Bradshaw's eyebrows raised in ire and repugnance. "How dare you . . ."

Lucas put his thumbs in his jean pockets but kept his voice even. "How dare I what? I've been informed your son's life is in danger. And I can assure you the source is reliable."

The sheriff whistled and shook his head. Lucas couldn't tell if he was amused or in agreement. Did he know something?

"And," Lucas added, "I can also assure you that there's little chance your son will make it home alive tonight. Should he venture outside without some protection."

Bradshaw's jaw dropped, and he appeared to be fumbling for a retort. Walter sat there stricken. *Oh, he knows right well what I'm talking about.* Walter stared off, avoiding meeting anyone's eyes. *As if he could make himself invisible. He could use some of Sarah's everlasting powder.* He felt sorry for Walter at that moment—a man who had so much of the world's comforts and so little of its smarts.

The sheriff laid a heavy hand on Bradshaw's arm and glared at Walter. "I'm thinking this is not the place for a discussion like this." He glanced quickly at the curious biddies nearby who seemed all too eager for a bit of gossip. "Gentlemen, follow me."

Lucas hung back and let Mr. Bradshaw yank his son from his seat. Walter dropped his head and walked behind the two men, and Lucas took up the rear. He caught a quick glimpse of Eli and LeRoy by the front door, looking about to head out. LeRoy tipped his hat at Lucas. Good, they knew he was here and had Walter covered. He knew they would be on the prowl for the ranchers.

The sheriff led them all into a large pantry room, with wraparound shelving stacked with stores and dishes and cooking pots. Big glass windows streamed in sunlight, making the space stuffy, but Lucas shut and locked the door behind him.

"Let's hear it," the sheriff said, nodding at Lucas as they faced off in the middle of the room. Mr. Bradshaw was sweating in his fine suit, and he looked plenty uncomfortable—no doubt for a number of reasons. *Fine, let him sweat. He needs to hear this, and understand this is no joke.*

Instead of confronting Walter's father, hitting him head-on with this news, Lucas spoke directly to the sheriff, catching Walter's scowl in the corner of his eye. He wasted no words to soften up the truth and make it palatable. He wanted its poison full strength.

"Last night, Walter Bradshaw was down in Evans, drinking whiskey at Myer's Saloon—with Gus Woodson."

The sheriff made a grunting noise, but Bradshaw looked puzzled. Lucas doubted he had any idea of the many times his son snuck out of town for a drink with his "pals." He continued. "Apparently the two of them got a bit drunk, being pals and all. When Rusty Dunnigan and Caleb Dixon found them, they heard Gus bragging to Walter here about how they'd killed that Indian boy in LaSalle and dumped his body in the river—"

"He's lying!" Walter said, lunging for Lucas.

Bradshaw, to Lucas's surprise, grabbed his son with two strong arms and jerked him back. "Let him finish. Then you can tell your side."

The sheriff scrunched his face and nodded. "Go on," he told Lucas, once he saw Walter was complying. Although, Lucas could tell those fists were coming his way soon.

"Apparently Dunnigan got his dander up with Gus for his blabbing. Later, outside the saloon he was heard threatening Gus— and punching him—for spilling about the murder of that Indian." Lucas told the rest of the story, but left out the part about the threat to Sarah's ranch. That was something he'd tell the sheriff, if he had to. For now, keeping Walter and his family out of danger was his priority. Mr. Bradshaw's face turned ashen when Lucas said they had no choice but to silence Walter—for good.

"It's not true—not a word of it," Walter protested, putting on what looked like his best innocent face. Lucas was sure he'd used it many times with both his father and his wife. Drunks always told lies to cover their indiscretions.

Mr. Bradshaw scowled and crossed his arms. "So if I ask Lynette where you were all last night, she'd tell me you were home?"

Walter fussed with his tailored vest buttons. "I . . . went out for a long walk, to get some air—"

His father made a noise of disbelief. "Do you know these men Mr. Rawlings is talking about?"

Walter shot a look at the sheriff. "I-I've met them a time or two. They were at the Fourth picnic."

His father frowned, then turned to the sheriff. "Mitch, you know those men? Who are they?"

It was evident then to Lucas that Bradshaw was friends with the sheriff—just as LeRoy had said.

The sheriff chewed his lip before he spoke. "Well, what Lucas here says troubles me. These ranchers run a lot of cattle on the Front Range, all around Greeley. They were here before the town was built. So they feel like they own the land and resent anyone crossing them. Now, Caleb Dixon was seen arguing with that Indian boy shortly before the disappearance. Plenty o' folks saw that. And there've been other incidents—before you moved here. Of people seen confronting Dunnigan or his rancher buddies. *Last* seen, I should amend." He gave Walter a warning look. "People who cross Dunnigan seem to disappear. Although no one's been able to put proof to the claims."

Mr. Bradshaw shook hard, his fists wiggling at his sides. He spun and got close to Walter's face. "What have you done? You've put this whole family at risk. Your own wife!"

Walter hung his head. "I don't remember," he said. "I don't know what Woodson told me . . ."

Bradshaw scowled and mumbled something under his breath. As much as he tried to keep his upper-class composure, at heart he was a father first and a wealthy businessman second. Lucas felt a bit sorry for him too. He turned to the sheriff and said, "So what do we do?"

The sheriff rubbed his chin and thought. "Well, this is a lot of hair in the butter. I'd advise you to head home now—not wait until dark. Or else stay overnight somewhere here in Fort Collins, if you can find a room, or two."

Lucas noted Bradshaw not liking any of this. Walter kept his mouth shut. *Finally learning—a little late, albeit—the wisdom in such an action.*

"And round up some protection to travel with you." The sheriff looked at Lucas, who nodded.

"I'll escort you all the way back." *And if Eli and LeRoy are still around, them too. But if not . . .*

He met eyes with Mr. Bradshaw, who seemed scared and entirely at his mercy. A shiver of fear ran up his spine. *What if I'm not able to protect his family? Protect Emma? Is this where I'll lose her?* He steeled his resolve. He would not lose Emma, nor allow her family to be hurt. He'd find able-bodied men to ride back with them. Or they'd stay right here in this building all night, and Lucas would stand over them, rifle in hand. He wondered if Emma's father had ever shot a gun.

A knock at the door startled them all. Walter jumped back and pressed his back against the wall. Lucas almost let out a chuckle, then grew serious. He fingered his gun and shared a look with the sheriff, who laid a hand on his pistol as well. Weyburn nodded at Lucas to go open the door.

"Charles? Walter? Are you in there?"

Lucas heard Bradshaw give an audible sigh. Lucas opened the door to Mrs. Bradshaw, whose relieved look turned to worry at the sight of the men standing in the center of the pantry.

"Why on earth are you in here?" she asked, stepping inside. "My, it's hot in here. I asked around, and someone told me they'd seen you come this way . . ." Her gaze flitted from one man to the next. When she lighted upon Lucas, her expression changed to one of suspicion.

Lucas knew then that Emma's mother had heard about the kiss. He suddenly remembered Sarah's admonition for Lucas to find a way to win over Emma's family. Well, he wasn't getting very far on that account. But maybe if he could get them all home safely he'd win some respect in their eyes. But even if they chose to hate him forever, that wouldn't keep him from marrying Emma. It'd be nice—for Emma—if her family accepted him, even if they didn't like him all that much. But if not . . .

He brought his attention around. "Why don't you get your family—"

Mrs. Bradshaw looked at her husband. "Charles, Lynette is feeling unwell. As much as I'd love to stay, perhaps we should head home. So she can get some rest."

"I see," Bradshaw said, making clear to the men in the room he had no plans of revealing the danger they were in to his wife. *Smart decision*, Lucas thought, having heard from Emma about her mother's propensity to overreact to the slightest thing. How would she react to a real danger? He didn't want to know.

As Bradshaw joined his wife and led her out of the room, he shot Lucas a look that seemed equal parts apology and fear. Then, as Walter quickly scooted out the door behind his father, the light in the room dimmed. Both he and the sheriff swiveled their heads to the window. That black, ominous cloud that had hovered over the twin peaks had swept in, just as Lucas had feared. The windows rattled as if a train were barreling down the street. Hail slapped hard against the glass panes.

Lucas's heart lurched. Maybe they should stay in town, spend the night. Surely they'd be safe here. He'd feel a whole lot better holing up until this storm passed over them. It may only last a short while and move on.

But when Lucas followed the sheriff out and went to look out the back door he'd come in through, his throat tightened as if someone had strung a noose around it. He'd only seen a sky this mean twice. And both times had gone on record as the two worst blizzards of Colorado history. One was that first winter he'd moved to the Front Range. A number of folks—and animals—died in that blizzard. The stories came tumbling into his head. Of people frozen where they stood, whisked into drifts and found weeks later.

But it hadn't started to snow yet, and the hail lightened up and a patch of blue peeked through. Lucas figured it was about one, maybe two, o'clock. There was time to make it back to Greeley if the snow held back.

First things first, though. He would look for LeRoy and Eli. He needed them by his side. And it wouldn't hurt if the sheriff came along with them.

He stepped outside, closing the back door behind him, then walked around to the front. His countenance dropped when he saw Eli and LeRoy's horses gone. *What does that mean? They either found Dunnigan or they're looking for him.* He didn't think they would leave without a lead. *Someone must have told them where Dunnigan was—or they spotted him.*

Lucas put his hands on his hips and let out a long pent-up breath. He watched the sky awhile, noting the storm tugging to the south, the slight breeze confirming his observation. Not a flake spun in the sky. All right, so maybe a reprieve? He still felt uneasy, but he might look the fool trying to convince Emma's family they shouldn't go home to their houses, which would be best for Lynette if she was feeling poorly. Her doctor in town could look in on her.

He stroked Ransom, taking a moment to compose himself before going in to face Emma's family—and Emma. He had to keep his wits about him, and he knew how hard that was going to be with her close by. But he couldn't afford any distractions. He looked around him at the few people leaving and getting into carriages and walking briskly down the street. *Trying to head off the storm.* He could tell he wasn't the only one bothered by the ugly sky.

He couldn't stall any longer. By now Mr. Bradshaw had probably gotten his family ready to leave. But before Lucas would lead them home, he wanted at least three other men riding with him. Maybe he'd have to pay them. Well, he figured Emma's father would pay any named price at this point, if the men were handy with a gun. But Lucas didn't know anyone here. Would he be able to find anyone? Most of these folks either lived here or had families with them. Well, he'd just have to ask around, keeping one eye out for Dunnigan and his men.

Ransom nickered and Lucas turned to look behind him. His breath snagged.

Emma stood a few feet away, her face flushed with joy at seeing him.

Chapter 28

BEFORE HE COULD SAY A word, she flung herself at him and wrapped her arms around his waist. "Oh, Lucas, you're here." She sounded breathless.

Suddenly his fear rose into his throat. He couldn't lose her, he just couldn't. *I'll do whatever I have to to keep her safe.*

"Emma, Emma . . . ," he whispered, his hands touching her all over, as if he couldn't believe she was here, in his arms. He didn't care who saw them. Not even her father or mother. Nothing mattered at this moment but drinking her in.

His lips found hers, and her mouth was sweet and warm. Lucas's knees buckled as passion ignited every pore in his body. He pulled her head closer, his desperate need for her coming through his kisses, his tongue exploring every inch of her lips and mouth, teasing and playing with her. She made a sound of ecstasy that sent a shudder through his loins. He pressed hard against her, wishing all those clothes weren't between them. Wishing he could run his hands over her soft skin, exploring the secret places he'd dreamed about and lusted over.

He knew he had to rope in his thoughts or he would completely lose control. He couldn't think of a worse time or place to be feeling the way he did right now, but he couldn't help himself. He needed and loved her more than life itself.

"Lucas," she managed to say between his kisses. She gently pulled back, and he watched her pant in shallow breaths, her face heated with desire. He dove into the blue pools of her eyes and drowned again, wishing nothing more than to sink to their depths and stay there forever.

But he had to wait. *There will be time for all this and more. So long as he got her home safely.*

The sobering truth of the looming danger finally won over his passion and corralled it for now. He stepped back and tore his gaze away from her face long enough to see, gratefully, that none of her family was outside. He rested his hand on her hot cheek.

"My sweet love," he said, shaking his head in wonder at her beauty and her spirit. He stepped back and dropped his hand, wishing a cold rain shower would blow in over his head. It would take some work to snuff out the fire she'd ignited in his body.

Emma wiped a loose strand of hair out of her face. Lucas longed to pull out all her hairpins and watch her hair tumble down her shoulders. Her naked shoulders . . .

He shook the image of her naked body out of his head and said, "We need to get going." He hated to keep her in the dark about Dunnigan, but he didn't want to alarm her. Her frown added to his unease. "What is it?"

"I'm worried about Lynette. Would you take a look at her?"

"Of course," he said, finally shaking off his passion and squeezing her hand. "Tell me what's wrong." He followed her inside, where the auction was now going full swing. To the left, over at the far side of the room, an auctioneer was rattling on about an item he was holding up. Emma led Lucas over to a table close to the door, where her family was sitting. He didn't see the sheriff anywhere, but didn't want to ask Mr. Bradshaw about him in front of his family. They were sitting on an emotional fire keg waiting to explode, and Lucas could tell Emma's father and brother were keeping as pokerfaced as they could.

Mr. Bradshaw stood. "Well, I'll go ready the carriage. It'll be out front when you're done here." His calm tone couldn't mask the fear Lucas saw in his eyes, although Lucas figured no one else saw it; they were fixed on Lynette. Bradshaw left, and Lucas knelt in front of Lynette.

His face tightened as he studied her. She looked pale and had a touch of a grimace on her mouth. *It's more than discomfort; she's in pain. Labor?* Walter sat on a chair next to Lynette but wouldn't meet Lucas's eyes.

Mrs. Bradshaw was sitting on Lynette's other side, holding out a glass of water, which Lynette was ignoring. Walter said to Lucas, "I asked around for a doctor." He shrugged, not as concerned over Lynette's condition as his mother was. Mrs. Bradshaw was in a full fret, and Lucas was sure that wasn't helping Lynette. He politely asked Emma's mother if she might step back a bit. She did a bit begrudgingly, wringing her hands.

"Is she in labor? She's not due for another month," Emma's mother said.

He shot a glance over to Emma, who clasped her hands in front of her and waited.

"Tell me what you're feeling, Miz Bradshaw," he asked Lynette.

She sucked in a breath, like a swimmer coming up for air. "There's a bit of tightness around my waist . . . and my back has been hurting all day. Yesterday as well."

Lucas nodded, watching her. "Lower back?"

"Yes. And I'm a bit nauseated."

Lucas chewed his lip. "You figure you can stand another long carriage ride home? If not, I'm sure we can find a place for you to spend the night." *And I'd be standing watch outside your door.*

"I'd prefer going home—if you think I'm up to it." She mustered a smile for him, and he appreciated it. Walter didn't deserve such a kind, gentle woman. Maybe in time, though, he'd learn to appreciate her. For her sake, Lucas hoped so.

"You've had no . . . spotting? Your water hasn't broken?" He hated asking such delicate questions, but she didn't seem to mind. She shook her head. "Well, then, I think you'll be fine. But I'd have your doctor back in Greeley check you over tomorrow, if you still feel poorly. It might just be the long, rough ride coming all this way. But a little shaking and rattling won't hurt the baby." He gave her a reassuring smile, which seemed to set her at ease.

"Then, we must be off," Mrs. Bradshaw declared, clearly anxious to get her daughter-in-law home. She was the most distressed over Lynette's condition.

At that pronouncement everyone stood and gathered their belongings. Lucas looked pointedly at Walter. "Wait with the ladies at the front door until I come fetch you."

Emma threw Lucas a questioning look, but he said nothing. He added, to Walter, "I may be a few minutes." Walter knew what Lucas needed to do—round up some other men to ride shotgun afore and behind the carriage.

He surveyed the room, irritated the sheriff had conveniently disappeared, which made Lucas wonder just where he'd gone. Home? Off to town, so he wouldn't have to put himself in mortal danger should Dunnigan show up? Everyone in Greeley knew the sheriff was just a figurehead. Why, there hadn't been any crimes in town in so long, the jail was presently rented out to the tanning factory and was filled to the brim with buffalo hides.

But he'd rather keep guard on his own than have any chicken-livered riders along who might just make a worse mess of things. He hoped Eli and LeRoy had already found the ranchers. If not, Lucas wouldn't discount the real possibility that those ruffians were lying in wait somewhere along the only road back to Greeley. If they'd been watching Walter, they knew which carriage he'd come in, which made Lucas wish he could switch the family out into someone else's. But that would raise problems and questions, and Lucas had time for neither. No, enlisting a couple of guns to ride along was his best choice. He'd done it plenty of times in the war—protecting deliveries and horses from rustlers.

After a moment of sizing up the men in the room, Lucas settled on two likely prospects. He worked his way through the crowd, the loud voice of the auctioneer drowning out the conversations around him. The bad feeling he'd had all day was growing into a boulder in his gut, but there was nothing he could do about it. He would face whatever threat was out there—and nothing could be as bad as what he'd faced in the war. But this time much more than his own life was at stake. And that was what made his legs shaky. Emma was at stake. And if he lost her, he may as well lose his life.

Emma looked out the carriage window as the day darkened. They'd only been riding an hour or so when the sky turned menacing. A strange warm wind blew in through the window, but quickly turned cold. Lynette, looking more miserable by the minute, wanted the fresh air, so Emma wrapped herself up in her shawl and huddled next to her mother, who seemed to have run out of words, for a change.

Walter had his arm around Lynette, his expression concerned, as she made little noises of discomfort—especially whenever the carriage hit a bump. At one point she cried out, which alarmed Emma's mother, but Lynette held out a hand to say she was all right. She closed her eyes but gritted her teeth. Emma noticed her knuckles were white as she clenched the wool scarf draped around her.

Through the window Emma saw Lucas on Ransom, riding at a trot about ten feet in front of the carriage. She wondered about his comportment, for he seemed nervous, glancing from side to side, instead of riding in the easy manner she was used to seeing. Something was worrying him. And she puzzled over the other rider up further ahead. He was keeping pace with the carriage instead of riding off, as one would expect of a cowboy on a fast horse in uncertain weather. They'd passed a few buggies on the road heading into Fort Collins, but other than that the afternoon was quiet and the ride, so far, uneventful.

Emma began to doze off, when suddenly she heard a loud roar, as if a train were chugging down the road behind them.

"What in heaven's name is that?" her mother asked jerking forward and looking out the windows to see if anything was out there.

Walter scowled and gripped Lynette tighter. He'd been oddly nervous, and sweat beaded on his forehead. If she didn't know better she'd think he was terrified of something. But maybe he was just struggling with not having had anything strong to drink of late. Emma noticed Lynette's eyes were still closed, but she wasn't asleep. She looked like she was concentrating hard. As if she was in pain.

Emma's stomach soured with worry. She gripped the armrest and craned to see out the window nearest her. The sky was as dark as charcoal, and heavy clouds moved at a fast clip over the landscape. The roaring grew louder, and the horses whinnied.

For some reason her father pushed the horses to go faster, which caused the carriage to jostle uncomfortably. Lynette let out an audible moan and clutched her belly.

Emma's heart pounded. Something was wrong. Everything felt wrong. The weather, her brother's strange expression, Lynette's health, Lucas's odd behavior.

Suddenly, a storm engulfed them. The roaring was like a mighty waterspout in her ears, and a vast wall of clouds sped like a whirlwind over them. Snow, as fine as flour, fell in sheets, whitening the air and erasing everything outside the window. The carriage came to an abrupt stop. Lynette let out a mournful cry. Walter and her mother leaned over to console Lynette. Emma hurried to close both the windows as snow spun into the carriage.

Within minutes the temperature plummeted. Her breath shot out clouds of frosty steam, and a chill settled in the carriage that neither her clothing nor the blankets they'd brought could dispel.

The carriage door flew open, and her father peeked inside.

"This storm," her mother said, "how bad is it? Can you keep going?"

"I'm not sure. We might have to turn around and go back."

Lynette let out another cry. "What's wrong with her?" Walter asked, almost pleading.

Emma's mother rested a hand on Lynette's bulging belly. Her face looked stricken.

Emma got Lynette to look at her. "Lynette, are you feeling contractions?" *Oh, God. Please no. Not here, not now.* She tried to keep calm—since she seemed to be the only one in the carriage not falling to pieces.

"I . . . I don't know." Lynette took shallow breaths. "Ow . . . it's my back. It hurts a lot."

Emma didn't know what that meant. And her mother didn't say anything, just shook her head from side to side. Emma looked at her father, who still had his head inside the carriage. But just that crack in the door was letting in blasts of snow. The small space was turning into an icebox.

"Father, can you get Lucas in here?"

He nodded wearily and closed the door. Walter scowled at Emma. "He's just an *animal* doctor. He doesn't know anything about women's . . . problems."

"He was married at one time," Emma argued, not wanting to tell him more—and certainly not about his wife dying. "And he's medically trained."

"Let him . . . come in," Lynette squeezed out between short gasps.

By the time the door opened and Lucas climbed inside, she was more relaxed and breathing easier. He asked her again what she was feeling and she answered. After looking her over a moment, he said, "Just hang in there, Miz Bradshaw. We'll keep going. I'll get you back to Greeley in one piece."

Lucas's soft, kind words had a calming effect on Lynette. She nodded and closed her eyes. Lucas then looked at Emma, and she saw beyond his considerate smile. Underneath, he was worried. Very worried. Which made her heart flutter in fear. They still had many miles to go. What if this storm stranded them? She pushed the thought out of her mind, reminding herself that Lucas would never abandon them. He'd promised to get them home safely, and she knew he'd make good on that promise.

Lucas strained through the whiteout, but he couldn't see a thing. Ransom danced around, and Lucas kept him on a short rein, waiting. The carriage horses snorted and tossed their heads, but so far weren't panicking. Finally he could see about twenty feet in front of him. But already the road was buried in a half-foot of snow, and the sky was dumping steadily.

The man he'd hired to keep watch with him rode over. His sorrel quarter horse pawed the snow as the man shook the powder off his hat, then stuffed the hat back on his head.

"I can't go any further with you," he said. "It'll be iffy as it is whether I make it back to town without freezing to death." Even dressed as warm as he was, this skinny cowboy's teeth were chattering. Lucas was cold, but he'd been this cold plenty of times before. He'd spent many days and nights in threadbare clothing in the trenches in the war during harsh winters. Maybe his body had acclimated to the cold—and besides, Colorado was a dry kind of cold. It didn't bite as hard as other places. But right now, Lucas was starting to feel it in his hands and feet. And although Ransom had a thick winter coat already, if this blizzard got any worse, he'd be in trouble. He needed to keep moving.

"I understand," Lucas said, glad he'd paid the man in advance, and grateful for his help. "If there's anyone out here hoping to ambush this carriage, they won't last long. And probably won't even be able to spot it. I'm much obliged. Go ahead and tell your friend back there"—he gestured down the road behind them—"to head to town with you. You'll fare better if you stay together."

The man thanked Lucas and rode off, disappearing in a wall of white. Lucas blew out a breath. He wasn't afraid anymore that Dunnigan would attack. No doubt if he and his pals were hoping to waylay their carriage, they would have given up by now. Probably sitting in some saloon in Fort Collins, warm and dry and planning a new attempt on Walter's life. Lucas scowled. Emma's brother would never be out of danger until those men were either dead or arrested. Lucas didn't care which.

No, this storm was as frightening as any outlaw. And just as unpredictable.

The cold chewed at Lucas's cheeks as he rode over to Emma's father, who was bundled up in a thick buffalo hide, his hat pulled down so that only his eyes were exposed to the cold.

"I think we can get moving again," Lucas told him. "I'll stay right in front, in the middle of the road. Just follow directly behind me." It made no sense to head back; they were almost halfway to Greeley. Neither way would guarantee a way out of the storm.

Bradshaw nodded and jiggled the reins. The horses reluctantly plowed through the growing snowdrifts, but followed Lucas and Ransom. Lucas patted his horse's neck. "We're just going to have to hunker down and get through this, pal."

As he trotted steadily, straining to make out bushes and shapes that told him where the sides of the road were, his thoughts rested heavily on Sarah and her sons. Had they made it back to the ranch? Was Sarah alone? Just where were Dunnigan and Dixon? His heart was torn. He wanted to be here, making sure Emma and her family got home safely, but he hated leaving Sarah without help at the ranch. No doubt she'd gotten the horses all secure in the barn and had a blazing fire going in the hearth. He imagined her loaded rifle and pistols lay nearby on the table, within arm's reach. Hopefully the sudden snowstorm would delay Dunnigan's plans. He grunted. Maybe it was a blessing in disguise.

Then he thought about Lynette. If he didn't know better he'd swear she was in labor. Some women started with back pains; Alice had. He'd been trying hard not to think about his wife, but seeing Lynette in distress, her burgeoning belly . . . it brought it all back to him. And now was not the time to allow his mind to wander to that place of pain and sorrow. Lynette still had a month to go; she was probably experiencing false labor. *But Alice went into labor early too . . .* He gritted his teeth. It was all too familiar, and he didn't like that one bit.

He pressed Ransom harder. He couldn't put him in a run because the carriage horses would never be able to keep up. Even getting them into a fast trot jostled the carriage about, and he knew that had to make Lynette more miserable. But the snow kept falling, harder and harder in a fury, and again he was having a hard time seeing more than a few feet in front of him. He had to make sure he stayed on the road or they'd all end up in a ditch, and the carriage could flip.

Tension shot up Lucas's neck, and he tightened his grip on the reins. He couldn't feel his face any longer, and his fingers were numb in his gloves. Icicles were forming on Ransom's mane. Lucas grumbled under his breath. There was no way they'd make it to Greeley if this kept up.

The snow muffled all the sounds. The horses' hooves clomping through the snow sounded far away. He worried what Emma was feeling right now. Was she freezing in the carriage? Angry at him for agreeing to let them leave town? He should have known the storm would blow in. He should have trusted his instincts and told her father no. He was the one that understood the dangers on the Front Range, and they depended on his wisdom and experience. Now he hoped they wouldn't all pay for his mistake.

He turned when he heard the carriage horses running up to him. Emma's father was waving at him as he pulled the carriage to a stop. Lucas reined Ransom in. All the horses were working hard to keep warm, stomping their legs. Steam erupted out their noses, and the whites of their eyes showed their fear. He could sense their anxiety as he slid off his horse and walked over to Bradshaw.

"What's the problem?" Lucas asked, irritated at the delay. They had to keep moving; didn't Bradshaw understand?

"Lynette," was all Bradshaw said, his eyes telling all. Snow blew like grit into their faces, and they both winced.

Lucas's gut wrenched. Sarah's words slammed into his mind, about having to face his worst fear. His skin crawled with icy ants as the understanding swelled over him like a giant fearsome wave.

He'd been wrong. All this time he thought she was talking about Emma. His fear over losing her. But that wasn't his greatest fear, for he knew they were meant to be together. Sarah had told him she was the one he would marry, and he hadn't married her yet.

No, Sarah was talking about the fear that lay lodged deep in his soul. The fear that had encased his heart in ice. It wasn't just about losing Alice and his son . . .

His throat choked up as the memories of that night assailed him. But instead of batting them away, he let them rail at him. And along with the memories came the guilt and shame. The horrible anguish of defeat and failure.

The fear was wrapped around his belief that he had been to blame. That he had been the cause of their deaths. And his greatest fear was that he might do it again. That someone else might die because of his failure.

A pained groan escaped his lips as he realized just what Sarah had seen. And what fiery trial he would have to go through. *Anything but this, Lord.* He thought of Jesus in the garden of Gethsemane, asking for the cup of trial to be taken away. *But not my will, your will.* If this was God's will for him, then he had no choice.

He opened the door to the carriage and one look confirmed his hunch. Emma's eyes were seared with her own fear, but Lucas laid a hand on her arm, not caring what her mother or brother might think. But no one was looking at him except Emma. Lynette was panting hard, holding her belly. She was in full-blown labor now.

"I'll get us to a place where we can get inside out of the snow," he told her, and then shut the door.

He hoped to God he wouldn't have to deliver her baby in that carriage. *Lord, you provided a manger for your Son. Where's that manger now, when I need one?* The storm groaned around him, throwing snow into his eyes without letup—like a big schoolyard bully.

Just then he saw a flickering light through the whorls of flying snow. A slice of clearing in the storm showed him where he was, and he recognized the few buildings half-buried in the not-too-far distance. A flare of hope lit up his heart. Hilton's halfway house.

J. L. Hilton was a wheat farmer, and he'd built this place a couple of years back. Lucas made out the flour mill and its conical peak next to the house. Even if Hilton wasn't there, he could break in, make a fire. There'd be food, firewood, supplies. It was the only house near the road between Greeley and Fort Collins. A tiny spiral of smoke rose above the roofline. *Thank you, Lord.* This was a mite better than a manger. He let out a sigh of relief and quickly mounted Ransom, who sidestepped impatiently. "Come on, boy, let's go get warm."

He urged Ransom into a fast trot, grateful for the clouds shredding enough for some light to shine through. A wide, glowing ray of sunshine struck the road ahead of him, like an arrow leading the way. *Not a star in the heavens, but it does the trick.* Despite the relief Lucas felt, knowing shelter was minutes away, the dread continued to grow in his gut. He doubted perchance there would be a doctor holed up at Hilton's house. And he also doubted there'd be time for him to wait out the storm and fetch one.

No, as much as he longed to deny this cup, he knew he was going to have to drink it. And a bitter drink it would be. Of that he had no doubt.

Chapter 29

EMMA HELPED EASE LYNETTE DOWN from the carriage as snow pelted her numb face. "Just a few steps to the door. That's it," she said, taking one arm while Walter took the other. Emma's mother groaned as if in her own agony, mumbling under her breath behind them. By the time they shuffled through the path Lucas had made through the snow, already two feet deep, they found the front door open and a blast of warm air seeping out.

Oh, thank God. She caught Lynette's brief look of relief, which quickly turned into a grimace of pain. Lynette gritted her teeth and hissed, "It's too early . . . for this . . ." Emma heartily agreed.

Emma followed them in and found Lucas standing in the hallway, speaking to a grizzled older man with a gray-speckled beard. His bifocals wiggled on his nose as he bobbed his head while listening to Lucas. His head swiveled to her when they came in, his smile revealing two missing front teeth.

"You kin git her settled in that room back thar," he said loudly. Emma guessed he was hard of hearing by the way he spoke. He pointed down the hall to the right. Walter nodded and helped Lynette walk.

Lucas turned to Emma, his face strained. She could tell he was working to stay calm, but his nervousness was evident. *No wonder he's nervous.* Her throat tightened thinking of what he must have gone through with his wife. Trying to save her and the baby and failing. Emma pushed down her own terror. It didn't appear that Lynette had very long before the baby would come. How could this be? She'd heard first babies took hours, even days, once labor began. Would they have time to find a doctor to deliver the baby? Or would Lucas have to? Oh, she hoped not. Maybe the storm would blow past as fast as it had come in. But if not . . . A cold shudder ran up her spine.

"Name's Hilton, but you kin call me J. L."

Emma jerked her head, unaware the man had come up beside her. She tipped her head and said, "Thank you so much for allowing us in out of the storm."

"It's what neighbors do," he said. "Now, I better git out thar and help your pa with the horses. They'll be jes fine in the barn with mine. Plenty of hay and water and straw."

He took rickety steps to the door. "You jes look around and find what you need. Thar's water in the urn—the pump's right froze up but should be enough. And you kin always git some snow and melt it over the stove. Rags, towels in that cupboard thar"—he pointed behind her—"and food in the ice box if'n ya git hungry."

"Thank you, Mr. Hilton," Emma said, the heat in the house now causing perspiration to bead up on her forehead. She took off her hat and coat and set them over the arm of a ratty chair, then unbuttoned the top two buttons of her blouse. She wiped her face with her sleeve and went to get a glass of water for Lynette, only to find her mother wandering around the kitchen, fretting and mumbling.

"Mother, why don't you go sit down? You look flushed." If Lynette's baby was coming, her mother would be more trouble than help. Was anyone else in this house? Or would she be the only one to help Lucas deliver the baby? The thought sent terror through her, and her knees threatened to buckle. *But he'll need me—calm and focused.* She let out a hard breath and found the water urn. She filled two glasses and gave one to her mother, then turned and hurried down the hall.

The room they were in was tiny, with only a bed and a dresser, and hardly any standing room. Lynette was sitting up on the bed, with pillows propped behind her and breathing hard. Walter was holding her hand, his eyes wide and his face painted with a sheen of sweat. When Lynette let out a cry and scrunched her face, Lucas watched her carefully, his lips moving. Emma realized he was counting.

When Lynette finally relaxed and sucked in a desperate breath, he turned and said to Walter, "Count the time between the contractions."

"But . . . how long is this going to go on?" Walter asked.

"I don't know yet. She's progressing fast."

Emma put a hand to her throat. *So the baby is coming.*

"Well, how fast is fast?" he demanded. "Someone needs to go find a doctor."

Lucas sighed. "I don't believe there's time for that."

Walter jumped up from the edge of the bed. "What are you saying—that *you* are going to deliver our baby? There is no way in the—"

Just then Lynette let out a wild scream, and Walter's face turned deep red. Lynette panted hard, and they all waited. Then she relaxed again, throwing her head from side to side.

"You have to . . . have to let him, Walt," Lynette barely got out.

"No," he said, crossing his arms. "You go find a real doctor—now!" He glowered at Lucas.

Emma said, holding back her anger, "Walter, Lucas knows what he's doing. He's helped deliver hundreds of babies—"

"Horses!" Walter spat out. He turned to Lucas. "You ever deliver any *human* babies?"

Emma's throat closed up, fearful of what Lucas would say, or do. But he remained curiously calm, as if he'd found some divine strength to face all this.

"I have," was all he said.

Walter shook his head hard from side to side. "I am *not* letting some horse doctor look at my wife undressed or touch her—"

Just then Lynette yelled at Walter, her face red and blotchy. "Get out! If you're not going to help, you'll . . . just be in the way. Mr. Rawlings will do just fine. He *will* deliver my baby!"

Emma was shocked. She'd never heard Lynette even raise her voice in all the years she'd known her. And maybe Walter had never been scolded like that either. His jaw dropped, and he just stared at Lynette as if seeing a ghost. Then, fuming, he turned and stormed out the room. Emma blew out a breath. Some help he was going to be.

Lynette turned a tired head to Emma and pointed at her. "Water . . ." She gulped.

Emma rushed over and helped Lynette sip the water. She'd forgotten she was holding the glass.

Lucas went to the window and opened it a crack. The cold air that seeped in was refreshing and dispelled some of the stuffy heat. He then came over to Lynette and said softly, "It looks like I'm going to deliver this baby, Miz Bradshaw. I know this is uncomfortable for you, in many ways. But Emma is here and she'll assist me, and I'll show you the decency and professionalism you deserve. We'll try to keep things as . . . modest as we can. But having a baby, well . . ."

Lynette's face began to scrunch up again, and she gripped the bedcovers so hard her knuckles turned white. Emma found a wash towel on the dresser by the water pitcher and used it to dab Lynette's forehead, her own hands shaking.

While another hard contraction rippled across Lynette's belly, she said to Lucas through gritted teeth, "No . . . matter . . . Just do what's needed . . . I'm grateful . . ." She panted in short bursts, even harder this time, then threw herself back against the headboard of the bed, looking thoroughly exhausted — and annoyed.

Emma couldn't imagine this going on for hours, but she knew some women suffered horribly long labors. She prayed the baby was in the right position and there'd be no complications. Oh, if anything happened to Lynette or the baby . . . she couldn't bear to think about it. She wouldn't know what to do if something went wrong. How could she help Lucas? What if he fell apart? She knew in her heart Lucas could never recover if Lynette or the baby died. *Don't think those thoughts!*

She went over to Lucas and took his hands; they were clammy and warm. Even now he smiled at her, trying to instill hope and confidence in her. Her heart swelled with so much love for him, she could hardly bear it.

"Tell me what you need me to do," she said. She locked eyes with his, hoping to encourage him. "You'll do fine; I know you will. I'll help you through this." She knew that *this* was about much more than delivering a baby.

His face softened in relief at her words. He leaned over and kissed her, a soft, quick kiss on her lips. When she pulled back his eyes were closed, and he stood unmoving for a moment as if in prayer. Then his face grew serious.

"Fetch all the towels you can. I need hot water, so find some pots and boil some. I'll need scissors, twine or yarn, soap—whatever you can find." He rolled up his sleeves to his elbows, showing his muscular forearms. She pulled her gaze away from his glistening skin. "Keep everyone else out. Maybe you can get your mother busy boiling water. She can do that, right?"

Emma smiled. "Yes, she knows how."

Lucas smiled in return, then got busy with Lynette, beginning with untying the laces on her shoes. Without turning he told Emma, "When you get back, I'll need help undressing her."

Emma met her father in the hall. Snowflakes melted in his hair as he stripped his coat and vest off. Walter was nowhere in sight. Emma could see other rooms off the hallway, and there was a small back staircase shadowed in the recesses that she'd missed, leading to upstairs rooms.

Her father's face was stricken with worry. "How is she? Walter is . . . upset."

Emma kept her expression and voice even. She had no time for her father's objections. "Lynette is going to have her baby, and Lucas will deliver it. I'll be helping him."

His cheeks became as pale as the snow outside. He stood unblinking for a moment, stiff as a tree, and then said, "There aren't many options here, so we'll do our best with what we have."

Emma saw the defeat written on his face. "Lucas is medically trained. He knows what he's doing."

She could tell he did not like this at all, but what choice did he have? One look out the window showed the snowstorm was gaining force, not letting up a bit. The wind kept up a steady roar and rattled the glass panes. "Is there anyone else here in this house—besides Mr. Hilton?" she asked.

He shook his head. "But he's been gracious to accommodate us. And the horses are warm and fed."

"Good. Now, if you'll please deal with Mother, and keep her out of the back room, I need to help Lucas." She spun around to head to the kitchen, but her father took her arm. His face loosened, and he gave her a weak smile. "I suppose we should be grateful Mr. Rawlings is here."

Emma studied her father's face. She couldn't imagine her father trying to help Lynette give birth. But if Lucas wasn't here to help, he'd probably have to. *It's understandable he's grateful.* She answered a bit curtly, "Yes, we should."

Just then a mournful wailing filled the house. Her father's face turned even whiter. Her mother came running over to them, flapping her arms like wings.

"Oh my, oh my. Charles, whatever shall we do?"

She fell into his arms and started sobbing. Emma rolled her eyes as her father patted her mother's head and tried to soothe her. She left them and hurried to the kitchen to start the water boiling, sending fervent prayers to heaven that all would go well with the delivery. *Please, Lord, give Lucas the strength of mind and heart to get through this. And let him deliver a healthy baby. Keep Lynette safe from harm so she can hold her baby in her arms.*

And help me keep from fainting, she added.

Chapter 30

"THAT'S IT, BLOW OUT," LUCAS instructed. "You're doing just fine."

Sweat poured down the sides of his face and neck as he tried to keep his pounding heart from exploding. *Everything's normal, going as expected*, he kept reassuring himself. He'd only attended one woman in labor, and that disastrous occasion clouded his thinking. He knew well that women experienced a great deal more pain than animals did; the Good Book said a woman's birth pangs would be greatly multiplied. Seeing how much Lynette seemed to be suffering made him glad he'd been born a man. It took mighty courage and inner strength not to buckle under such a trial. He doubted few men — himself included — could weather the ordeal of labor without going out of their mind.

He looked over at Emma, who watched Lynette intently, attending to her every need. Lynette's screams and volatile temper just seemed to roll off her; Lucas was proud and impressed with how Emma was holding up. He'd lost track of the hours, but behind all the snow and clouds he could sense the shift of day into night.

Another contraction gripped Lynette, and she seethed in agony, her face scrunched tight. They were coming back-to-back now. It was time to check her dilation again. So far, to keep Lynette from too much discomfort, he'd had Emma check for him, explaining what to look for. There was no need yet for Lynette to expose her body to him. Although, the way she was feeling, she cared for nothing at all but getting her baby out.

Emma had helped Lynette out of her clothes and into a big old nightshirt she had found in the dresser while Lucas had taken a quick break to get some more cold water and clear his head. When he'd passed Emma's parents, who were sitting in a foyer at the front of the house, they lifted their heads and inquired how Lynette was doing. He reassured them all was well.

All is well, he reminded himself. So far, normal. The baby's head was engaged in the birth canal, Lynette's water had broken about an hour ago. There were no signs of eclampsia, no bleeding. He kept praying for a steady hand and heart, knowing he needed divine help to get him through this.

Fear crouched on his shoulder like a grizzly eager to devour him. He felt it there, breathing on his neck, whispering in his ear as he stood to the side and waited for Emma to check how much further along Lynette was. Sarah's words replayed in his head. *"Fear slumbers beneath the rocks, like a bear in hibernation. And when disturbed, it roars. Don't be afraid to face your fear. For if you stare down the bear, it will turn and lumber away, never to bother you again. Only then will you be free of it."*

He so wanted to be free of this fear. It had lassoed him and kept him tightly bound, and he knew Sarah was right. He would never truly be free to love Emma with all his heart, to be the man she needed him to be, until he loosed that fear. It would forever stalk him, steal his peace, rattle him in the late hours of night. No one wanted to stare down their fear—there was nothing more terrifying. But he understood now something he never had before—that going through the fear and coming out the other side was worth every bit of agony. In a strange way Lynette's pain mirrored his own. She would, as well, come out on the other side, victorious—with a baby to show for all her hard work. He blew hard through his nostrils and willed his hands to stop trembling.

And with the Lord's help, I'll be victorious too.

"Lucas, I see the head!" Emma moved aside and gestured him to come over. Lynette's legs were spread wide, and she threw her head back once more, writhing and moaning. Emma held the lantern that she'd brought into the room, and Lucas took a look. To his relief, he saw Lynette was almost fully dilated, and the head was beginning to bulge out of the cervix. A head full of dark hair. The sight made his heart skip.

"I see your baby. You're in transition now, Lynette," he told her, brushing wet hair back off her forehead. "Not much longer. You're almost there."

Her eyes darted until she found his face, and she nodded furiously. "I . . . I have to push . . ."

"Not yet!" he said, laying a gentle hand on her arm.

Lynette threw it off. "I. Have. To. Push!"

"Emma," Lucas said, "help prop her up better." While Emma did that, Lynette panted hard in bursts, like a steam engine chugging up a hill. He wiped the sweat off his forehead and used a towel to dry his stinging eyes.

"I . . . can't . . . hold back . . ." Lynette snorted. Emma kept talking to her in a soothing tone while Lucas went to the wash basin and scrubbed up again. He closed his eyes and swallowed. *Almost there. Hang in there, cowboy.*

He turned back to Lynette and sat on the end of the bed, between Lynette's open legs. He nodded, and tears pushed out the corners of his eyes.

"All right, you're ready. Start pushing when you feel the urge —"

Lynette said through her clenched teeth, "About time . . ."

She gave out another loud roar, which was more like a grunt, her face straining so hard the cords in her neck tightened like ropes.

"That's it . . . that's it . . . ," he said.

Lucas choked back a sob as the slippery wet head began to emerge, face up, the color good — not like the sickly blue-gray color of his son's skin, with his wife listless, almost incoherent and unable to push. He'd had to pull his unresponsive son from his wife's weak body, the horror of it now rippling through his body, the memories mercilessly assailing him.

He shook his head hard, flinging them away. Flinging away his fear and terror and guilt and shame. He heard Lynette give another sharp long cry, and the warm, wiggly body of a healthy baby boy practically fell into his waiting hands. Tears streamed down his face as he beheld this gift from God. A gift in more ways than one.

He looked at Emma, whose face awaited anxiously for his news.

His smile stretched his face so wide, it hurt. "You've delivered a fine baby boy, Miz Bradshaw."

Lynette and Emma burst out in joyful noise.

Emma came rushing over to him with towels. "Oh, he's beautiful. Lynette, wait till you see him."

Lucas looked at Lynette. She looked fine. Tired, happy, but as fine as could be. Lynette met his gaze, her gratitude spilling from her heart. "Just hang on there a minute, and we'll get your baby to you." She nodded and closed her eyes.

Without any help on his part, the baby was already breathing, moving his little arms and legs, reacting to the changed environment. Emma laughed and kissed Lucas on the cheek while he carefully wiped the baby down, then tied off the umbilical cord close to the baby's naval when it stopped pulsating. He looked at Emma, drinking in her joy and longing for the day when he'd see their firstborn child come into the world. He hoped that day wouldn't be too far off.

He snipped the cord with the sterilized scissors and handed the baby to Emma. Her eyes reflected her amazement as she leaned in close to the baby's face.

"He looks like you, Lynette," she said, taking the baby over to the mother's waiting arms.

"Oh. Oh!" Lynette shook her head, flinging tears on Emma, who was crying as well. "My baby, my baby."

While the women cooed over the new arrival into the world, Lucas kept a careful eye on Lynette, waiting for the afterbirth. The cord looked healthy, now shriveling up, so he gave a tiny tug, knowing it could help the placenta release, but too hard a tug could rip it from the uterine wall and cause hemorrhaging. They'd come this far; he couldn't bear for anything to go wrong now.

He let out a long breath in relief as the placenta moved. Lynette stiffened and looked at him. "Just need a little push," he told her, then gave her a smile. "Nothing like before."

She bore down and pushed, and the placenta slipped out all in one piece. More fluid followed, but no blood.

It's over. He looked down at his hands as if seeing them for the first time. They had brought life into the world a thousand times over. But not one instance compared to the deep joy and satisfaction he felt now, with this birth, in this moment. He could almost feel Alice's smile on him, and instead of breaking his heart, it healed it. He felt reborn on this day of birth.

"Is everything all right?"

Lucas turned to the closed door when he heard Emma's mother yelling and knocking.

"It's gotten quiet in there."

Lucas chuckled, picturing Emma's mother with her ear up against the door. He looked at Lynette and covered her up so she was decent. "You ready for visitors? I can usher them out once they see the baby."

Lynette nodded, eagerly watching the door, no doubt looking for Walter. But only Emma's parents came in.

"Where's Walter?" Lynette asked, frowning.

Her father and mother hurried over to Lynette's side. She had the baby in her arms, and they ogled him excitedly. Walter was nowhere in sight.

"Father, where's Walter?" Emma asked.

Her father turned to her, distracted by the sight of his first grandchild. He made a sour face. "Upstairs. With Hilton."

Lucas wondered what was going on. Why wasn't Walter eager to see his son?

Emma said, "I'll go get him." Lucas nodded. Maybe Walter didn't want to face him after those harsh words he'd spoken. Hopefully once Walter saw his son, though, his anger would melt away. Maybe he'd even feel some gratitude . . . but Lucas wasn't going to hold his breath for that. But he didn't really care what Walter thought of him—as much as it might help to smooth things between him and Emma's family. All that mattered right now was that mother and baby were healthy and strong. Funny, for a woman who always seemed weak and sickly, Lynette sure displayed some inner strength. She looked hale now, although understandably tired. But, really none the worse for wear.

After a few minutes of the Bradshaws admiring their grandson and cooing over him, Lucas suggested they step out so Emma could help Lynette wash up when she came back into the room, and then allow the new mother some rest. Emma's mother gushed to Lynette, praising her for a job well done, then she turned to Lucas.

She gripped both his hands and shook them up and down. "Oh, Mr. Rawlings, we are soooo thankful. Oh, thank the Lord for sending you to aid us. You're an angel, Mr. Rawlings. We're forever in your debt." To Lucas's surprise, she threw her arms around him and wept. Her husband carefully extricated his wife from her tight embrace. He threw Lucas an apologetic look, then escorted her out the door. A moment later he came back in alone and faced Lucas.

"I'm greatly indebted to you," he told Lucas.

"No sir. I'm just glad I could help and that everything went well."

Bradshaw shook his head. "I'm . . . sorry for the way I've treated you. I . . . didn't know if you were an honorable man, and the way Emma—"

Lucas held up his hand, then glanced over at Lynette, who was touching her baby's face, so enamored with her son she paid no attention to their conversation. Lucas whispered, "We can talk later, Mr. Bradshaw."

Bradshaw nodded and smiled. He looked over at Lynette, and Lucas saw his face radiant with pride and relief. Maybe this whole ordeal *had* been a gift from God. Lucas couldn't think up a better way to get Emma's family to think highly of him. Although, he thought with a stab of despair, there was Randall Turnbull to consider. And Emma's engagement to him—which Lucas doubted Emma's parents would forget about. But he couldn't be bothered with that now.

Just then the door blew open, and Emma rushed in. His heart jolted when he saw the upset expression on her face.

"What is it?" her father demanded. "Where's Walter?"

"Upstairs," she said, her tone seething and agitated.

"He's been drinking," her father said gloomily, as if it was no surprise.

"Yes, but . . . that's not the problem." She threw a frightened look at Lucas. "Lucas, you have to talk to him. He's a mess, terribly upset. He said something about having to warn you. I kept asking him what he meant, and it finally came out." She grabbed his arm and looked at the window. Even in the dark he could see the snow still steadily falling.

His gut soured with dread. "Tell me, Emma."

"Those ranchers you told me about? They're planning to kill Sarah and her sons." She could barely get the next word out.

"Tonight."

Chapter 31

"So, I heared the baby's bin born," Hilton said gleefully, then held up his glass of whiskey, "Let's drink t' that."

Emma scowled at Walter, who was hunched over in a ratty armchair, and grabbed the glass out of his hand. She sputtered with indignation, "Tell Lucas what you told me."

Walter hung his head. They were in a small upstairs sitting parlor, and by the nearly empty liquor bottle on the table between the two men, Emma guessed they'd had plenty to drink. Emma was incredulous. Here he sat, getting drunk all the while his wife was in labor, giving birth to *his* son. And he was too drunk to have the presence of mind to go see his wife and baby.

Lucas was buttoning up his coat and pulling on his gloves. He settled his hat on his head, ready to bolt. Her eyes snagged on the gun belt strapped around his waist. Emma wished he wouldn't go. He'd be in grave danger facing those violent men — if he didn't get lost or freeze to death first while trying to ride back to the ranch in the dark in a blizzard. He'd quickly explained to her who these men were and how Walter knew him, but his brief telling left her with more questions than answers. But Lucas had no time for further talk. Sarah's ranch—and her life—was at stake. And Lucas was as furious as she'd ever seen him.

He strode over to Walter and yanked him up off the seat by his collar. Walter's eyes widened with fear. Lucas demanded, "What are they planning? How many men? When?"

Walter shook his head, pulling back. "I . . . I don't know." He sounded utterly dejected, but Emma felt no pity for him. He'd known about this for some time. How long? How could he know evil men were planning such crimes and not tell someone? A more horrific thought came to her mind. Was Walter meant to be a part of this travesty? She wanted to throttle him.

Walter stuttered, "I-I don't think it's many. Dunnigan. Dixon. Two or three others." He gave Lucas a sorrowful look. "Look, I'm sorry. I'm so sorry . . . you saved my wife . . . my baby—"

Walter let out a loud gasping sob and then wept into his hands. Emma's jaw dropped. She'd never seen him cry—or show such remorse. But it only made her more angry. She turned to Lucas, and seeing the determination and courage in his face, her heart ached. She heard her parents talking downstairs—more like arguing—about Walter. If only she could go with Lucas. She couldn't bear staying here in this house in the middle of nowhere, not knowing if Lucas was safe.

He caught her eyes and gave a sweet smile that made Emma want to cry. But she swallowed back the tears lodged in her throat. She needed to stay brave for him—again. Whining for him to stay would only make leaving more painful for him. But she knew he must go.

She threw her arms around him, unheeding of what anyone might think. "Lucas, I know you have to leave. But promise me you'll be careful. I can't lose you. I love you too much."

He stroked her cheek, the touch sending shivers all over her body. "I have every intention of coming back to you. I wouldn't have it otherwise." His eyes burned with a love so hot she felt he could melt all the snow in Colorado.

Then he kissed her and ignited her soul in a flame of passion. His lips held on to hers in desperation, and his arms pulled her tight, his muscles tense and rippling. He whispered hot in her ear, "I love you so much, Emma, more than you'll ever know." His mouth drifted down to her neck, his tongue playing across her skin and making her moan. "I'm coming back. You just wait."

Emma's knees gave out—from his touch and from the long, exhausting hours of Lynette's labor. But he held her up, her chest pressing against his and feeling his heart beating. She considered how hungry and tired he must be. "You should pack some food. You haven't eaten for hours."

"No time," he said, letting her down gently into a chair. "Watch after Lynette. Make sure she drinks plenty of water and that she rests." He threw a glance down the stairs. "Don't let anyone disturb her. And better wait until Walter sobers up before you let him in to see the baby." He added with a smirk, "I'm sure Lynette will understand."

Emma found that remark puzzling. He seemed to know more about Lynette than he let on.

With a last firm kiss to her forehead, Lucas said good-bye and skipped down the stairs. Her throat choked up as he left her arms. She followed him to the door and watched him run to the barn in the scantest of light, the flurries of snow catching in her hair. The snow was a good three feet deep all around. *How in the world will he make it to the ranch?* Lucas had told her it was only about four miles—not that far a ride on a clear, warm day. But slugging through thick snow in the dark? Would Ransom be able to keep going with his legs frozen? Could he even see the road?

Emma shuddered. It wouldn't help to worry about it. Nothing would help. All she could do was hope and pray. And she didn't like it one bit.

Not long after Lucas saddled up and started pushing Ransom along through the sea of snow, his eyes adjusted to the faint light. And then, in answer to his prayers, a sharp breeze kicked up and blew open a patch of clouds, letting moonlight spill down across the prairie. The pristine sight of millions of sparkles across the expanse would normally awe him, but he had no time to dwell on the beauty. His first thought was to find the quickest, easiest path to Sarah's ranch. And now that the snow trickled to a halt and he could see enough to get the lay of the land, he spotted just the field he'd cross to make better time.

A heavy boulder of worry lay in his empty stomach. All his nerves tingled in anticipation of what he'd find at the ranch. Was he too late? That fear ate at him, and his frustration grew while trying to find shallow patches of snow he could gallop through. But he could only push Ransom so hard, and by the time he found his familiar deer track along the Platte, he was sure an hour had passed, at the very least. An hour that felt like a year, with every second agonizing him with worry. Ransom was a trooper though, clearly just as anxious to get home as he was.

By the time the river curved south and he knew he was less than half a mile away, his entire body was almost frozen. But along this stretch of cottonwoods, the snow was sparse enough to allow him to lope the last leg to the ranch. He let Ransom pick the speed, surprised the horse still had spunk. By now the clouds had shredded apart, and a crescent moon hung in the east, dangling like a charm on a necklace. But the clearing also gave him a distant view of the land ahead, and what he spotted in the quiet of night stabbed his gut.

Tongues of fire tickled the sky and sent dark smoke and sparks aloft. Lucas gasped. He had no doubt the flames were coming from the ranch.

Heedless of the danger, praying Ransom would find purchase for his hooves in the snow-piled road, he kicked his mustang for all he was worth. The wind stung his eyes so badly tears squeezed out, but he set his sights ahead and raced without letup. When he got to his cabin sequestered in a copse of trees, he slid off his horse and stopped to think. The air was choked with smoke and ash, and now Lucas heard the panicked whinny of horses.

The sound made his pulse pound his ears, and his throat went dry. He couldn't imagine men so cruel as to kill horses, but he wouldn't put it past Dunnigan and his pals. He wanted to wring their necks—and hoped he'd get the chance.

In seconds he had his rifle untied from behind the saddle and loaded, then he threw Ransom's reins over the post by the door, telling him to stay. Ransom looked so tuckered out, Lucas knew he wouldn't wander far, if at all.

The little bit of moonlight cast shadows all around, and Lucas hugged those shadows as he cut a wide arc to the east of the horse barn. Upon coming out from the trees, his heart leapt to his throat. The barn was ablaze!

He had to restrain his feet from racing to save the horses, who clearly were locked in the barn. *Why, those dirty ruffians are going to pay for this!*

As much as his heart bled for the horses, his first concern was Sarah. Were Eli and Leroy here? He wished he knew. He had to get to the ranch house—where he assumed Sarah was. Or she could be outside, or in another barn. There was no telling. And he had to be careful he didn't get shot—either by the ranchers or accidently by his friends. In the dark, no one would know who he was. A good and bad thing, he reasoned.

Fortunately the house wasn't on fire—yet. And the barn fire looked to be set only moments ago. He formed a quick plan that would swing him around the back of the horse barn so he could at least get the back door open.

He crouched low and ran from shadow to shadow, cradling his rifle. When he got behind the small toolshed, he propped the rifle up against the siding, knowing in close range the Colt was what he needed. He hoped he wouldn't need to come back for the rifle. For that matter, he hoped he wouldn't have to use the pistol, but he would if he had to. He'd shot guns more times than he'd like to remember back in the war. He killed plenty of men too, but only when they were about to kill him. Sometimes it had been harder to kill the injured and suffering horses than it was to kill those men— who were, for the most part, only a few years older than he had been.

He thought he'd left the bloody battlefields of war behind him. But now he was afraid he was about to engage in another war. A trickle of nausea rose to the back of his throat but he pushed it down. The irony of this night hit him—going from the joy of birth, of new life, to a fight that might result in death—maybe even his own. But he refused to think of failure. *I promised Emma I'd come back alive. And I mean to do so.*

All the years in the war—the hiding and fighting and attacking—came back to him, heightening his senses. He called upon the wisdom he'd gained through the effort to survive the bloodbaths he'd found himself in. He'd wriggled his way out of every scrape then, and he'd do so now.

So he closed his eyes and listened, filtering out the loud noises of the horses' panic, the crackle of the fire eating through wood. Then, underneath it all he heard a flutter of wings, and then a crack of a stick—or a rifle's lever being pulled back. Whoever was out here wasn't concerned about getting found. Their mistake.

He kept low and trod softly. Thankfully the snow muffled his steps. But he knew just where the shooter was, and he hoped to God he got to him before the villain fired off a shot—at whoever he was aiming for.

There! A dark shape leaned against a tree, taking aim toward the house. Lucas was close enough to the barn to feel the heat on his right side. The horses' cries and banging against the barn's sides made him sick. *He had to save the horses!*

He sucked in a breath and ran. Before the man was able to turn, Lucas knocked him down, causing his rifle to fire into the air. He punched the man, who grunted and swung, but missed Lucas's face by an inch. Lucas grabbed the rifle that had fallen within reach and swiveled it around.

The man lunged for him, but Lucas faced the rifle backward and smacked his attacker on the side of the head with the butt, twice. The man fell over. Lucas checked to make sure he was out cold. Then he ran, stumbling, to the back of the barn.

The flames were eating up the front carriage doors and siding. Smoke billowed and blew around him. He pulled his shirt over his mouth and breathed shallow breaths. He tried to open the door, but it was latched from inside. A kick did nothing to bust the door open.

He took the rifle he still had in his hand and smashed it into the window that opened in his medical room. In seconds he had all the glass out, and more smoke poured out in ugly black whorls. He closed his eyes and threw himself headfirst into the room, shoulder-rolled to his feet, then crouched low and ran to the back door.

The smoke gathered along the inside of the canted roof, thickening close to the horses, who pawed at the gates of the stalls and screeched. He cringed as memories of shot and bleeding horses assailed him. The back door was padlocked. Lucas pulled out his pistol and shot it off, then threw down the pieces and yanked open the door. Fresh, cold air streamed in.

He then ran to the stalls, throwing them open one by one, careful to keep out of the way of stampeding hooves. The barn was huge, and all fifty-plus head were inside, where Sarah had put them to stay warm and safe from the storm. *Those ranchers would have figured she'd do that. And no doubt had set fire to the barn to draw her out.*

But Sarah hadn't come out. He could imagine how hard it was for her to resist running out and saving them. But she knew what he knew—that had she come out, she would have been killed.

He had no time to stand around and figure out his next steps. He had no idea where the other men were. He had to assume the worst and assume they were already in the house.

Once he knew every horse had made it out safely, he ran hard, zigzagging as he aimed for the porch. He was exposed now, but there was no cover between the barn and the house. He couldn't afford to wait until he saw someone—or heard someone scream.

And then he heard a gunshot. Then another. It sounded like a rifle, those two shots. Then another volley of shots followed. Lucas could tell those were two different guns. Three guns. But whose? And the shots were coming from somewhere near the house, maybe even from inside. He couldn't tell.

He crouched when he hit the porch, then snuck around the north side, where the overhang made a dark shadow. There he could listen and figure where to go next. His heart thumped hard, hoping he wouldn't find Sarah dead. He knew she was clever, though, and hoped she'd found a strategic place to defend herself.

Where on earth are Eli and LeRoy? They were supposed to track these hooligans down and stop them. He gulped hard. If they weren't here, they could already be dead. Maybe Dunnigan caught them following him on the way over here.

Lucas pushed down his rage. If Emma's family had just stayed home, none of this would have happened. But if they had, Lucas wouldn't have delivered Lynette's baby and discovered Dunnigan's plan. Lucas realized that if Walter hadn't gotten mixed up with these ranchers, then Lucas and Sarah would never have known what danger they were in. *Lord, you sure work in mysterious ways.*

Another shot rang out, but this time he heard a voice. Dunnigan's.

"Jes come on out here now, if you don't want to die. I know you're in there, Banks."

Lucas gritted his teeth. He didn't think Dunnigan was talking that way to Sarah. Had to be Eli. Which meant Eli was inside, maybe LeRoy too. Thinking they might be alive gave him hope, but not for long. He heard another voice, and it was Dixon's.

"I'm going in," he said to Dunnigan.

Lucas couldn't see a thing from around the corner, but he gauged the distance based on the sound of Dixon's voice. He was maybe ten feet from him — Dixon was at the kitchen door. He could hope Dixon would open that door to a gun pointed at his face, but he didn't want to chance it. Eli could be wounded, for all he knew. Lucas had to stop Dixon.

He set down the Winchester he'd been lugging around. *It might come in handy still.* His Henry was back behind the toolshed.

He calmed his nerve for a second, then spun around the corner. He took three long leaps, then dove for Dixon's legs. Dixon hollered, then shook himself free. He turned and aimed his gun right in Lucas's face.

Lucas jerked to a stop. There was nowhere to run. He lunged for Dixon and with his elbow knocked his pistol-toting arm, which fired a bullet into the side of the house. They tussled hard on the snowy ground, exchanging punches. Dixon scrambled to his feet. Lucas tried to grab his legs, but Dixon ran around the side of the house, where Lucas had come from.

Lucas scurried to pull out his Colt, when a shot rang out. A flash of hot pain seared his right arm. He fell on his face, then scrambled up and managed to fling himself over the threshold of the kitchen door, which had eased open in their scuffle. He slammed the door, latched it, and crawled into the sitting room, holding the wound with his hand. It hurt like the dickens, but he could tell the bullet had gone clean through. If that was the only damage he suffered tonight, he'd be glad.

But he was far from safe. Those men were either going to storm in or set the house on fire and flush them out. Lucas had no intention of waiting for either occurrence.

He called for Sarah, and then her sons. Then realized they weren't in the house. If Dunnigan had seen Eli or Leroy come inside, the boys had snuck back out. Smart move. He didn't know much about other Indians, but these three knew how to blend into the darkness and move silently. And they knew every inch of ground of this property. Lucas was sure they had themselves positioned right where they wanted to be.

But who had been shooting at whom a while back? Just Dunnigan and his pals shooting at shadows? Or trying to scare Sarah? Dunnigan obviously knew nothing about his opponents. Sarah's boys might be young, but they were cunning and adept at knives, guns, lassos, and evasion. Lucas almost chuckled thinking of how Eli often tried hard to evade his mother but rarely succeeded.

His shoulder throbbed and his head grew dizzy. Blood leaked out the wound. He ripped the lower part of his shirt and bunched it up to use as a compress. He wouldn't die, but if he lost too much blood he'd get too woozy to think straight. He wiggled his fingers. At least he could still fire his gun.

With his right hand holding his Colt, he pressed the cloth against the wound. He ran over to the door leading out to the porch, when he heard more shots. This time he couldn't tell how many guns were firing. But now he had an idea where Sarah and her sons were. LeRoy had once showed him the small hollow down the road, pointing out what a good vantage point it gave of the house and road, but you couldn't be seen.

If that's where they were, then Lucas determined from the reports where the ranchers and their cronies were. Depending on how quick he was, he might take down two or three before they knew what hit them.

Lucas went back to the front kitchen door, then slipped out and listened. The firing continued, and a cry erupted—from the ranchers' camp. With his pulse hammering in his ears, and his shoulder on fire, he crawled over to the front fence and scooted behind a big stump. From there he inched his way around, through thick bushes buried in snow, and got in position. He couldn't make out anything but dark shapes wielding rifles. Which told him just where he needed to aim.

He hated to kill anyone, but he couldn't take a chance on shooting to disarm—not in the dark. A miss on his part could cost him his life. And maybe Sarah's and her sons'.

He breathed deep, held his breath, and said a prayer. Then he aimed and squeezed the trigger—once, twice, three times. He saw all three shapes fall, and his heart hurt. Why did men have to be so evil? He scowled and waited.

The night grew quiet, with the faint hissing and crackle of the barn burning to the ground. From where he crouched, he couldn't see flames, but the air carried the smoke and sparks into the heavens, almost like an offering. He went over and checked—all dead. Dixon, Woodson, and one other cowboy Lucas had never seen. He pursed his lips, feeling sad for these men and wondering what had set their feet on a bad road.

He then heard one more shot, coming from near where his friends hid. Lucas ran around the house and down the road, yelling. "Sarah, LeRoy, Eli—you there?"

They'd know it was him. He had no doubt they'd known the moment he rode in on Ransom. He grunted. Sarah probably knew he would show up to save the horses and that's why she didn't risk going out. He shook his head. As much as Sarah's insights bothered him sometimes, tonight he was glad for them. Maybe her invisible everlasting powder really worked. For he saw the three of them come out from the hollow and walk toward him as if materializing out of thin air.

Then he saw a shape on the ground near the entrance to Sarah's ranch. He could tell by the hat lying next to the body that it was Dunnigan.

Eli said, "He thought he was being sneaky, coming around from the road."

At least Eli wasn't gloating. As much as Sarah's sons wanted those ranchers stopped, they weren't killers. Sarah had told them to try to avoid killing, but she'd also advised wisely: Do what you have to. He figured Eli had taken Dunnigan down. He was a good enough shot that he could have wounded him instead. But Lucas had to believe Eli had done what he felt would best protect his family.

He blew out a breath. He'd killed three men himself. What would Emma and her family think? He pictured her mother being so horrified, she'd make them all hop on the next train back to New York. He smiled. Emma wouldn't leave, though. No, whether she knew it or not yet, she was made for the Front Range. A true

Colorado gal at heart. He couldn't wait to get back to her, knowing how worried she must be. Just thinking about her sweet face and luscious lips invigorated him.

"You're shot," LeRoy said, looking at the bloody shoulder in the moonlight.

"I'll live," Lucas said, smiling. "I'm glad to see you all—alive."

"Helps to be invisible," Eli said with a twisted grin. His mother elbowed him.

"Don't make fun," she said. She reached out and touched Lucas's face. "The horses?"

"I got 'em out." He looked over to the barn, which he could make out partly from where they stood. "Looks like we'll need to pick up more siding in LaSalle," he joked. The horses were probably out in the pastures, which were now completely fenced with all that new barbed wire. They'd be safe.

Sarah nodded. "We'll hire some help. Get a new barn built. Plenty of time before the next storm."

Lucas shook his head. He didn't dare ask her how she knew what the weather would be like for the next month. Or was it more like she put in a request and it was seen to?

She nudged him and smiled. "The baby? He's good?"

"How did you—?" Lucas scoffed, and LeRoy let out a laugh. "Never mind. I should know better than to ask." He scowled at her playfully. "Just why *do* you ask—when you already know everything?"

She shrugged. "Makes for good conversation."

Lucas rolled his eyes, then hugged her with his one uninjured arm.

"Her family—they now think you're something, right?" Sarah chuckled.

"What is she going on about?" Eli asked.

Lucas shook his head, the exhaustion hitting him hard. "I'll tell you in a bit. First, you two need to go check out the guy who set the fire. I knocked him out, over by the toolshed. Got his rifle around the side of the house. My Henry is back behind the shed."

"We'll take care of him," Eli said, a little too eagerly.

Sarah grabbed his arm. "Tie him up. Don't hurt him. Bring him in so he can tell the sheriff."

Eli looked disappointed, but LeRoy cuffed him and they got going, their rifles in hand.

Sarah turned to Lucas, her dark eyes sparkling. "A difficult night, yes? But a good one."

Lucas thought she had an odd way of looking at things. "I suppose."

She looked him over. "Let's get you inside. Cook you up some supper and make some nice hot coffee. Clean and treat that wound."

His mouth watered at the mention of food. Weariness seeped into his bones, making walking hard. His shoulder now smoldered like a hot ember. The smoke smell dissipated, and Lucas figured with all the snow, they didn't need to worry about any other buildings catching fire.

As they approached the kitchen door, Ransom stood blocking it, his reins dragging on the ground. A pang of guilt hit Lucas.

"Hey, sorry, Ransom—I completely forgot about you." *I was a little busy.*

His horse nuzzled him and nickered. Sarah slid his headstall off, then uncinched the saddle. She pulled it off and set it on the ground, then said to the horse, "Go find LeRoy and Eli. In back of the barn."

Ransom nickered again and trotted off—making a beeline for what was left of the barn. Lucas shook his head. How come Ransom never obeyed him like that?

"The horses will be fine outside now," she said. She smiled wide and laid a warm hand on his good shoulder. "The storm's over, Lucas."

He knew she wasn't talking about the weather. He blew out a shaky breath, the aftermath of the last twenty-four hours beginning to sink its hooks in him. He was spent. And starving.

"Yep, Sarah. It is."

Chapter 32

EMMA JERKED AWAKE IN THE dark, forgetting momentarily where she was. Then, last night's ordeal came rushing back to her, and her body trembled as she threw the strange bedcovers off and sat up. The house was quiet except for the rattle of a snore she heard through the walls, and a glimpse out the small transom window in her upstairs room showed a tiny hint of dawn smearing the far horizon. The whole world was buried in a blanket of cottony snow. From what she could tell, the sky was clear and calm.

Lucas! Had he gotten home safely? Did those ranchers attack? What if Lucas was hurt—or had been killed? She clutched the big men's shirt she'd worn for a nightdress and jumped out of bed. *I have to go to him. I couldn't bear it if anything happened . . .* Lucas had promised her he'd be careful. And that he'd come back to her. Well, she wasn't going to wait; she'd go to him.

She rushed around the room, flustered. She had nothing with which to brush her hair, no clean clothes to wear. Her costly silk dress and petticoats lay strewn over the wingback chair in the corner. This wouldn't do at all. She would have to find some warm appropriate clothes, and use one of the horses to ride to Sarah's ranch. She huffed. It wasn't likely she'd find a lady's sidesaddle in Hilton's barn. But none of this mattered.

Her mind in a whirl, she washed up as best she could using the rough bar of soap and threadbare towel lying on the child-sized dresser. She rummaged through the dresser drawers, then the armoire standing in the corner. Nothing but men's clothing. She wondered whether Mr. Hilton had ever been married. But even if he had, he'd have no need to keep his wife's clothing. Emma was left with little choice. She gulped down her pride and found trousers, a belt, and a thick wool shirt. She could at least wear her own stockings and boots.

She dressed, thankful the clothes at least were clean, and had to roll up the pants cuffs a bit and hold the sagging waistband with the belt, but in a matter of minutes she was ready. She longed to peek in on Lynette and the baby, anxious to know if they were both all right. But she couldn't risk waking anyone.

She tiptoed down the stairs, went into the kitchen, and drank down a glass of water, feeling utterly foolish in her attire. In the closet by the front door, she found a long heavy coat, the sleeves of which hung so long, her hands were buried inside. *But that will keep them warm.* She found a thick pair of riding gloves—much better than using her thin lambskin ones she'd worn to the auction.

The affair in Fort Collins felt like ages ago. She shuddered thinking of the storm and how cold and terrified she'd been. Lucas had brought them to safety, and then delivered Lynette's baby without complications. Her heart swelled with pride and love for this wonderful, brave man. But she hoped he hadn't been foolishly brave last night. Emma knew Lucas would do anything to help Sarah and her sons. But the thought of them being attacked in the middle of the night . . .

She couldn't waste another minute, dreading what she'd find when she got there. Could she even locate the ranch? They'd passed her road yesterday on the way to Fort Collins. In her mind, she saw how the road had turned east, following the river. There was only one main thoroughfare, so how lost could she get? Although, if the snow was deep, she wasn't sure she would find her way. Hopefully others would be out on the road this early. If she could find horse or wagon tracks, she could follow those.

Just as she was about to rush out the front door to the barn, she heard footsteps on the old plank floorboards behind her. She spun around and faced her father. Her heart sank, and she put her hand to her throat.

He wore an old, ratty robe, and the sight almost made her giggle. Her father's hair stood askew, and his tired eyes attested to his lack of sleep. To her shock, he reached out a hand and laid it on her shoulder, smiling.

"You're up early," he said in a whisper, no doubt trying not to wake her mother. "Emma, where are you going?"

She hoped he wouldn't try to stop her, for she would not let anyone keep her from Lucas. Not now. *Not ever.*

"Father, I have to go. I must make sure Lucas and Sarah are safe." She hoped the pleading in her eyes would show him how serious she was. She pulled back and began buttoning up her coat.

He studied her for a moment, then frowned. "You must love him a lot if you're willing to ride through snowdrifts dressed like that."

Emma's jaw dropped. Words tangled in her throat. Did she hear him right? "I do love him, Father. More than the world. I know . . . I know Randall and I are to be married. But I can't marry him;

I don't love him. Please . . ." Tears threatened to fall, but she swallowed them back.

A smile rose on her father's face. He took her hands. "You did well last night—helping with Lynette. I'm so proud of you."

Her father's eyes glistened. Was he about to cry? First Lynette yelling at Walter, and now this? Her family was certainly changing—but in so many ways for the better.

He continued. "And I will be forever grateful to Mr. Rawlings for all he's done." He looked around the small entryway. "For finding us shelter from the storm. For saving Lynette and the baby. For having the courage to tell me about Walter and being willing to risk his life to protect us . . ." He let out a long breath, his eyes showing love for the first time in ages. "He's a good man, Emma. He's watched out for you from the moment he met you. At first I questioned his intent. How could I have known . . . ?" His face was apologetic, soft. She was seeing a side to her father she had never witnessed before. "You must understand, Emma, it's a father's job to protect his daughter. To—"

"You don't have to explain, Father. I understand." She leaned over and planted a kiss on his scratchy cheek. "I love you too."

He swiped at his eyes, then straightened. "But how will you get there?"

"I'll ride one of the horses. I'm sure Hilton must have a saddle or two in the barn."

Her father's face showed fear. Before he could protest, she said, "I'll be careful. And if I even get a hint of something wrong at the ranch, I'll ride straight to town and find the sheriff."

Her father nodded, but Emma knew he didn't like the idea of her leaving—not at all.

"Come back as soon as you can. I'm sure we'll be staying here today, and perhaps the next. Lynette won't be in any condition to travel for some time. I'd come with you, but your mother would throw a fit if we both left . . ."

Emma nodded. "I have to go."

He smiled again, adoration in his eyes. "I know you do."

She hurried out the front door, warmed by her father's unexpected words. She wanted to laugh for joy that he had finally seen what a good man Lucas was. In her heart, she knew her father wanted her to be happy, and he would allow her to marry Lucas now. Then she frowned and her stomach knotted. The fear that Lucas might have been hurt or killed seeped back in. *Oh please, Lord, let him be all right.*

After finding the privy out back, she ran through the two-foot-high drifts of snow to the barn. With her feet she kicked and pushed the snow from the doors, then finally pulled them open. She felt ridiculous in her attire but at least she was warm. The barn was dark, and she waited a moment for her eyes to adjust.

Next to Mr. Turnbull's two Cleveland Bay draft horses stood Mr. Hilton's two plow horses. Emma came over and petted them, assessing which might be the better horse to ride. Whatever saddles he had, they wouldn't fit the Bays well, so she'd have to go with one of Hilton's. She wasn't sure just what kind of horses they were, but they were both a bit smaller than the Bays, and both geldings. One seemed a little younger, and he was the friendlier one, so she chose him. Hopefully he wouldn't mind a stranger riding him—and one who'd never sat astride a horse before.

Emma grumbled as she found the tack and then led the horse out of the stall. She should have heeded Sarah's—and Lucas's—advice long ago and gotten a proper horse to ride. And learned to ride astride. It had taken her months to concede—due to her stubbornness and insistence on being "proper"—that if she was going to get around on the Front Range, she needed to ride the way people rode in the West. Well, today would be her trial by fire.

In minutes she had the horse saddled, bridled, and the stirrups adjusted. She stuck her foot in the stirrup and swung up and sat. She shook her head, amazed at herself. *Lucas will laugh his head off when he sees me.* She then remembered his words: *"Miss Bradshaw, you could be dressed in sackcloth with ashes streaked across your face and I don't think there'd be a more beautiful woman in all the earth."* Her chest fluttered, recalling how she felt hearing those words.

She kicked the horse and got him trotting out the barn, stepping lively in the snow to dawn streaking pink and orange on the horizon. The new day glowed bright, and the snow sparkled like diamonds as far as she could see. The beauty of the open prairie draped in such jewels astonished her. A soft cool wind tickled her ears, promising a mild day. Songbirds began trilling in the few bare trees, and the dry air smelled of pine and wood smoke coming from someone's hearth. *As beautiful as a Christmas postcard.*

Emma hoped the calm new day boded well for what she'd find at Sarah's ranch. To her relief, wagon tracks left deep ruts in the road, for as far as she could see. Fence posts peeked out from the drifts on either side. At least she would have no trouble staying on course.

She kicked hard and hugged the sides of the horse with her thighs, noting how much more secure she felt riding astride than sidesaddle. It may not be very ladylike, but it was practical. And she was learning that practical often was the better choice when it came to surviving in Colorado Territory.

With hope and dread fighting each other in her heart, she galloped down the road—holding on to the saddle horn, just in case.

Lucas downed his coffee faster than he'd have liked, but he wanted to get back to Emma, and check on Lynette and her baby. He'd intended to get up before dawn, but whatever Sarah had given him for the pain last night made him drowsy, and he'd had to drag his body out of bed as if it were a bag full of rocks. The moment he stood up, his shoulder reminded him he'd been shot clean through with a bullet, but the pain had dulled to a bearable throb. When he finally washed up and dressed, he'd found Sarah in the kitchen and breakfast already made. She informed him her boys were still asleep, and the kid they'd tied up was in the room with them— probably getting little shut-eye, seeing as he had to put up with LeRoy's snoring, which was torture enough.

Lucas took his cup and empty breakfast plate to the sink. "So, do you know who that kid is?" he asked, figuring Sarah had grilled their captive a bit last night, after Lucas had gone to bed.

"No. But he's young. Maybe sixteen. Still time for him to correct his path. Maybe after last night, he'll think twice about wanting to be an outlaw." She went into the sitting room and came back with a small leather pouch. "LeRoy will go fetch the sheriff. Probably when you get back here, he'll want to question you."

Lucas nodded, then thought about the four bodies that had been left out in the cold all night. "What will you do with the dead men?"

"Nothing. Best to let the sheriff see where they fell. Explain what happened."

Lucas whistled. "This is going to make some news."

"Plenty," Sarah said. "Those men—some of them—had wives, family. They owned a lot of cattle, property. Influential men."

Lucas worried how this would affect Sarah and her ranch. When word got out that "red savages" killed a prominent rancher . . . It couldn't bode well. They might want to hang Eli for what he did. Well, Lucas could claim he'd killed Dunnigan too, but he knew that it was not only wrong to lie but that Eli wouldn't stand for Lucas covering for him like that.

Sarah smirked. "The sheriff will see—the fire, the ambush. Self-defense. Besides, we have the boy. He'll tell the truth." She added, "He's got a lump the size of an apple on the side of his head."

Lucas winced. At least he hadn't killed him. How in the world did someone so young get tangled up with a man like Dunnigan? He hoped he could be set straight. Probably came from a no-good home and felt the need to prove himself a man. Lucas had seen enough of those types in the war, with kids that age enlisting, thinking to prove themselves heroes. They just ended up dead for their stupidity.

"I'll talk to the kid when I get back," Lucas offered. Maybe he could find a way to knock some sense into the wanna-be outlaw. It was worth a try.

She gestured Lucas over to sit again at the table. "All the horses are out in the south pasture. Fed and watered. Glad to be out of the barn."

"Sarah, I really need to get a move on," he said. "Emma must be worried sick over me."

"Sit. There's no hurry. Let me look at your wound." Her eyes held a secret, and he almost felt she was laughing at him. What was going on in her mind? Well, whatever it was, he didn't want to know. He just wanted to hurry to Emma's arms and waiting lips.

He sighed in resignation, knowing Sarah would pester him if he protested. He sat, then stripped off his shirt, moving his right arm with care, wincing at the effort. She examined the bandage and pulled one edge back. She grunted.

"It's healing well. Try not to shoot any bad guys today." A big smile came up on her face. "Or hug anyone too hard . . ."

At that moment Hoesta started barking loudly outside the house. Lucas could tell the dog was running down the road. Someone was coming.

Lucas tensed, the night's shoot-out setting off warnings in his head. More of Dunnigan's men? His hand went to his gun at his side. But Sarah kept smiling.

"Who?" he asked her. Who would be here this early, after that snowstorm? Most people would be busy shoveling snow off their walks, if they were even out of bed yet.

The barking grew loud again. Hoesta had followed someone to the house. He stood and waited alongside Sarah, who made no move to open the door. He narrowed his eyes at her, puzzled.

The door blew open, and some strange man in baggy clothes ran in. Sarah laughed.

"What . . . ?" It wasn't a man. Emma?

It *was* Emma—dressed like a man. Lucas laughed, but not because of her clothing. He was stunned and delighted to see her here.

"Lucas!" she said, running into his arms. "Oh, you're safe. Thank God!" She kissed his lips and ran her hands through his hair.

Lucas gritted his teeth as pain shot down his side. Sarah was right about hard hugs.

Emma pulled back and looked at him. He still had his shirt off, and her eyes went wide. "What happened?" She turned to Sarah. "Are you all right? Your sons?"

Sarah nodded, chuckling—no doubt at Lucas's shocked expression.

Lucas said, "We're all fine. This is just . . . a scratch." He'd tell her later—everything. But for now he didn't want her upset.

He drank in the woman he loved—her long ebony hair tangled over her shoulders, her shining eyes and gorgeous smile, her strange men's clothing that hung on her slender frame. Not even those ugly clothes could hide her beauty. Then he realized if she was here alone, she must have come on horseback.

"You rode over here? On what?" He never imagined he'd ever see Emma like this. He thought back to the day he'd found her knocked off her horse. How concerned she was with her appearance, wearing all those fancy clothes and riding her hot-blooded Arab. How offended she was that he suggest she get a proper horse and learn to ride astride.

Emma laughed. "I'll show you." She took his hand and dragged him out the door. Sarah followed. "I apologize for my appearance, but my maid wasn't there to help me dress, and there were no proper women's clothes on hand."

Lucas chuckled. Then, when he stepped outside, he saw the horse she'd ridden. "You're kidding me," he said. Sarah clucked her tongue. "Emma, you are full of surprises."

She came to him and put her hand on his cheek, her eyes brimming over with love. "I couldn't wait for you to come back to me. I had to know you were safe."

Sarah laughed. "Come inside and I'll fix you some breakfast. There's coffee. And I have some things to give you before you go on your way."

Emma looked at Lucas. "Just coffee, thank you. We should hurry back to Hilton's. My father will be worried."

Lucas nodded. "How is Lynette, and the baby?"

Emma sat down at the table, and Sarah handed her a hot cup of coffee. "Oh, thank you. It was a cold ride." She turned to Lucas. "I don't know. They were asleep when I left. But I'm sure they are fine. The house was quiet."

"You snuck out? Did you leave a note?" Lucas asked.

"Well, I'd tried to, but my father caught me." She sipped and sighed. Lucas couldn't take his eyes off her. He reached over and pushed a wayward strand of hair out of her face, and she took his hand and rested it against her cheek. "But, Lucas, he said kind words about you. He admits he was wrong, that you're an honorable man. I told him I loved you and was going to marry you." Her smile lit up her face. "He wants me to be happy. I don't think he'll object now."

"But what about Randall?" Lucas asked. Emma had told him Randall was due back in a few days from Denver. He felt bad for him in a way, but Lucas knew Randall wasn't right for her, and she'd never truly be happy with him. He hoped Randall would understand—and would want Emma to be happy.

"I plan to meet him at the train. I'll tell him then." She tried to look confident, but he could tell she was nervous at the prospect.

"Here," Sarah said, laying some things out on the table. She opened a glass jar the size of her palm. "This is Prairie Puffball—to prevent chafing. For the baby. This pouch has milk medicine—to help her milk flow. And sweetgrass tea, for long life and health." She took a pinch of the dried sweetgrass and set it on a plate on the hot stove. Soon the room filled with a sweet aroma, like hay and honey.

"Thank you," Emma said. "I am sure Lynette will appreciate your gifts."

"The Cheyenne have many traditions tied in with the birth of a baby. There are blessings to be said over a newborn. And some plant a tree, which becomes the baby's life tree."

Emma's eyes suddenly widened. She became thoughtful a moment, and then said, "Would you be willing to do a blessing ceremony for the baby?" she asked Sarah.

Sarah questioned Emma with her eyes. "Here?"

"In Greeley. At my brother's house."

Lucas wondered what Emma was thinking, but he said nothing.

Sarah said, "If they would like me to come, I would be honored."

Emma thanked Sarah and stood, then frowned. "Is it possible you might have a better saddle—one I won't slide around on?"

Sarah chuckled and gestured her to follow her outside. "I have a better idea."

Chapter 33

"THIS IS HOONEVASANE. PROTECTOR," SARAH told Emma. "The horse I picked out for you."

Emma looked at the mustang Sarah had collected from the pasture, still reeling from seeing the barn burned to the ground. They stood near the charred remains, which were still smoldering in places, the caustic stench of the smoke wafting into her eyes.

The horse had beautiful paint markings and a much different conformation than Shahayla. Smaller, sturdier, calmer. Emma came over and stroked his muzzle that featured a white blaze running from his forehead to his nostrils.

"He's beautiful."

"Smart too," Sarah said. "Hoonevasane, how old are you?"

The horse threw his head back, then pawed the snowy ground four times. Emma's mouth fell open.

Sarah raised her eyebrows at Emma and handed her the lead rope. "Smart, right? And when Lucas isn't around protecting you, he will watch out for you."

Lucas said, "He hates snakes even more than Ransom."

Emma made a face. "I bet those two horses are the best of friends."

"If they aren't, they will be," Lucas said, "since they'll be together a lot now."

Hoesta danced around, running back and forth under Protector's legs. The horse paid the dog no mind. Emma shook her head. "Shahayla would never stand still like that, if a dog ran under her." She sighed. "She'd probably trample the poor thing to death."

"You have a fine Arabian mare, Emma," Lucas said. "She's a pretty brave horse to leave the comforts of the city and come out here to face the dangers of the open range head-on." He looked at her, and she knew he wasn't really talking about her horse. "In time, she'll get used to the wildness of the West, and maybe, who knows — she might just come to love it here."

"She won't want to go back to the crowded streets of the big city," Sarah added, her eyes twinkling. "Where there is no place to run free."

Emma's heart swelled with joy. She put her arm around Lucas's waist, and he bent to steal a kiss. Her face heated, knowing Sarah was watching them.

"Let's get you saddled up," Sarah said. "Luckily, we keep most of the saddles in the smaller barn." She threw Emma a look. "Sorry, only Western saddles. No fancy ladies' sidesaddle."

Emma laughed. "I guess I'll have to make do. Isn't that what living in the Wild West is all about?"

"Oh no," Sarah said, shaking her head. "We do much more than *make do* out here. We *live*."

Emma's heart raced in response. "Oh, and that's just what I want to do—live *my* life, free to do what I love."

Lucas swung her to him and pulled her close. "And I hope some of that includes me."

"All of it does," she said breathlessly in his ear. "For always."

The sun was high in the sky by the time they arrived at Hilton's halfway house. They'd had a glorious ride along the road, with the snow mostly melted, but not enough to make the riding muddy. Hoesta followed at their heels, unwilling to remain behind. As Lucas untied the rope he used to pony Hilton's horse, Emma slid off Protector and gave him a pat on the neck.

"You are certainly a wonderful horse, and I can tell already we're going to become great friends. I just hope Shahayla likes you—and doesn't get jealous."

The gelding whinnied and bumped her shoulder with his nose. Emma liked his spunk and playfulness. He was a young horse but well trained and responsive to her leading. Sarah had seen to that. He was the perfect horse for her—and the saddle was just her size. Which made Emma wondered if Sarah had been keeping it just for her. Had she bought it just for her? It was a bit small for Sarah, and her sons certainly wouldn't fit it. A truly generous gift—although, Emma planned to repay her. She doubted Sarah wouldn't take money for the horse, but Emma planned to have a talk with her father—about helping fund the rebuilding of Sarah's barn. She had a feeling he would agree.

Lucas came over and took Emma's reins. "I'll get these three in the barn for now, feed them a little before we head back. They missed breakfast."

"I did too," Emma said, feeling her stomach rumble. "In fact, I never ate dinner last night either. No wonder I'm so hungry."

"Well," he said, leaning over and giving her a long kiss that shot heat down to her toes, "I think ya worked hard 'nuff to deserve some vittles, miss. I'll rustle somethin' up fer ya once we git inside."

She laughed at his imitation of old Hilton's speech. "I never knew you had such a sense of humor," she told him.

He trailed kisses along her neck, and she shuddered, her body sparking with desire for him. He whispered hot in her ear. "There's a lot you don't know about me, Miss Bradshaw. But I rightly intend to show you."

Emma's chest fluttered, and she drew in a shaky breath. "Mr. Rawlings," she whispered back, "you'd best contain yourself. My parents are standing in the doorway."

Lucas turned around and saw them watching from the threshold. He gulped and tipped his hat at them.

Emma chuckled. At least they were smiling, for once.

Lucas gave her an embarrassed look, then headed with the three horses in tow to the barn. Emma skipped up to the house.

Emma's mother looked a bit horrified as she looked Emma over. Thankfully Sarah had given Emma a pretty tailored blouse to wear instead of the baggy cowboy shirt she'd put on earlier. But she still had on the wool trousers that were rolled up at the cuffs. And her hair was down, and no doubt a mess. But there would be plenty of time to bathe, brush her hair, and act the lady. Right now she wanted to know about Lynette.

She followed her parents into the house and learned Lynette was still sleeping. Emma listened to her mother go on and on about the baby and the weather and the horrible scare they'd all had as she scrounged around for something to eat. She turned to her mother. "Are you hungry?"

Her parents exchanged a look that told Emma they hadn't even thought about food. Were they hoping someone would show up and cook them their meals? Emma highly doubted Mr. Hilton had any servants. Or would be inclined to act as their cook during their stay here. Well, someone had to face the task, and she doubted she'd get any volunteers.

"I'll make us something to eat," she said.

"You?" her mother said, shocked.

"Yes, Mother. Unless you'd like to."

"Oh, I don't think that would be a good idea."

Emma was amazed at how quickly her mother got flustered and looked about to faint.

Emma left them to go relax in the sitting room and returned to the kitchen. There she found eggs and bread and butter, and stood there, wondering how to cook them into something edible. She hadn't ever cooked her own breakfast, but she supposed it was time to learn. How hard could it be to fry up some eggs?

"I'll make you breakfast."

She spun around and found Lucas with a cast-iron pan in his hand.

"You go visit with your parents. Let me know when Lynette's awake, so I can check on her."

"You mean to tell me you know how to cook?"

"Like I said, there's a lot you still don't know about me. I'm full of surprises."

Emma laughed. "I'm finding that out." She leaned into him and tickled his stomach playfully. "And I hope to find more."

He squealed when she pinched his sides, then swatted at her but missed. "Now, out of the kitchen and let me work. Looks like there's enough here for everyone. We'll have to replenish Hilton's pantry."

Emma nodded and went to her parents. She heard movement upstairs and wondered if Walter had slept up there or in the room with Lynette. But then the back bedroom door opened, and Walter came out, dressed and looking almost rested and awake. She was glad he'd been in with Lynette.

She walked over to him. "Walter, what do you think of your son?"

Tears were in his eyes, and his face beamed. "He's beautiful. The most beautiful baby in the world."

"You must be so proud," she said, hoping this portended a new day for Walter. Their baby promised a new start on a better future. New beginnings. For them all.

"I am. And, Emma, I want to thank you for helping Lynette. For . . . putting me in my place. I was so wrong. And rude to Mr. Rawlings."

"You were." Emma had no intention of letting Walter off that easily, not while he was being so uncharacteristically humble. She gestured to the kitchen. "He's in there, making us all breakfast." She grinned. "Maybe you'd like to help him."

Walter startled at the suggestion, but then he nodded and said, "I will. It's the least I can do after all he's done for me. I mean, for us."

Emma gave her brother a hug, which seemed to startle him even more. It had been years since she hugged him—something she did a lot when they were young. No reason they couldn't start again. It was a lot nicer than scowling.

She stood in the hall, eavesdropping. This was one conversation she didn't want to miss. Amid the clatter of pans and footsteps, and the wonderful aroma of bacon and eggs cooking, Emma listened to her brother speak to Lucas. Tears pushed at her eyes and her throat closed up, hearing Lucas's kind response and encouraging words to her brother, who seemed entirely remorseful for all his mistakes.

She peeked in and said, "I'm going to check in on Lynette and the baby." From the looks of it, it almost appeared as if the two men had become friends. Emma hoped so, with all her heart. "Oh," she said to Walter, "have you named him yet?"

He nodded as he worked at slicing a loaf of bread, being careful not to cut his fingers. "We're calling him Adam. Hoping he'll be the first of many." He smiled at her—a smile filled with hope.

"That's a perfect name," she said. "Adam Bradshaw."

A Colorado promise of more blessings to come.

Chapter 34

"EMMA!"

She spun around when she heard her name, and spotted Randall walking toward her along the depot platform.

"Randall, there you are."

He came to her and took her hands, and she was relieved he didn't kiss her. She felt awkward and uneasy in his presence, and although she had rehearsed over and over what she would say to him, now that he was near her, the words fled.

The train rumbled behind them, snorting out steam. People hurried through the crowded station, on their way to their families for Christmas. As joyful as she felt, with so many things to be grateful for, her heart hurt thinking how Randall might respond to her announcement. A terrible Christmas present for such a good friend.

"Come," he said, his face troubled, "let me take you out for some coffee. There's something I must tell you."

Her body stiffened. Was he angry? Had he somehow heard about Lucas? Her heart sank, knowing this would prove to be a much harder conversation than she'd expected.

All she could do was nod and let him take her arm. He walked with her in silence down the street, leaving behind the noise of the depot. The stillness in the morning air hung precariously like judgment. How could she tell him in a way that wouldn't break his heart and make him despise her forever? Would he ever speak to her again? She hated the thought that she'd lose his friendship, now that they'd found each other again.

He led her into the hotel they'd stayed at that first week they came to town. The lobby swept her back into the memories of that day, and how she'd felt so attracted to Randall, and so frightened to be in this new, strange place so far from home. It made her realize how much she'd grown and changed since then. How she had planted herself in the rocky desert soil of Colorado and truly bloomed. She'd never expected that, but she was glad for it.

They took a table by the window, and after the waiter poured their coffee and left, Randall looked at her intently. His face couldn't hide the sadness and disappointment he felt. How she had hurt him! She hadn't meant to, but what could she do? She loved Lucas with all her heart. She hadn't meant to fall in love with a Colorado cowboy, but she had.

"Randall, I—"

"Please, Emma. I need to say this before I lose my nerve. I don't know what you will think of me, and I hope you won't despise me." He drew in a deep breath and looked out the window.

Emma laid her hand on his. "It's my fault. I shouldn't have—"

"No," Randall said, giving her hand a little squeeze. "It's me. I'm . . . just not ready for marriage. I hate to tell you this—after the announcement of our engagement. I don't mean to bring shame on you, or embarrass you, but, Emma, I have to be truthful."

Emma's mouth went dry. What was he saying? Was he giving her a way out, so she wouldn't feel bad for breaking off the engagement? How did he know?

"It's been wonderful to see you again after all those years. And knowing you were here was a comfort to me. You're really the only friend I have in Colorado. So, it's understandable . . ." He blew out a frustrated sigh. "What I mean to say is, I apologize if in some way I led you on. I didn't mean for you to think I wanted to marry you. Please, don't misunderstand me—if I married anyone, I'd want it to be you. You . . . are so sweet and kind and wonderful. I truly do love you with all my heart. But as I said before I left, I . . . love you as a friend. And my father insisted . . . it was his idea for us to marry, and he went and spoke to your father and they arranged it all. I know you were as upset as I was . . ."

Emma finally understood what he was saying. She had been so sure he was upset with her, she'd discounted what she'd suspected all along, hidden in her heart. He never wanted to marry.

"Oh, Randall. I understand perfectly. I want us to be friends."

"You . . . seem happy out here. You've adjusted to life on the frontier. I know this is where you belong . . . with Lucas."

A pang of surprise stabbed her heart. Emma faltered. "I . . . was going to tell you—"

He smiled and shook his head. "No need. My father heard from your father and, well, I got a good chewing out for allowing my fiancée to be stolen by another man." He then clasped her hand tight. "But I stood up to him. Finally. Told him I could no longer work for him, and that I'm going back to New York."

Emma gasped. "You did? What did he say?"

He chuckled. "He was speechless for a moment—if you can picture that. Threatened to cut me out, disinherit me, etcetera. And you know what? I didn't care. It was very freeing, speaking my mind. I heard you'd done the same with your father." He gave her a sly, knowing look. "Your bravery inspired me."

Emma huffed, stunned and amazed. "I don't know what to say . . ."

"Just wish me well, Emma. I've landed a job with a book publishing house in the city. I'm a city man at heart. I would just wither and die out here, in time. Maybe someday I'll be able to publish your book of botanical illustrations of the plants of the Front Range." He looked deep into her eyes, and she could tell he was happy with his decision. "Don't give up your dreams, Emma. I know that someday your books will be used in universities around the country—required reading for botanists."

Tears came to Emma's eyes. Her throat choked with emotion. "Oh, Randall, I do wish you well. You deserve to be happy, to live the life *you* want."

"I hope you'll come visit me—you and Lucas and all your children."

Emma flushed. "I would love to. When are you leaving?"

"Tomorrow evening."

"But, that's Christmas!"

He grunted. "I can't think of a better Christmas present to give myself. A journey home."

Home. She had stopped thinking of New York as home months ago—after she met Lucas. Her home was truly here now. With Lucas on the wide-open prairie.

"Would you please come by the house in the morning and have Christmas cheer with us, so we can send you off properly? And I want to give you one of my illustrations." She added, "You can frame it and hang it over your desk at the publishing house—to remind you of your dreams."

"I'd like that. Will you walk me home?" he asked.

Emma nodded and took his arm, her heart glad for him. She turned to him and said, "What else did you say to your father? And what happened on your trip to Denver? I want to hear all the details."

He laughed, a deep hearty laugh. Then began to regale her with stories, just like he used to when they were children.

After helping her mother from the carriage, Emma reached in and carefully cradled her crape myrtle in her arms. The early April morning had a hint of spring in the air. Even though she knew it would probably snow again before winter gave up its last gasp, the ground was soft enough and ready for her tree to be planted.

She walked up the pathway to the front of Walter and Lynette's house and set down the pot. No one else had arrived yet, but that would give her a few minutes to play with little Adam, who was adorable and chubby and already had two front teeth. When she went inside, her mother had scooped the baby into her arms and was saying silly things to him. And her father sat there gleefully enthralled with the antics of his first grandchild. The sight brought a smile to Emma's face.

Ever since Adam had been born, her mother was a different person. She hardly fretted anymore—not even when the servants failed in their duties. Now her mother hummed through the house and puttered about town with her friends, busy with charities and helping Mrs. Edwards on various committees for all the many fundraisers and events the town put on each year. They were hard at work this month, getting ready for the biggest event of all—the Greeley One Hundred Grand—to celebrate the nation's centennial in July. And it had recently been announced that Colorado was about to become the thirty-eight state in the union. Colorado was proving to be a place of promise not just for her family but for the whole territory.

Emma was glad her mother had recovered from her melancholy. And her father couldn't be happier having an "heir" to his fortune. Emma knew, though, he was just as in love with Adam as his wife was, and he doted on the baby as much as she did. Which left Emma free to do what she wanted more than anything—spend time wrapped in Lucas's strong, warm arms.

Her parents were taken aback when she and Lucas announced they planned to be married on New Year's Day. It gave her mother no time at all to prepare the elaborate wedding she'd always wanted. Which was Emma's intent. She chose to have a small, cozy wedding, with just close family and friends—and they decided they'd have it at Sarah's ranch.

To her surprise, her parents voiced no objection. So under a full moon on an unexpectedly warm winter night, they'd exchanged vows under the big Colorado sky splattered with stars. Sarah had prepared a feast and sang a Cheyenne wedding song for them. Eli and LeRoy had decorated Ransom and Protector with feathers and paint for the occasion, and when the ceremony was over and everyone congratulated them, they feasted. Even the horses got a piece of Sarah's spice cake.

Then after the guests had gone home late in the night, Lucas had taken her for a short ride across the river and north of the ranch, to a place she'd never been. A small house sat alongside a bubbling creek up against a protective hill. When he took her inside, she found it beautifully furnished—simple and homey. He explained he'd bought this place a while back, hoping one day to move here. But he never felt right living in it alone. It needed a woman's touch, he'd told her. A woman's heart. And now it had one.

When he took her into the bedroom, she saw a big bed covered with thick comforters. A lantern was lit and cast a soft glow to the room. She noticed then he had brought some of her things over from her family's house—no doubt provided secretly by her mother. For he had all her favorite dresses and shoes, and a beautiful blue silk nightgown lay across the bed. He said he'd specially chosen it to match the two blue pools that were her eyes.

Her heart nearly burst with joy as he took her into his arms and kissed her. Long into the night he kissed her and loved her and showed her all those surprising things he'd promised he'd show her. She melted in his arms and let the passion they'd been holding back for so long sweep her away. Every touch of his hands, every brush of his lips, sent ripples of pleasure through her. And each kiss left her with the promise of more to come. What Lucas came to call his "Colorado Promise."

In the nursery, Emma smiled thinking back to their first night of passion. And then, as she played with Adam, she heard a commotion out the front door.

Everyone had arrived at the same time. After she and Lucas had eaten breakfast with Emma's parents, Lucas had gone to fetch Sarah, Eli, and LeRoy. Emma hurried outside. Sarah was dressed in a traditional Indian dress and knee-high boots, adorned with beads and feathers. Emma had never seen her in such garb, and it made her sad to know Sarah's people were no longer living on the Front Range, where they'd lived for centuries. Emma was so glad she'd had the opportunity to know her and was eager to learn more from her about the plants of the prairie, so she could keep painting and writing her book.

Emma waved hello to Violet and her family as they rode up to the house on their horses, dressed in comfortable riding clothes. The twins were prancing around on their ponies, eager to go for a ride.

"You'll just have to wait a little while," Violet told them. "Until the ceremony's over."

They grumbled and fidgeted, but Violet shot them a look, and they settled down.

Lucas chuckled and came over to where Emma stood on the cleared space that fronted the dining room window. He wrapped her in his arms and laid his cheek against hers.

"Oh, you're cold." She pulled back and searched his eyes. "But once you start digging, I'm sure you'll warm up." She handed him the shovel, and he laughed and took it.

Once the hole was deep enough, Emma planted the tree that was almost bursting from its small pot. It was more than ready to bloom where it was planted. Tiny buds clumped on the branches, promising new leaves and flowers later in the spring.

Lynette and Walter came out, Lynette cuddling Adam in her arms and Walter with his arm around her. Emma's heart sang at seeing how happy they were, and it jolted her thoughts back to the danger Walter had been in and how he might not have ever held his son. Now all the danger was past. Although Lucas had worried there'd be repercussions from the attack at the ranch, the truth won out and no charges or negative consequences had befallen Lucas or Sarah's family. Instead, many of the townspeople had been so incensed by the travesty, they joined in with money and labor to rebuild Sarah's barn. The project had only taken two weeks, and the new barn was bigger and better than the former one. Even Mr. Turnbull—to Emma's great surprise—had donated a nice sum to the rebuilding effort.

Emma patted down the soil and watered it. Then she stepped back and let Sarah perform her ritual. Sarah called Lynette to her side, and singing in the Cheyenne language, she sprinkled something on Adam's head. Then she danced around the tree, singing and tipping her head back to look to the sky. Everyone watched, enraptured, standing silent until she finished. She handed a small leather pouch to Lynette and said something to her, which

Emma couldn't hear. Lynette's face flushed. Emma grinned, wondering what she'd said that embarrassed Lynette. Then Sarah took a beaded necklace from her dress pocket and put it over Lynette's head. She walked over to Walter and gave him one too.

As Emma went over and put her arm around Lucas, the ground began to shake. She looked down and saw the soil jiggle, and noticed everyone looking around in confusion. An earthquake? They'd never had one here. Did they even have earthquakes in Colorado?

She looked over at her parents. Her mother gripped her father's arm, and fear streaked her face.

"What is it?" she asked in a shaky voice.

Lucas let out a laugh, and Emma spun and looked at him.

"Why are you laughing?" she asked.

He just shook his head and walked over to Ransom. After he swung up on the horse, he called over to the twins, who were holding on to their ponies' reins, standing still with puzzled faces staring at the ground.

"Well, what are you waiting for, Tex?" Lucas asked with a big grin.

The boys finally realized Lucas was talking to them. One of them answered, "What do you mean?"

"Haven't you been wanting to see the buffalo run?"

"Buffalo?" Emma's mother said, throwing a hand over her heart. "Where? Are they coming to town?" Emma swore her mother looked about to faint as the rumbling continued and the ground shook even harder.

Sarah and her sons looked west, toward the snow-capped Rocky Mountains that stood majestic and blue in the soft spring light.

"Over there." Lucas pointed.

Emma strained to see, but all she could make out was a large dark shadow in the distance. Lucas turned to her and said, "Honey, you better hurry and saddle up Protector. The buffalo aren't going anywhere fast, but I don't think these boys can wait much longer. They've been waiting all year to see this."

She hurried over to him as he sat on his horse. He leaned down and gave her a sweet kiss. She wasn't properly dressed for galloping across the open range, but it wouldn't be the first time.

"Give me two minutes."

The boys whined impatiently. Violet laughed along with her parents. Lucas looked at the boys' parents and said, "I'll bring them back to the house later, if that's all right with you. We hunters've got some hunting to do."

Mrs. Edwards patted Lucas's hand as the boys mounted their ponies, bouncing up and down in their saddles. "You sure do."

Emma rushed to the back, where she'd hobbled Protector. In under two minutes she had him ready to go. She mounted and rode over to Lucas, whose eyes shone with the excitement of a boy about to go see his first buffalo. His face glowed with his love for the land, for the open prairie, for her.

And the land embracing her mirrored her heart, showing her who she really was—a Colorado woman through and through.

Lucas was right. She had run from her past, but it wasn't until she ran *to* her dream that she came to feel at home on the Front Range. She had run to Lucas, who, thankfully, had caught her in his loving arms.

"You ready?" he asked. She knew he didn't have to ask the twins. They were already trotting down the street, waving wildly at Lucas to follow.

Emma nodded. She was ready—for anything and everything.

~The End ~

ACKNOWLEDGMENTS

I AM GRATEFUL FOR THE support and encouragement from so many. A heartfelt thanks to Marylu Tyndall for reading and instructing me in this genre that she knows so well. Her insights and edits were tremendously helpful. Thanks also go to my author friends, especially Pamela Walls, Elena Dillon, and Michelle Weidenbenner.

I couldn't have captured Greeley in the 1870s without the help of Greeley Museum curator, Peggy Ford. Her patience with my tireless questions about the locale and era, and the terrific bibliography she provided for me to use in my research, were invaluable.

A special thanks to my cover designer, Delle Jacobs, for creating a beautiful cover for me. Also to Ellie Searl, of Publishista.com, for her great help and patience in creating the look of this book, inside and out. And to Babs Hightower, for marketing and promotion, as well as being so helpful and encouraging.

Having lived in Greeley and other places along the Front Range for years, delving into the historical aspects of the region was enlightening and entertaining. My husband is to be thanked for many of the great plot ideas and his support and patience as I wrote long hours into the night.

CPSIA information can be obtained
at www.ICGtesting.com
Printed in the USA
LVOW07s1809200317
527826LV00006B/1448/P